NOPL@NORTH SYRACUSE
100 TROLLEY BARN LANE
NORTH SYRACUSE, NY 13212

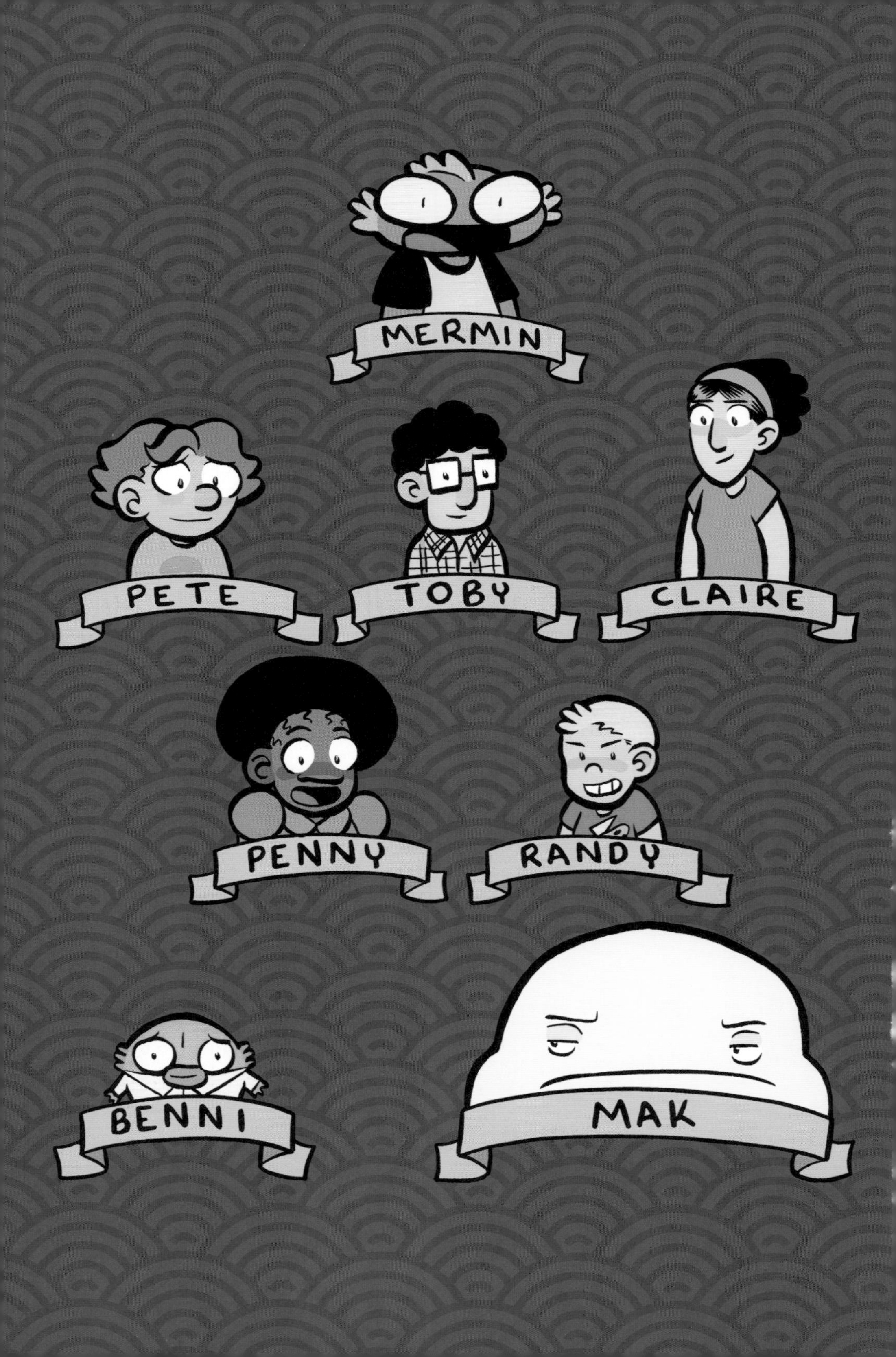
MERMIN
PETE
TOBY
CLAIRE
PENNY
RANDY
BENNI
MAK

MERMIN™

BOOK FOUR: INTO ATLANTIS

KING MERUS

QUEEN BLU

MERMA

OMER
(deceased)

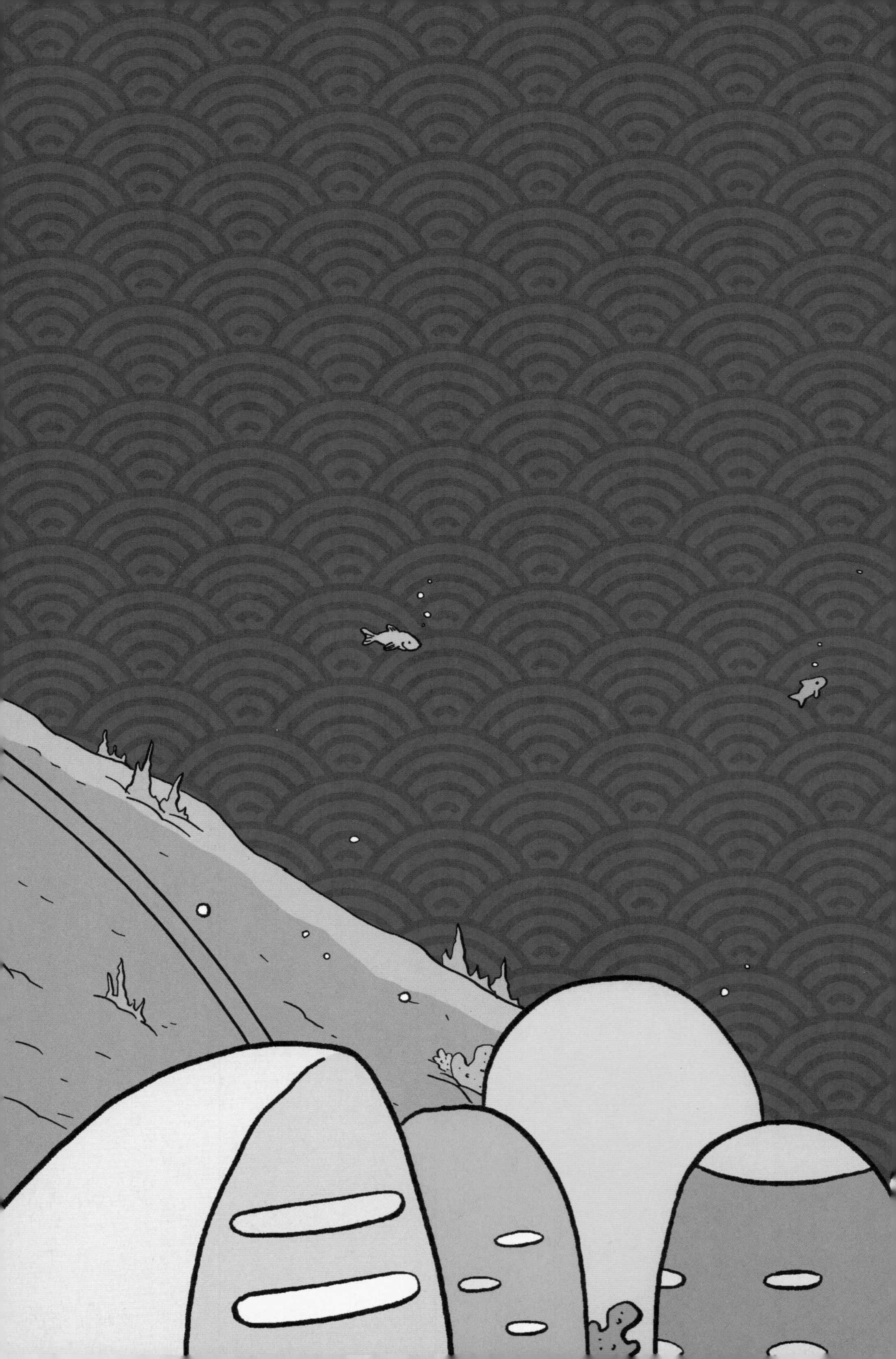

MERMIN™

BOOK FOUR: INTO ATLANTIS

Written and illustrated by
Joey Weiser

Colored by
Joey Weiser and Michele Chidester

Edited by
Robin Herrera

Designed by
Keith Wood
with
Hilary Thompson

Oni Press, Inc.

publisher, **Joe Nozemack**

editor in chief, **James Lucas Jones**

director of sales, **Cheyenne Allott**

director of publicity, **Fred Reckling**

production manager, **Troy Look**

graphic designer, **Hilary Thompson**

production assistant, **Jared Jones**

senior editor, **Charlie Chu**

editor, **Robin Herrera**

associate editor, **Ari Yarwood**

inventory coordinator, **Brad Rooks**

office assitant, **Jung Lee**

onipress.com
facebook.com/onipress
twitter.com/onipress
onipress.tumblr.com
instagram.com/onipress
tragic-planet.com

First Edition: September 2015
ISBN: 978-1-62010-258-9
eISBN: 978-1-62010-259-6

Mermin: Into Atlantis, September 2015. Published by Oni Press, Inc. 1305 SE
Martin Luther King Jr. Blvd., Suite A, Portland, OR 97214. Mermin is ™ & ©
2015 Joey Weiser. All rights reserved. Oni Press logo and icon ™ & © 2015
Oni Press, Inc. All rights reserved. Oni Press logo and icon artwork created
by Keith A. Wood. The events, institutions, and characters presented in this
book are fictional. Any resemblance to actual persons, living or dead, is purely
coincidental. No portion of this publication may be reproduced, by any means,
without the express written permission of the copyright holders.

Printed in China.

Library of Congress Control Number: 2012953664

1 2 3 4 5 6 7 8 9 10

CHAPTER ONE

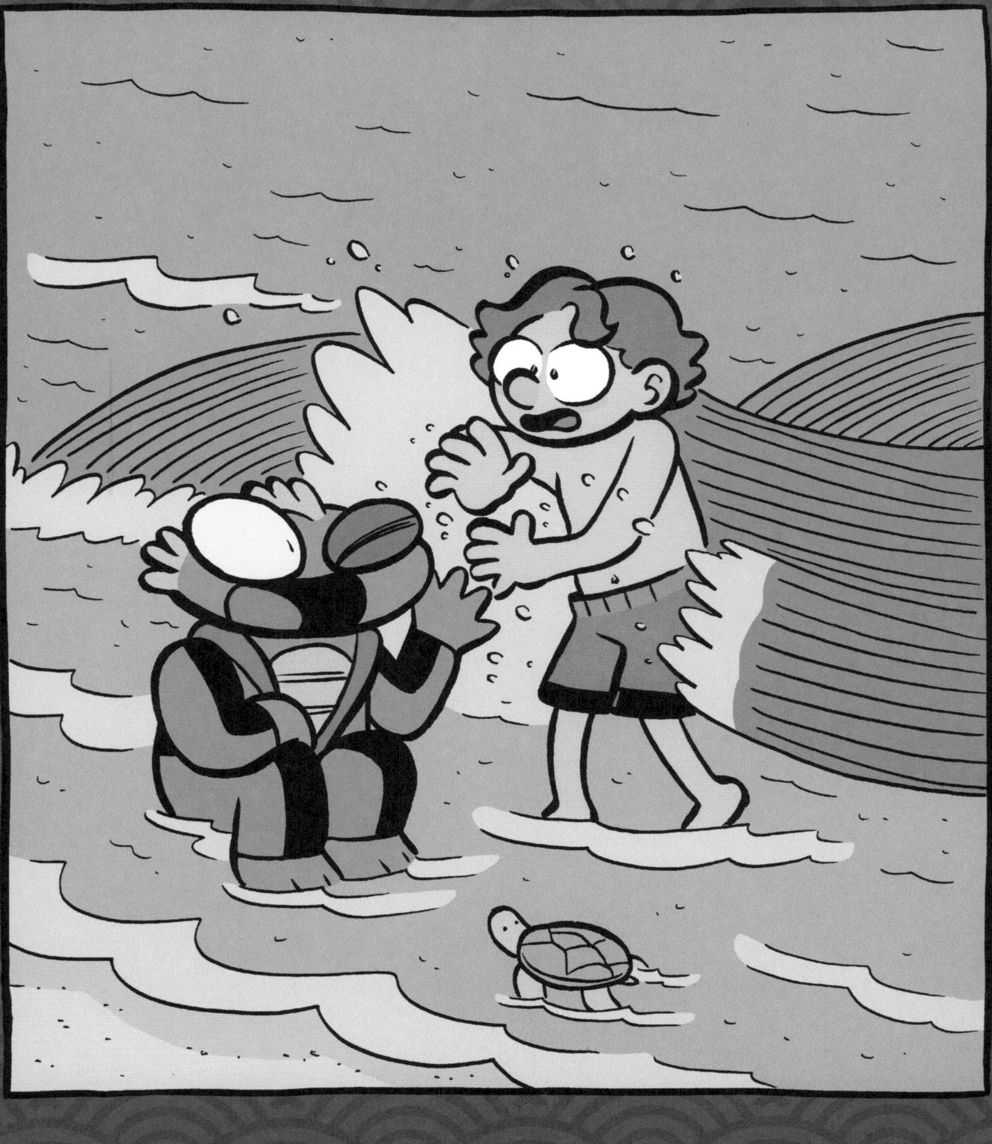

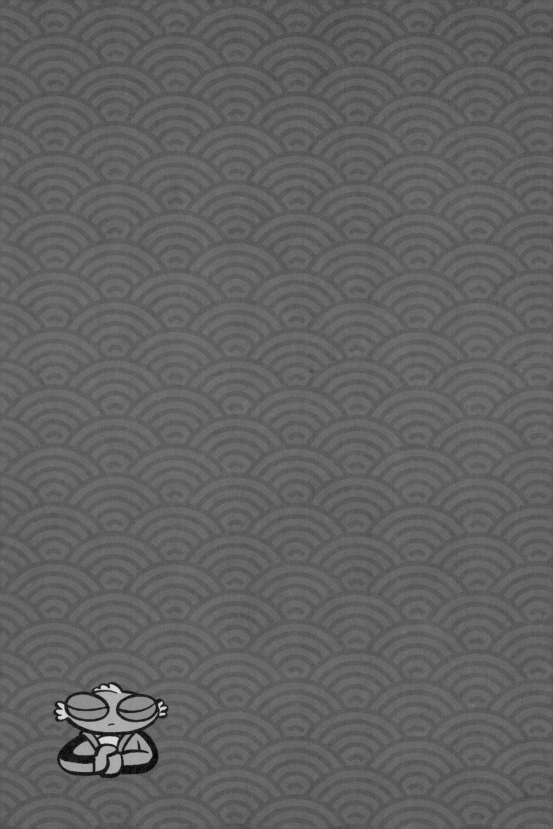

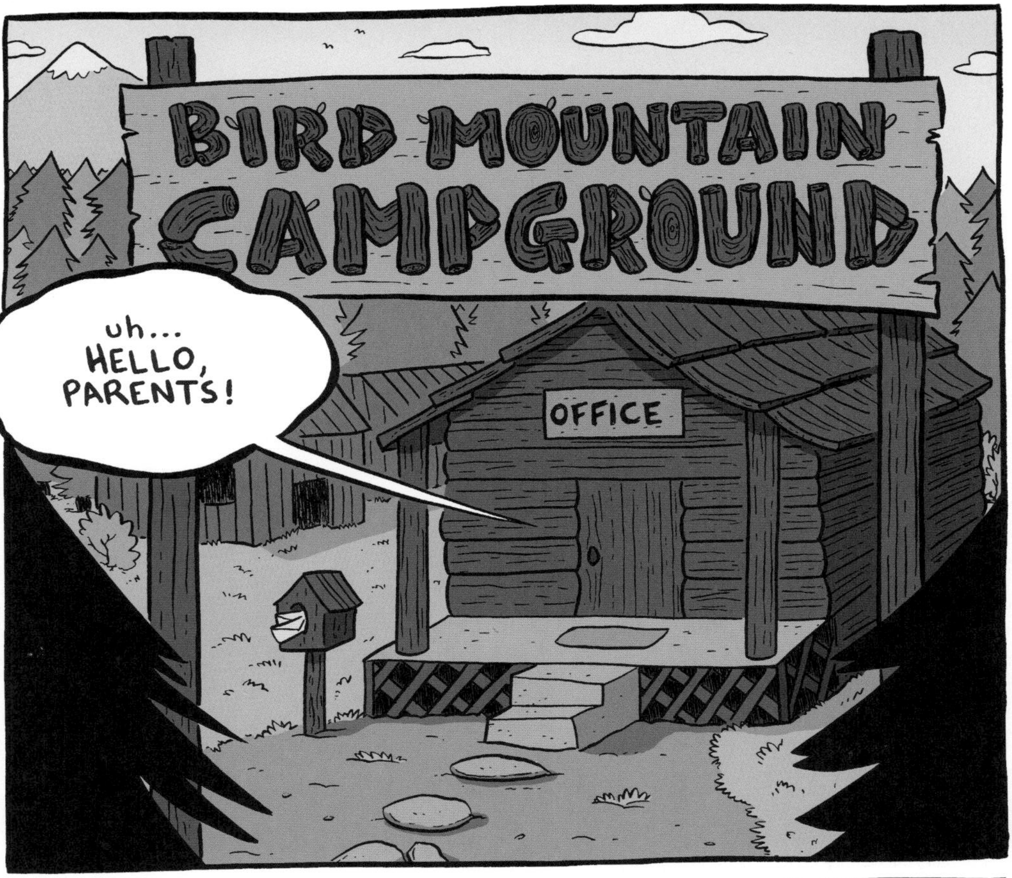
BIRD MOUNTAIN CAMPGROUND
uh... HELLO, PARENTS!
OFFICE

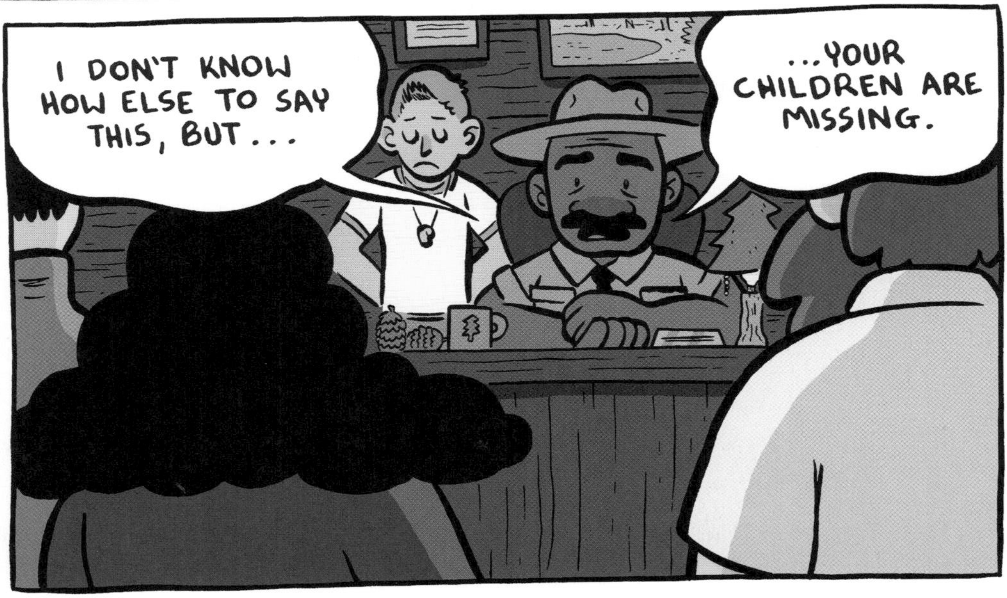
I DON'T KNOW HOW ELSE TO SAY THIS, BUT...
...YOUR CHILDREN ARE MISSING.

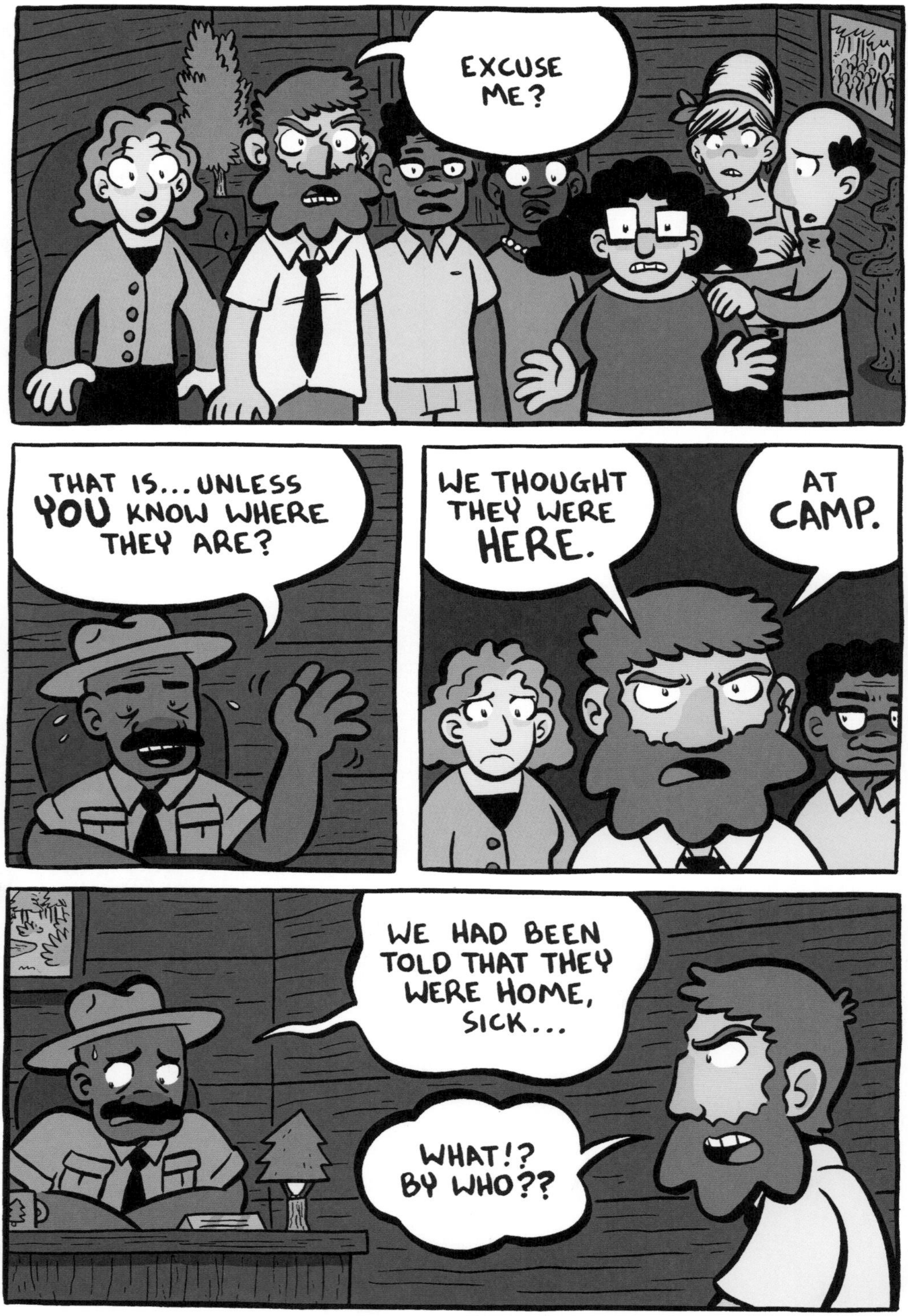
EXCUSE ME?
THAT IS... UNLESS YOU KNOW WHERE THEY ARE?
WE THOUGHT THEY WERE HERE.
AT CAMP.
WE HAD BEEN TOLD THAT THEY WERE HOME, SICK...
WHAT!? BY WHO??

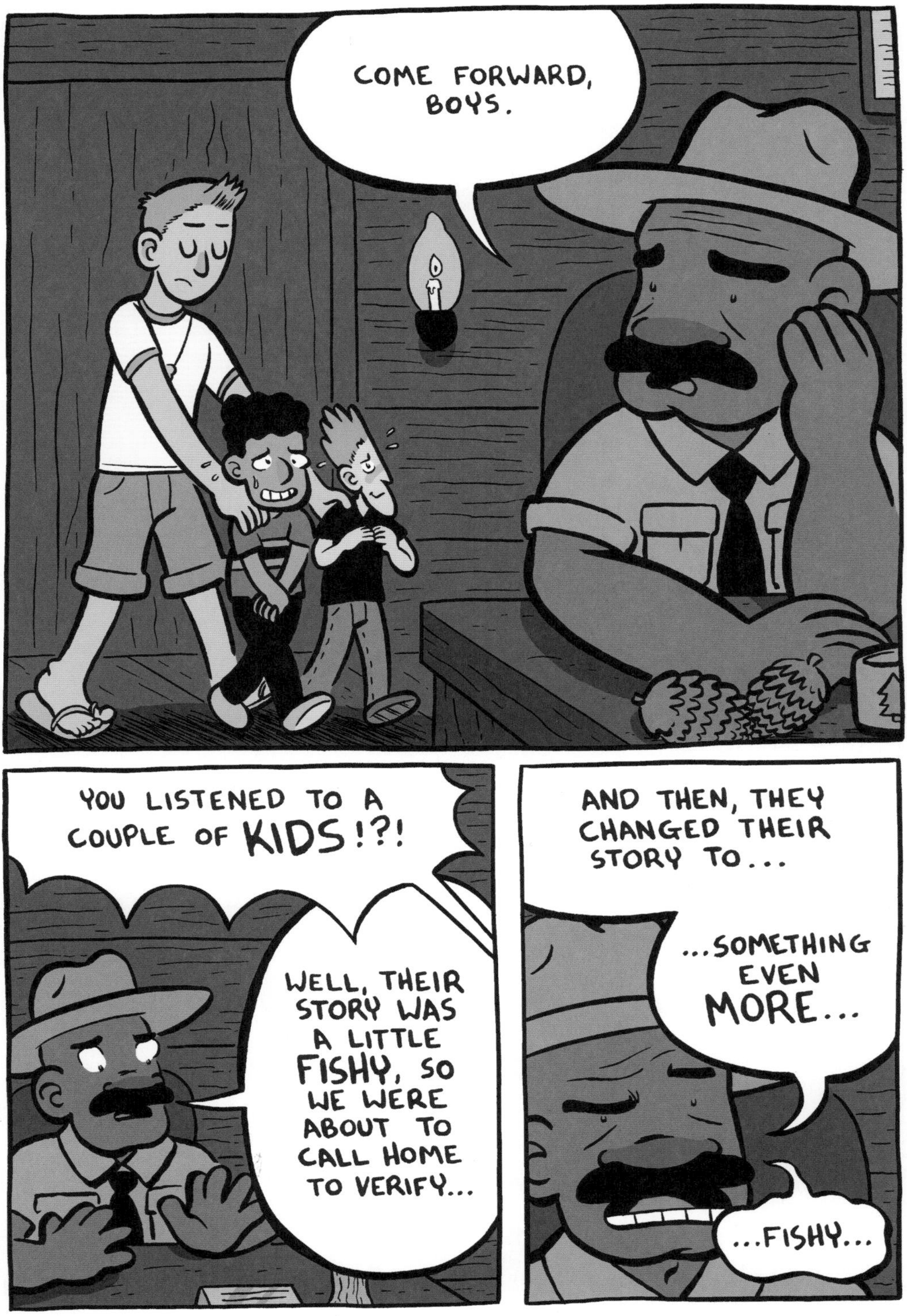
COME FORWARD, BOYS.
YOU LISTENED TO A COUPLE OF KIDS!?!
WELL, THEIR STORY WAS A LITTLE FISHY, SO WE WERE ABOUT TO CALL HOME TO VERIFY...
AND THEN, THEY CHANGED THEIR STORY TO...
...SOMETHING EVEN MORE...
...FISHY...

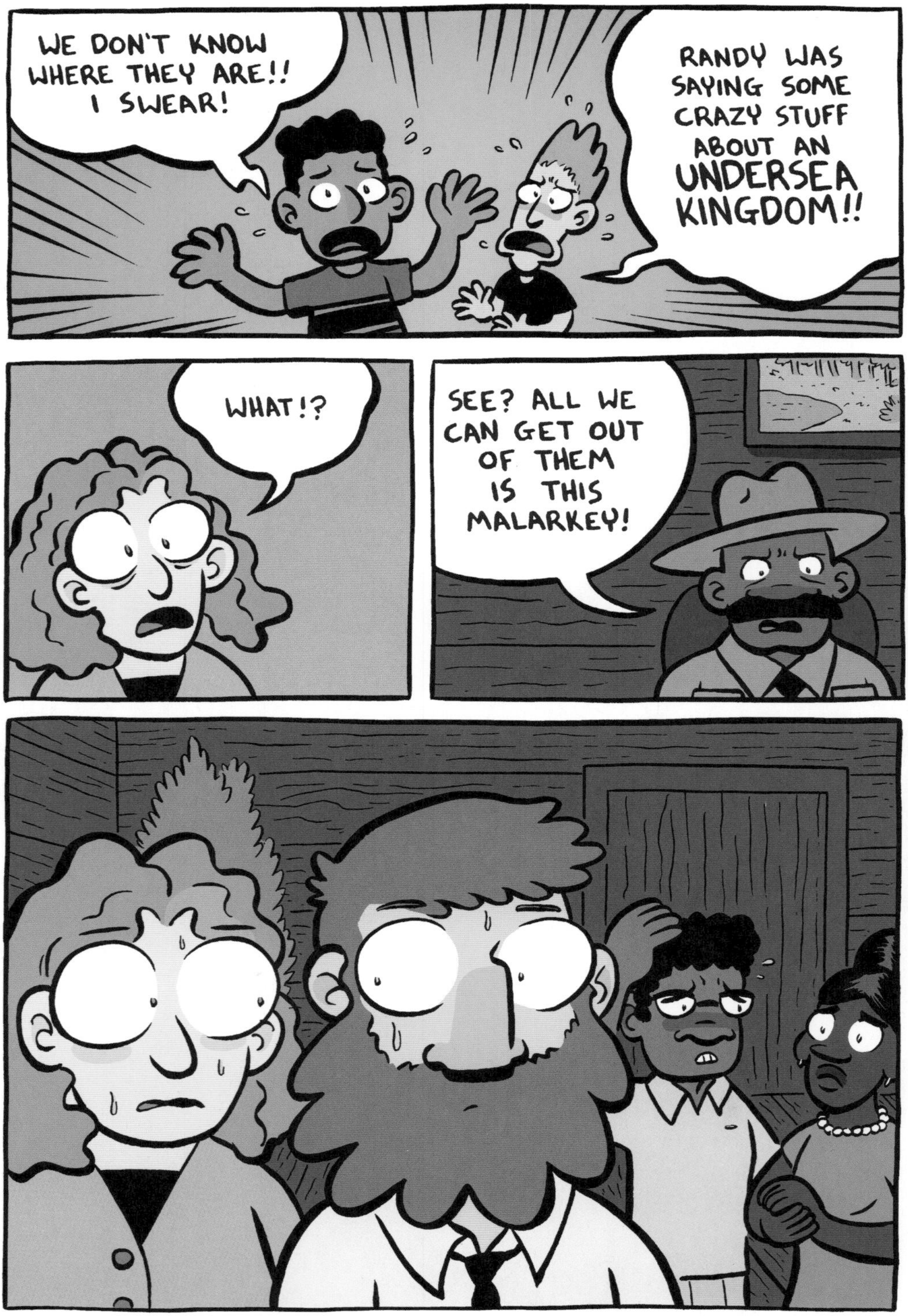
WE DON'T KNOW WHERE THEY ARE!! I SWEAR!
RANDY WAS SAYING SOME CRAZY STUFF ABOUT AN UNDERSEA KINGDOM!!
WHAT!?
SEE? ALL WE CAN GET OUT OF THEM IS THIS MALARKEY!

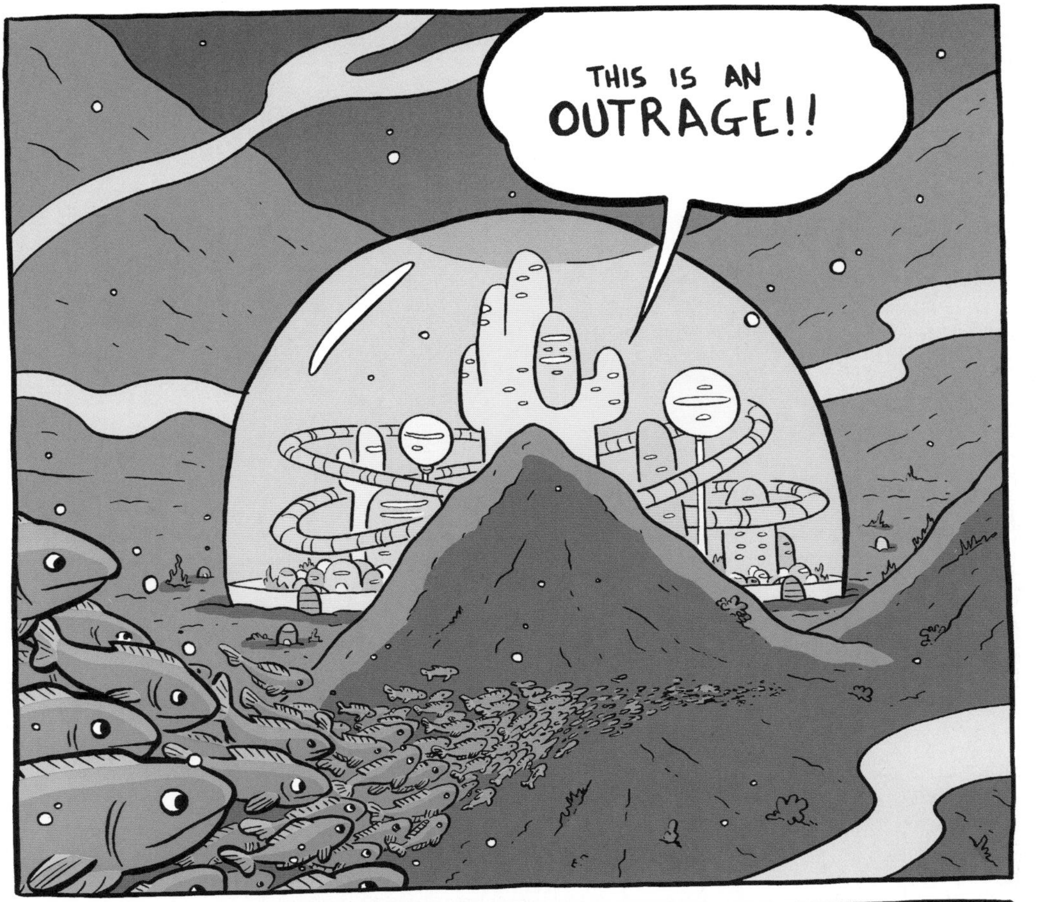
THIS IS AN OUTRAGE!!

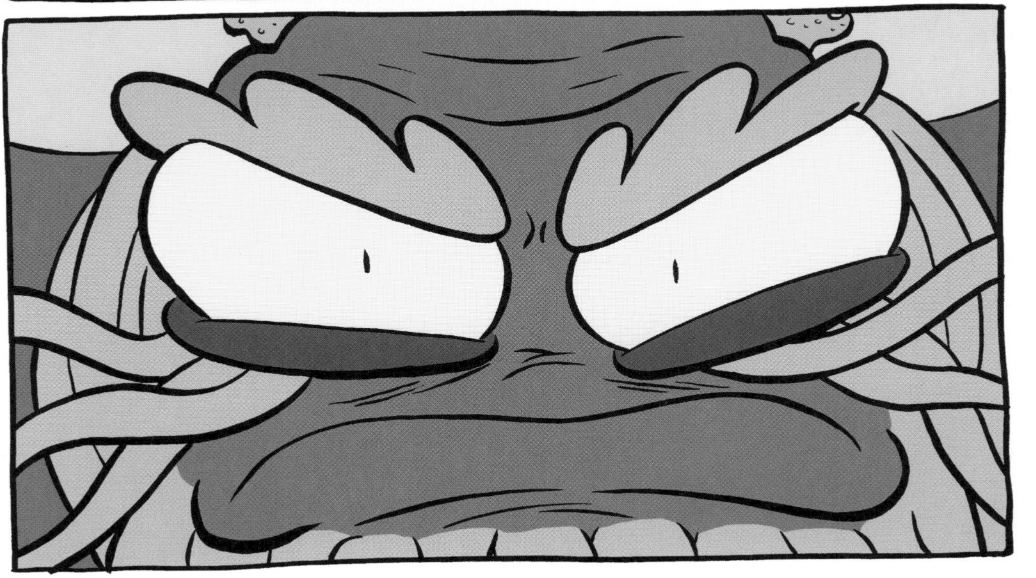

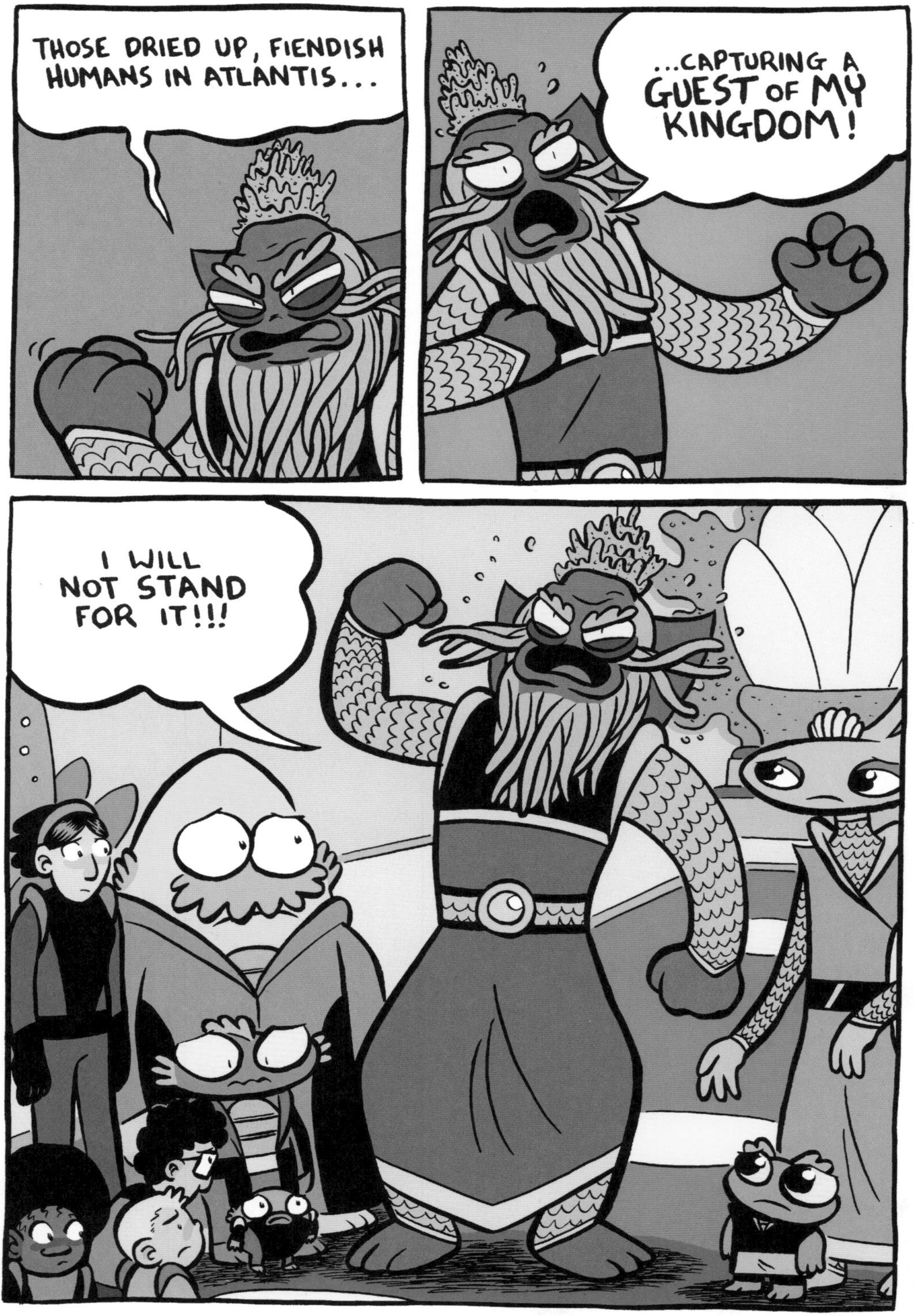
THOSE DRIED UP, FIENDISH HUMANS IN ATLANTIS...
...CAPTURING A GUEST OF MY KINGDOM!
I WILL NOT STAND FOR IT!!!

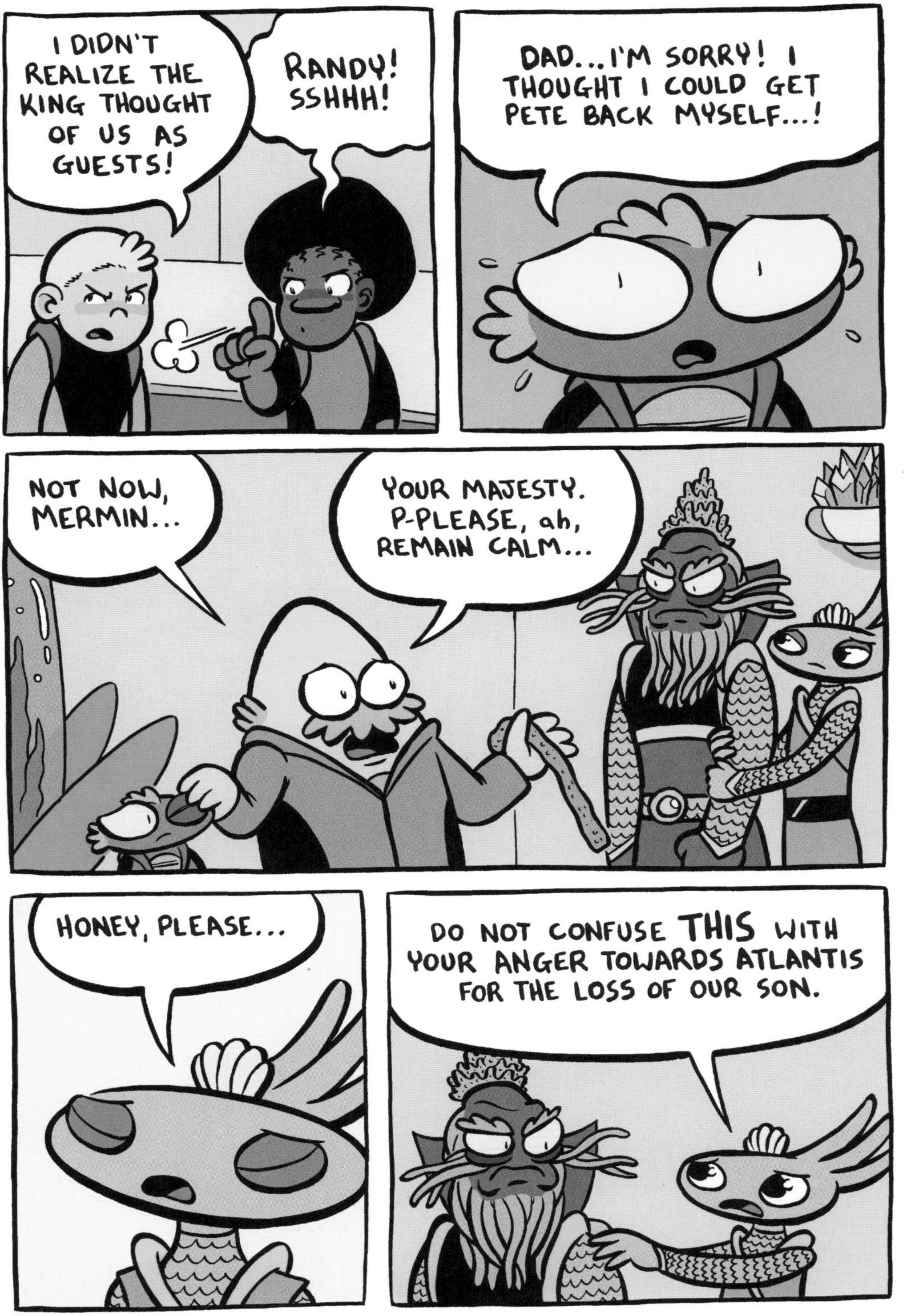
I DIDN'T REALIZE THE KING THOUGHT OF US AS GUESTS!
RANDY! SSHHH!
DAD...I'M SORRY! I THOUGHT I COULD GET PETE BACK MYSELF...!
NOT NOW, MERMIN...
YOUR MAJESTY. P-PLEASE, ah, REMAIN CALM...
HONEY, PLEASE...
DO NOT CONFUSE THIS WITH YOUR ANGER TOWARDS ATLANTIS FOR THE LOSS OF OUR SON.

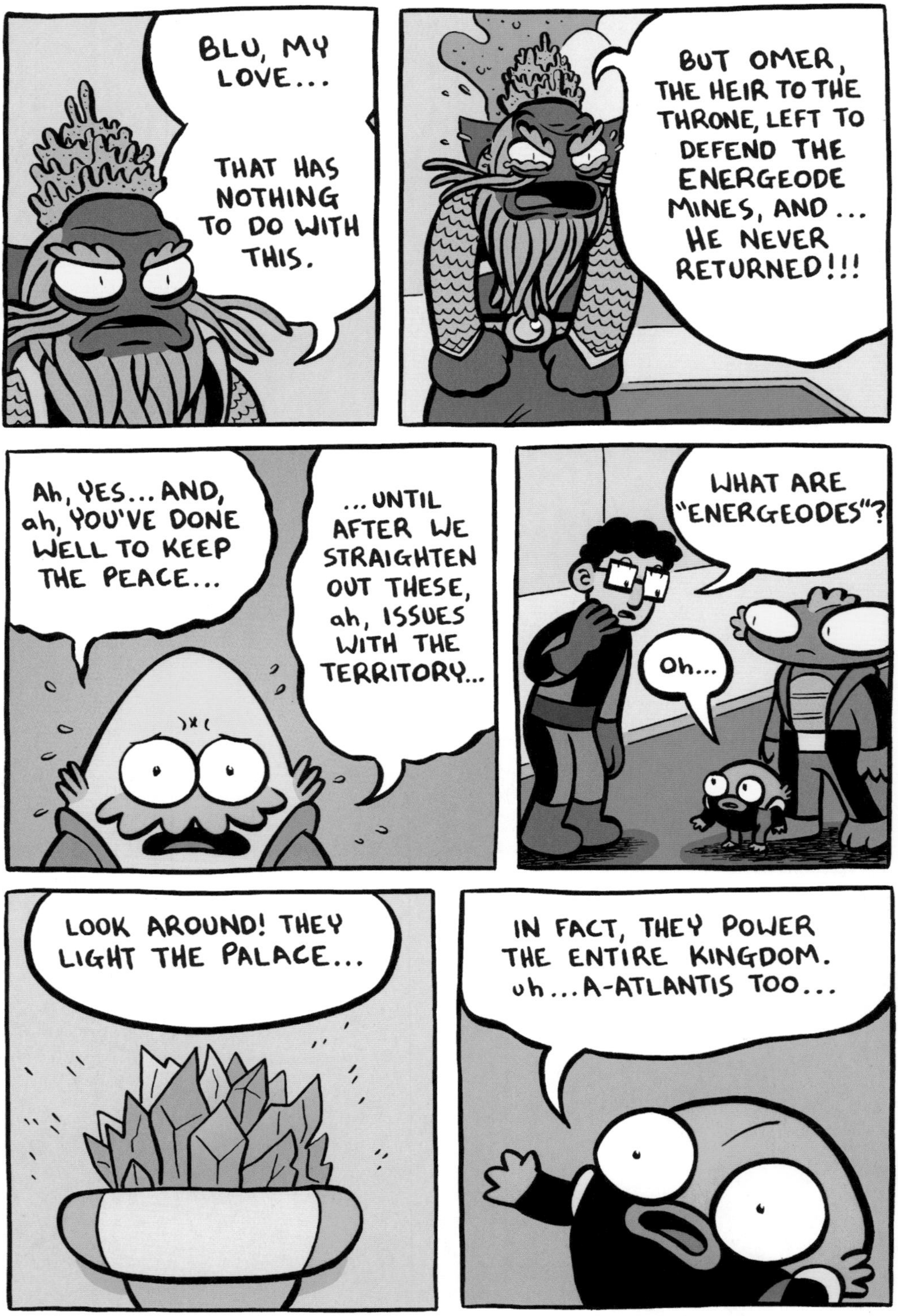
BLU, MY LOVE...
THAT HAS NOTHING TO DO WITH THIS.
BUT OMER, THE HEIR TO THE THRONE, LEFT TO DEFEND THE ENERGEODE MINES, AND... HE NEVER RETURNED!!!
Ah, YES... AND, ah, YOU'VE DONE WELL TO KEEP THE PEACE...
...UNTIL AFTER WE STRAIGHTEN OUT THESE, ah, ISSUES WITH THE TERRITORY...
WHAT ARE "ENERGEODES"?
Oh...
LOOK AROUND! THEY LIGHT THE PALACE...
IN FACT, THEY POWER THE ENTIRE KINGDOM. uh... A-ATLANTIS TOO...

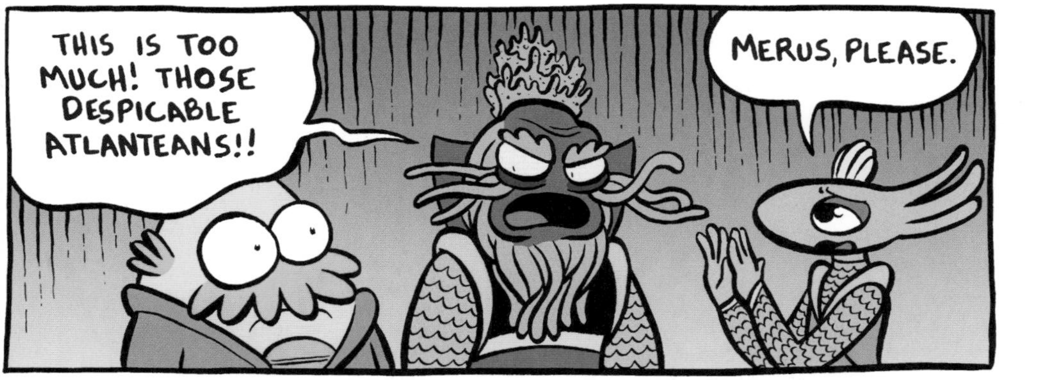
THIS IS TOO MUCH! THOSE DESPICABLE ATLANTEANS!!
MERUS, PLEASE.

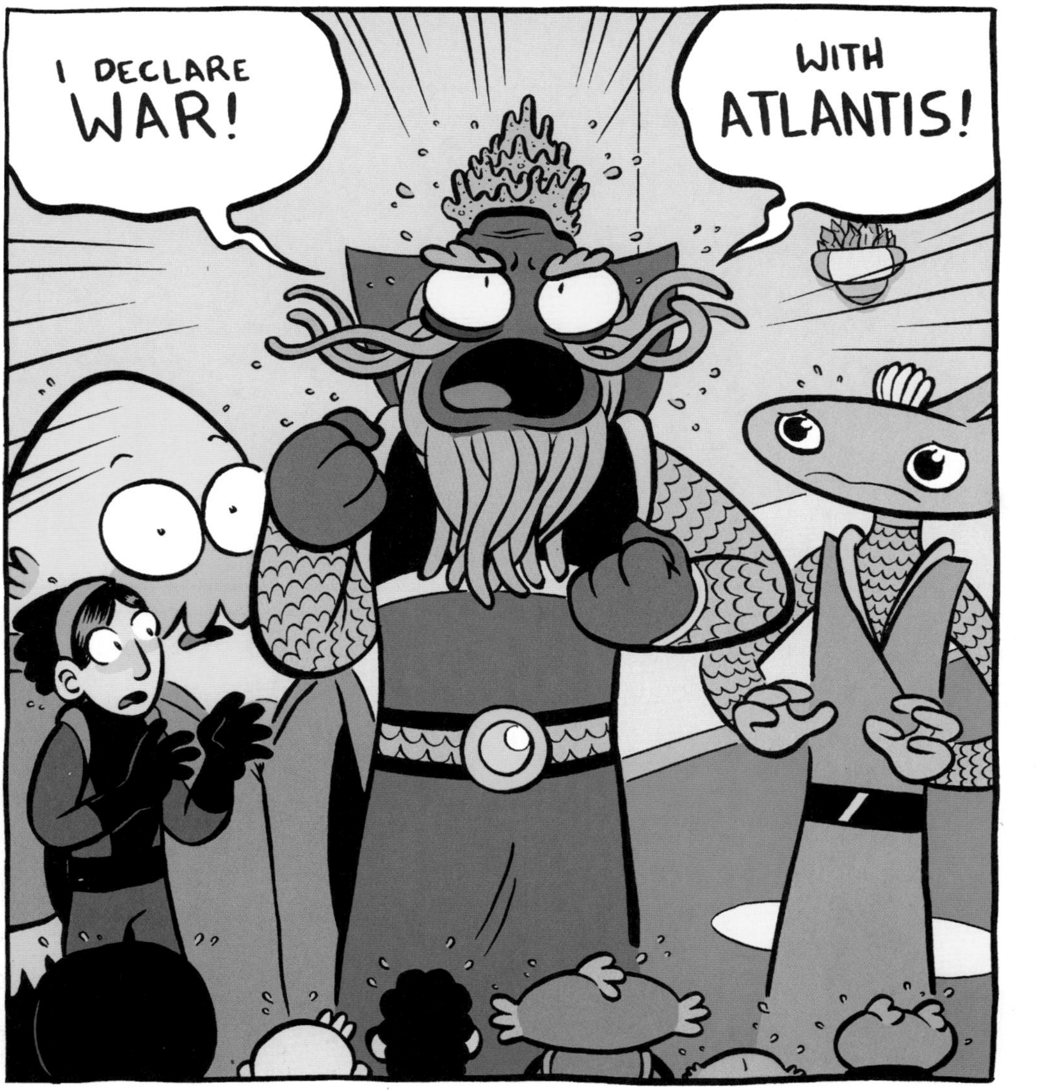
I DECLARE WAR!
WITH ATLANTIS!

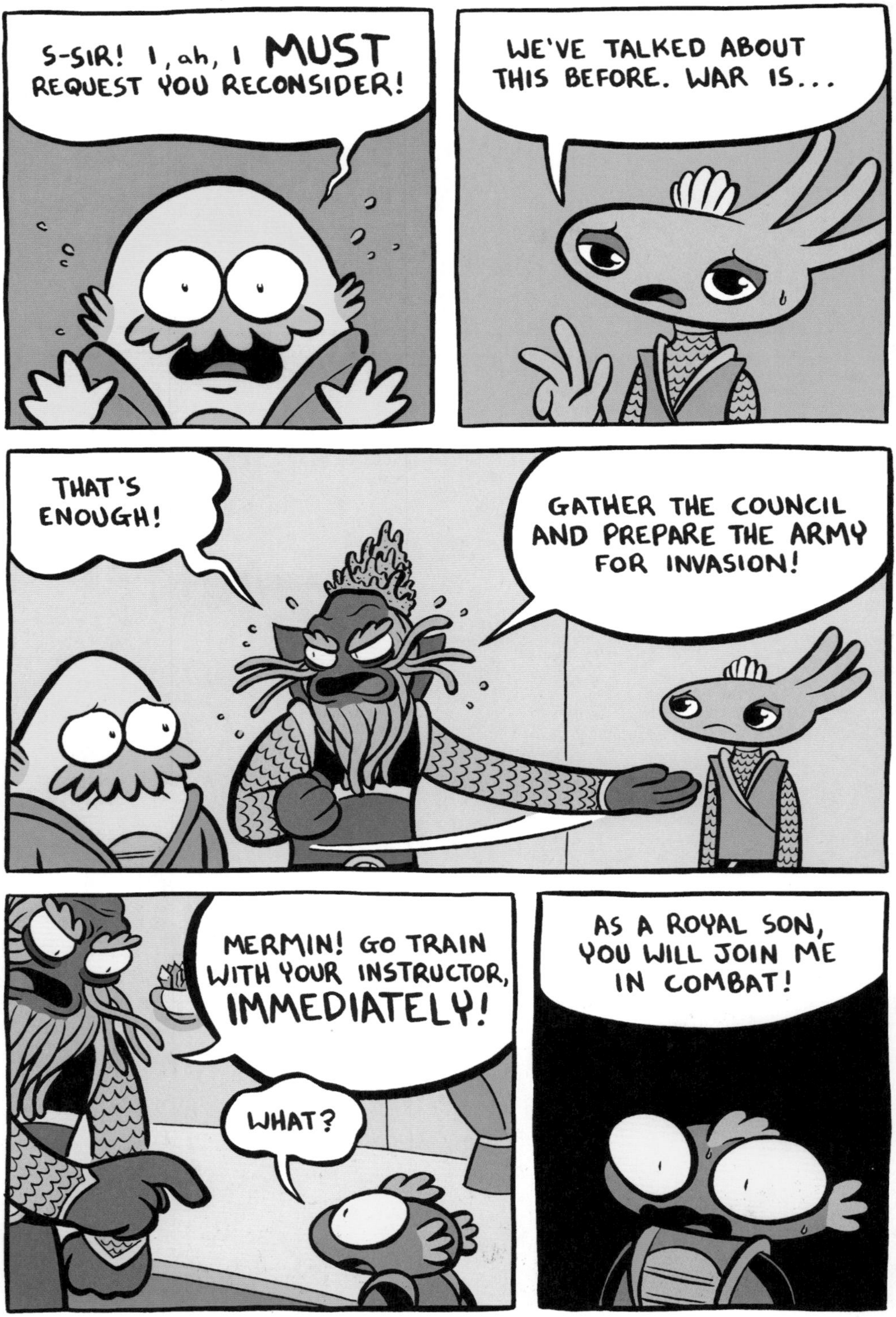
S-SIR! I, ah, I MUST REQUEST YOU RECONSIDER!
WE'VE TALKED ABOUT THIS BEFORE. WAR IS...
THAT'S ENOUGH!
GATHER THE COUNCIL AND PREPARE THE ARMY FOR INVASION!
MERMIN! GO TRAIN WITH YOUR INSTRUCTOR, IMMEDIATELY!
WHAT?
AS A ROYAL SON, YOU WILL JOIN ME IN COMBAT!

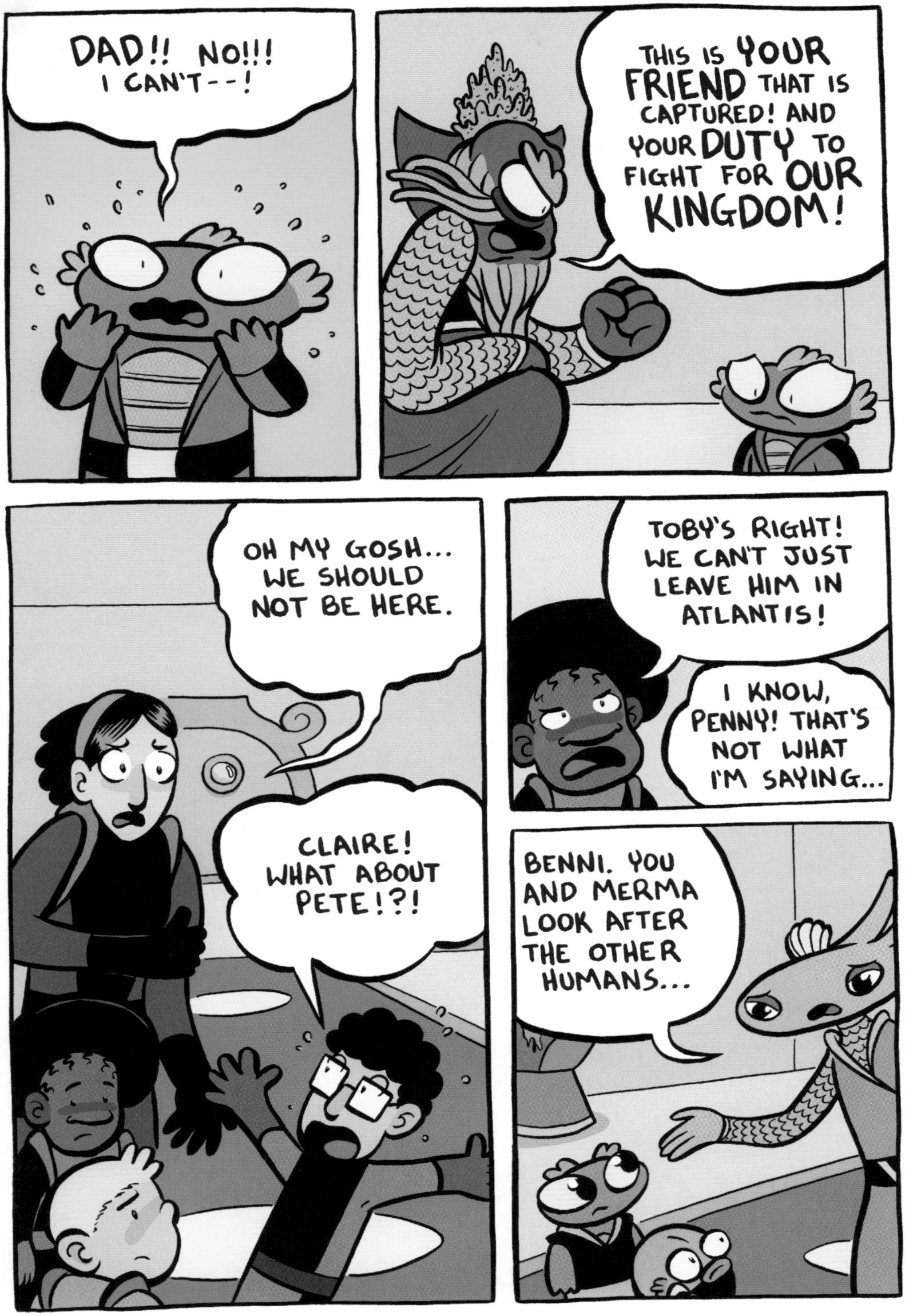
DAD!! NO!!! I CAN'T--!
THIS IS YOUR FRIEND THAT IS CAPTURED! AND YOUR DUTY TO FIGHT FOR OUR KINGDOM!
OH MY GOSH... WE SHOULD NOT BE HERE.
CLAIRE! WHAT ABOUT PETE!?!
TOBY'S RIGHT! WE CAN'T JUST LEAVE HIM IN ATLANTIS!
I KNOW, PENNY! THAT'S NOT WHAT I'M SAYING...
BENNI. YOU AND MERMA LOOK AFTER THE OTHER HUMANS...

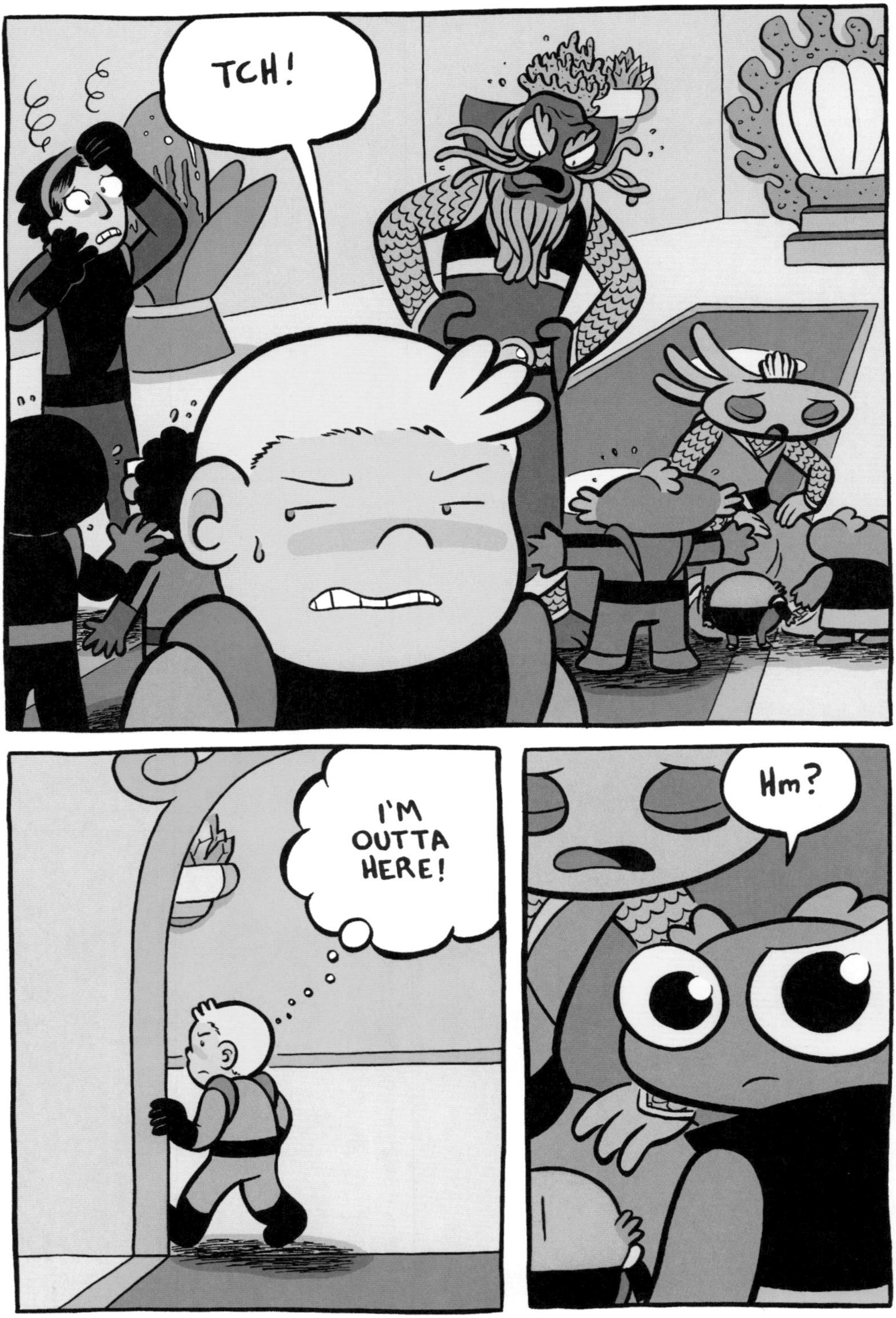
TCH!
I'M OUTTA HERE!
Hm?

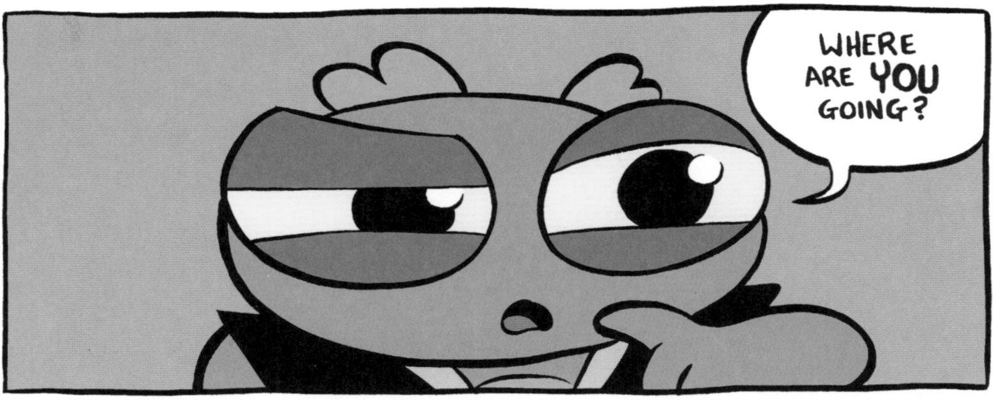
WHERE ARE YOU GOING?

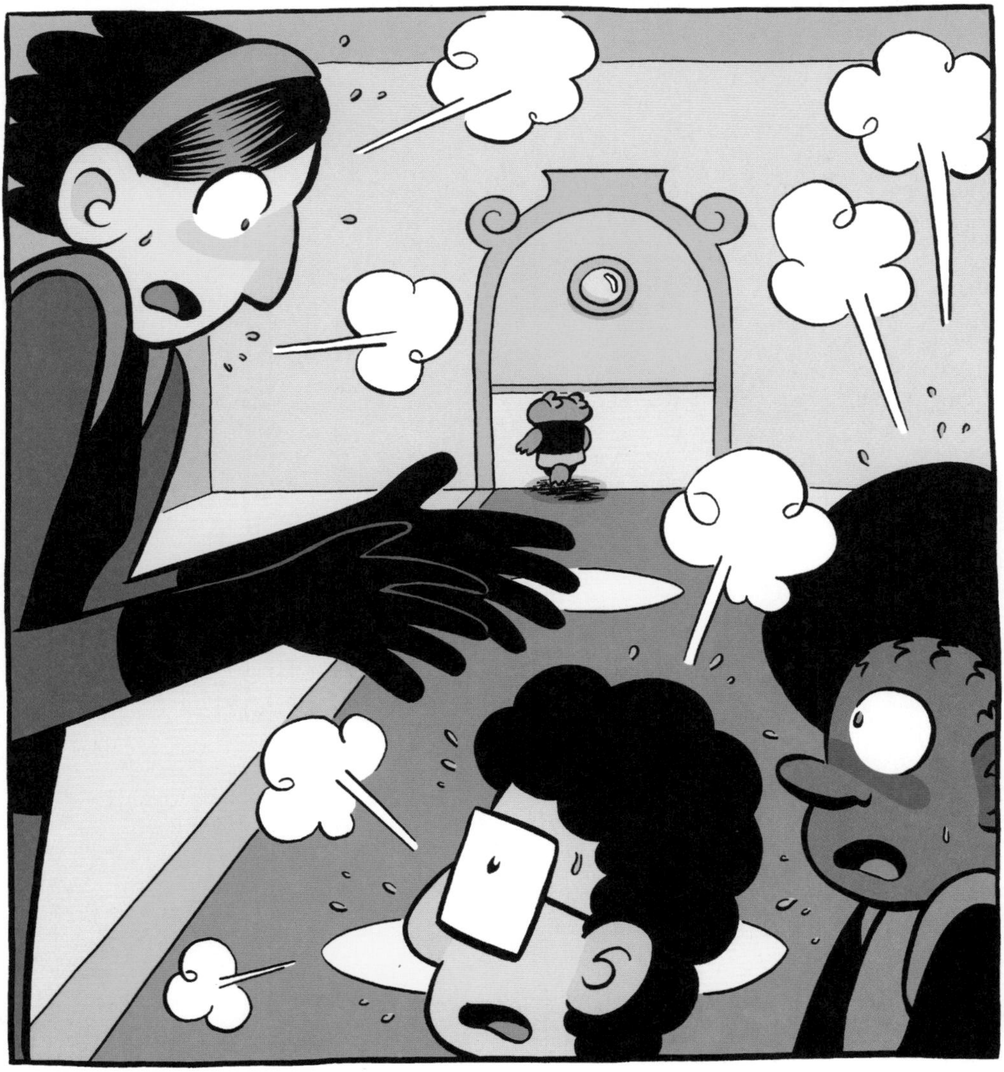

CHAPTER TWO

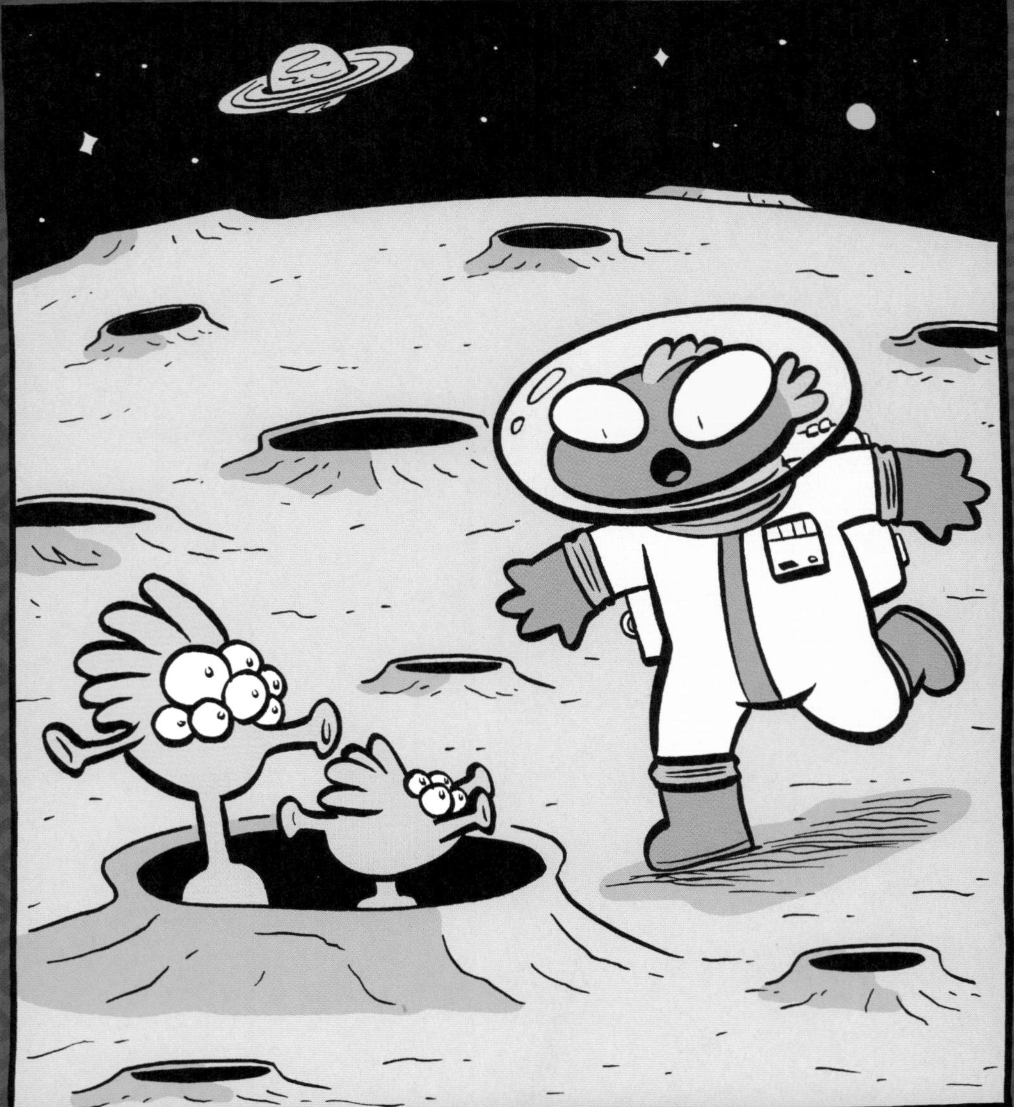

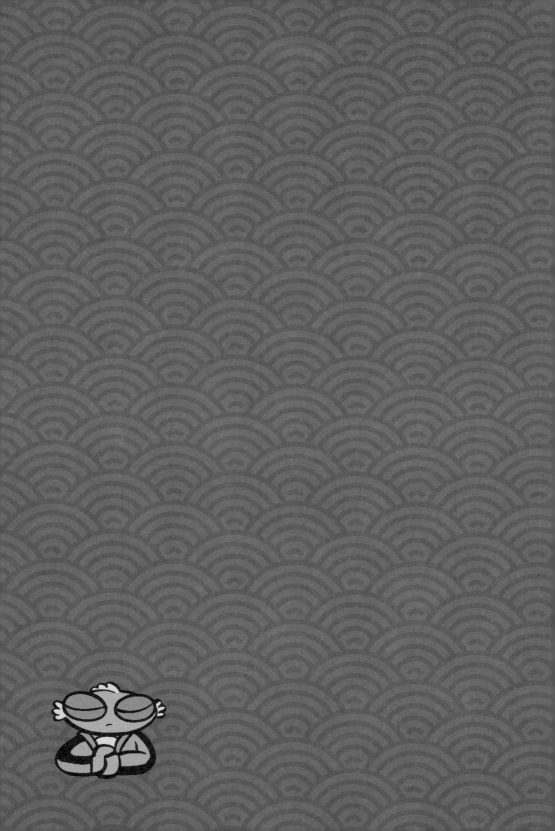

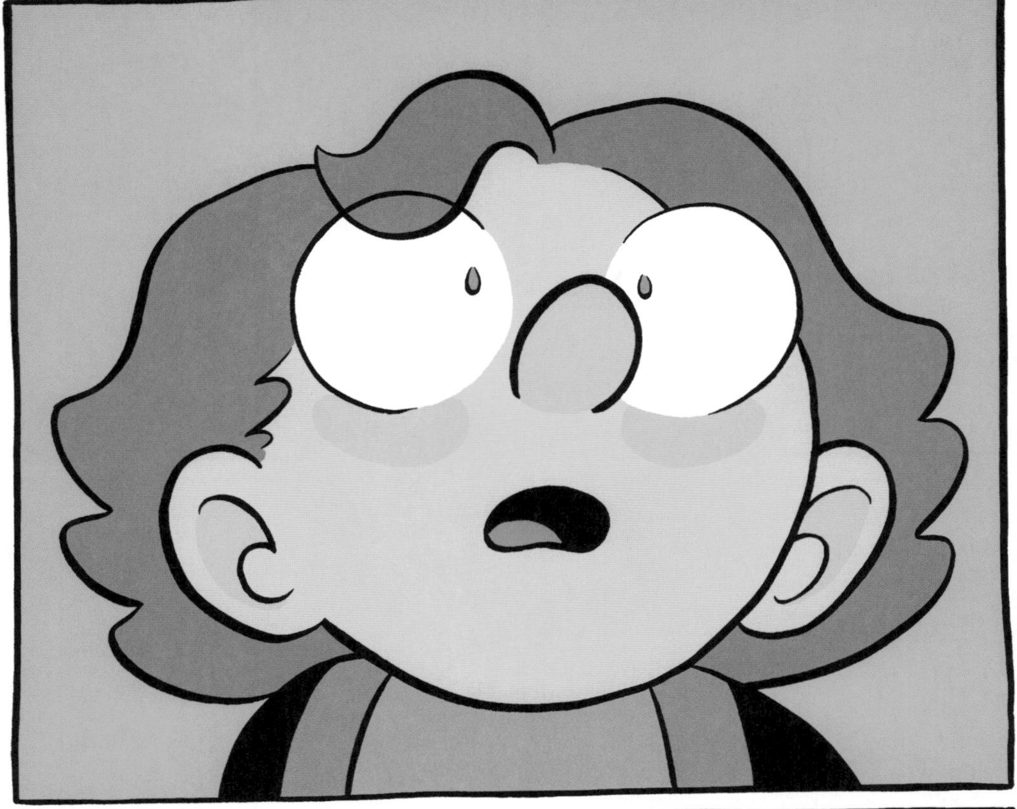

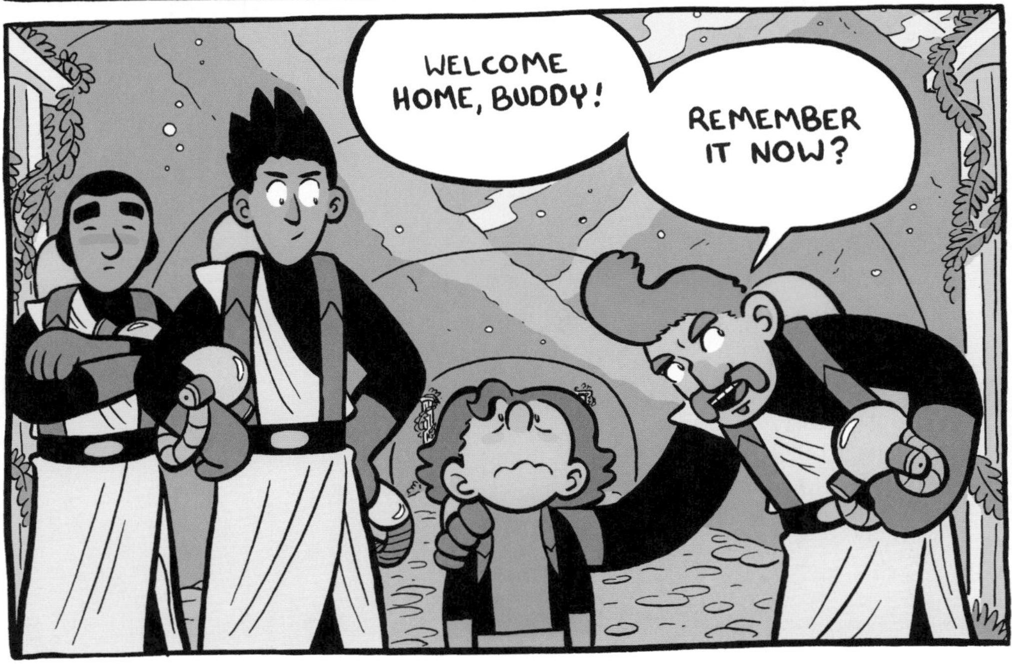
WELCOME HOME, BUDDY!
REMEMBER IT NOW?

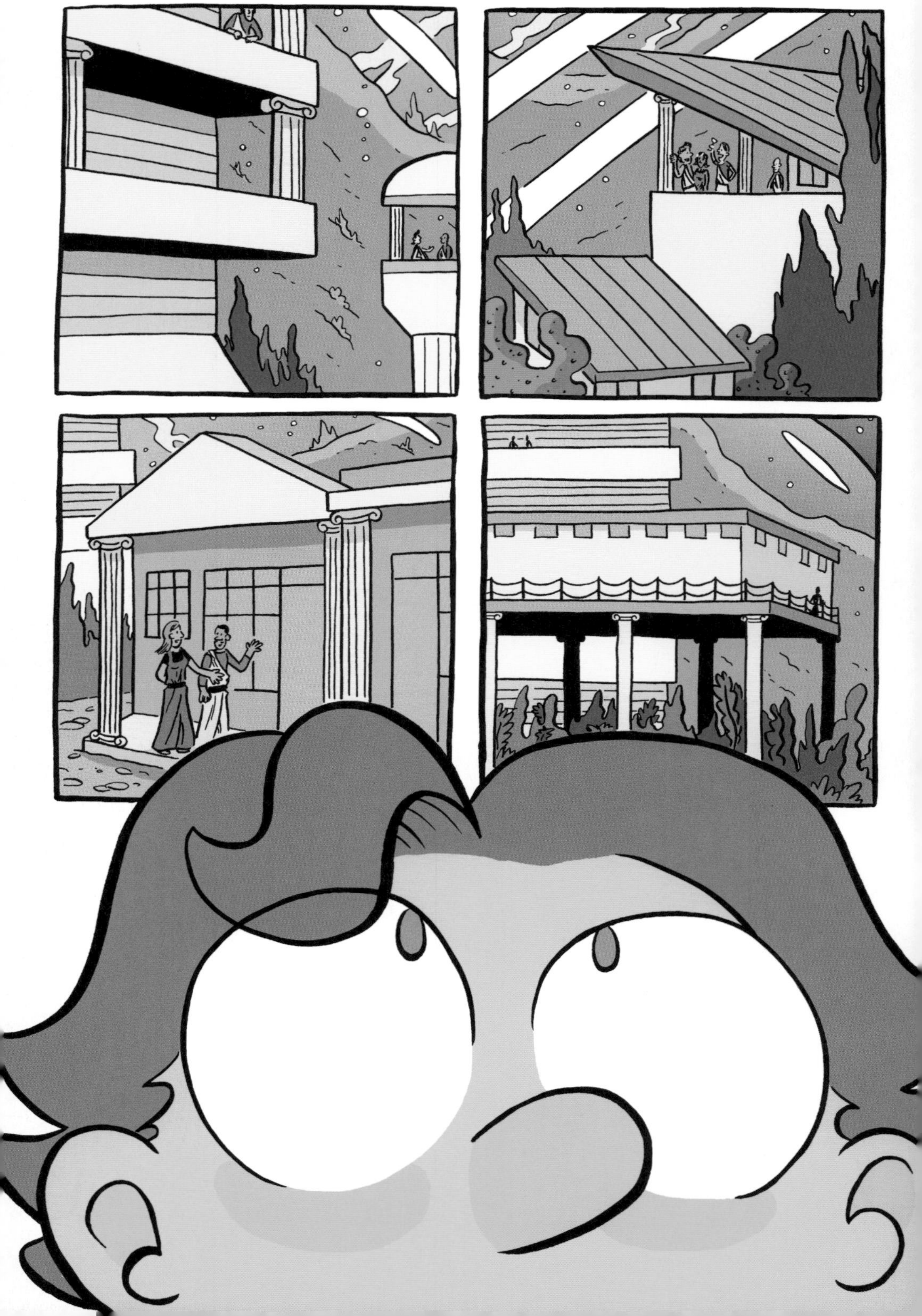

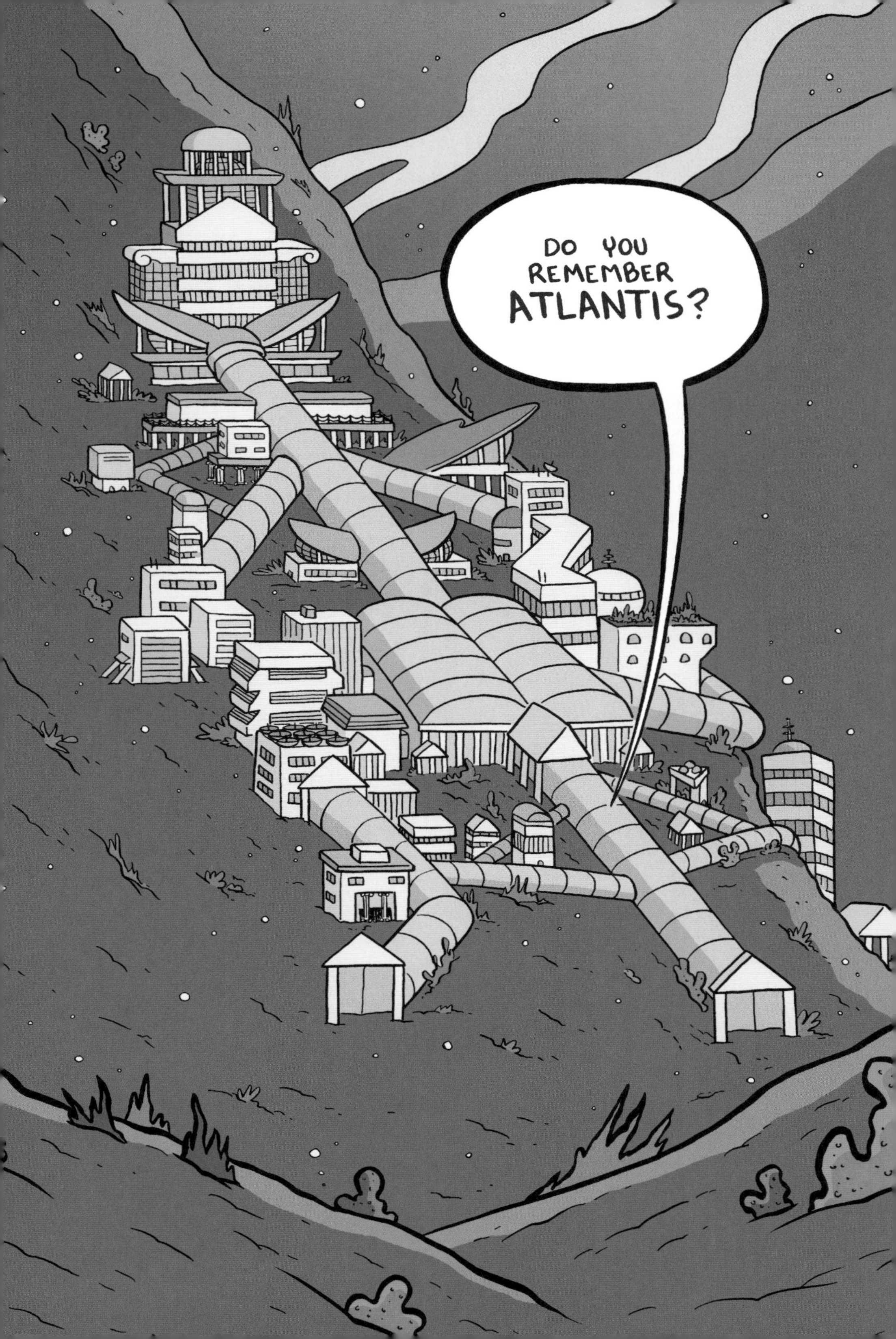
DO YOU REMEMBER ATLANTIS?

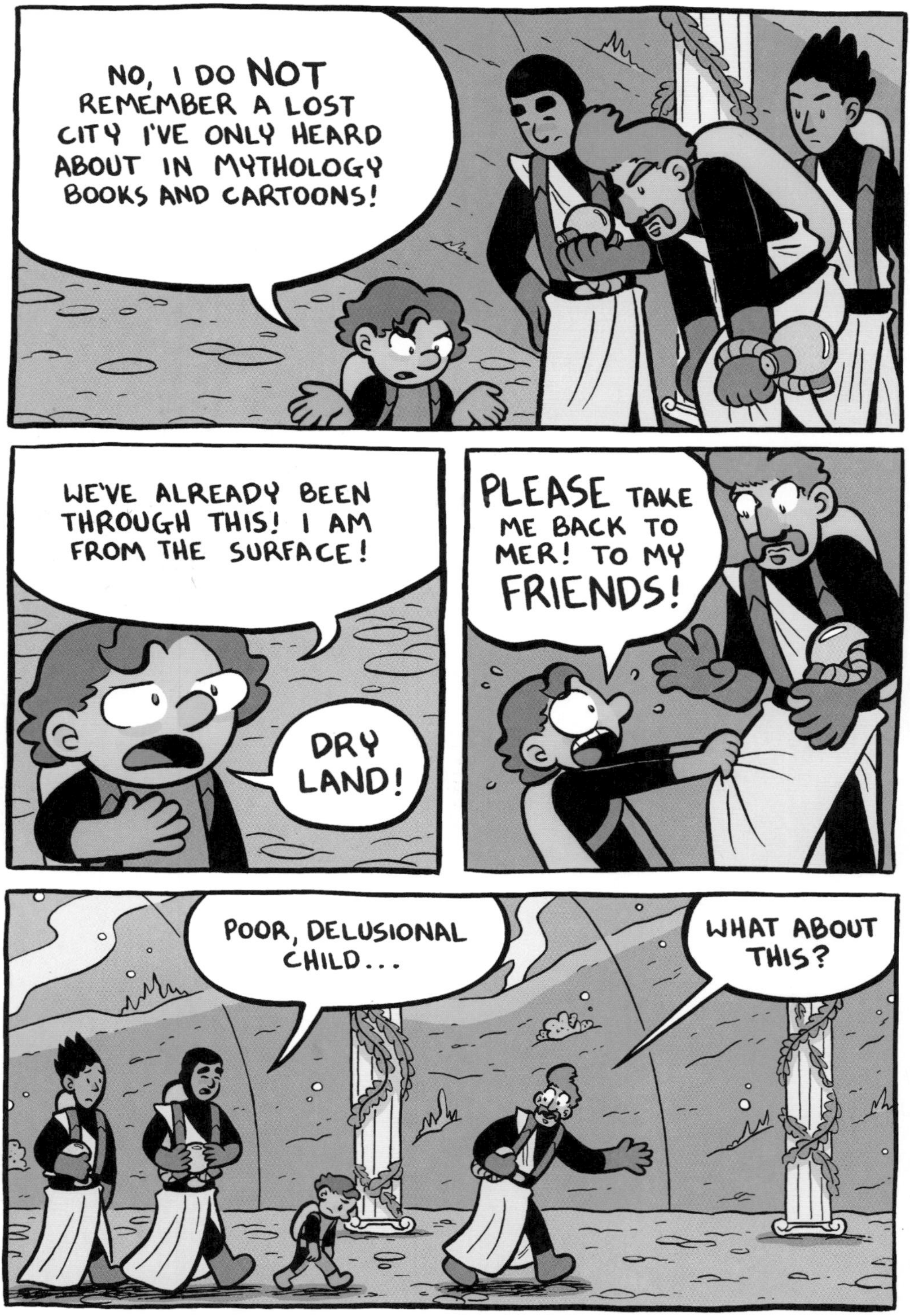
NO, I DO NOT REMEMBER A LOST CITY I'VE ONLY HEARD ABOUT IN MYTHOLOGY BOOKS AND CARTOONS!
WE'VE ALREADY BEEN THROUGH THIS! I AM FROM THE SURFACE!
DRY LAND!
PLEASE TAKE ME BACK TO MER! TO MY FRIENDS!
POOR, DELUSIONAL CHILD...
WHAT ABOUT THIS?

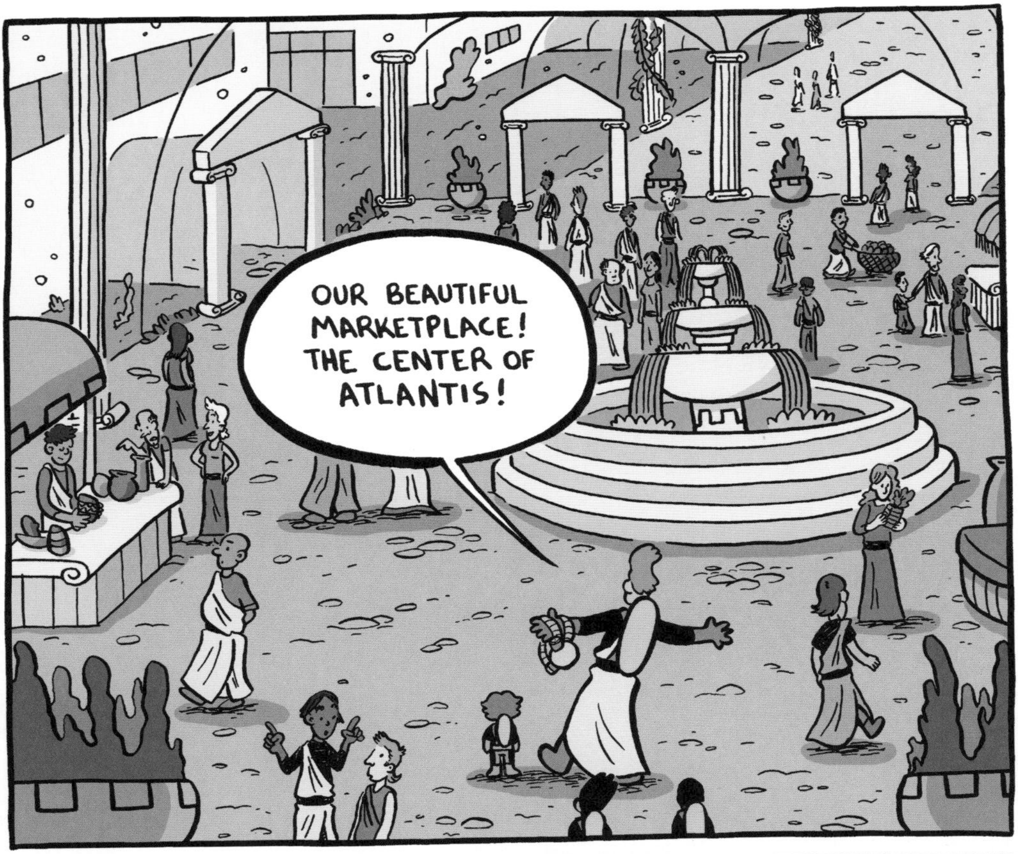
OUR BEAUTIFUL MARKETPLACE! THE CENTER OF ATLANTIS!

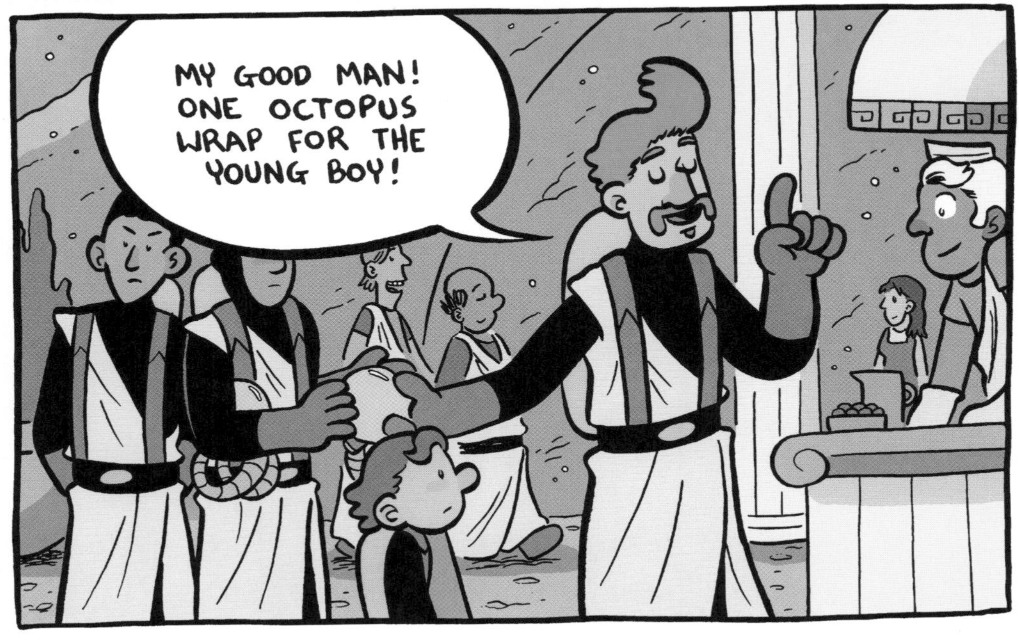
MY GOOD MAN! ONE OCTOPUS WRAP FOR THE YOUNG BOY!

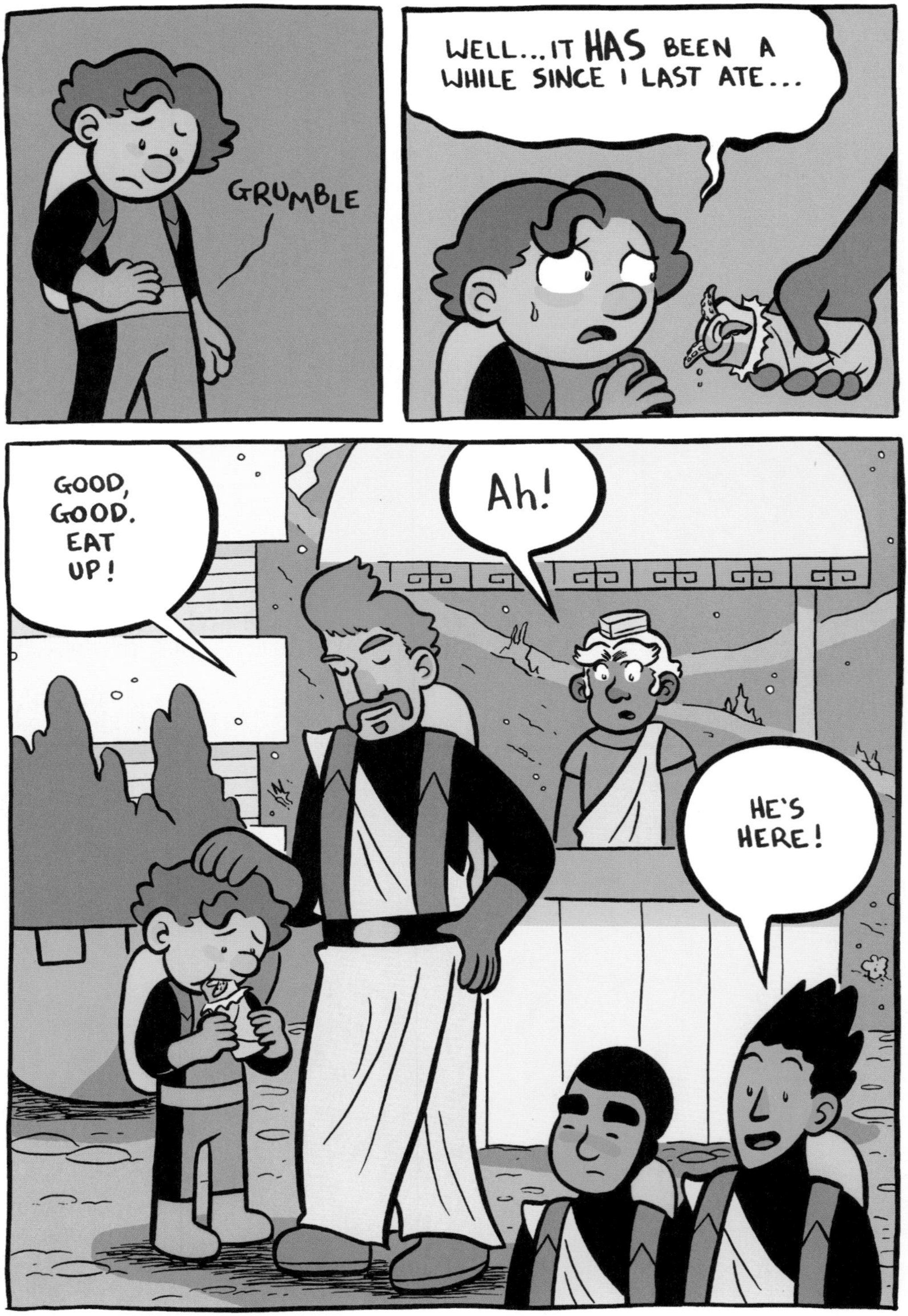
GRUMBLE
WELL... IT HAS BEEN A WHILE SINCE I LAST ATE...
GOOD, GOOD. EAT UP!
Ah!
HE'S HERE!

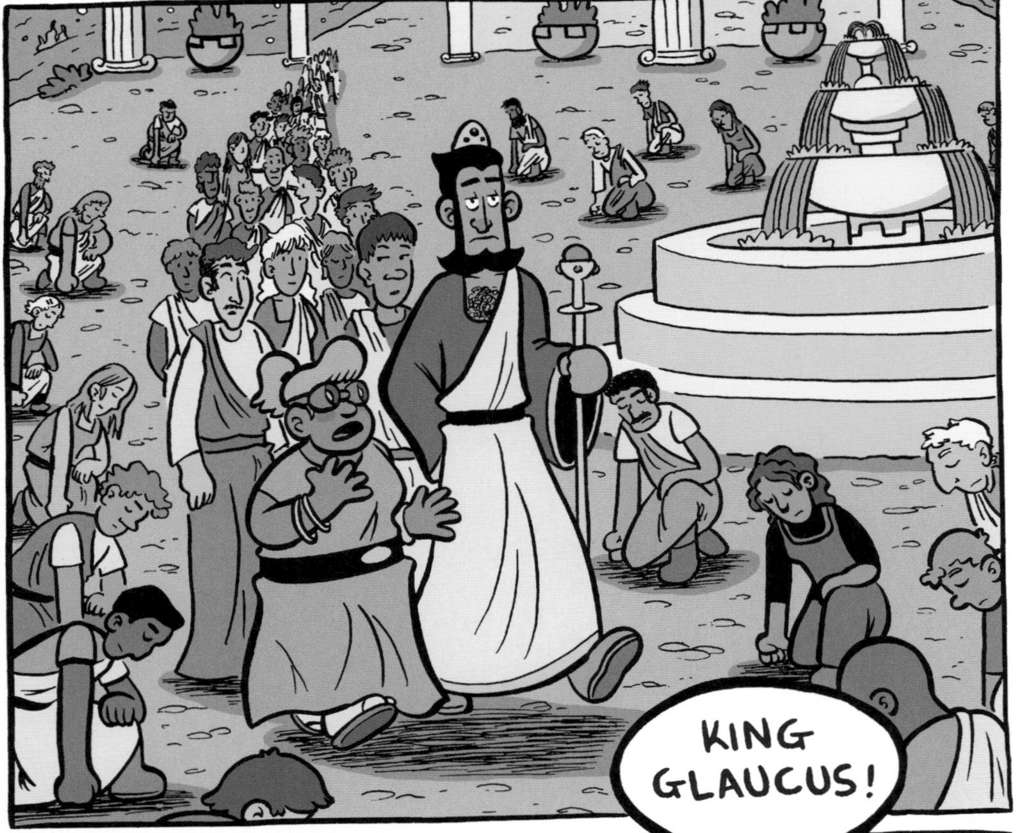
KING GLAUCUS!

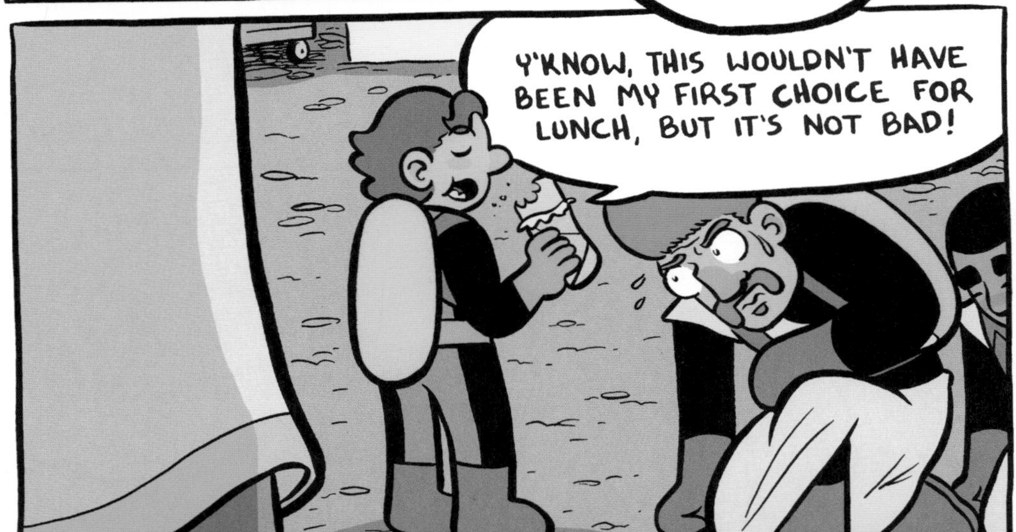
Y'KNOW, THIS WOULDN'T HAVE BEEN MY FIRST CHOICE FOR LUNCH, BUT IT'S NOT BAD!

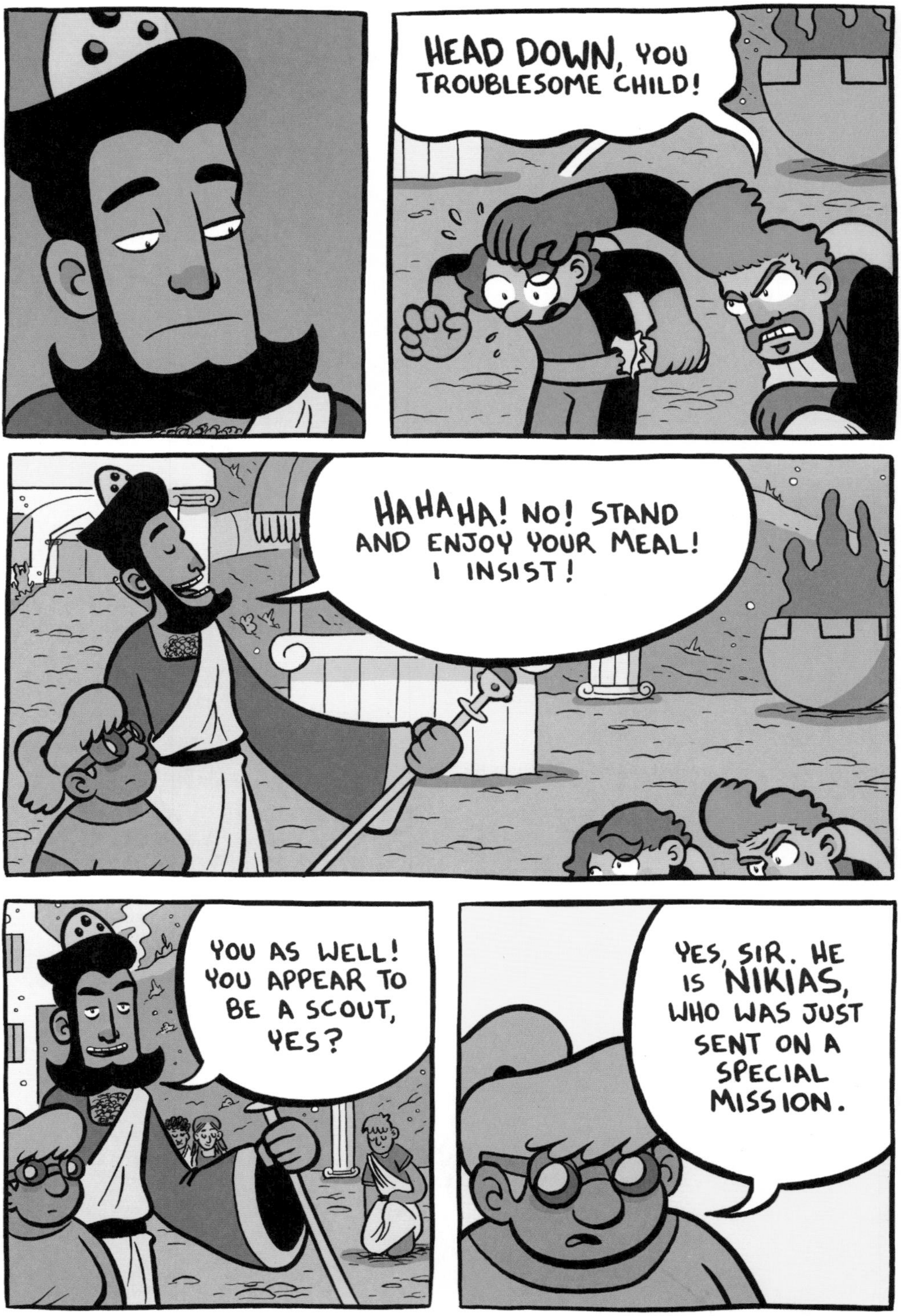
HEAD DOWN, YOU TROUBLESOME CHILD!
HAHAHA! NO! STAND AND ENJOY YOUR MEAL! I INSIST!
YOU AS WELL! YOU APPEAR TO BE A SCOUT, YES?
YES, SIR. HE IS NIKIAS, WHO WAS JUST SENT ON A SPECIAL MISSION.

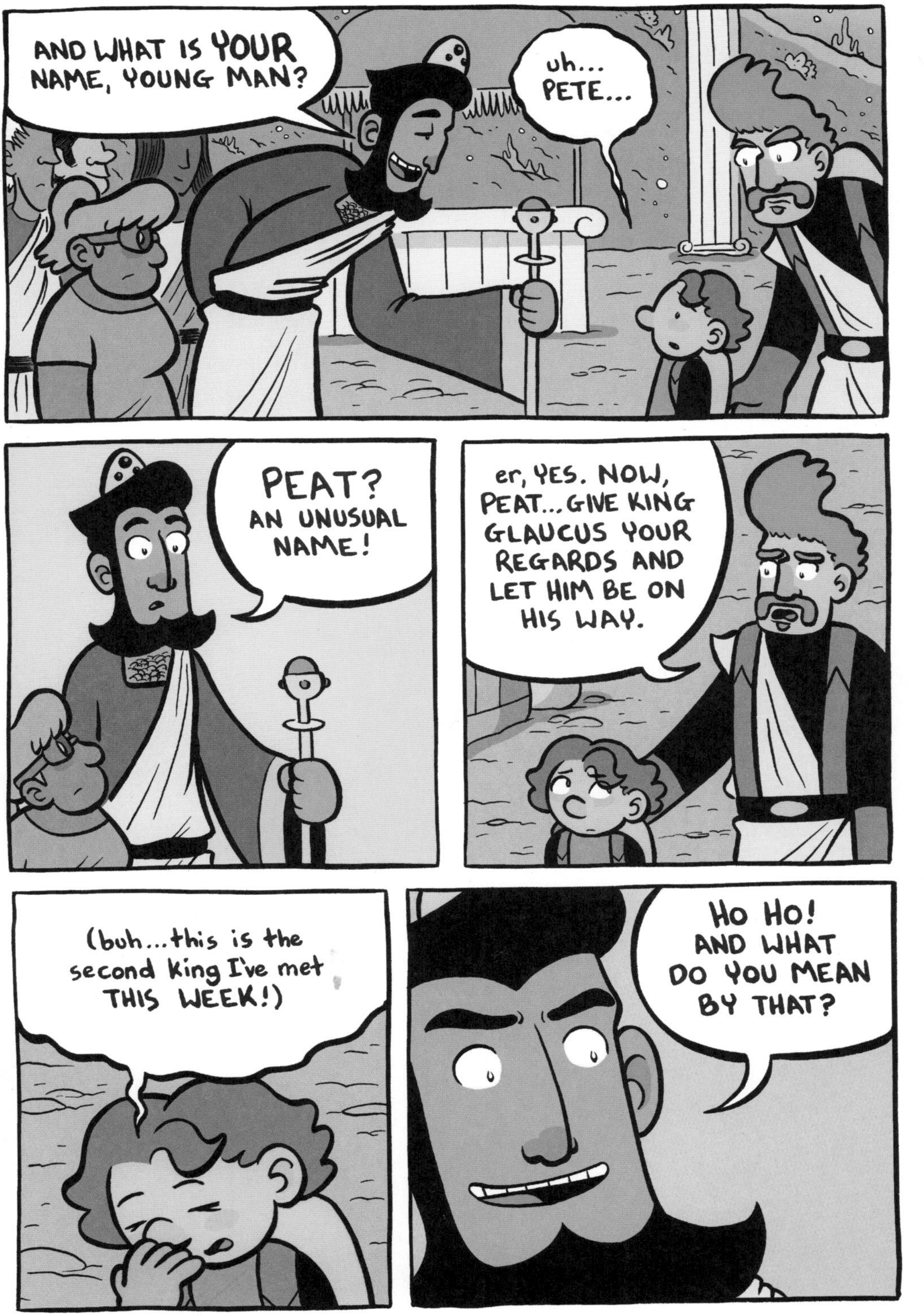
AND WHAT IS YOUR NAME, YOUNG MAN?
uh... PETE...
PEAT? AN UNUSUAL NAME!
er, YES. NOW, PEAT... GIVE KING GLAUCUS YOUR REGARDS AND LET HIM BE ON HIS WAY.
(buh... this is the second king I've met THIS WEEK!)
HO HO! AND WHAT DO YOU MEAN BY THAT?

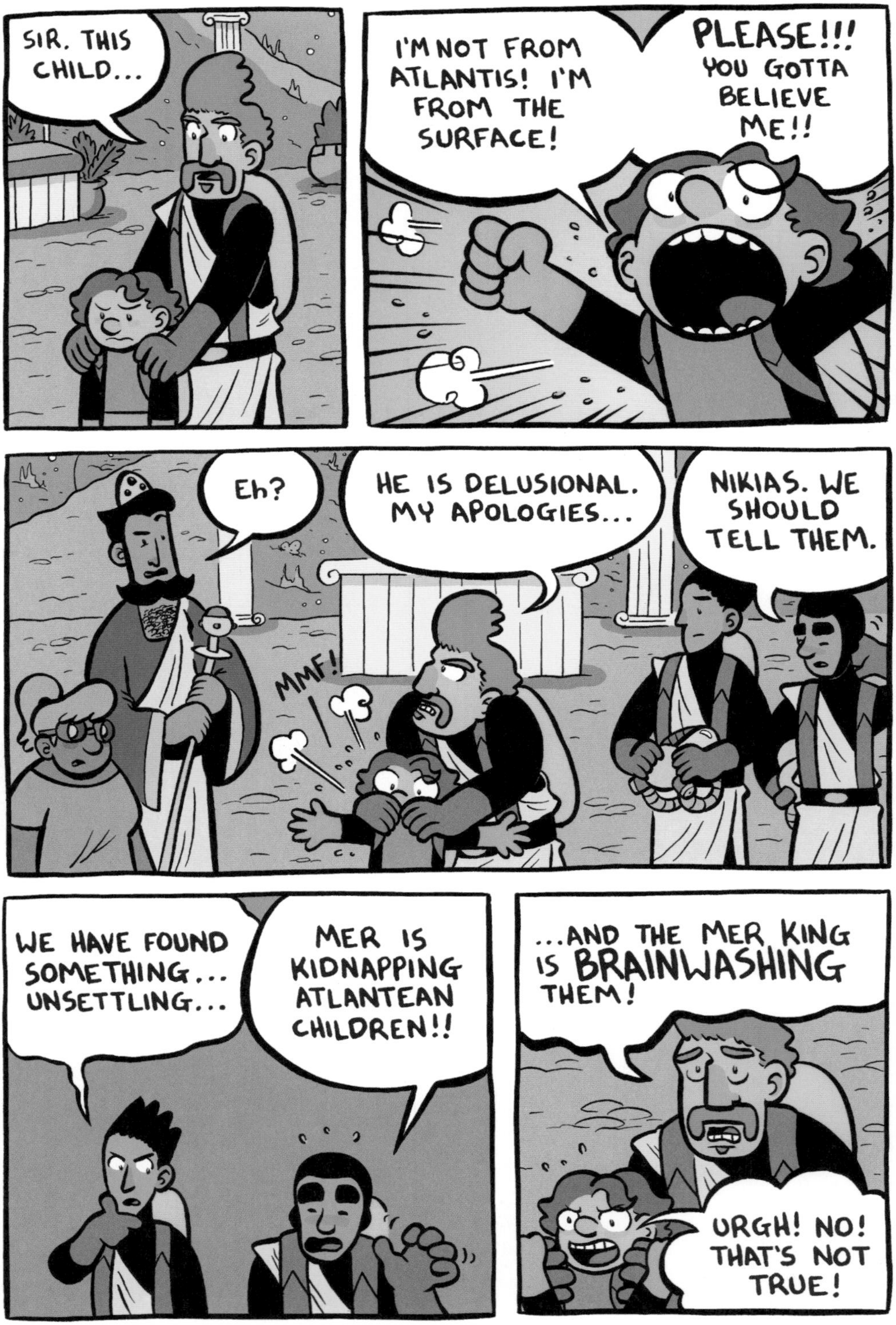
SIR. THIS CHILD...
I'M NOT FROM ATLANTIS! I'M FROM THE SURFACE!
PLEASE!!! YOU GOTTA BELIEVE ME!!
Eh?
HE IS DELUSIONAL. MY APOLOGIES...
MMF!
NIKIAS. WE SHOULD TELL THEM.
WE HAVE FOUND SOMETHING... UNSETTLING...
MER IS KIDNAPPING ATLANTEAN CHILDREN!!
...AND THE MER KING IS BRAINWASHING THEM!
URGH! NO! THAT'S NOT TRUE!

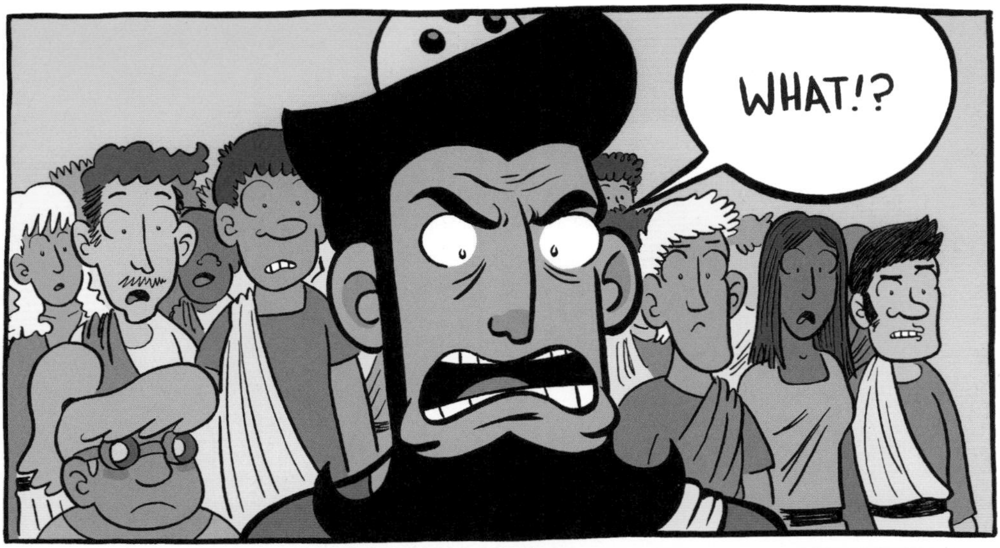
WHAT!?

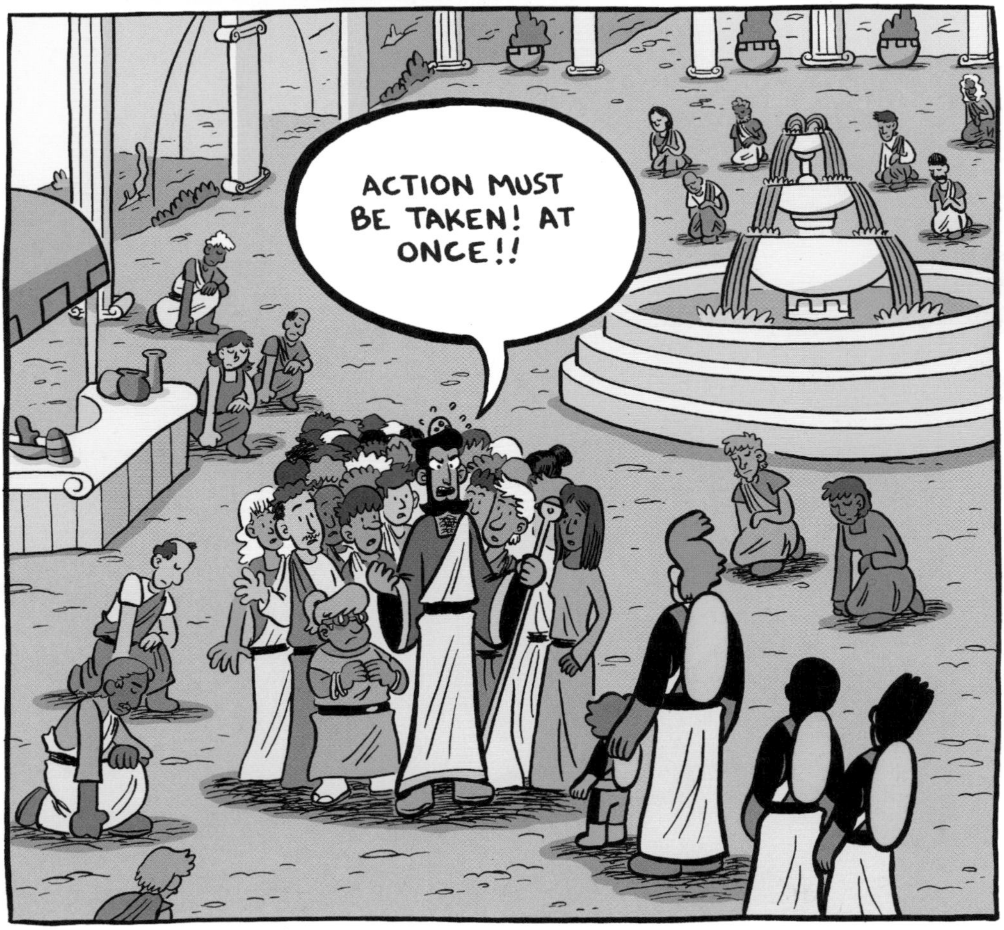
ACTION MUST BE TAKEN! AT ONCE!!

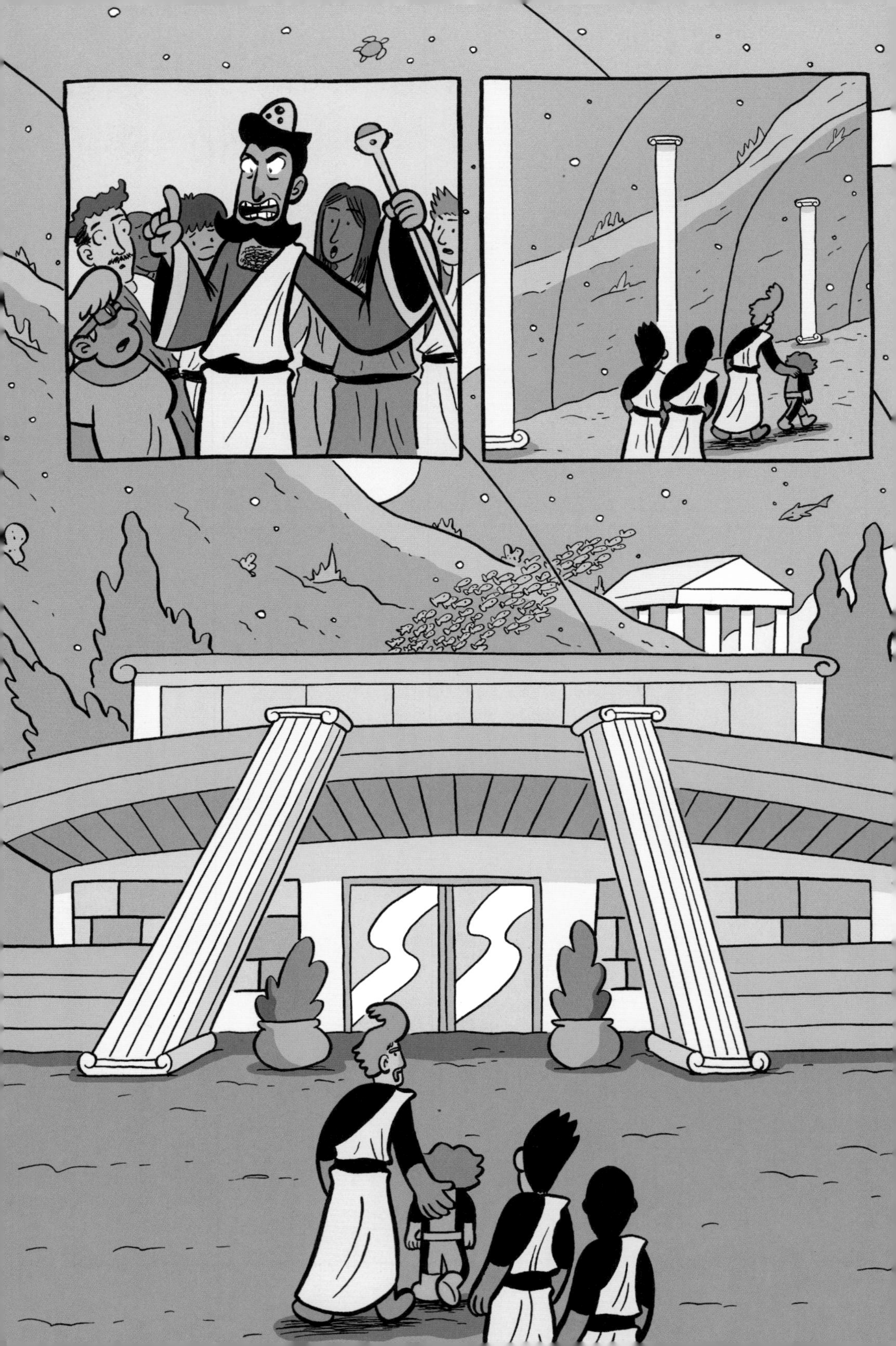

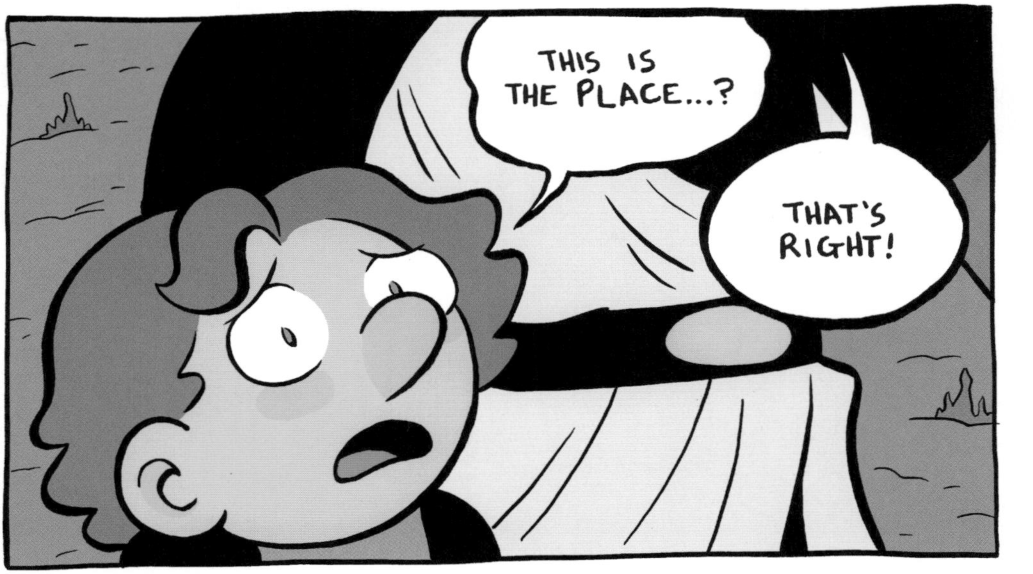
THIS IS THE PLACE...?
THAT'S RIGHT!

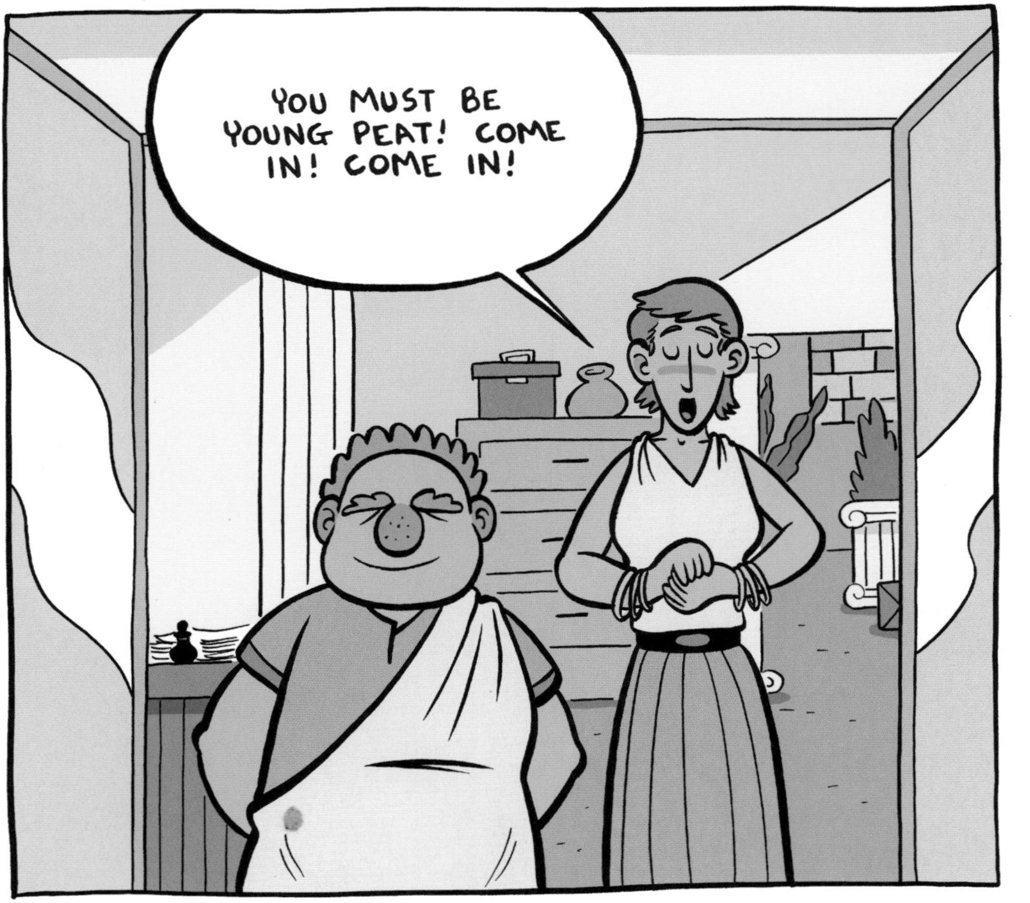
YOU MUST BE YOUNG PEAT! COME IN! COME IN!

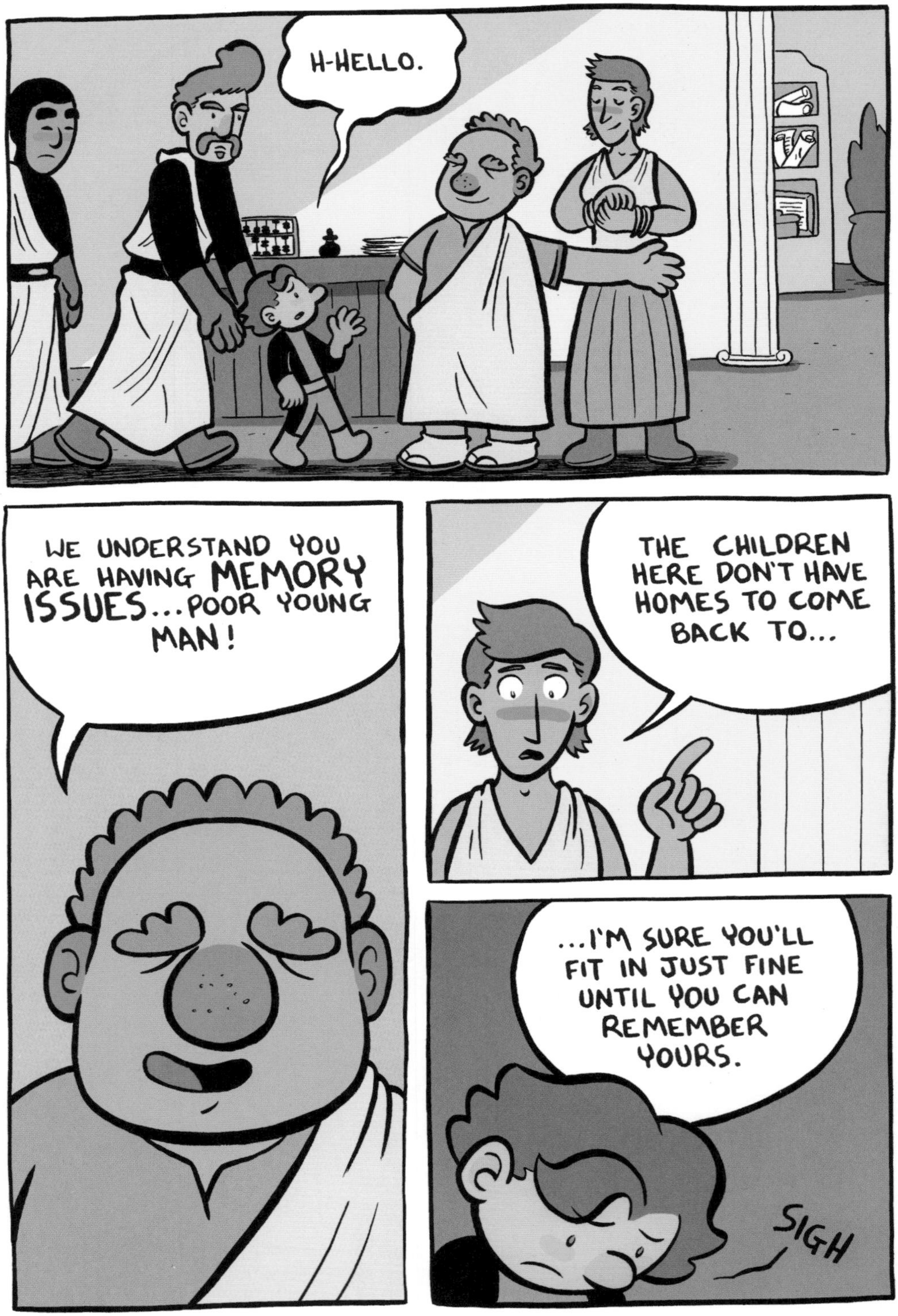
H-HELLO.
WE UNDERSTAND YOU ARE HAVING MEMORY ISSUES... POOR YOUNG MAN!
THE CHILDREN HERE DON'T HAVE HOMES TO COME BACK TO...
...I'M SURE YOU'LL FIT IN JUST FINE UNTIL YOU CAN REMEMBER YOURS.
SIGH

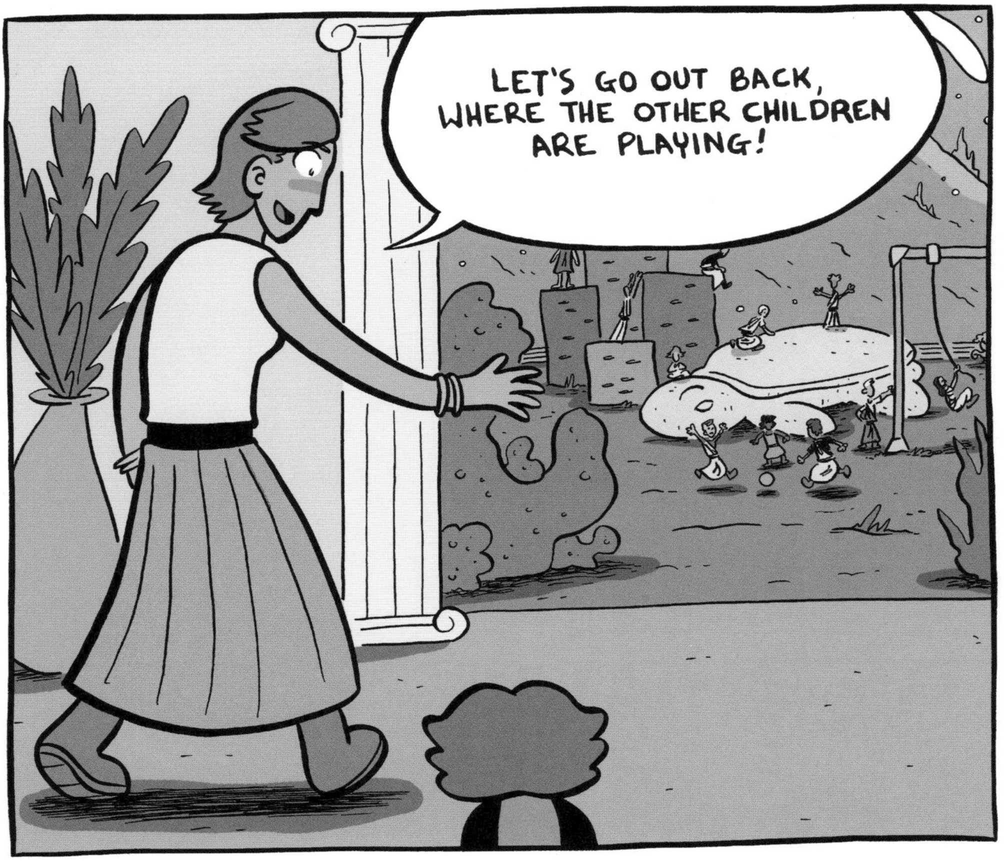
LET'S GO OUT BACK, WHERE THE OTHER CHILDREN ARE PLAYING!

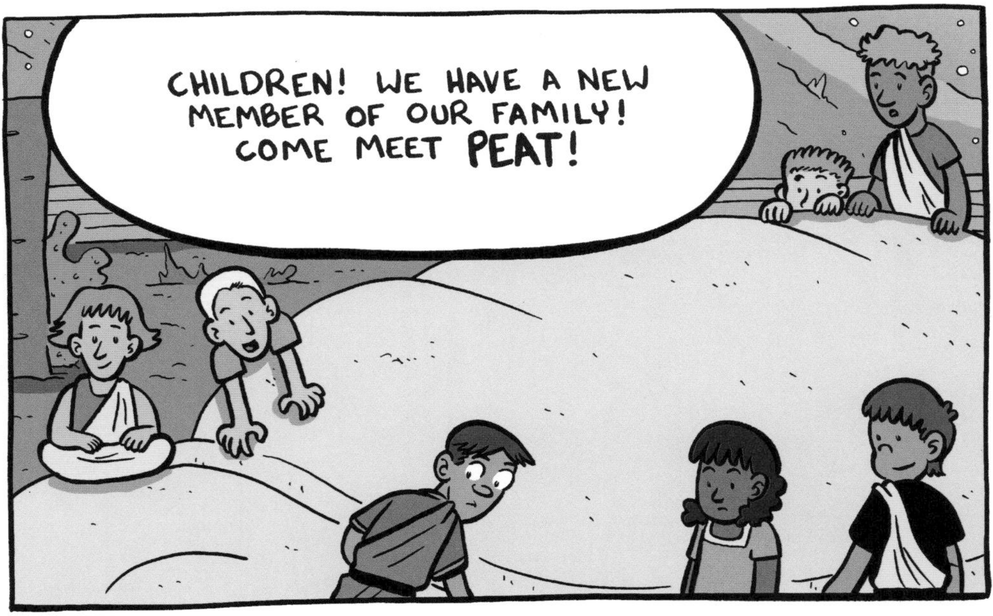
CHILDREN! WE HAVE A NEW MEMBER OF OUR FAMILY! COME MEET **PEAT**!

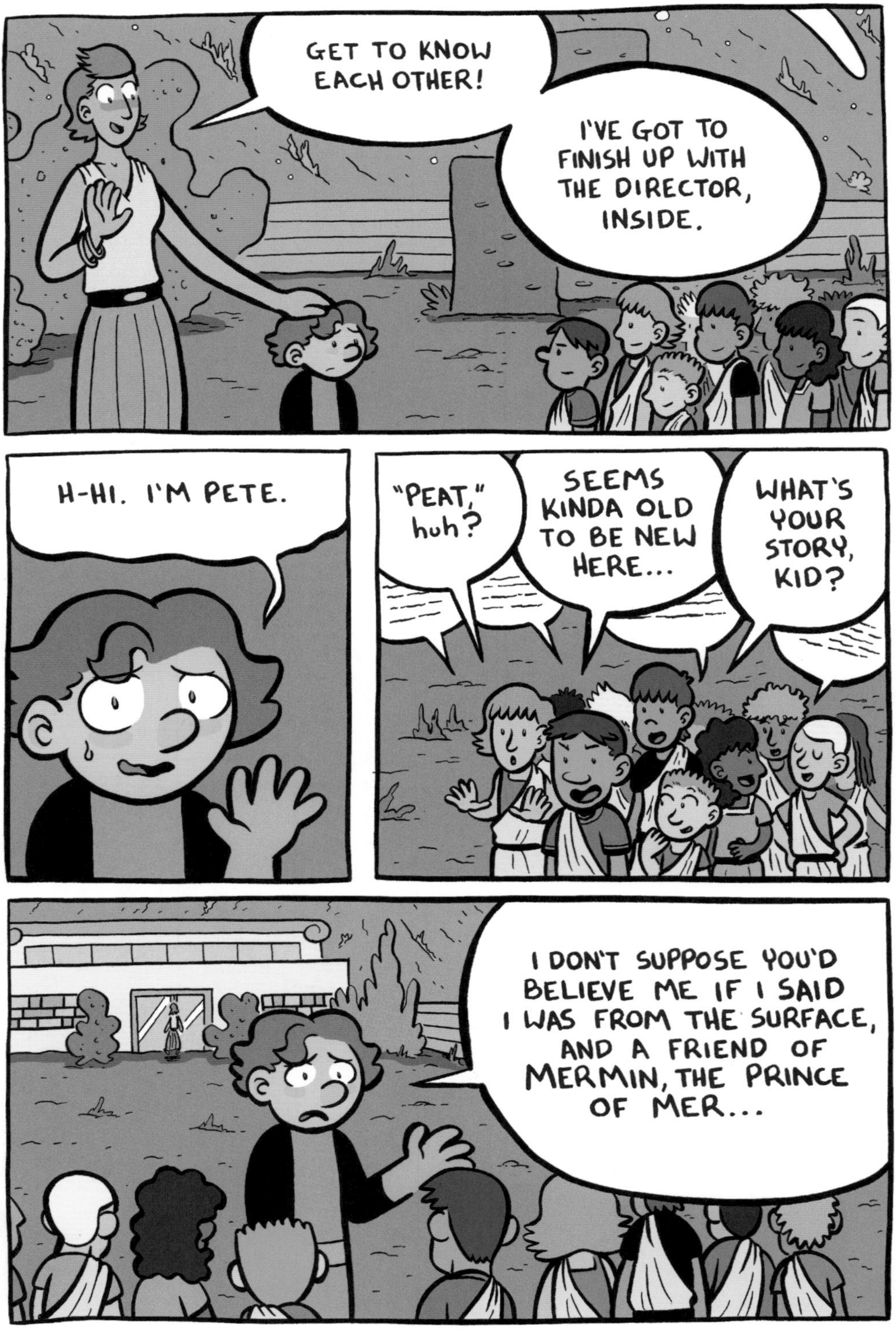
GET TO KNOW EACH OTHER!
I'VE GOT TO FINISH UP WITH THE DIRECTOR, INSIDE.
H-HI. I'M PETE.
"PEAT," huh?
SEEMS KINDA OLD TO BE NEW HERE...
WHAT'S YOUR STORY, KID?
I DON'T SUPPOSE YOU'D BELIEVE ME IF I SAID I WAS FROM THE SURFACE, AND A FRIEND OF MERMIN, THE PRINCE OF MER...

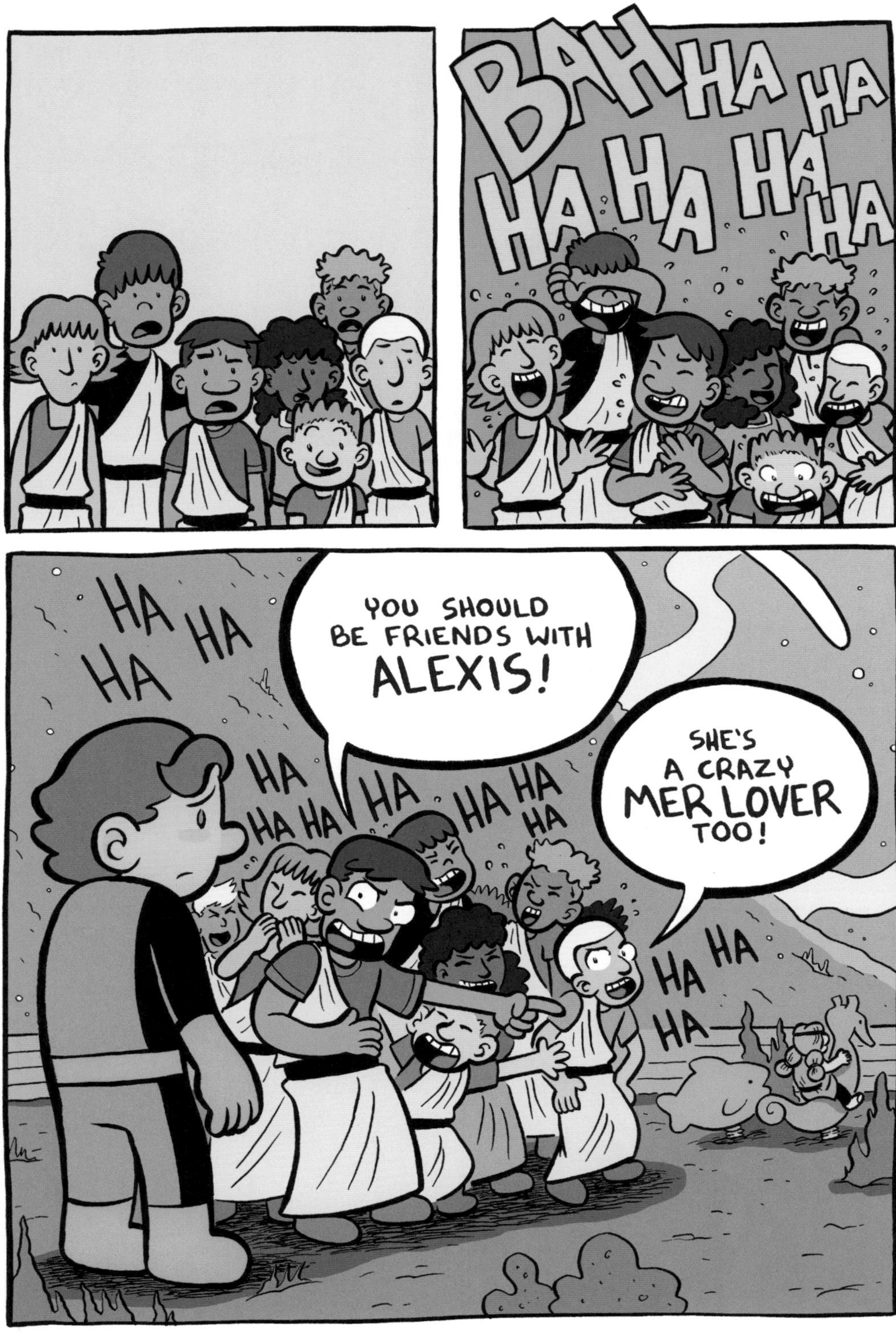
BAH HA HA HA
HA HA HA HA HA HA
HA HA HA
YOU SHOULD BE FRIENDS WITH ALEXIS!
HA HA HA HA HA HA HA HA
SHE'S A CRAZY MER LOVER TOO!
HA HA HA HA

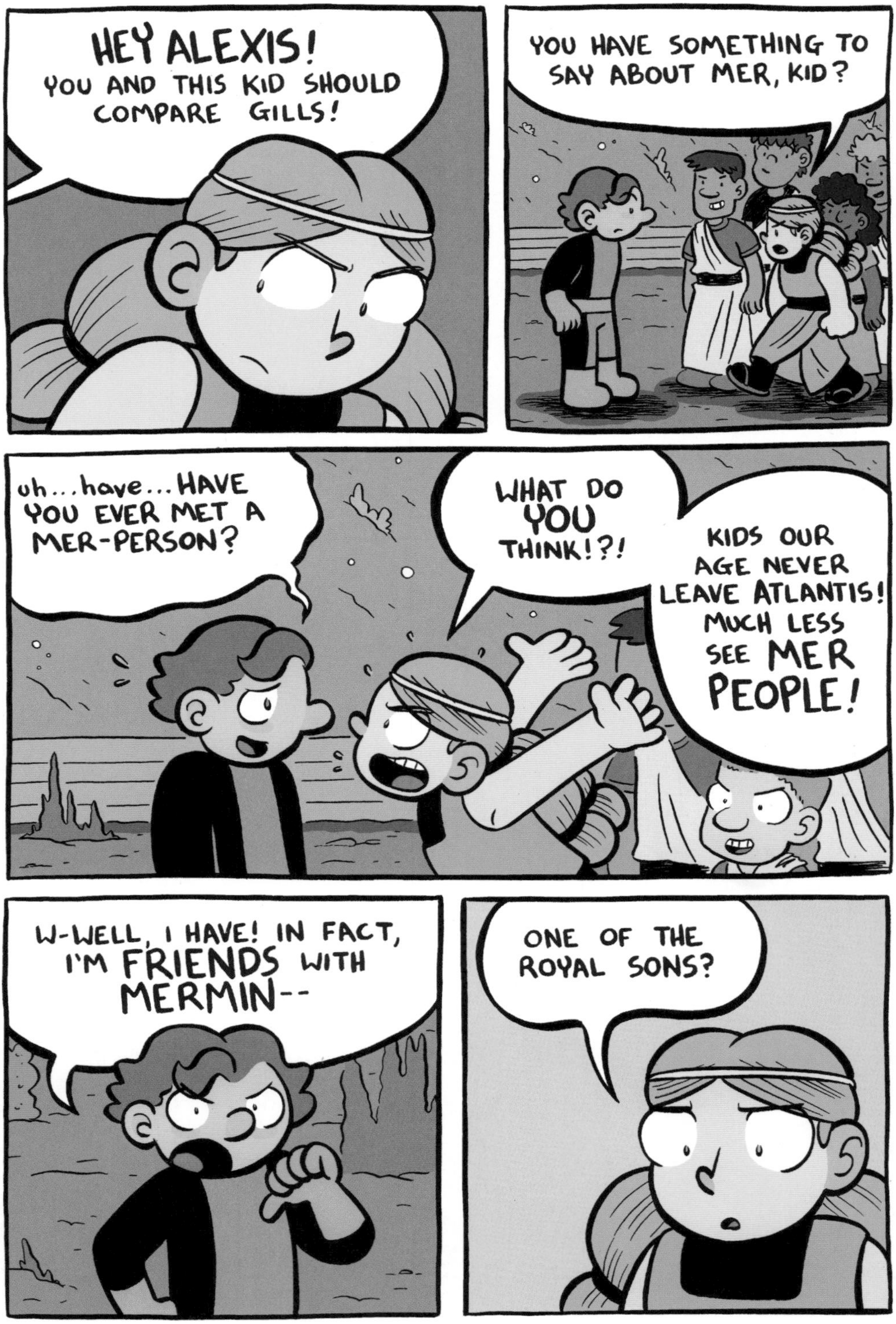
HEY ALEXIS! YOU AND THIS KID SHOULD COMPARE GILLS!
YOU HAVE SOMETHING TO SAY ABOUT MER, KID?
uh...have...HAVE YOU EVER MET A MER-PERSON?
WHAT DO YOU THINK!?!
KIDS OUR AGE NEVER LEAVE ATLANTIS! MUCH LESS SEE MER PEOPLE!
W-WELL, I HAVE! IN FACT, I'M FRIENDS WITH MERMIN--
ONE OF THE ROYAL SONS?

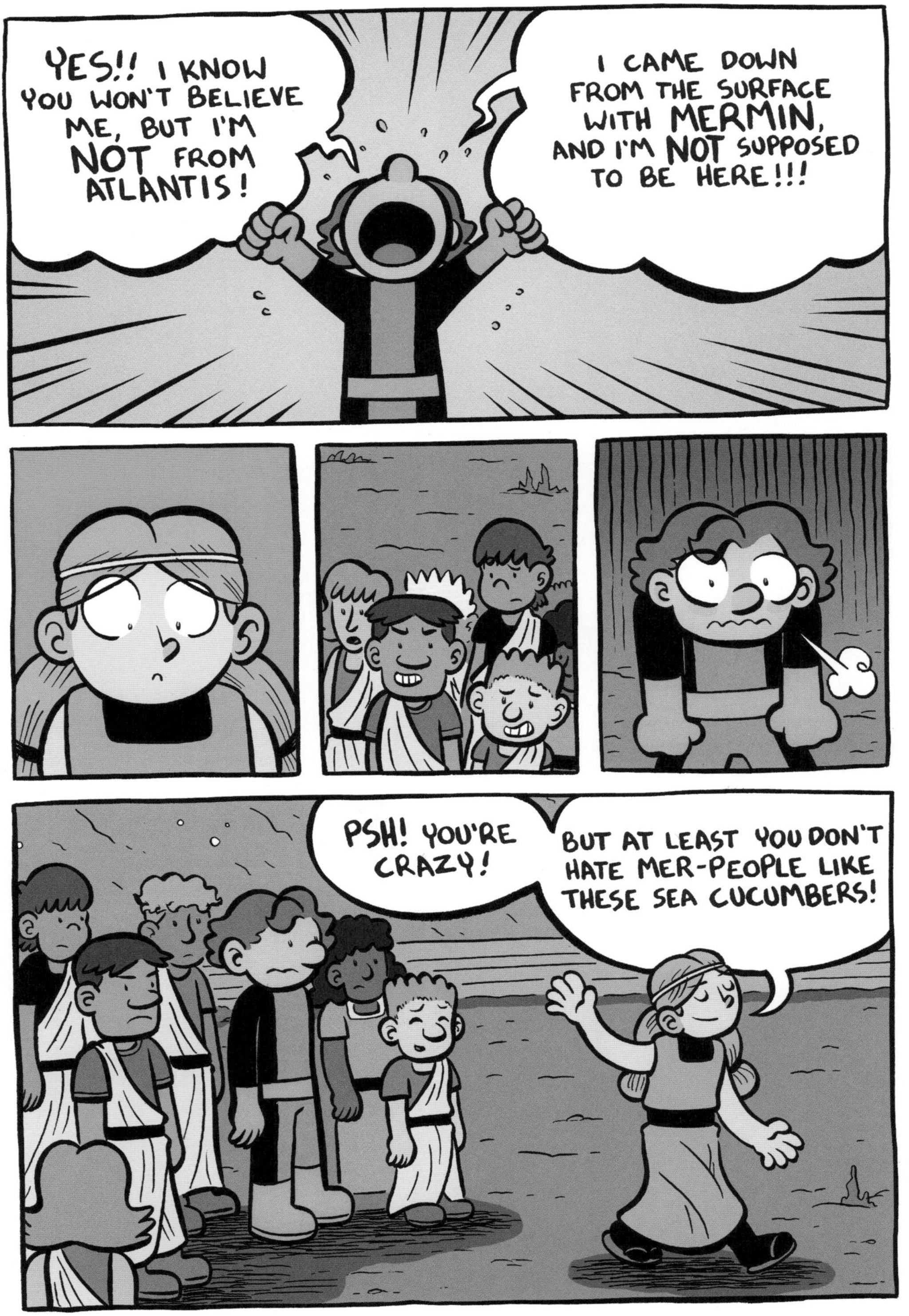
YES!! I KNOW YOU WON'T BELIEVE ME, BUT I'M NOT FROM ATLANTIS!
I CAME DOWN FROM THE SURFACE WITH MERMIN, AND I'M NOT SUPPOSED TO BE HERE!!!
PSH! YOU'RE CRAZY!
BUT AT LEAST YOU DON'T HATE MER-PEOPLE LIKE THESE SEA CUCUMBERS!

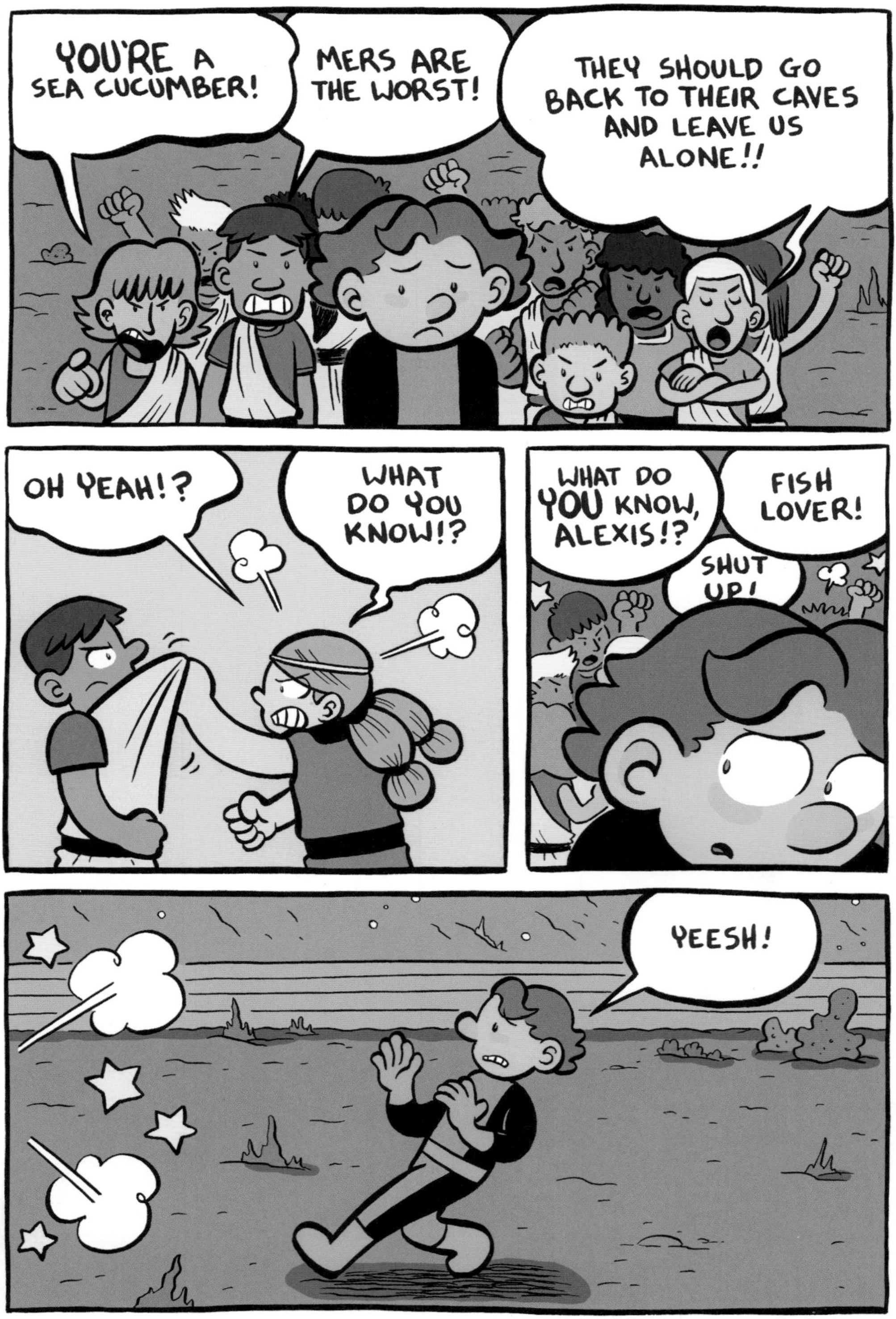
YOU'RE A SEA CUCUMBER!
MERS ARE THE WORST!
THEY SHOULD GO BACK TO THEIR CAVES AND LEAVE US ALONE!!
OH YEAH!?
WHAT DO YOU KNOW!?
WHAT DO YOU KNOW, ALEXIS!?
FISH LOVER!
SHUT UP!
YEESH!

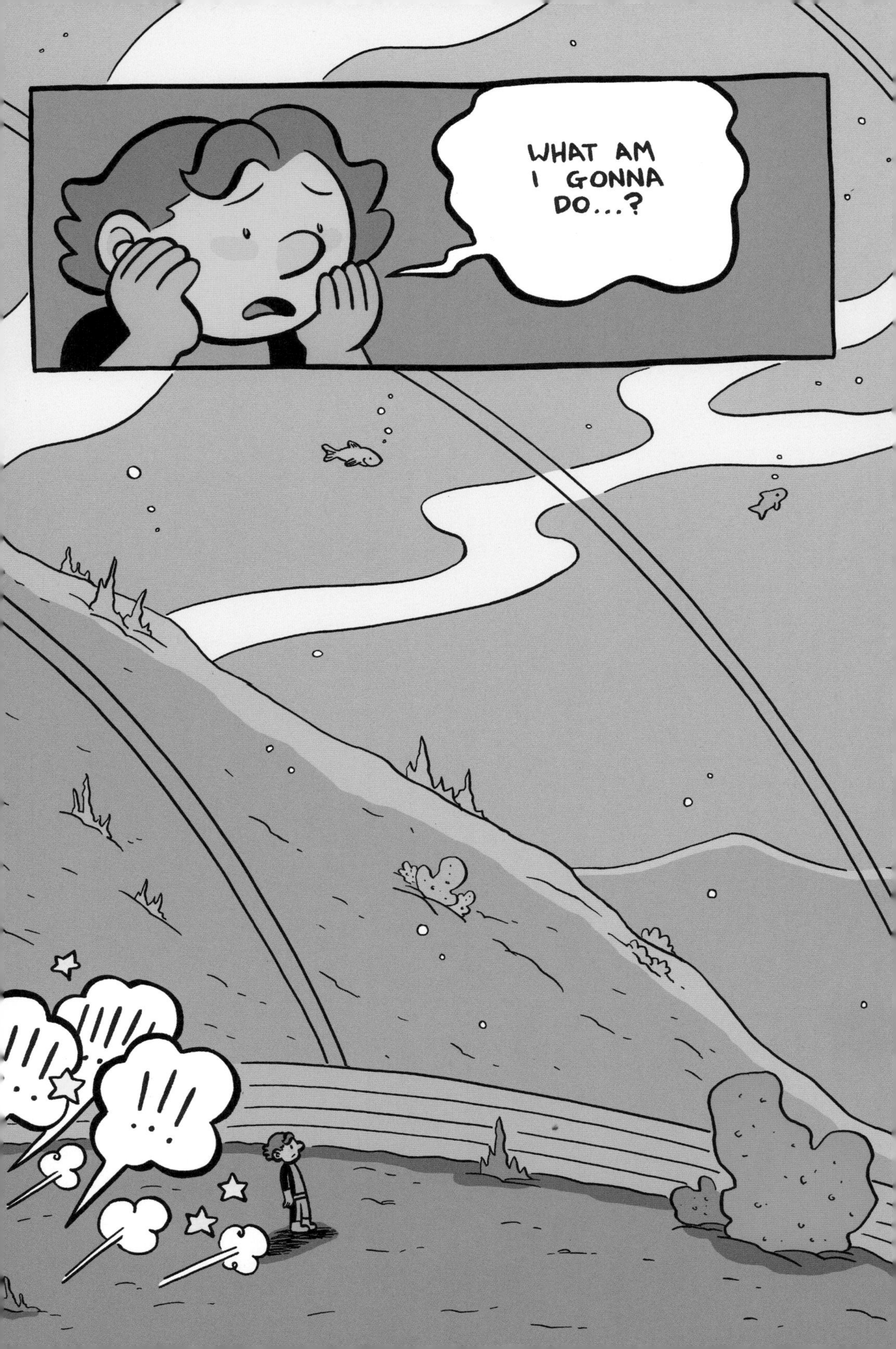

WHAT AM I GONNA DO...?
!!!
!!!
!!!

CHAPTER THREE

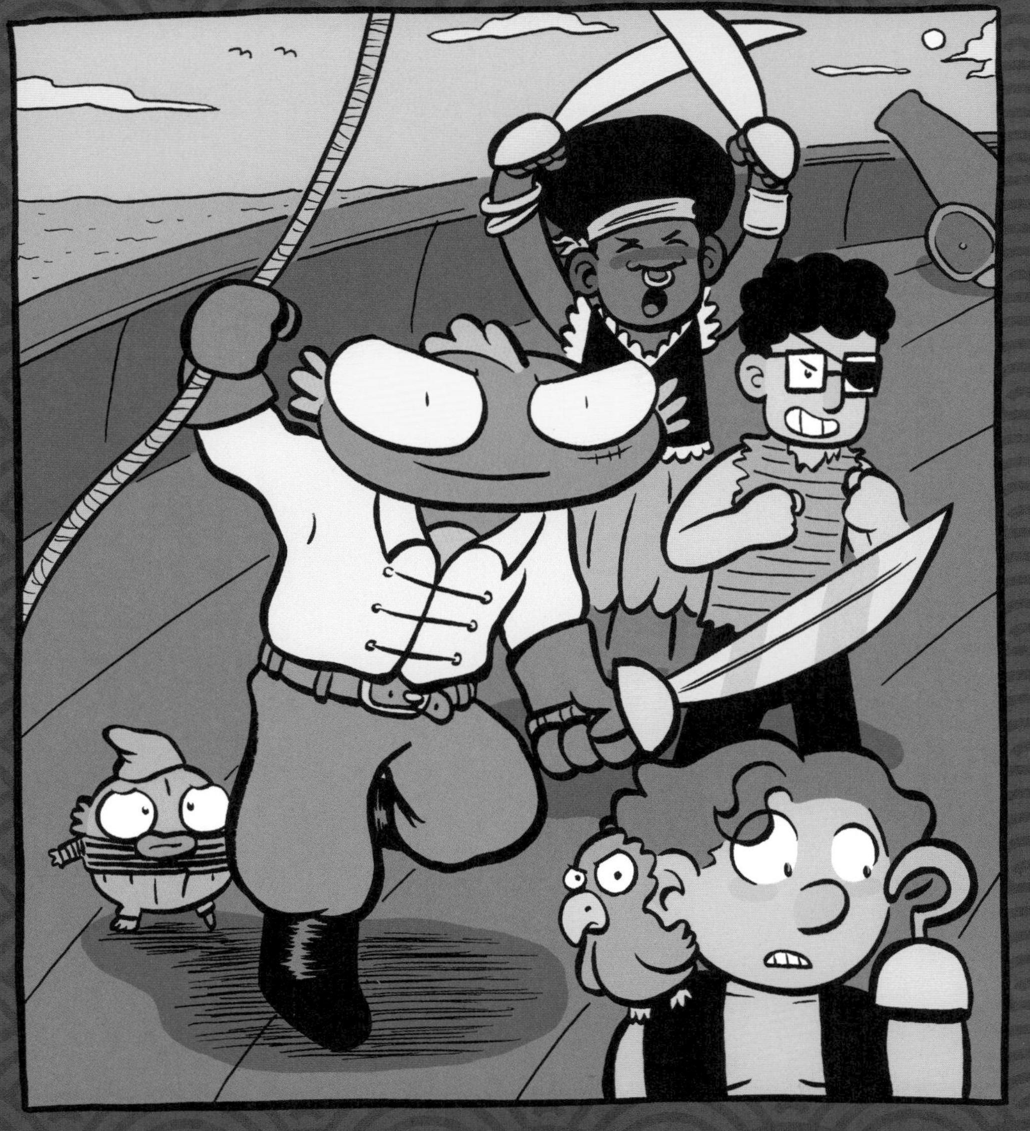

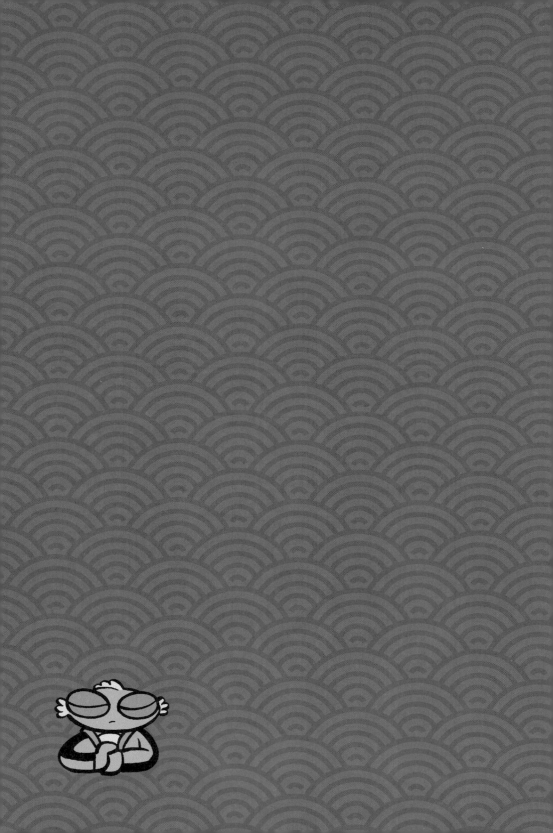

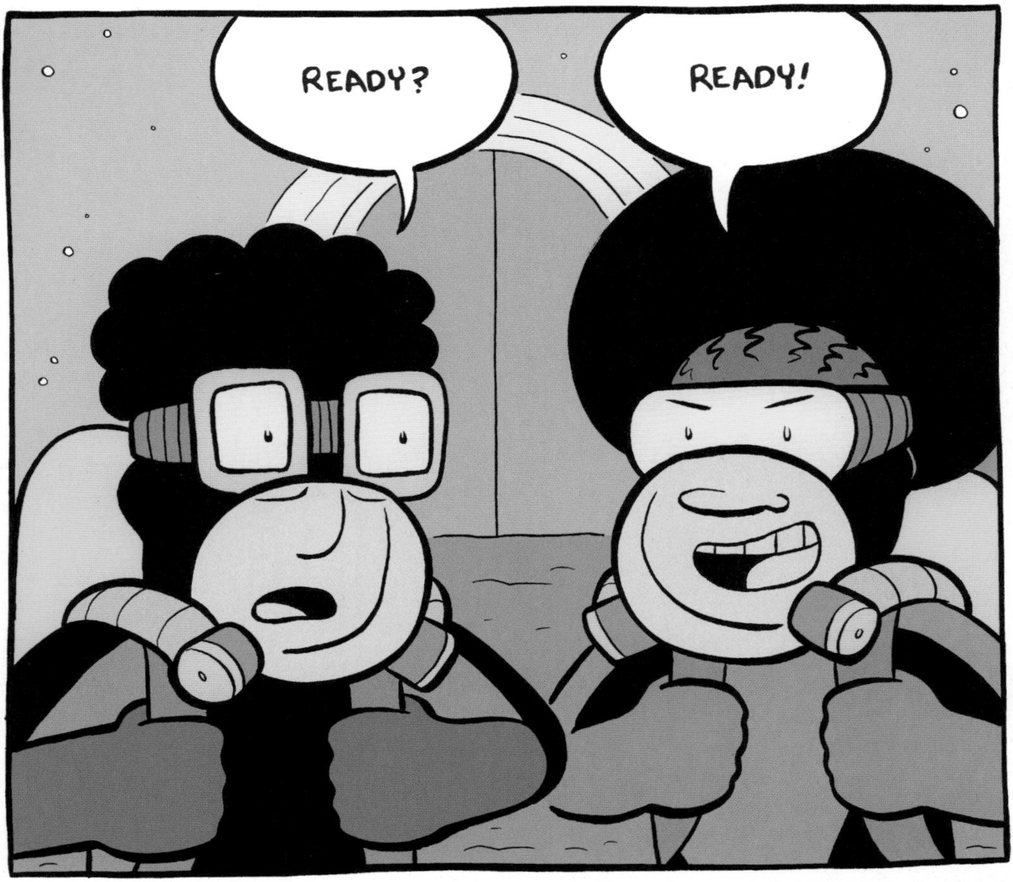
READY?
READY!
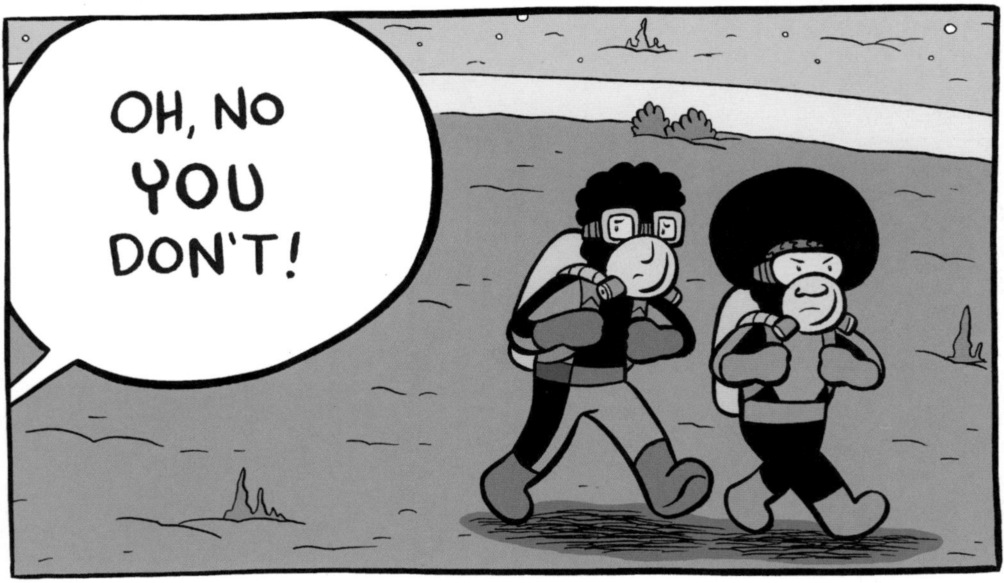
OH, NO YOU DON'T!

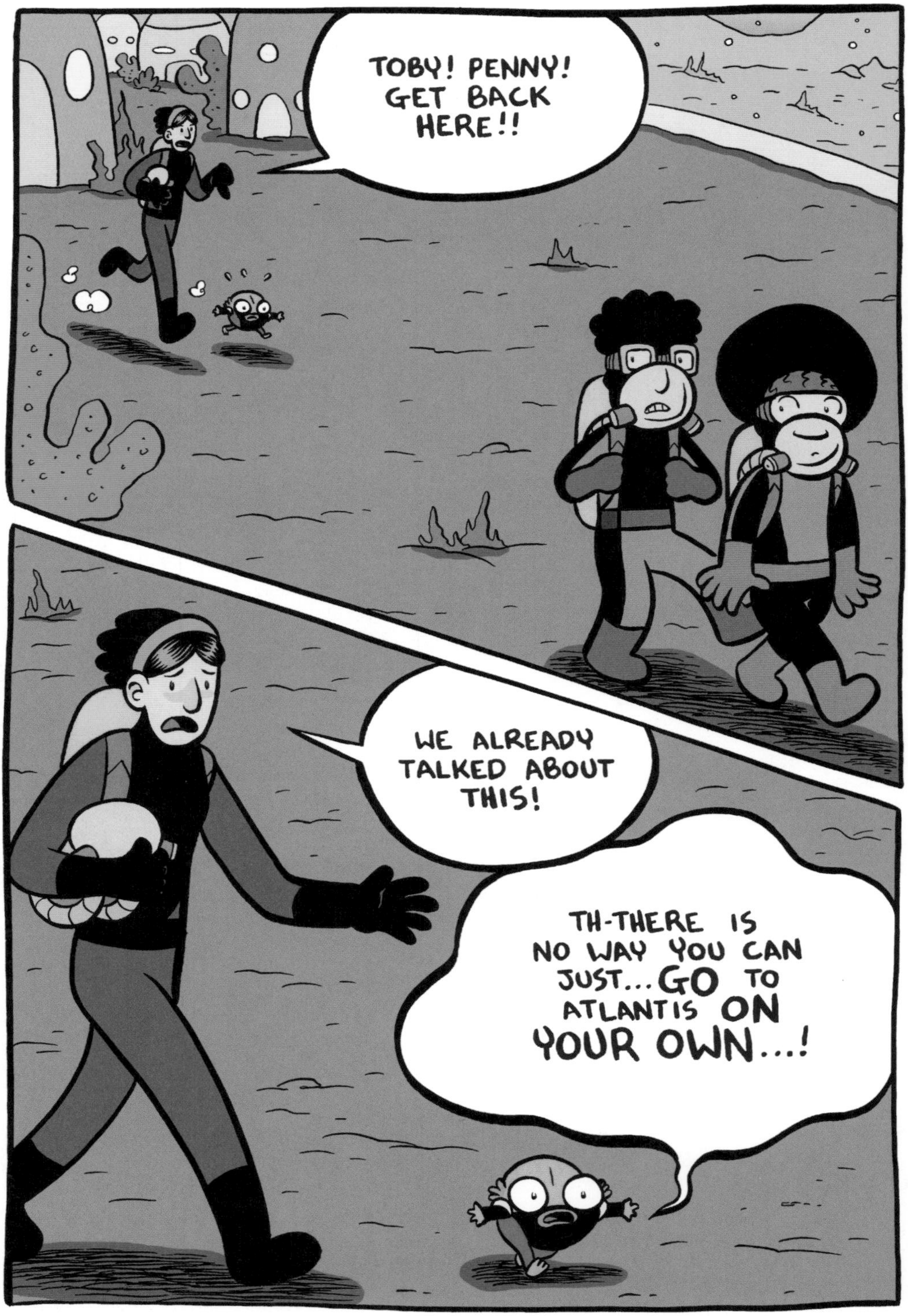
TOBY! PENNY! GET BACK HERE!!
WE ALREADY TALKED ABOUT THIS!
TH-THERE IS NO WAY YOU CAN JUST... GO TO ATLANTIS ON YOUR OWN...!

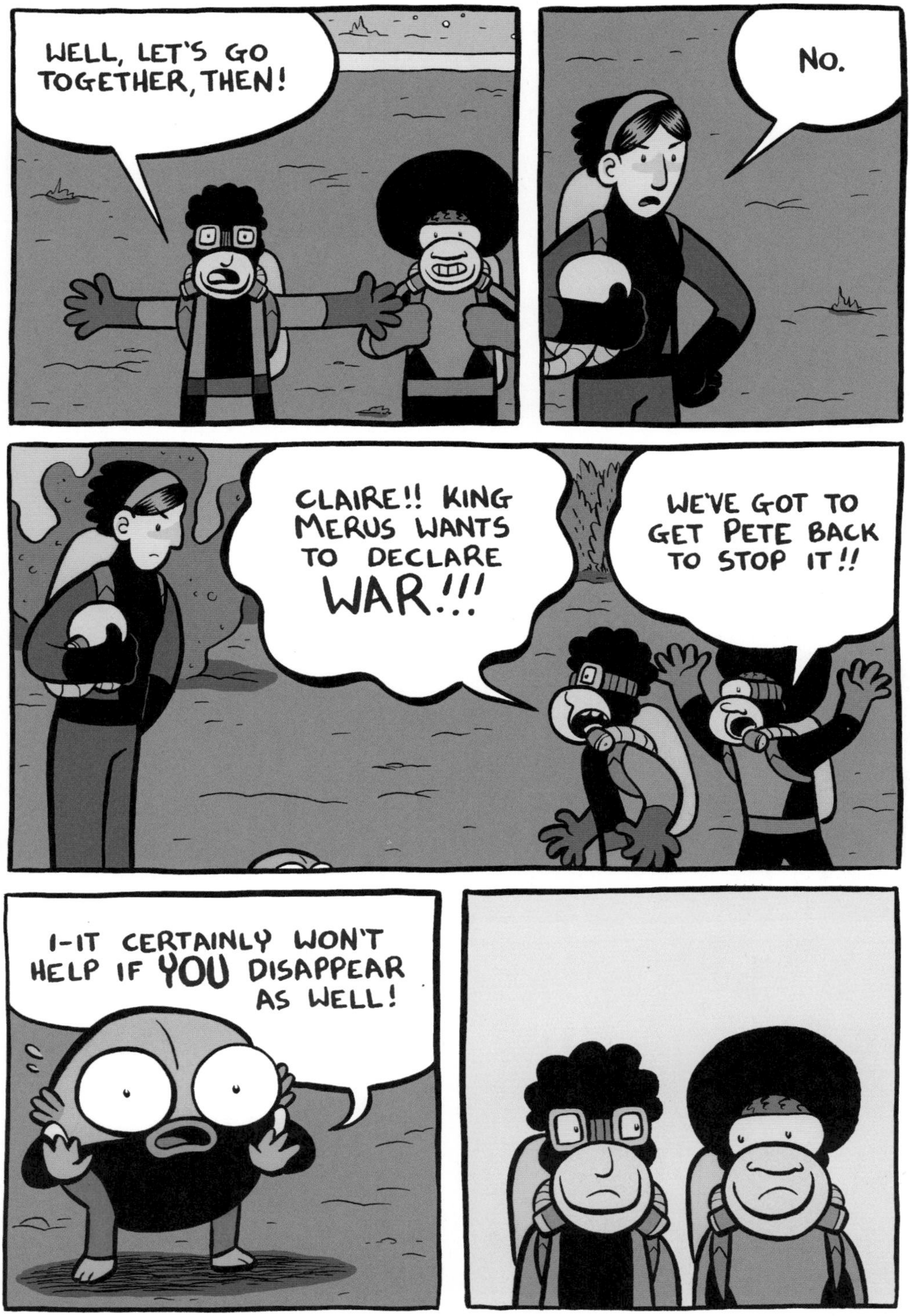
WELL, LET'S GO TOGETHER, THEN!
NO.
CLAIRE!! KING MERUS WANTS TO DECLARE WAR!!!
WE'VE GOT TO GET PETE BACK TO STOP IT!!
I-IT CERTAINLY WON'T HELP IF YOU DISAPPEAR AS WELL!

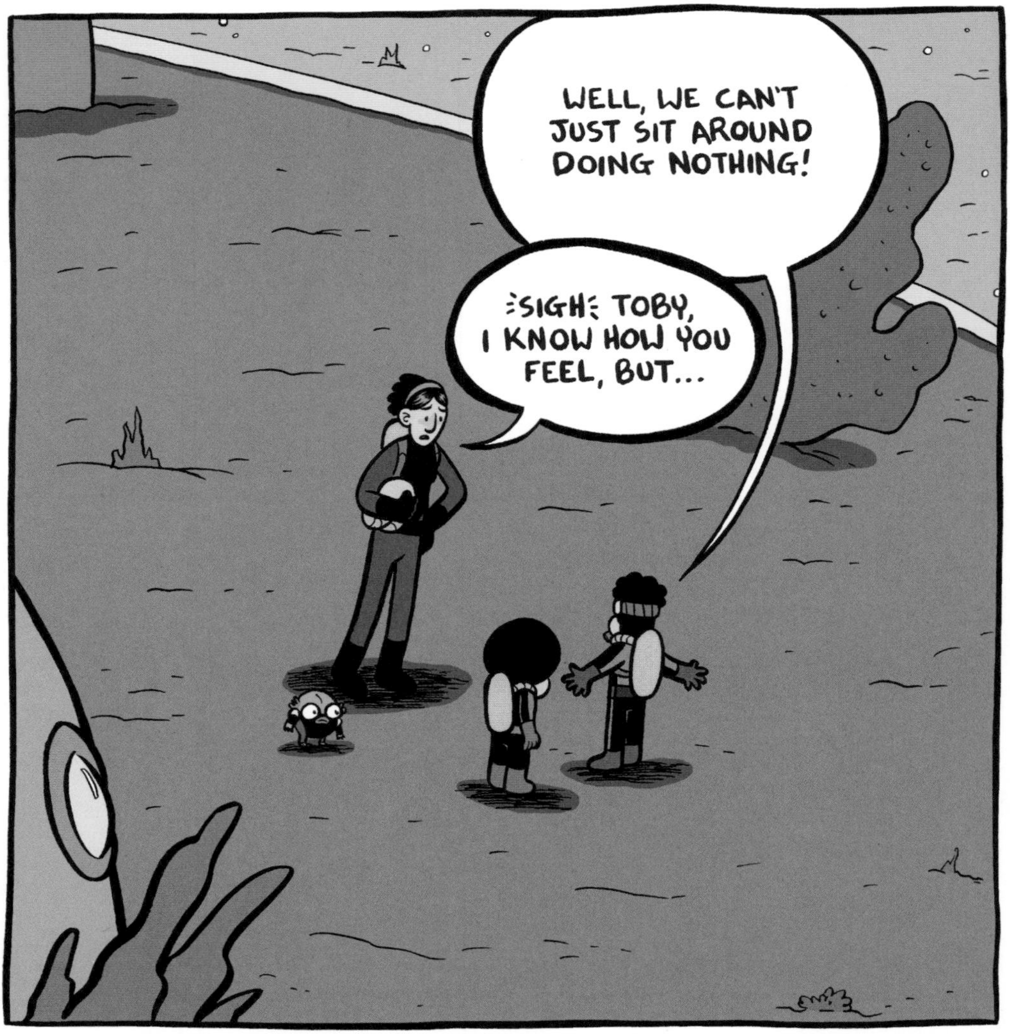
WELL, WE CAN'T JUST SIT AROUND DOING NOTHING!
SIGH TOBY, I KNOW HOW YOU FEEL, BUT...

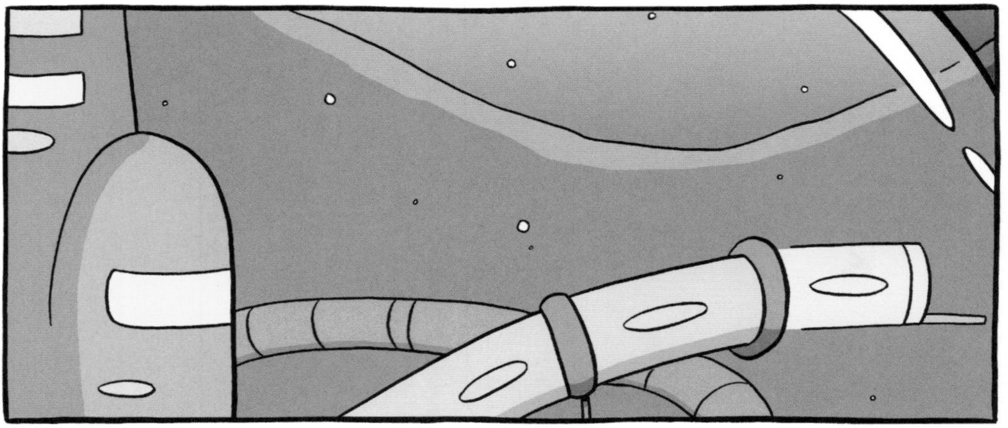

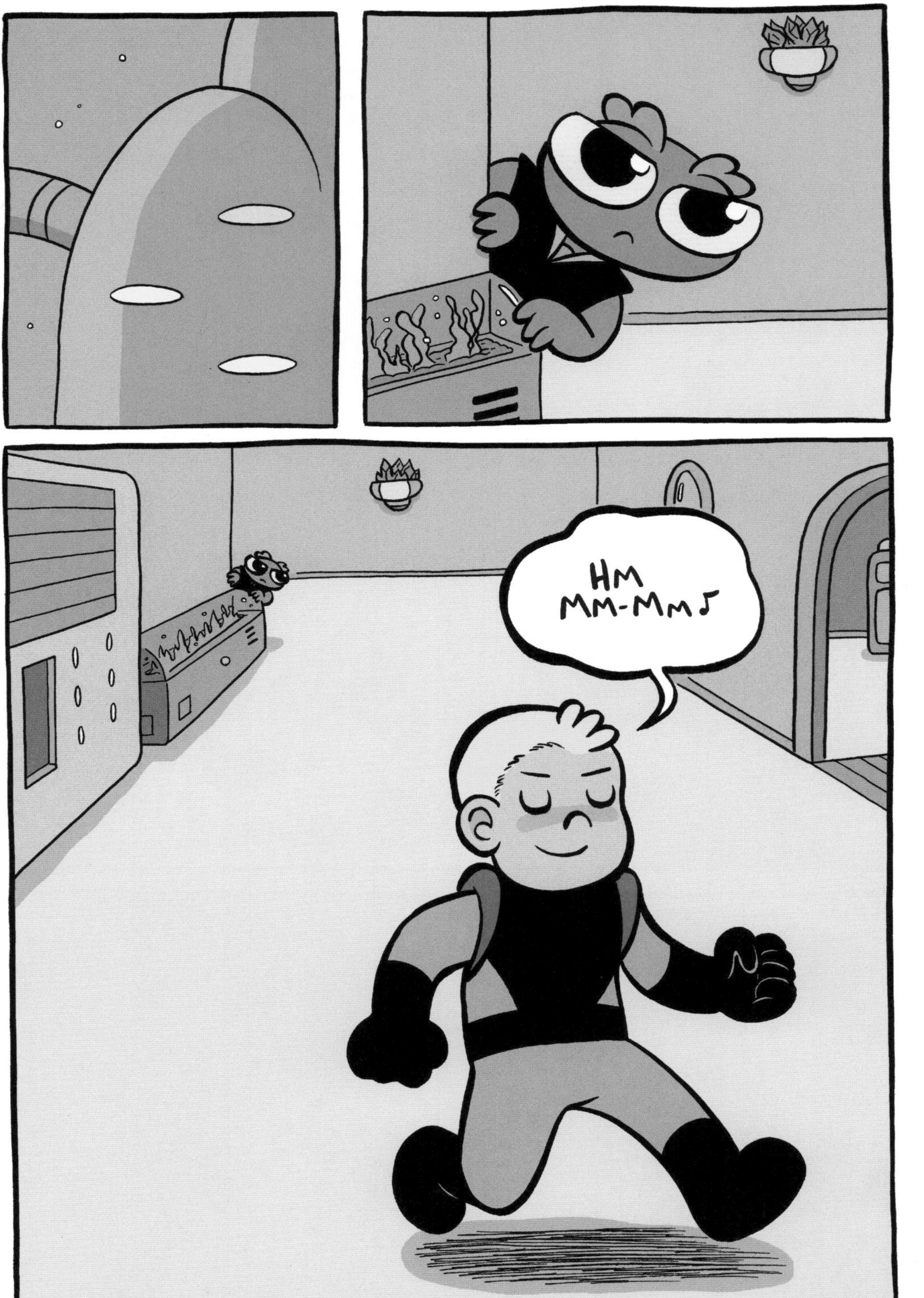
HM MM-MM♩

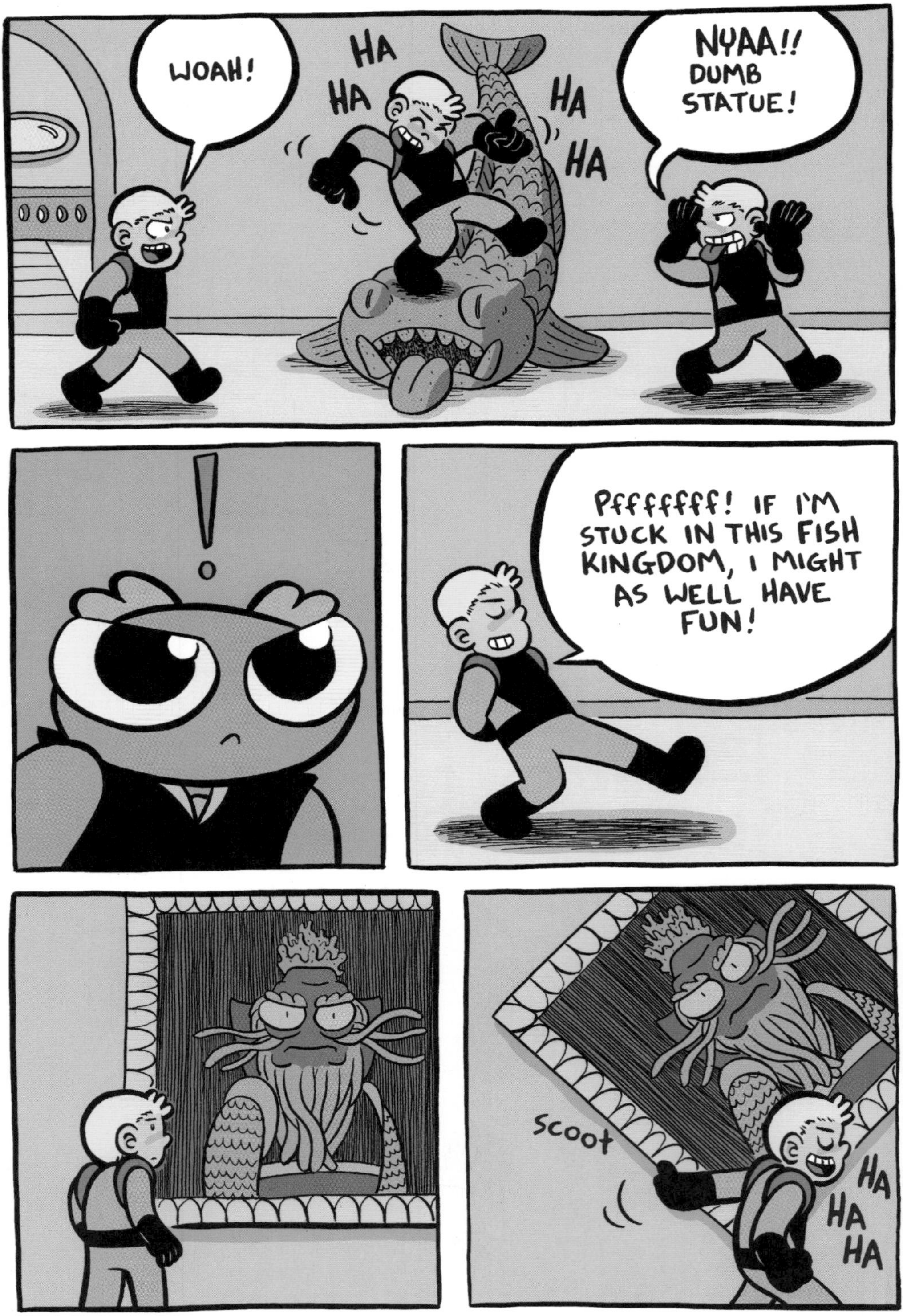
WOAH!
HA HA
HA HA
NYAA!! DUMB STATUE!
!
Pffffff! IF I'M STUCK IN THIS FISH KINGDOM, I MIGHT AS WELL HAVE FUN!
scoot
HA HA HA

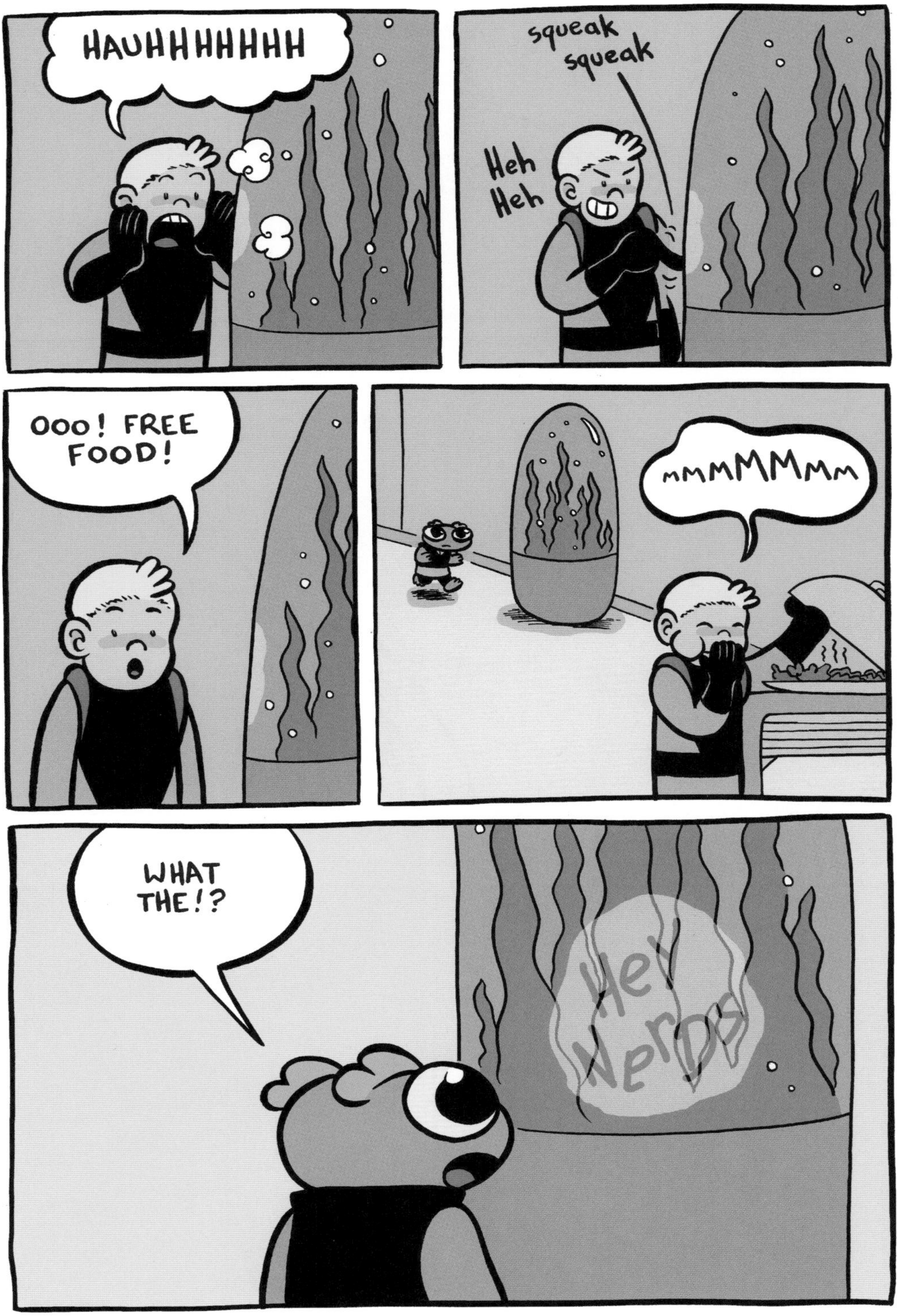
HAUHHHHHHH
squeak
squeak
Heh
Heh
OOO! FREE FOOD!
mmmMMmm
WHAT THE!?
Hey Nerds

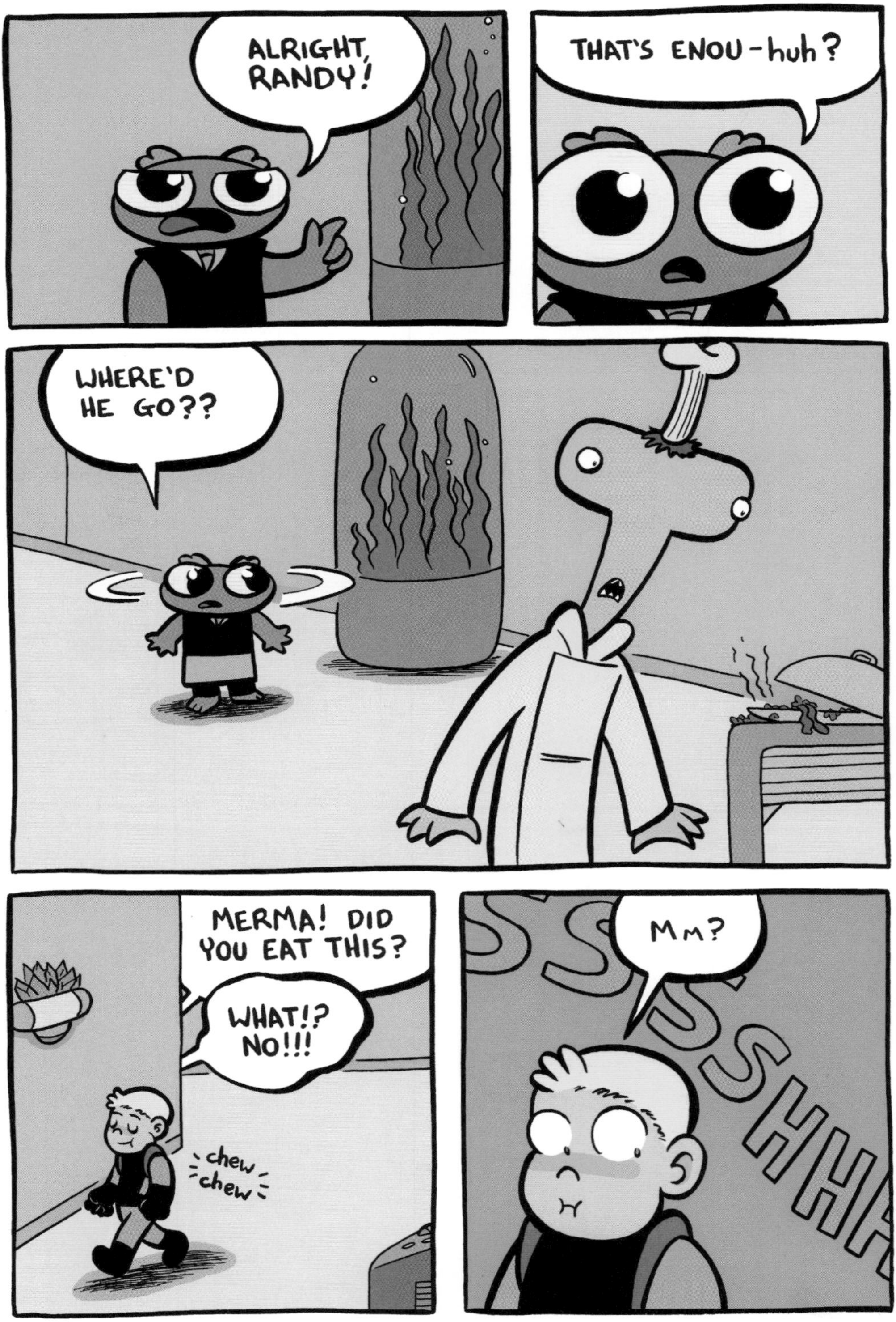
ALRIGHT, RANDY!
THAT'S ENOU-huh?
WHERE'D HE GO??
MERMA! DID YOU EAT THIS?
WHAT!? NO!!!
chew chew
Mm?
SSSSHHH

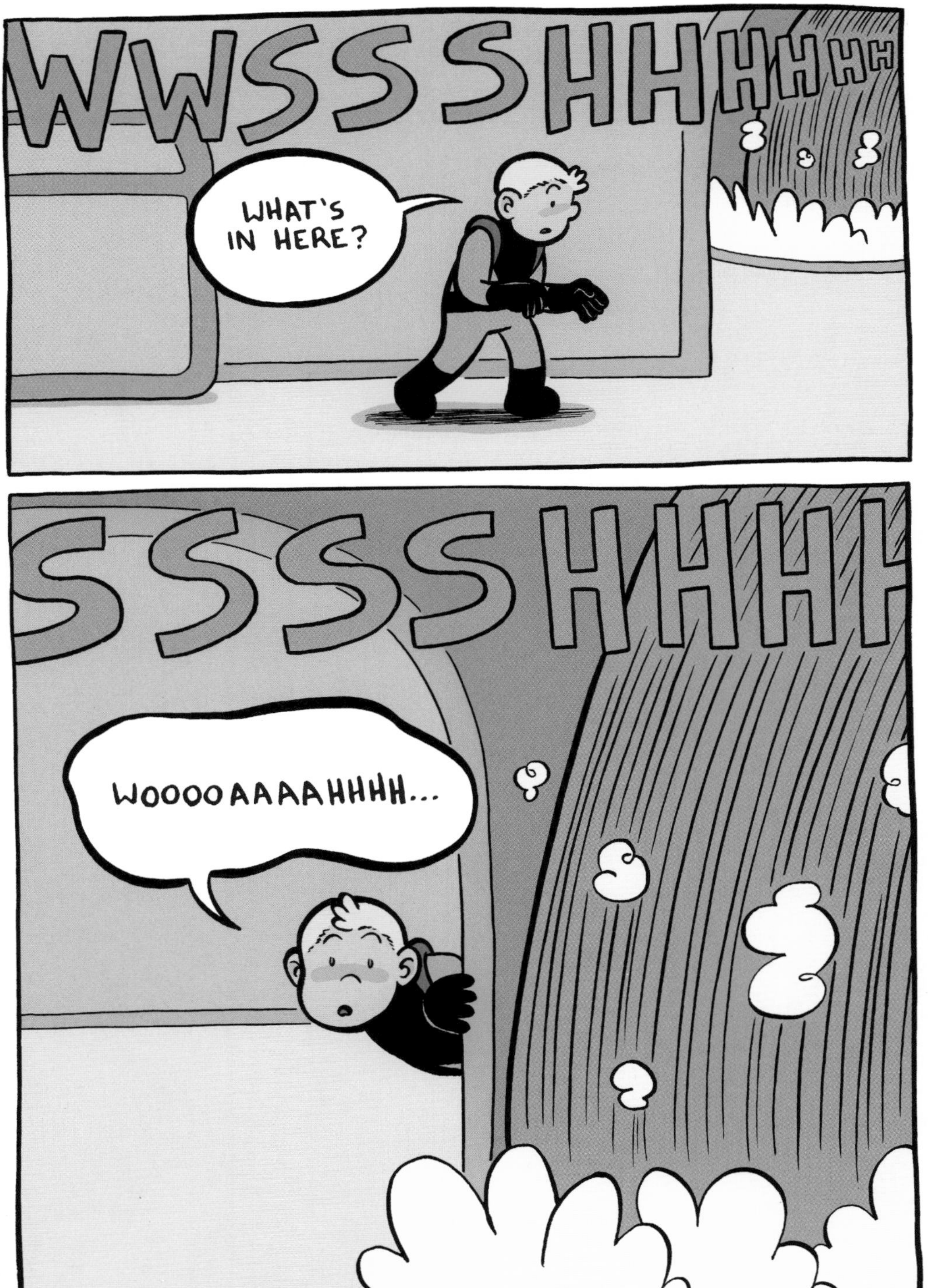
WWSSSSHHHHHH
WHAT'S IN HERE?
SSSSSHHHH
WOOOOAAAAHHHH...

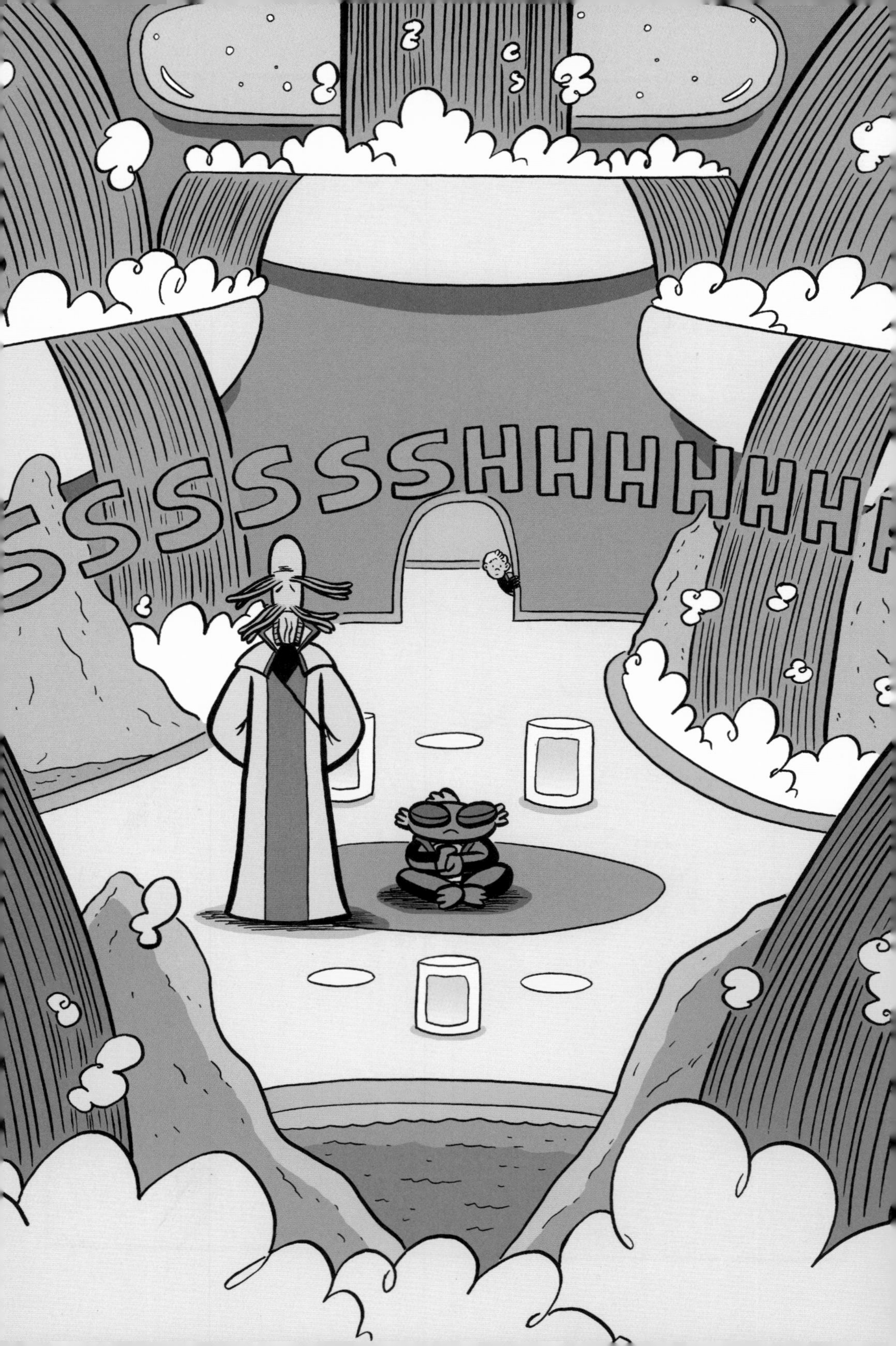
SSSSSSHHHHHHHH

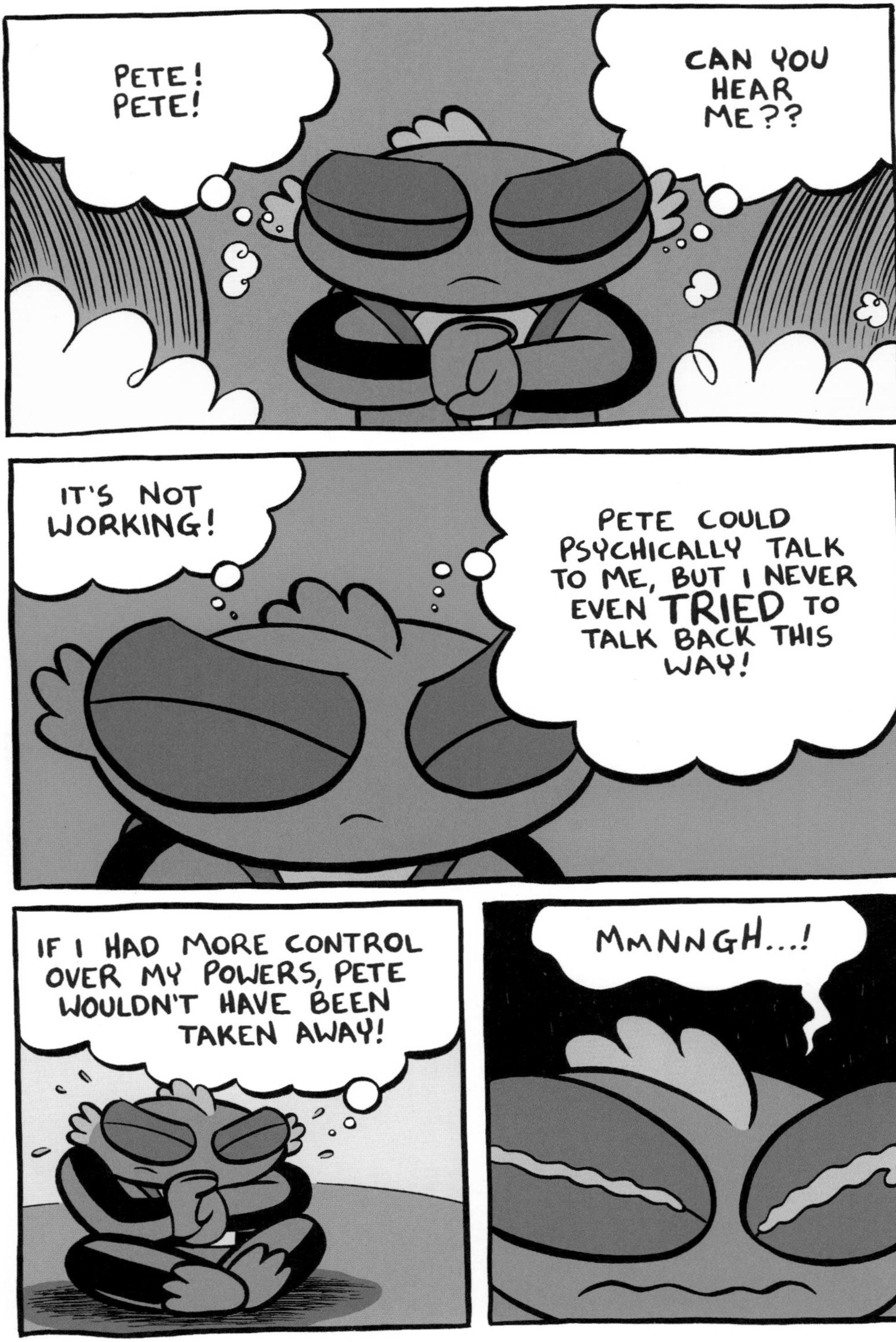
PETE! PETE!
CAN YOU HEAR ME??
IT'S NOT WORKING!
PETE COULD PSYCHICALLY TALK TO ME, BUT I NEVER EVEN TRIED TO TALK BACK THIS WAY!
IF I HAD MORE CONTROL OVER MY POWERS, PETE WOULDN'T HAVE BEEN TAKEN AWAY!
MMNNGH...!

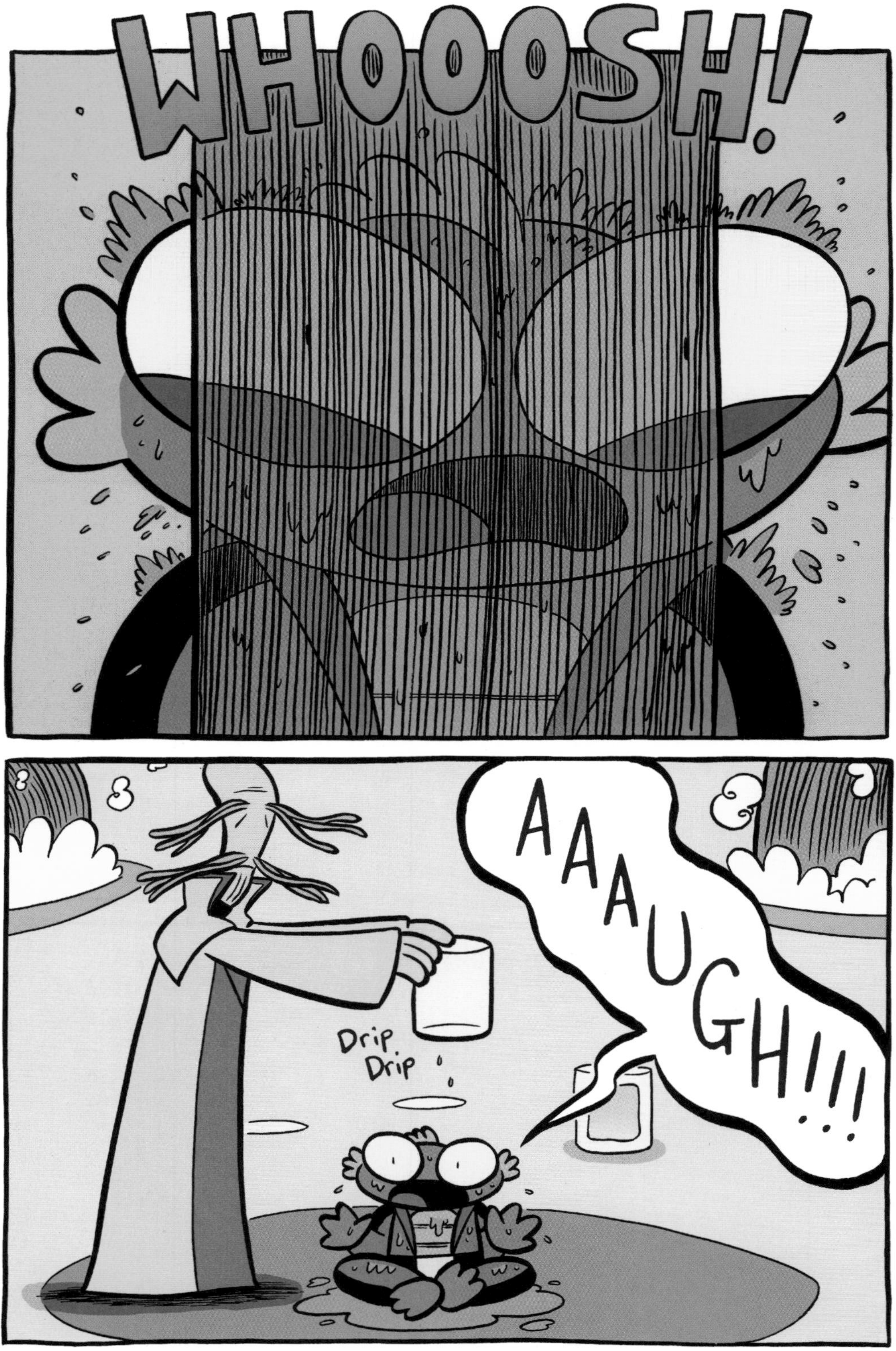
WHOOOSH!
Drip
Drip
AAAAUGH!!!!

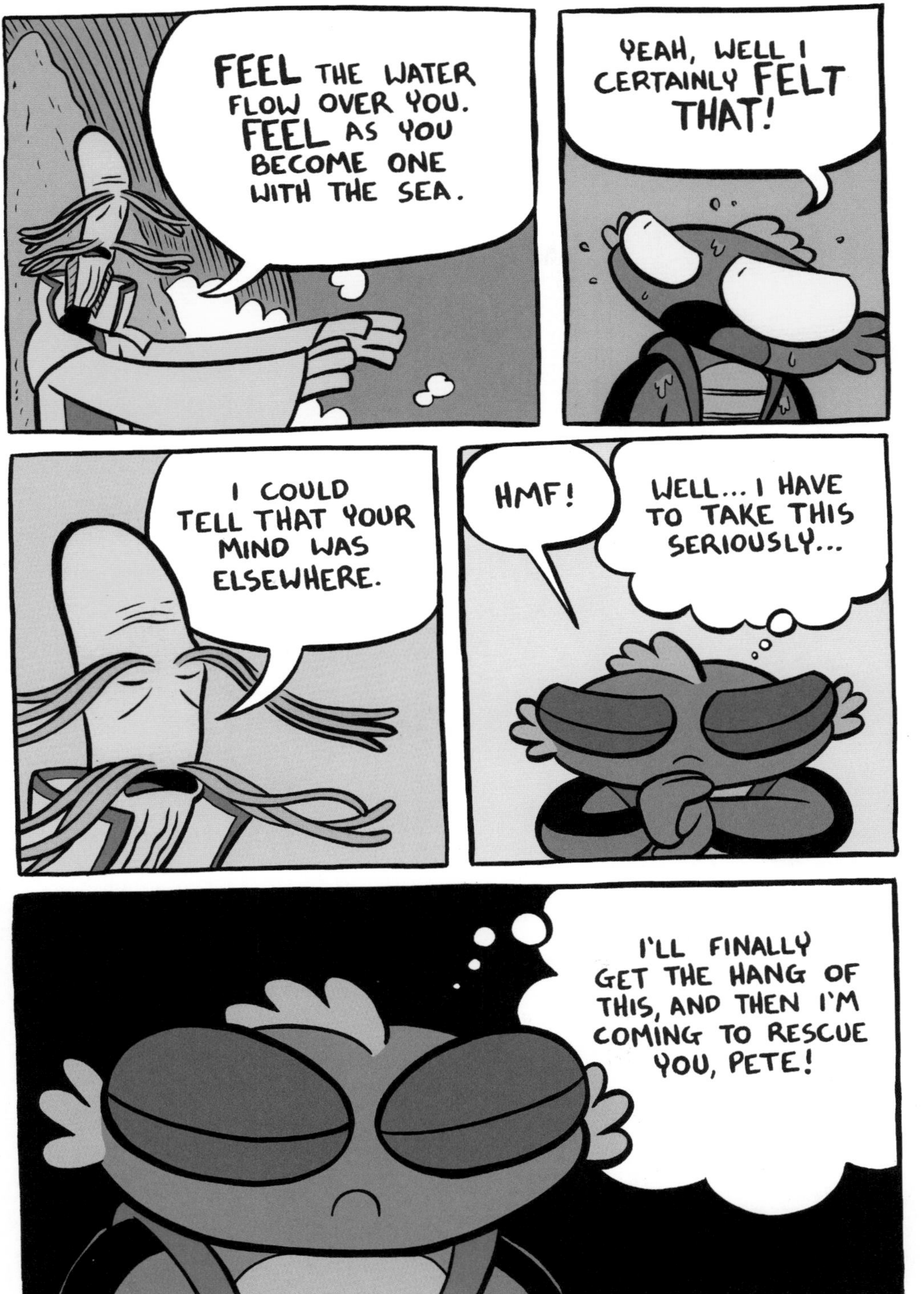
FEEL THE WATER FLOW OVER YOU. FEEL AS YOU BECOME ONE WITH THE SEA.
YEAH, WELL I CERTAINLY FELT THAT!
I COULD TELL THAT YOUR MIND WAS ELSEWHERE.
HMF!
WELL... I HAVE TO TAKE THIS SERIOUSLY...
I'LL FINALLY GET THE HANG OF THIS, AND THEN I'M COMING TO RESCUE YOU, PETE!

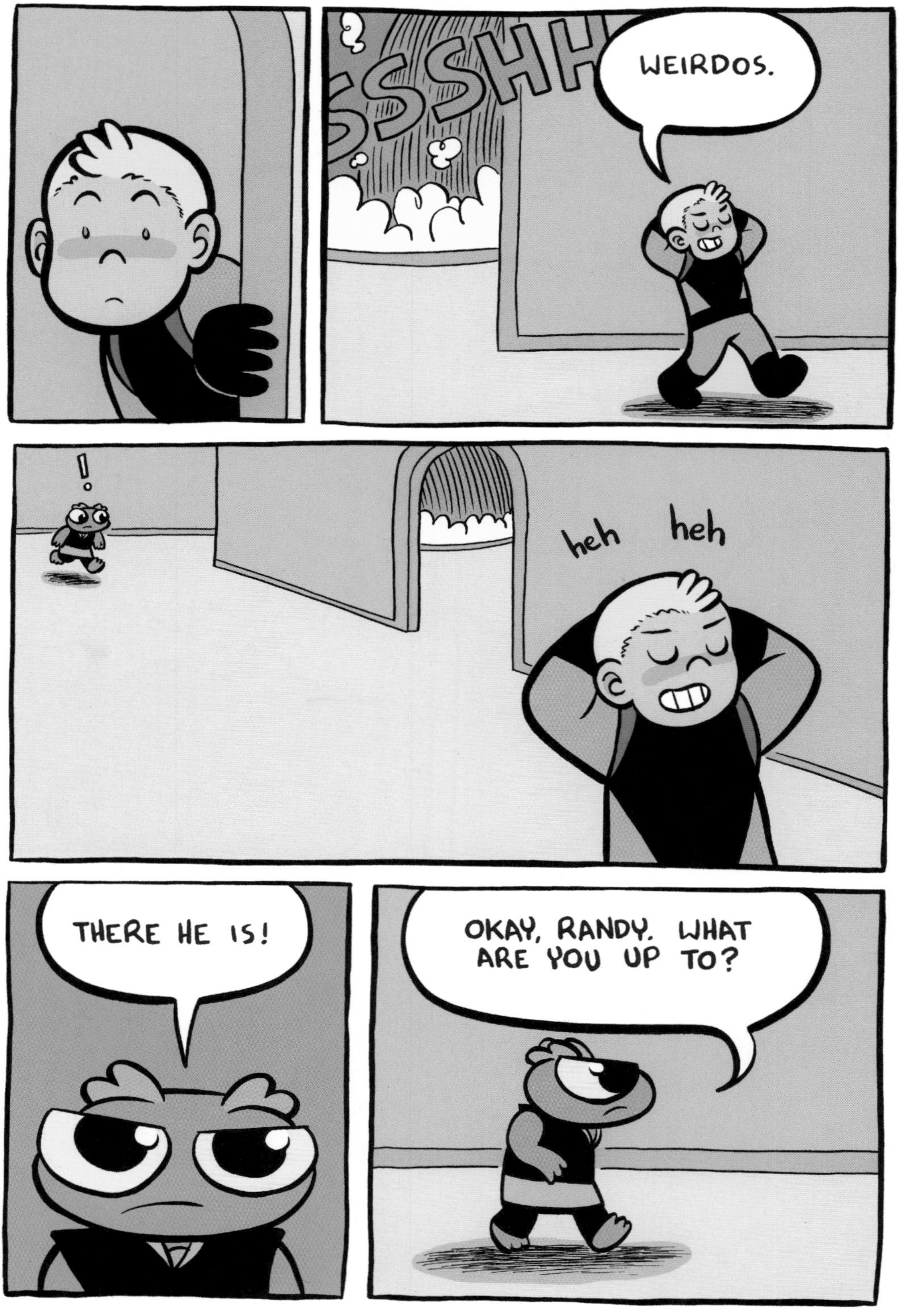
SSSHH
WEIRDOS.
heh heh
THERE HE IS!
OKAY, RANDY. WHAT ARE YOU UP TO?

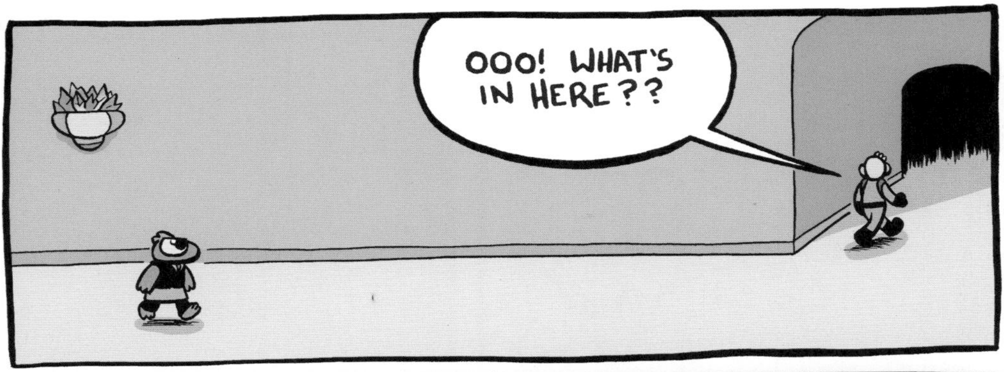
OOO! WHAT'S IN HERE??

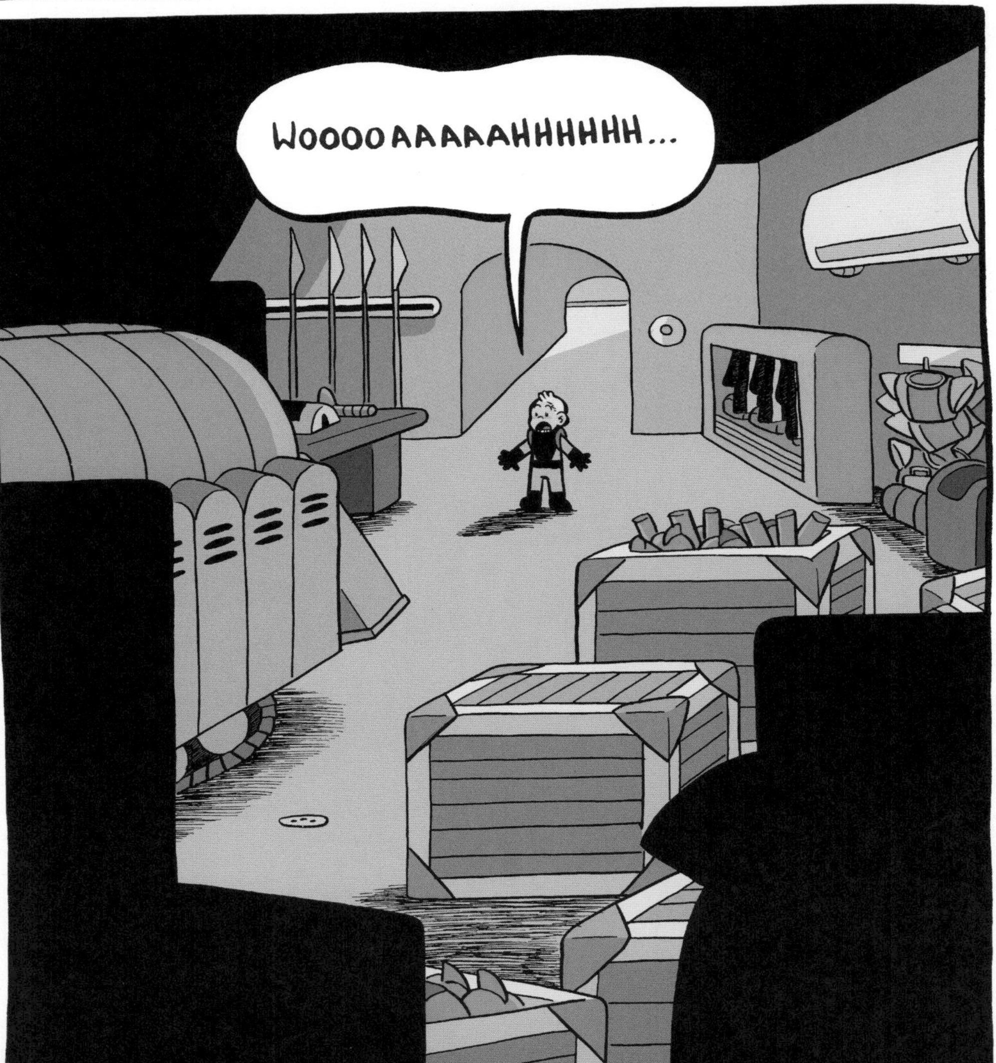
WOOOOAAAAAHHHHHH...

LOOK AT ALL THIS STUFF!

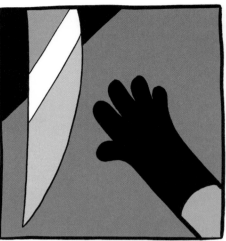

RANDY!! STOP RIGHT THERE!!!

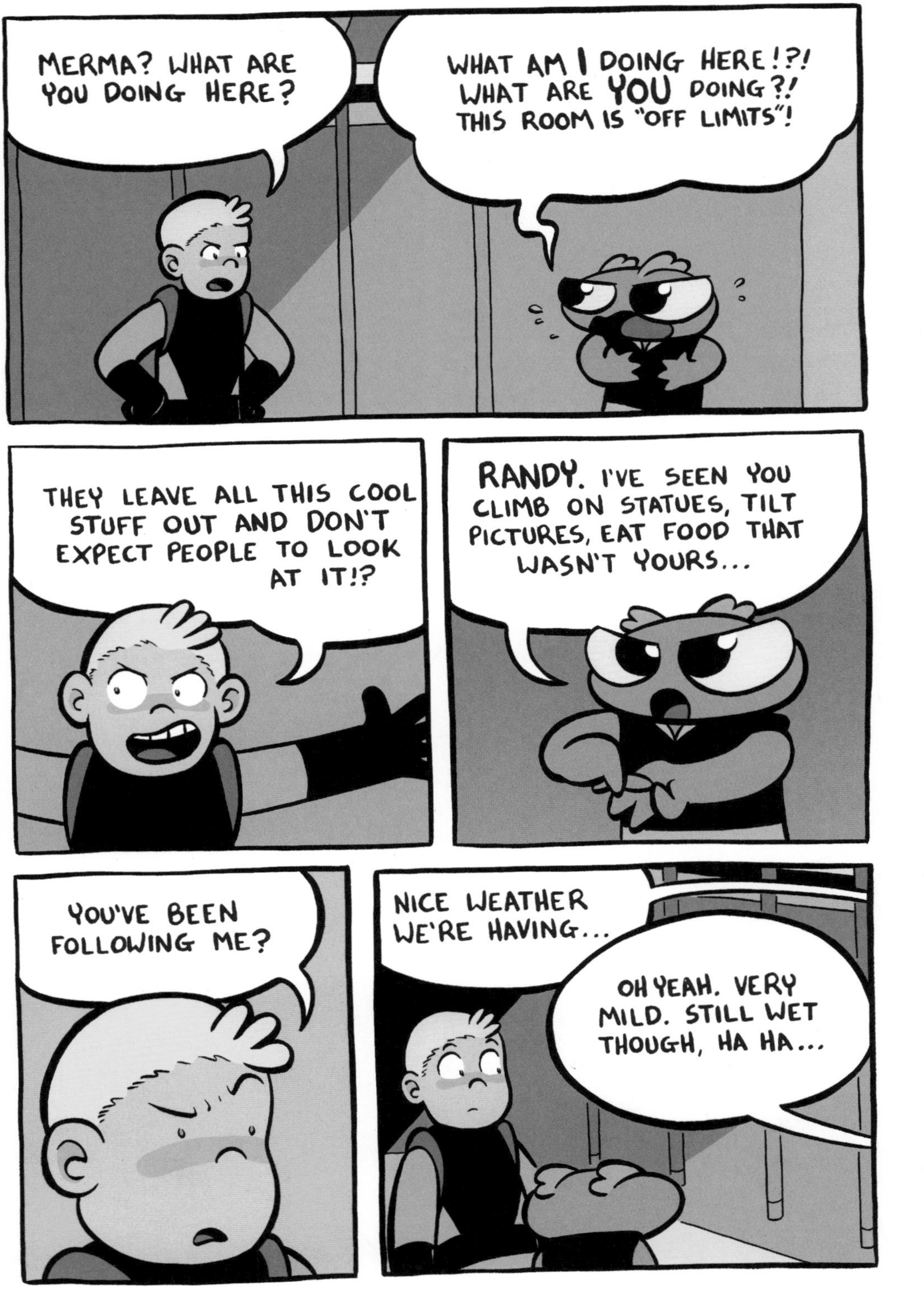
MERMA? WHAT ARE YOU DOING HERE?
WHAT AM I DOING HERE!?! WHAT ARE YOU DOING?! THIS ROOM IS "OFF LIMITS"!
THEY LEAVE ALL THIS COOL STUFF OUT AND DON'T EXPECT PEOPLE TO LOOK AT IT!?
RANDY. I'VE SEEN YOU CLIMB ON STATUES, TILT PICTURES, EAT FOOD THAT WASN'T YOURS...
YOU'VE BEEN FOLLOWING ME?
NICE WEATHER WE'RE HAVING...
OH YEAH. VERY MILD. STILL WET THOUGH, HA HA...

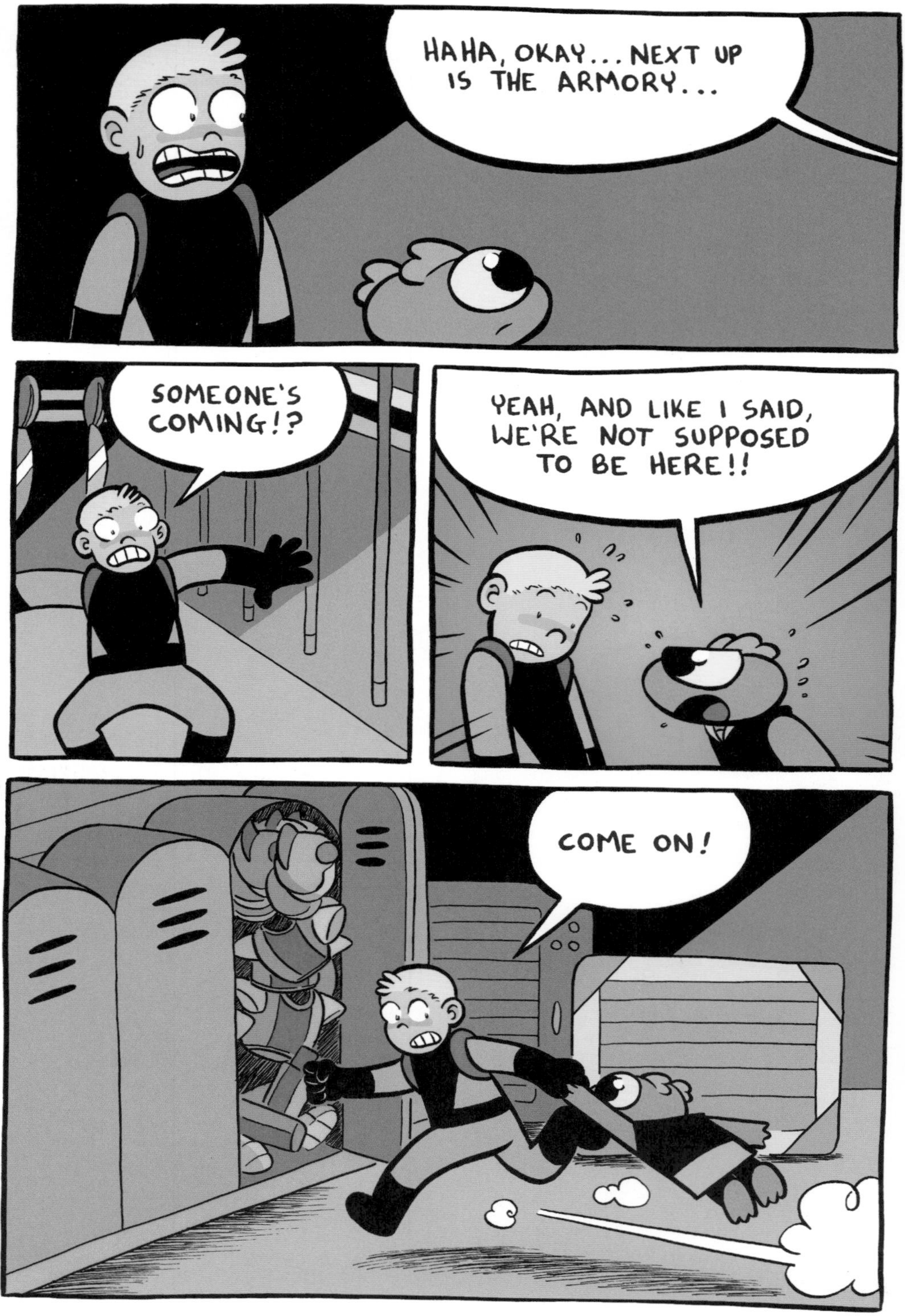
HAHA, OKAY... NEXT UP IS THE ARMORY...
SOMEONE'S COMING!?
YEAH, AND LIKE I SAID, WE'RE NOT SUPPOSED TO BE HERE!!
COME ON!

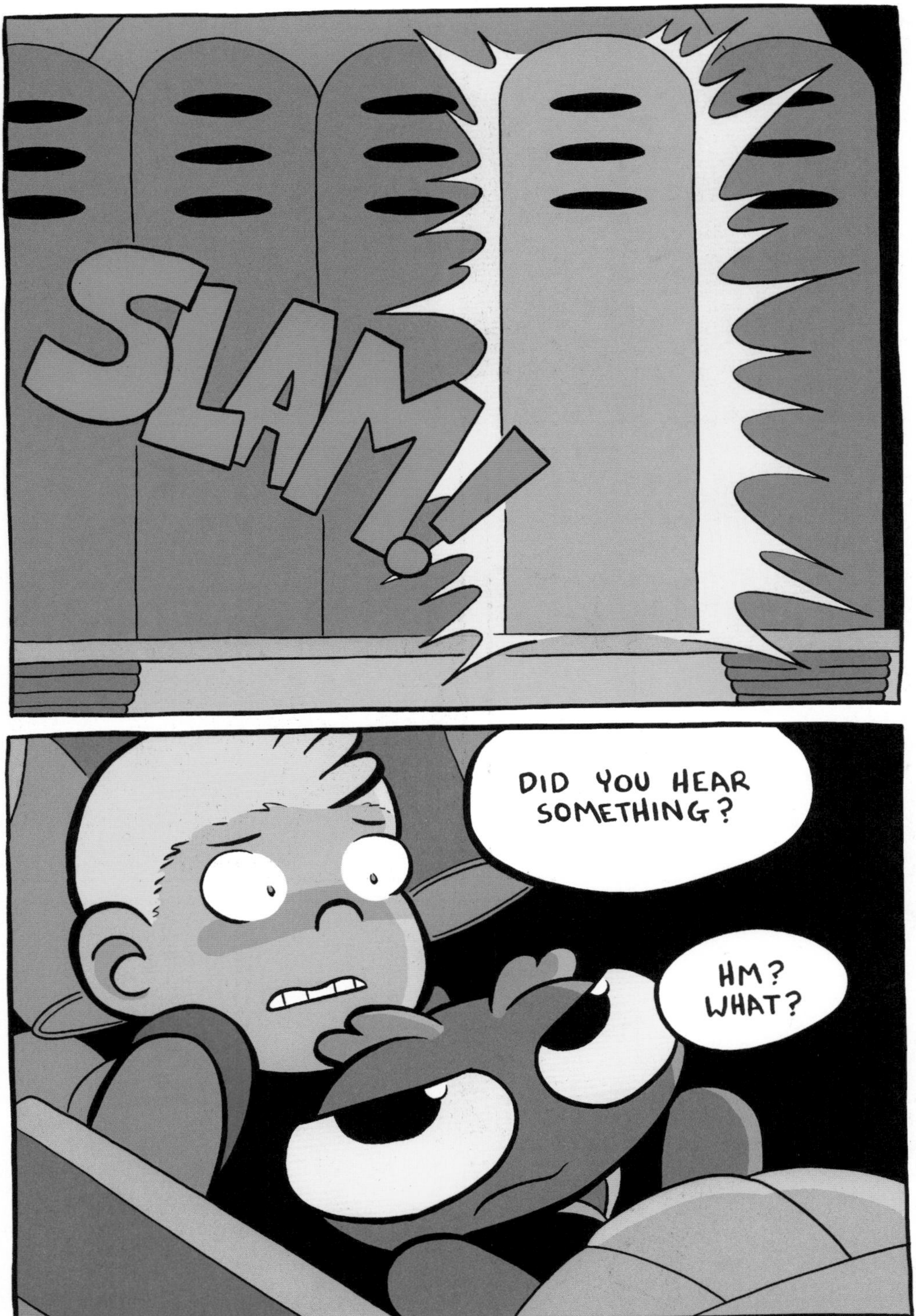
SLAM!
DID YOU HEAR SOMETHING?
HM? WHAT?

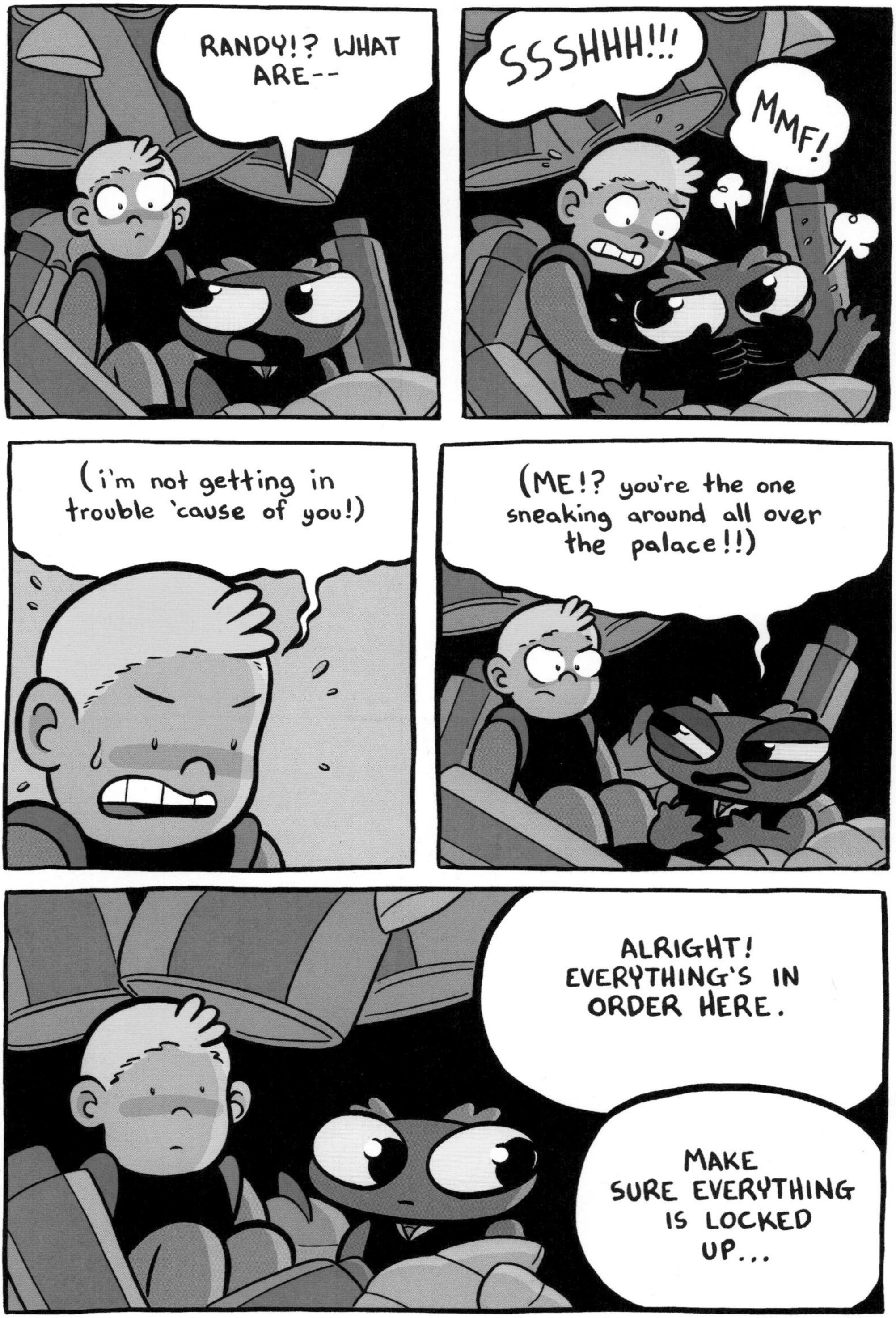
RANDY!? WHAT ARE--
SSSHHH!!!
MMF!
(i'm not getting in trouble 'cause of you!)
(ME!? you're the one sneaking around all over the palace!!)
ALRIGHT! EVERYTHING'S IN ORDER HERE.
MAKE SURE EVERYTHING IS LOCKED UP...

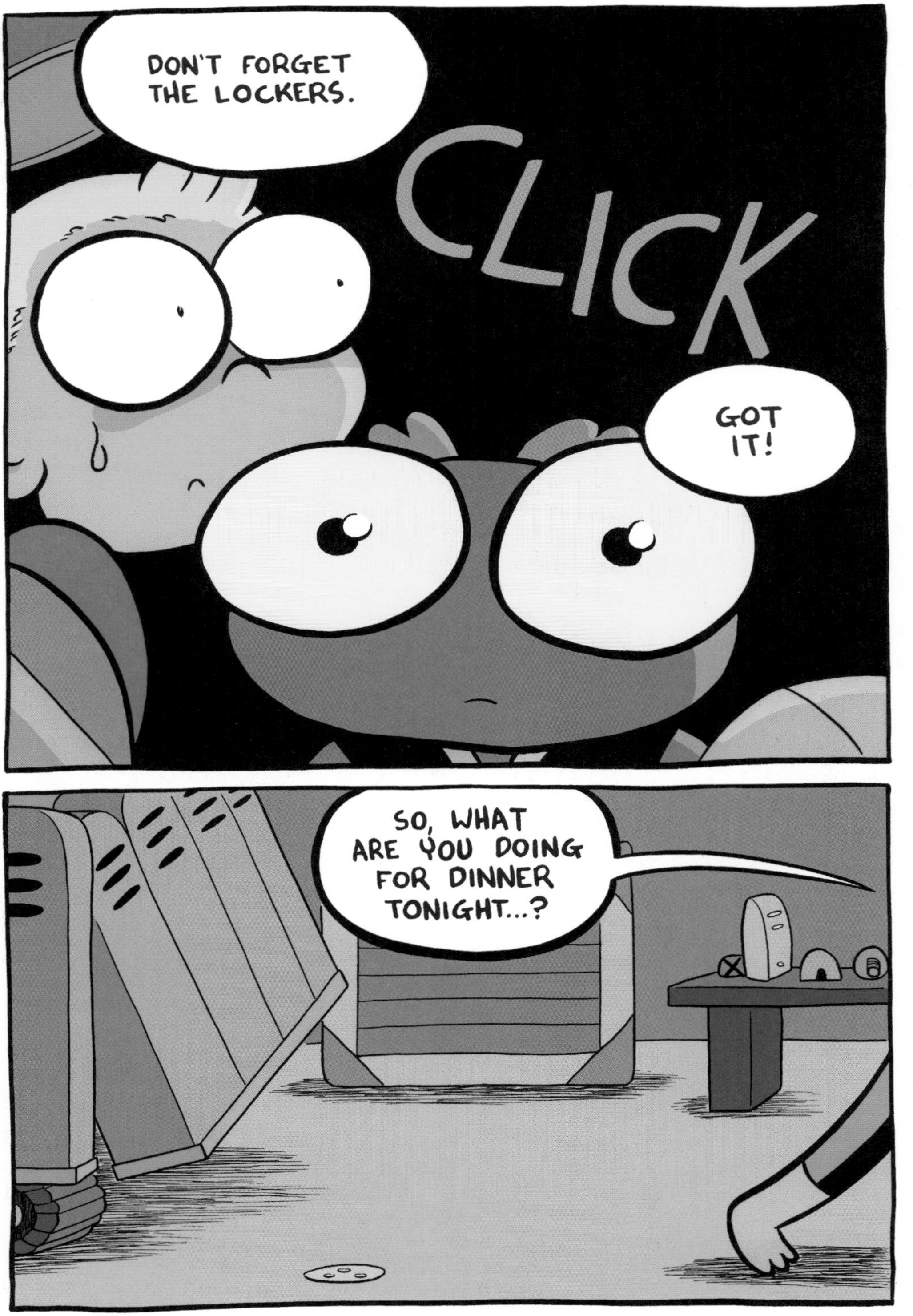
DON'T FORGET THE LOCKERS.
CLICK
GOT IT!
SO, WHAT ARE YOU DOING FOR DINNER TONIGHT...?

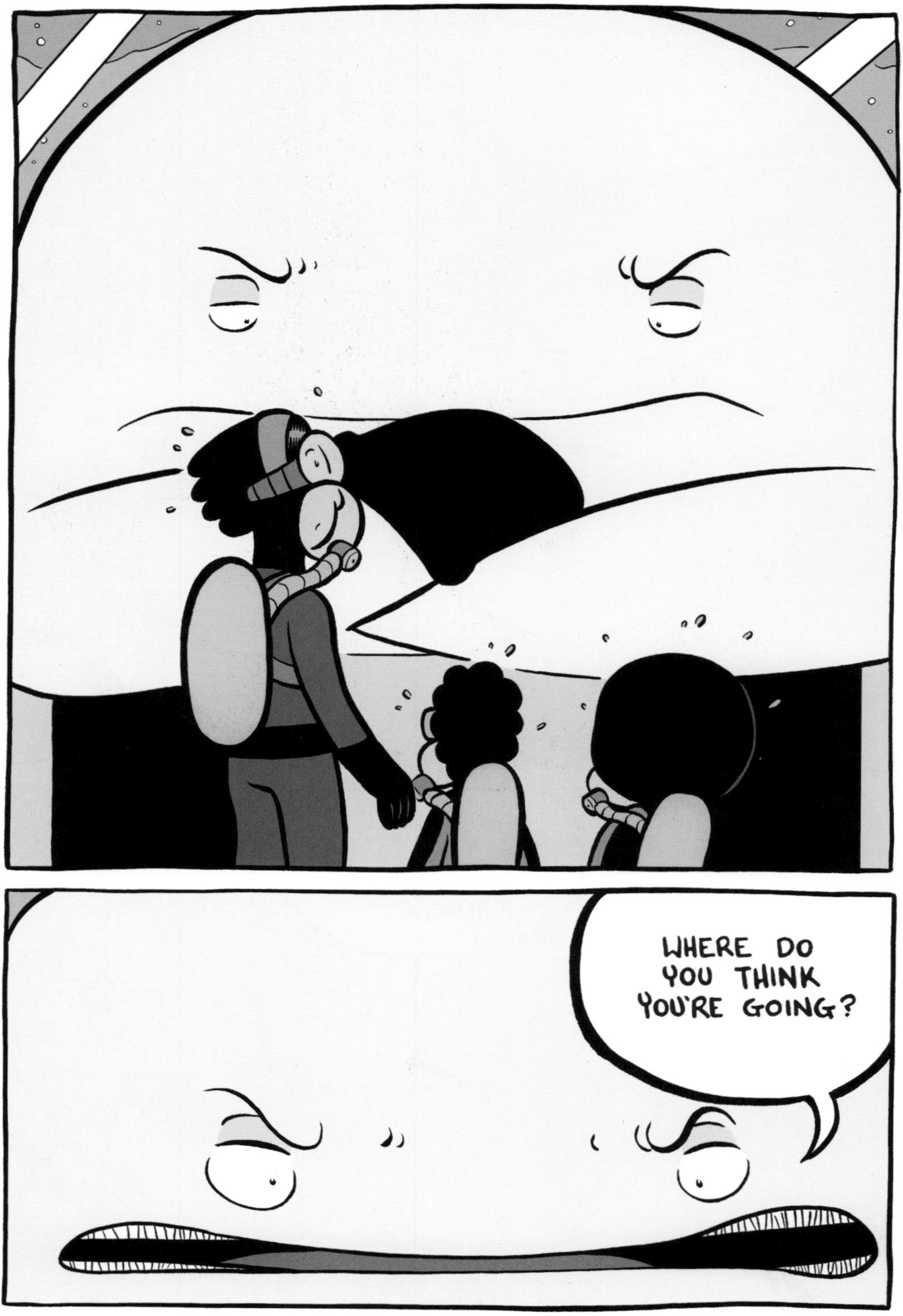
WHERE DO YOU THINK YOU'RE GOING?

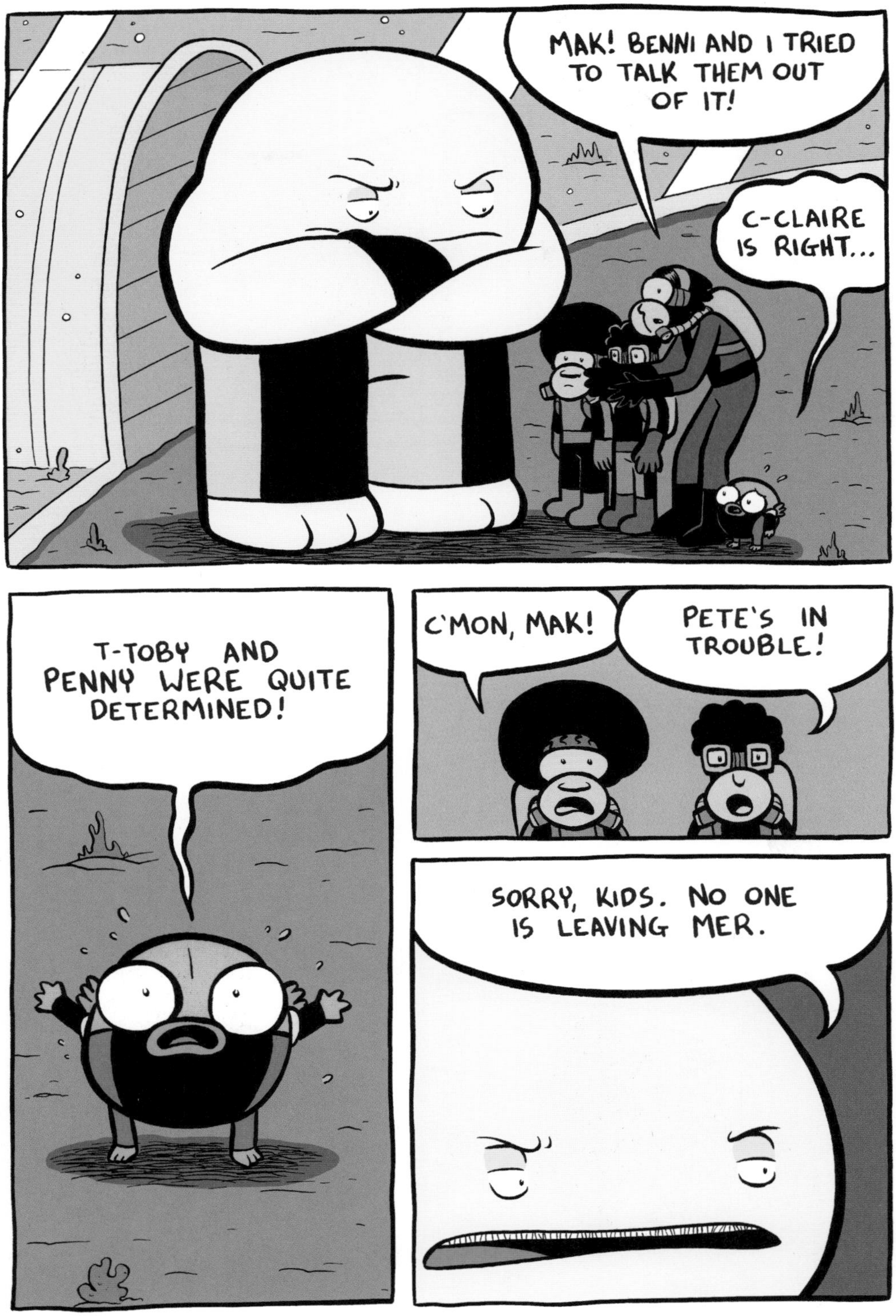
MAK! BENNI AND I TRIED TO TALK THEM OUT OF IT!
C-CLAIRE IS RIGHT...
T-TOBY AND PENNY WERE QUITE DETERMINED!
C'MON, MAK!
PETE'S IN TROUBLE!
SORRY, KIDS. NO ONE IS LEAVING MER.

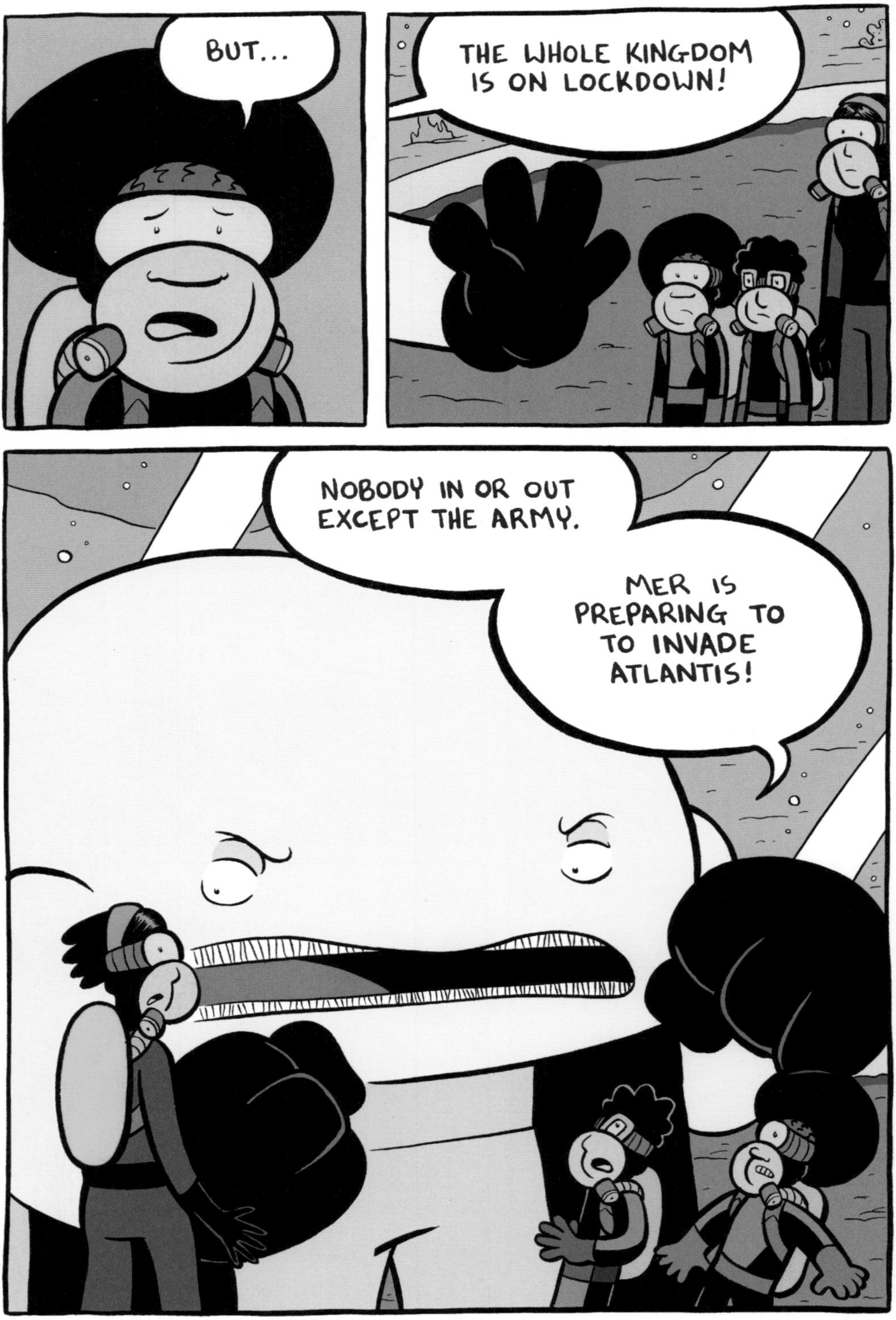
BUT...
THE WHOLE KINGDOM IS ON LOCKDOWN!
NOBODY IN OR OUT EXCEPT THE ARMY.
MER IS PREPARING TO TO INVADE ATLANTIS!

CHAPTER FOUR

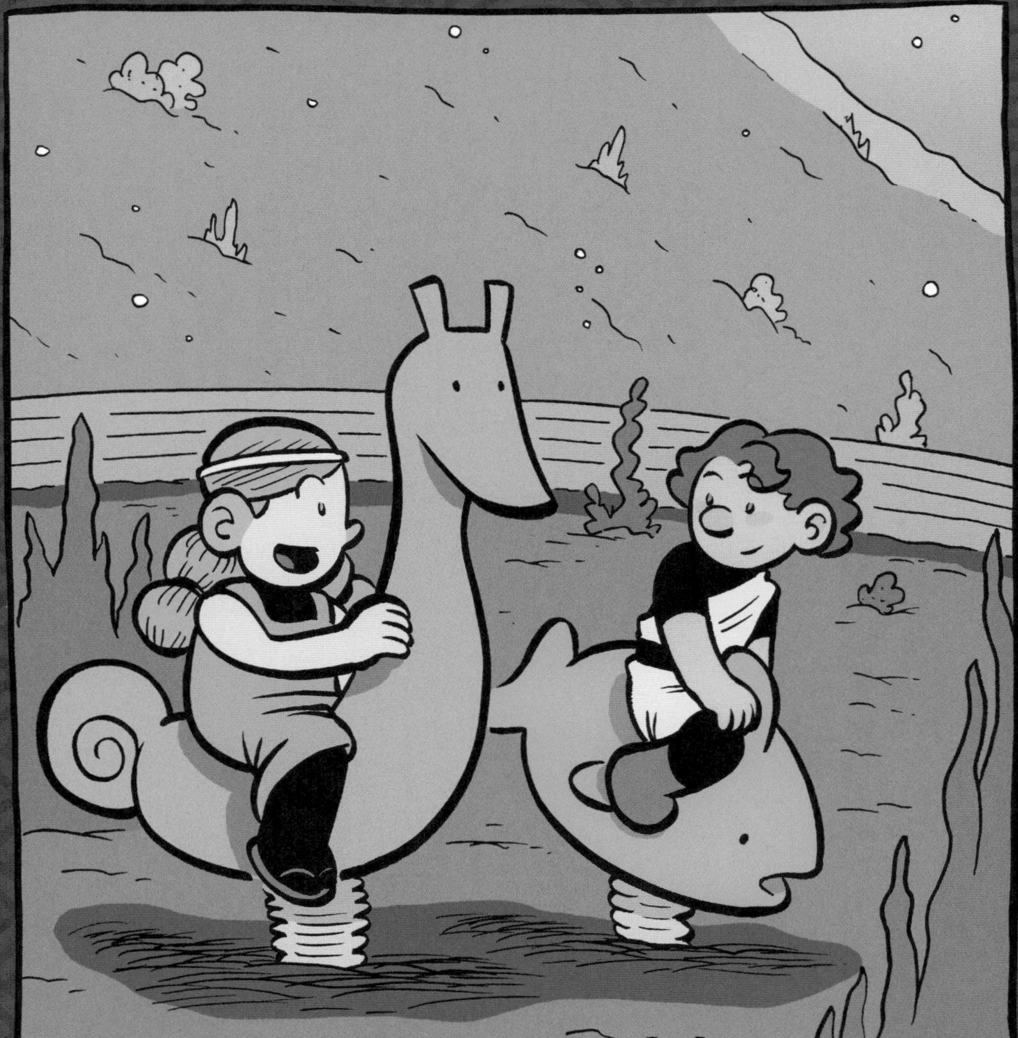

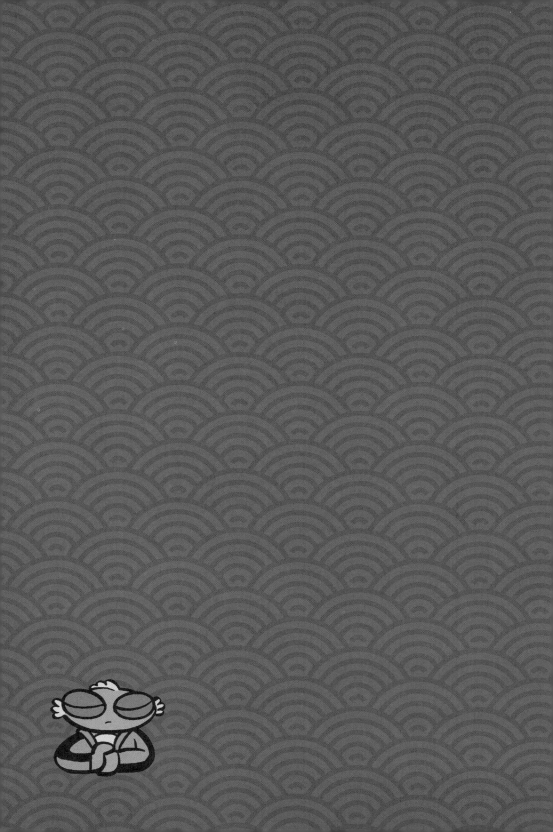

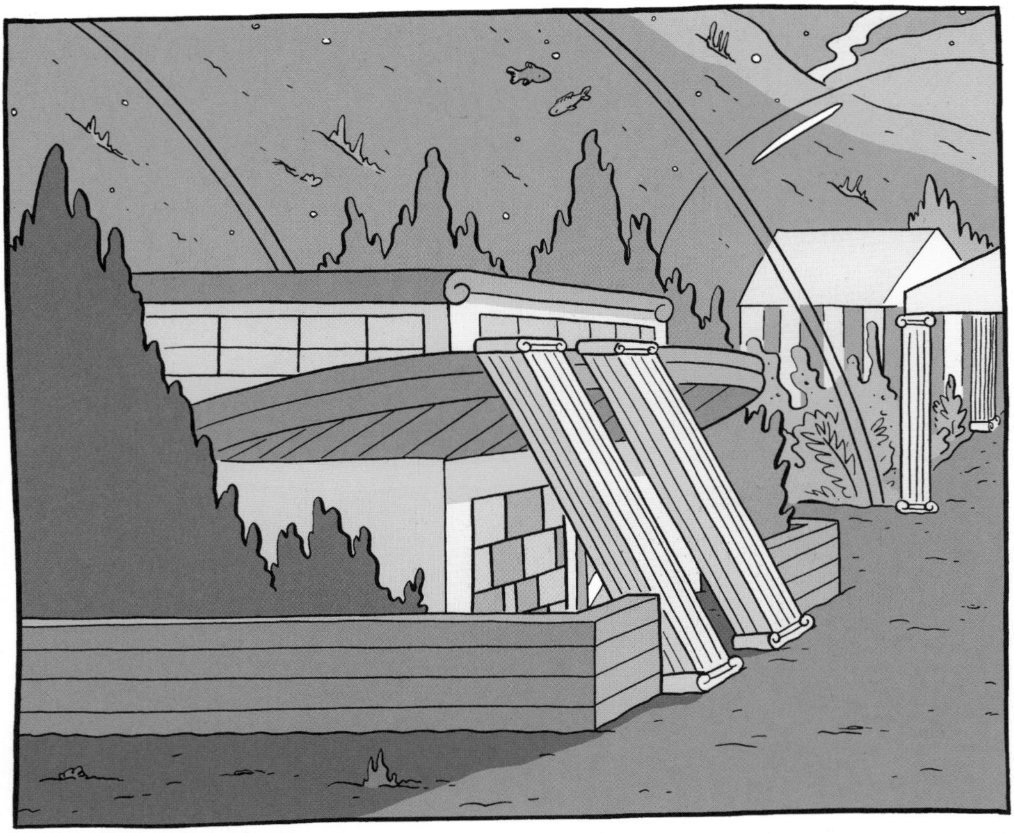

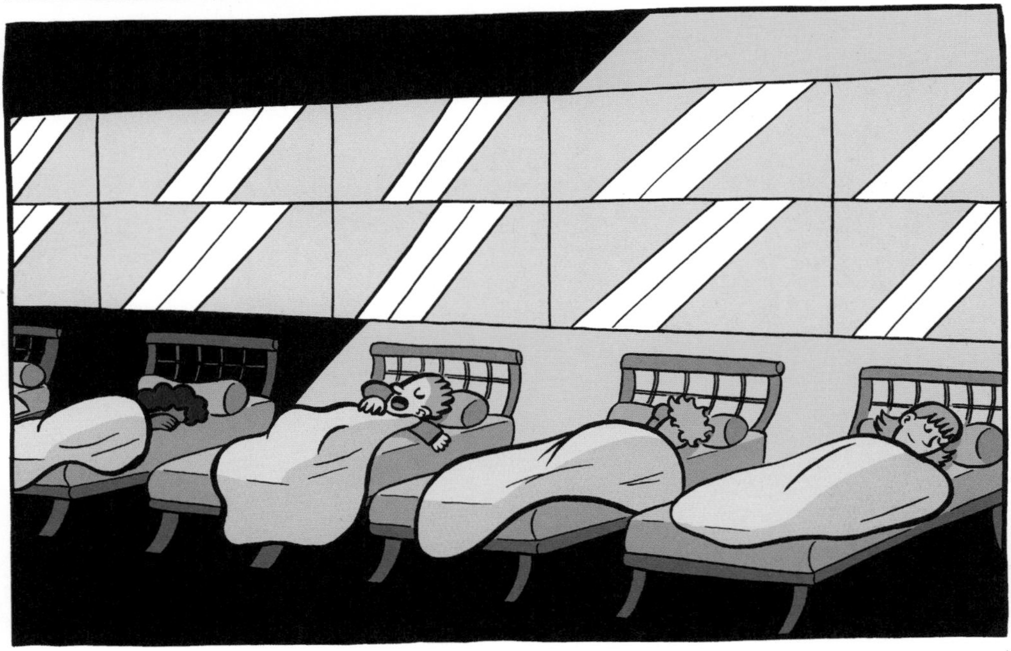

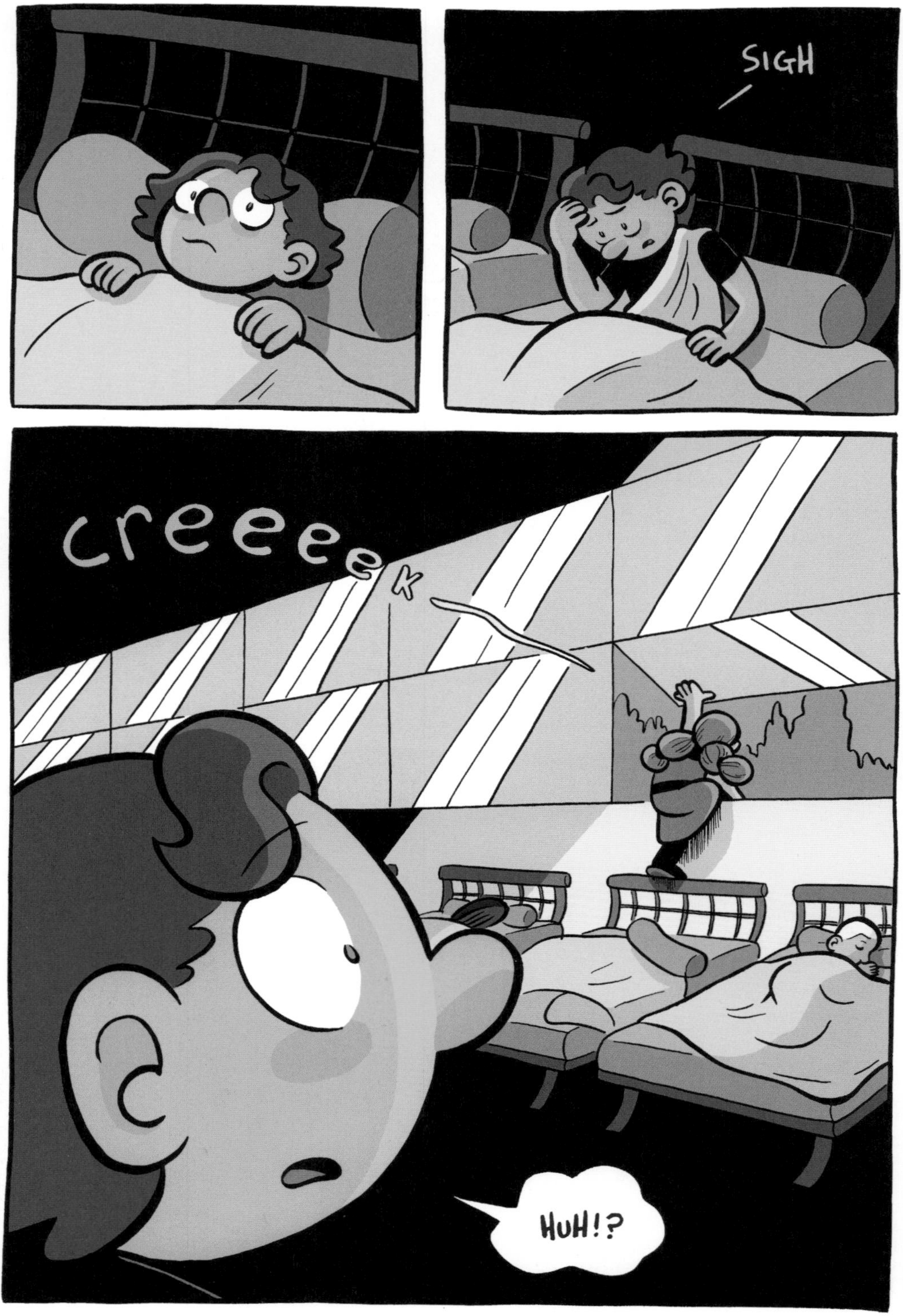
SIGH
creeeek
HUH!?

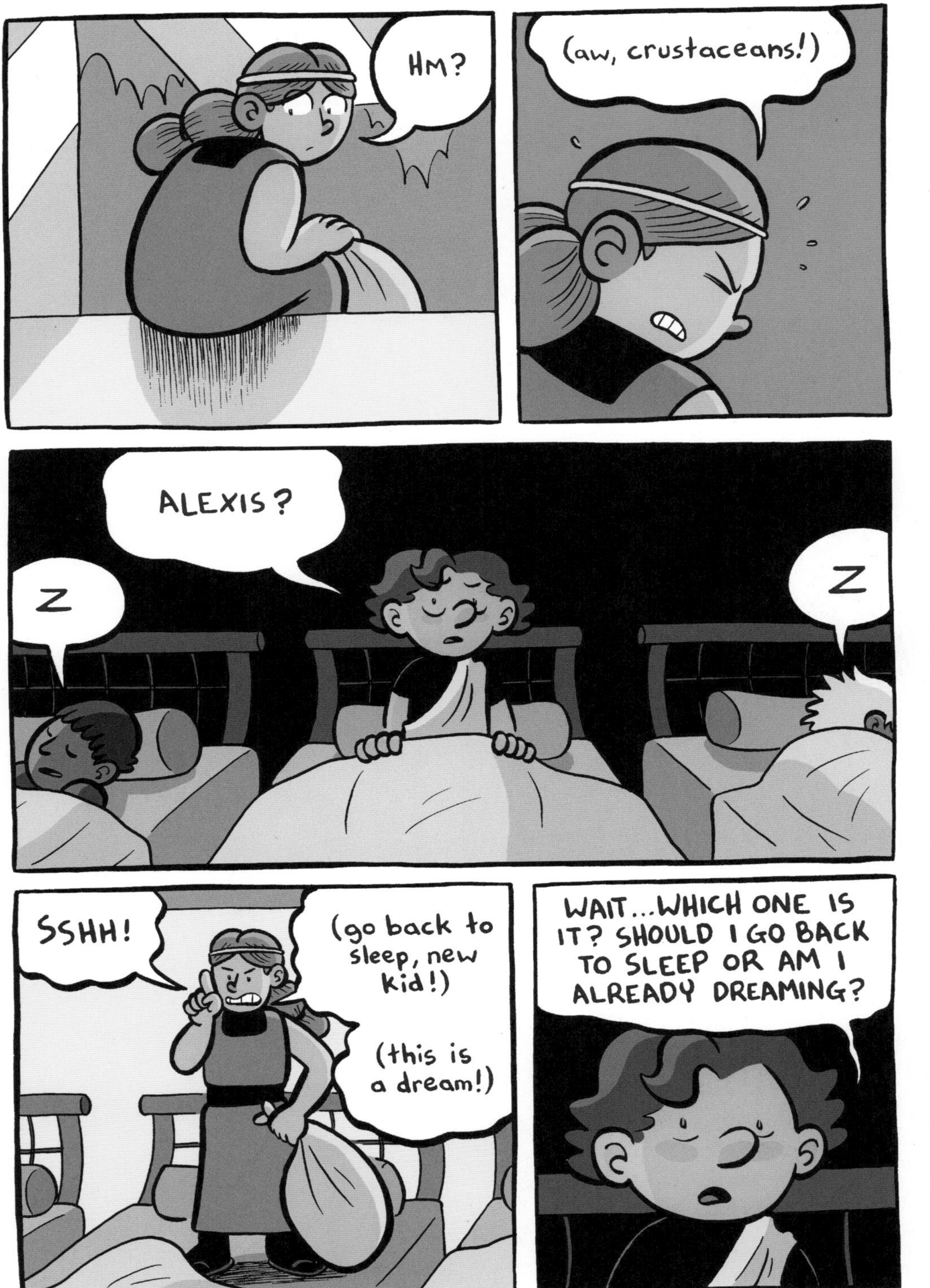
HM?
(aw, crustaceans!)
ALEXIS?
Z
Z
SSHH!
(go back to sleep, new kid!)
(this is a dream!)
WAIT...WHICH ONE IS IT? SHOULD I GO BACK TO SLEEP OR AM I ALREADY DREAMING?

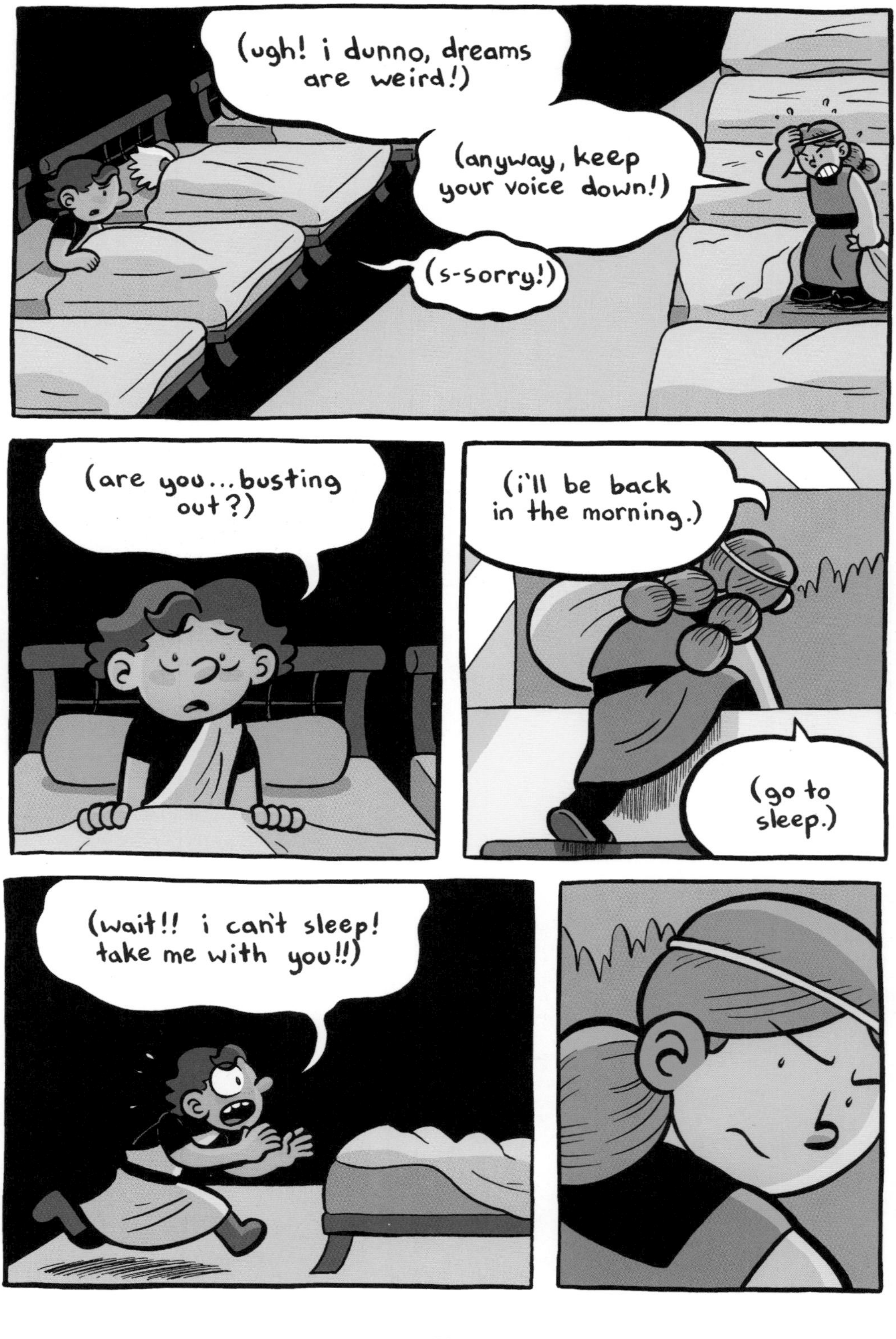
(ugh! i dunno, dreams are weird!)
(anyway, keep your voice down!)
(s-sorry!)
(are you...busting out?)
(i'll be back in the morning.)
(go to sleep.)
(wait!! i can't sleep! take me with you!!)

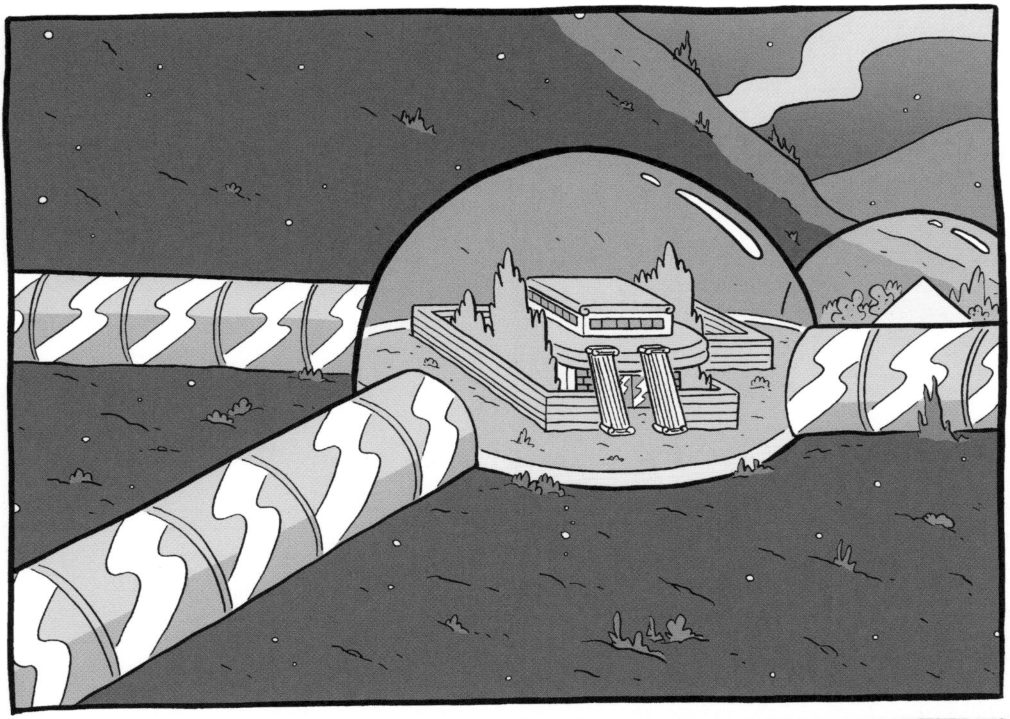

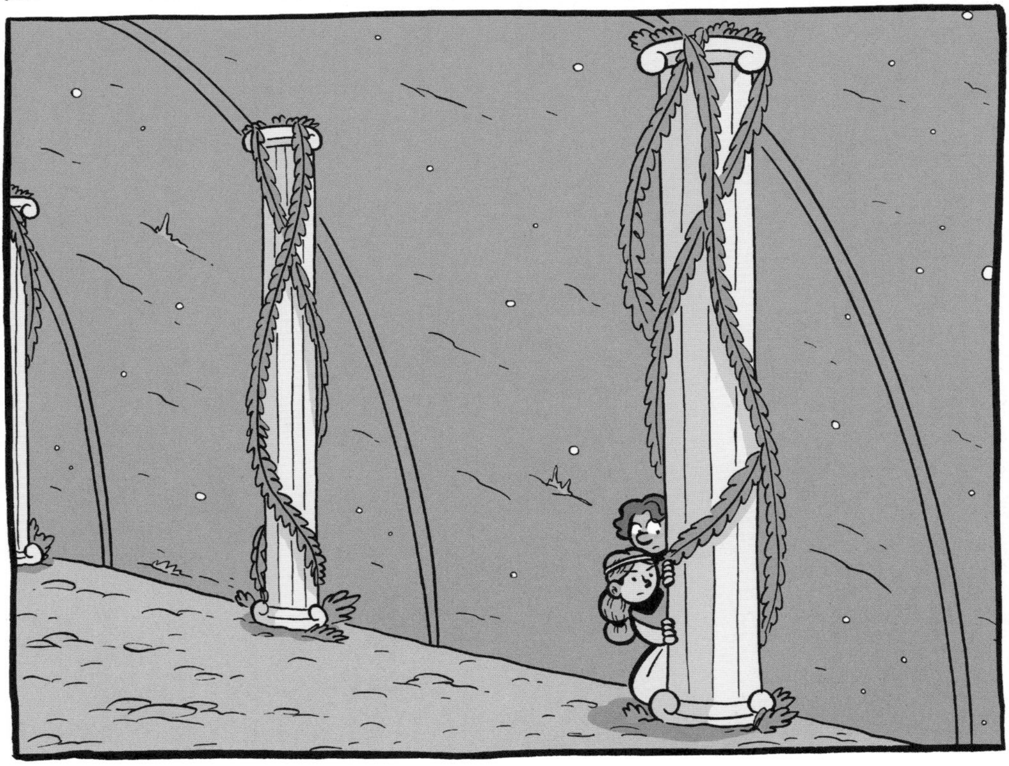

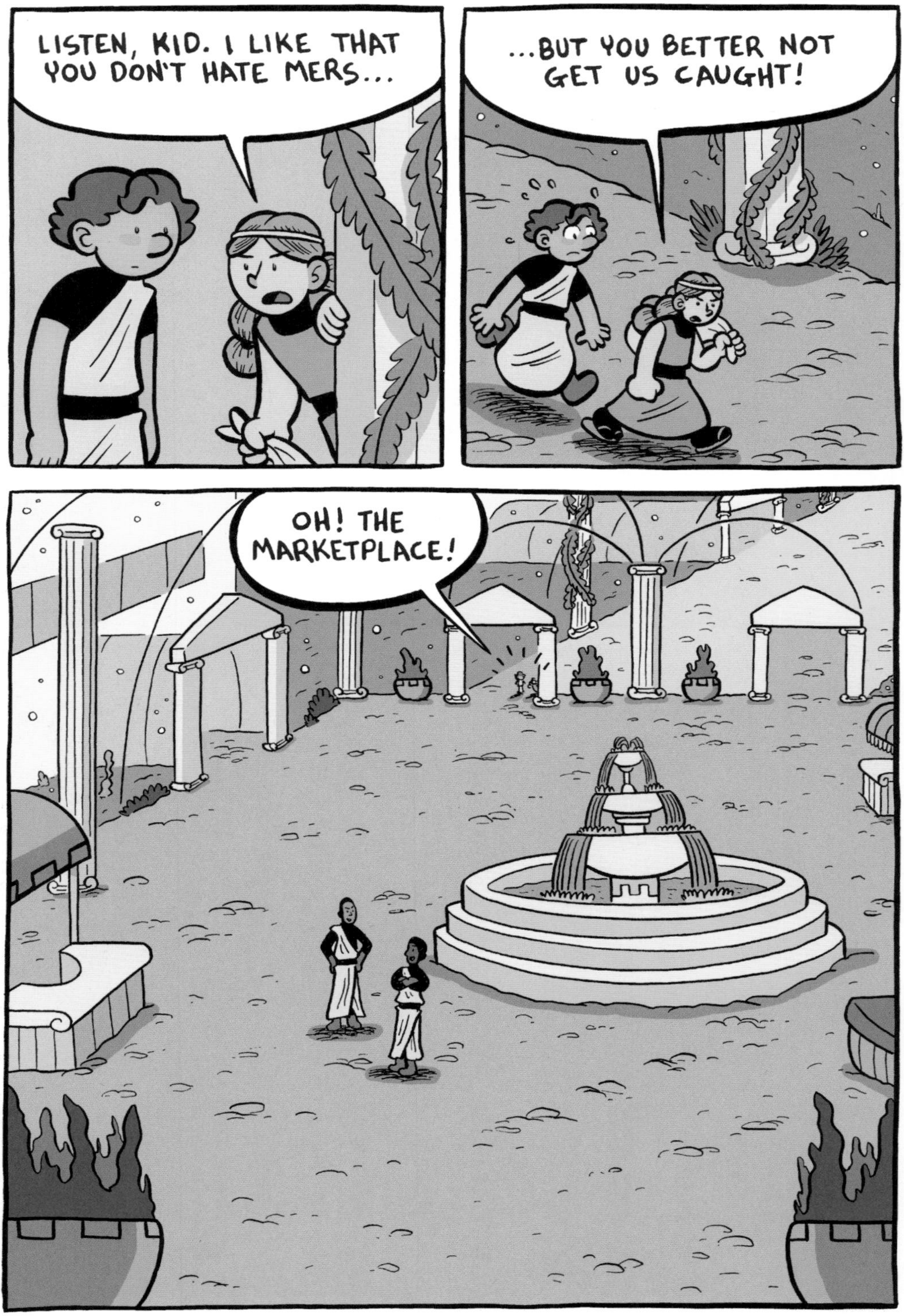
LISTEN, KID. I LIKE THAT YOU DON'T HATE MERS...
...BUT YOU BETTER NOT GET US CAUGHT!
OH! THE MARKETPLACE!

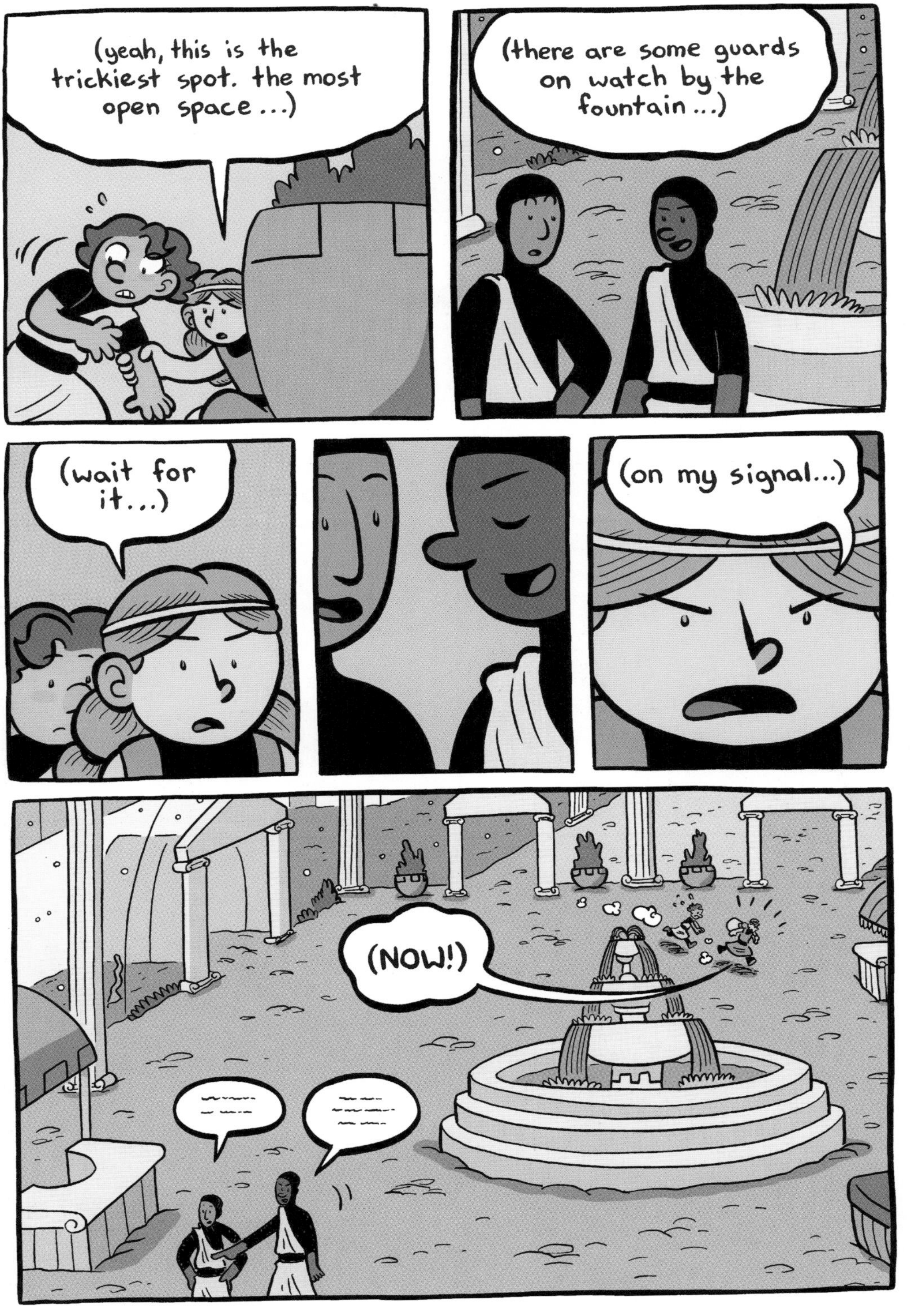
(yeah, this is the trickiest spot. the most open space...)
(there are some guards on watch by the fountain...)
(wait for it...)
(on my signal...)
(NOW!)

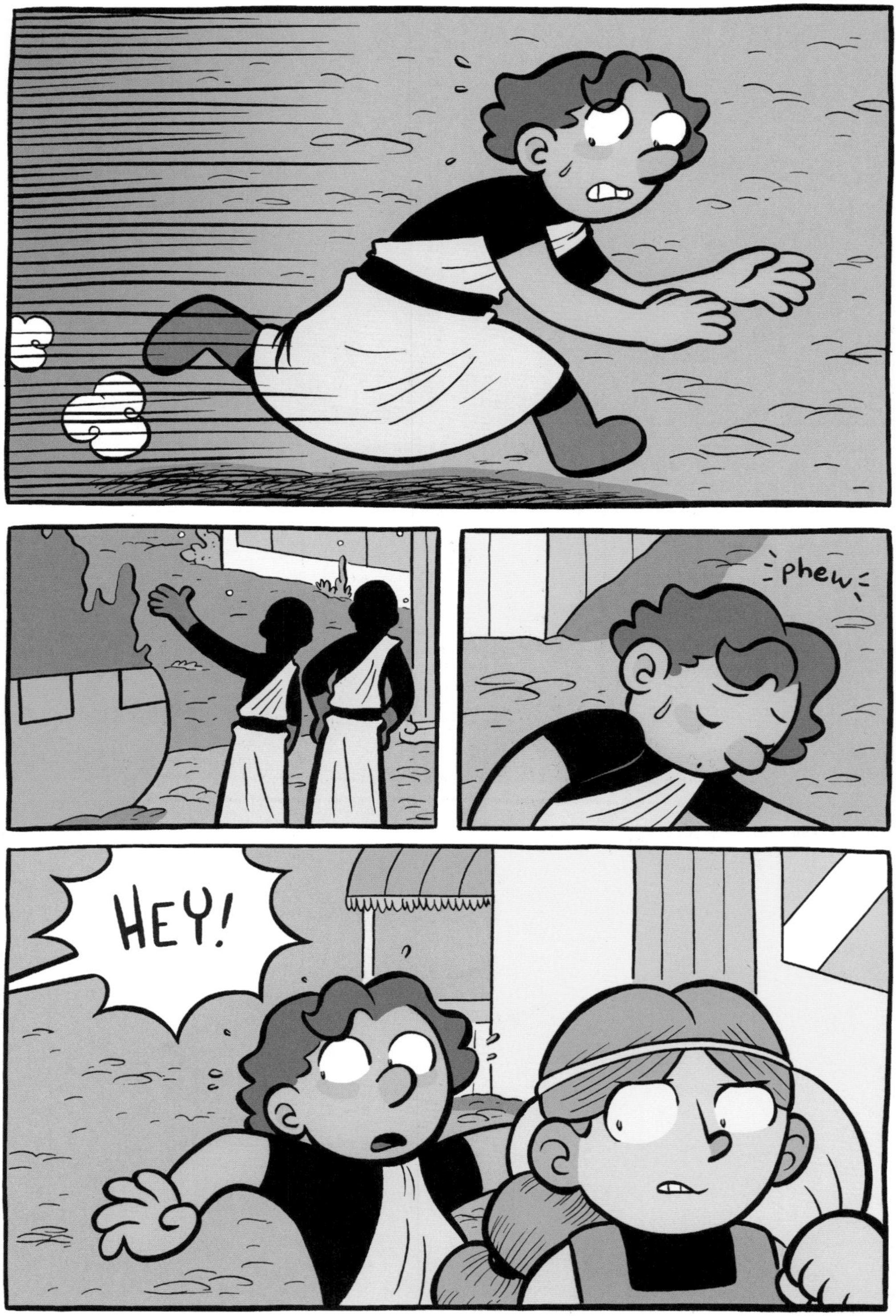
phew
HEY!

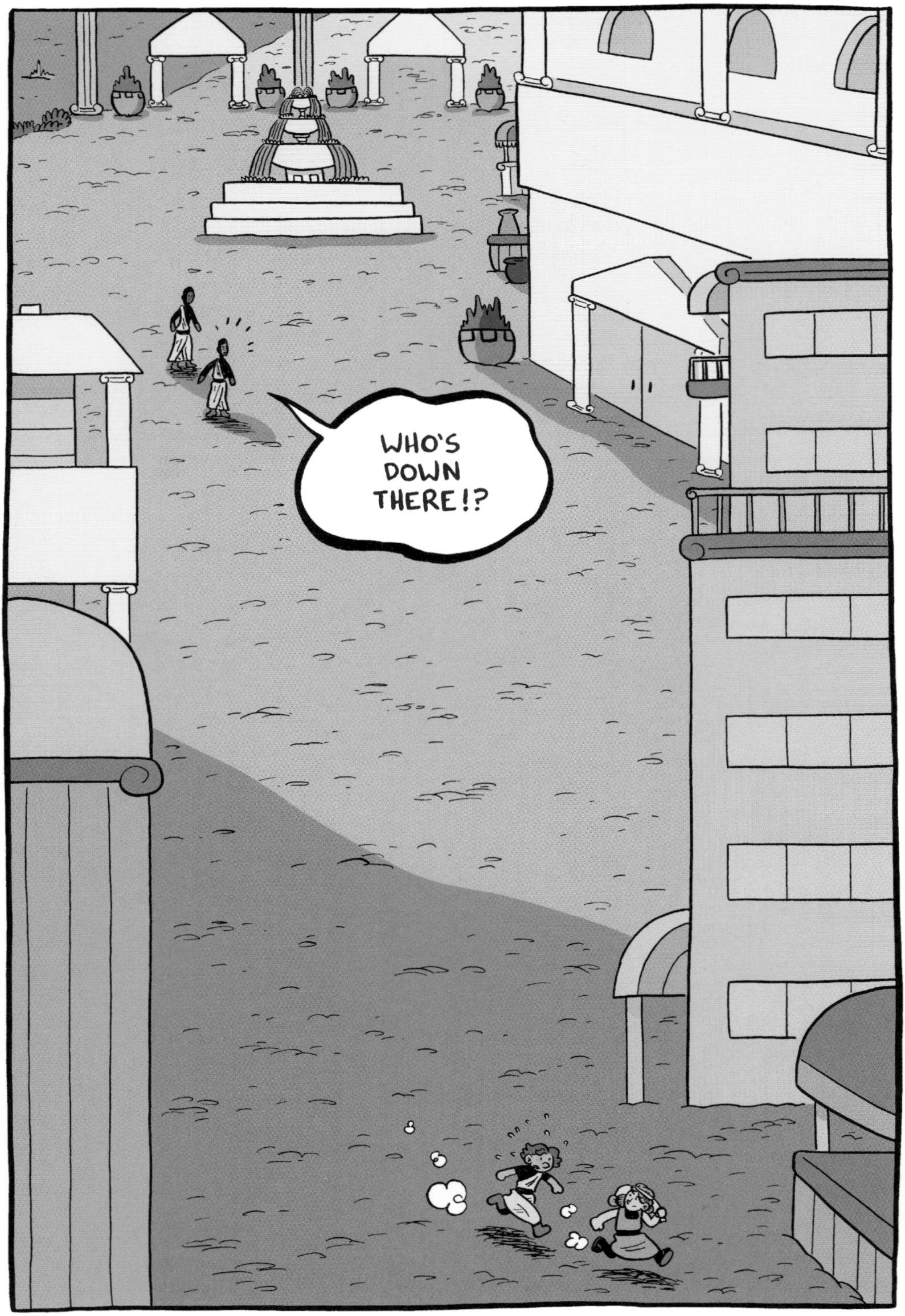
WHO'S DOWN THERE!?

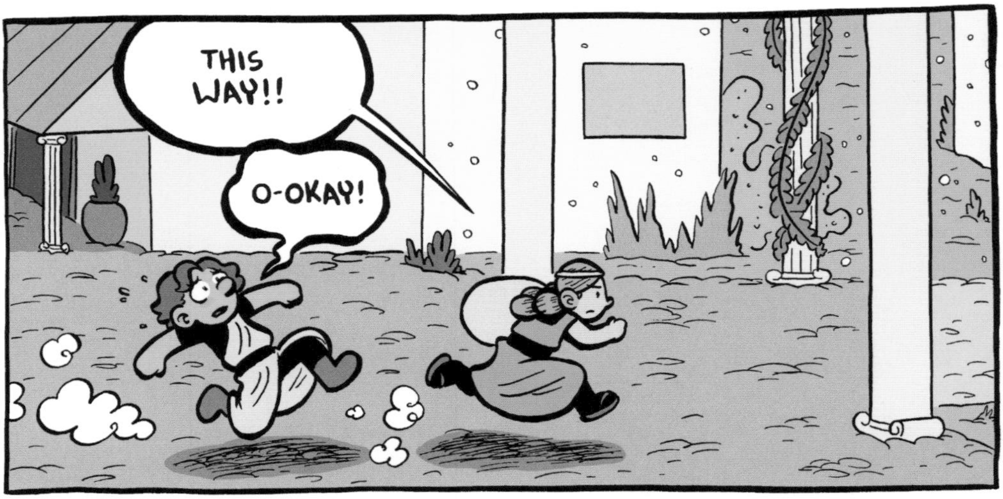
THIS WAY!!
O-OKAY!

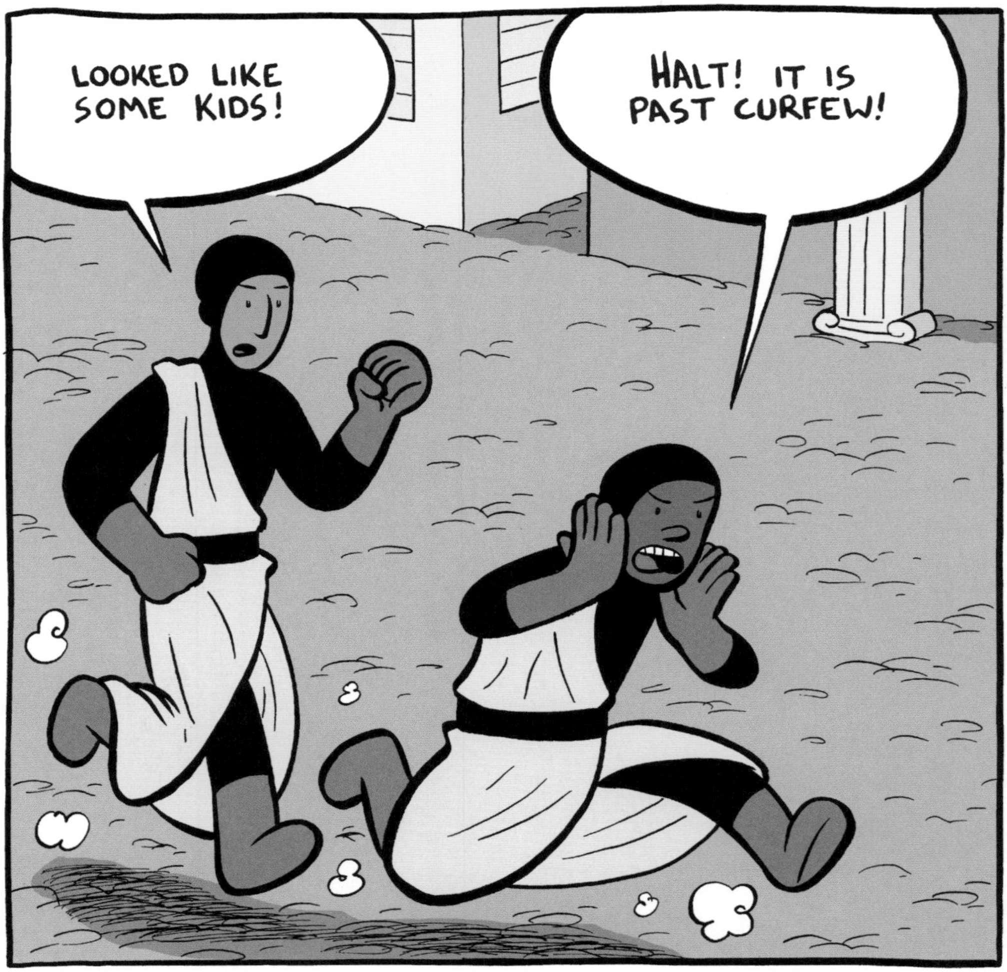
LOOKED LIKE SOME KIDS!
HALT! IT IS PAST CURFEW!

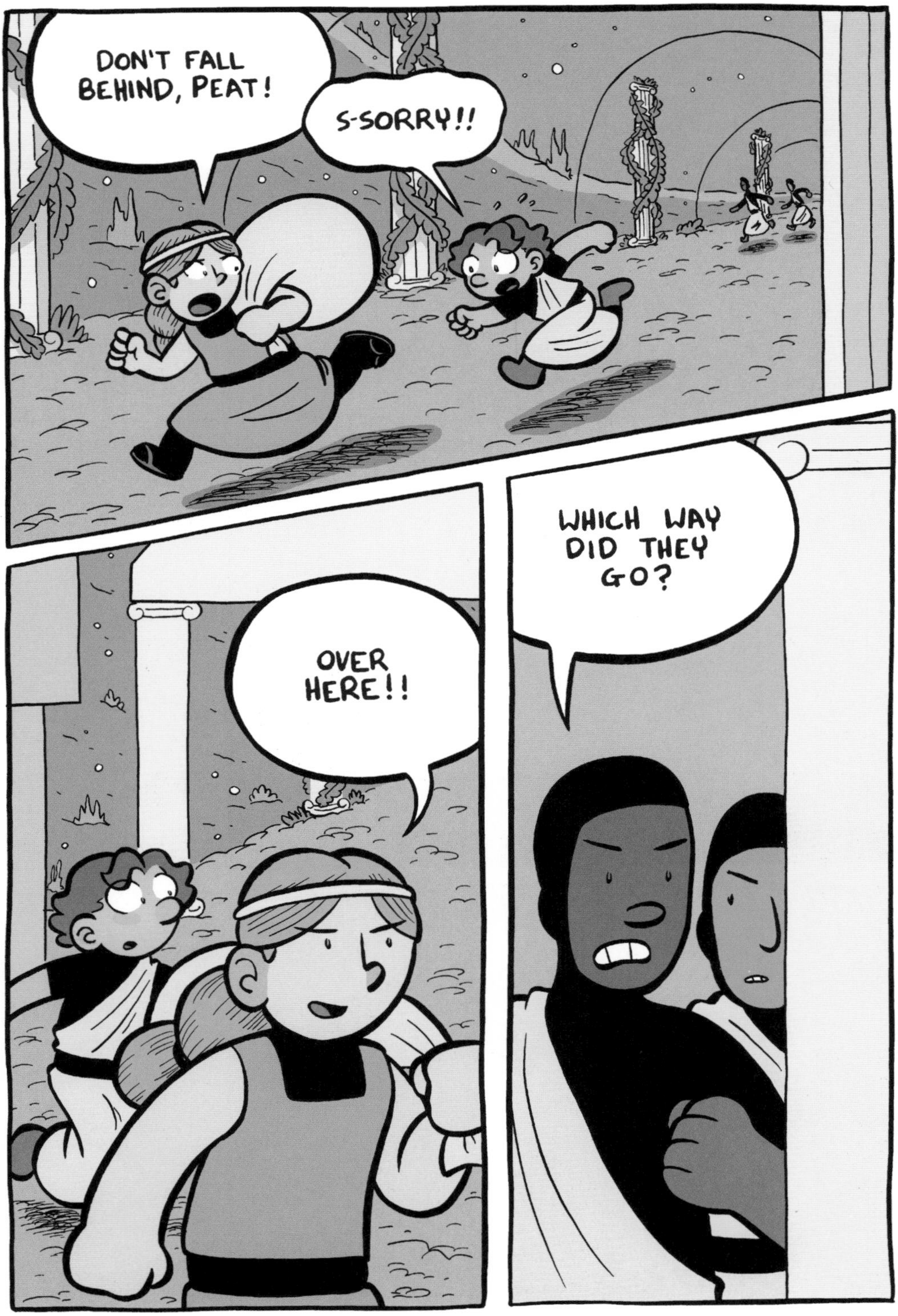
DON'T FALL BEHIND, PEAT!
S-SORRY!!
OVER HERE!!
WHICH WAY DID THEY GO?

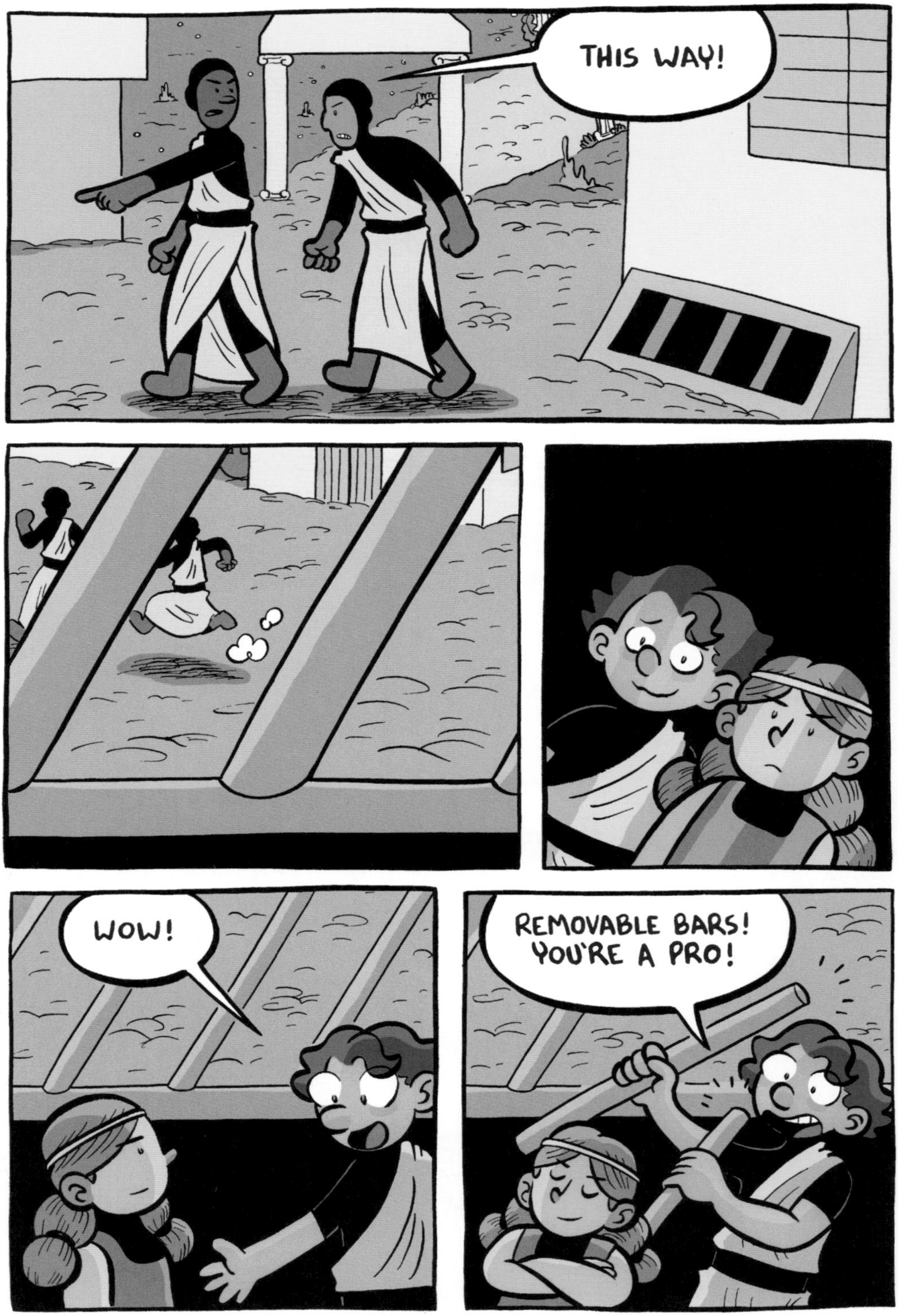
THIS WAY!
WOW!
REMOVABLE BARS! YOU'RE A PRO!

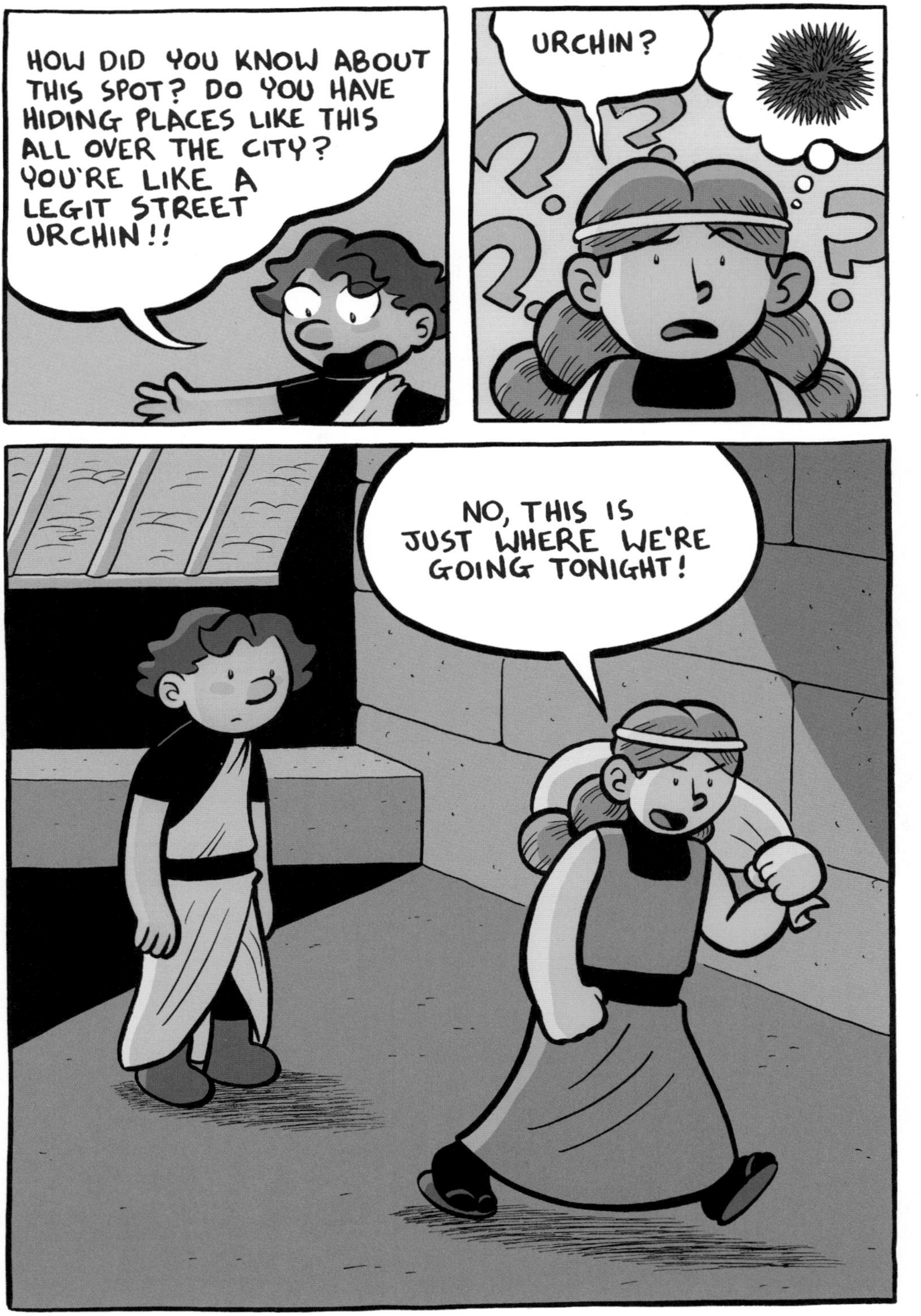
HOW DID YOU KNOW ABOUT THIS SPOT? DO YOU HAVE HIDING PLACES LIKE THIS ALL OVER THE CITY? YOU'RE LIKE A LEGIT STREET URCHIN!!
URCHIN?
NO, THIS IS JUST WHERE WE'RE GOING TONIGHT!

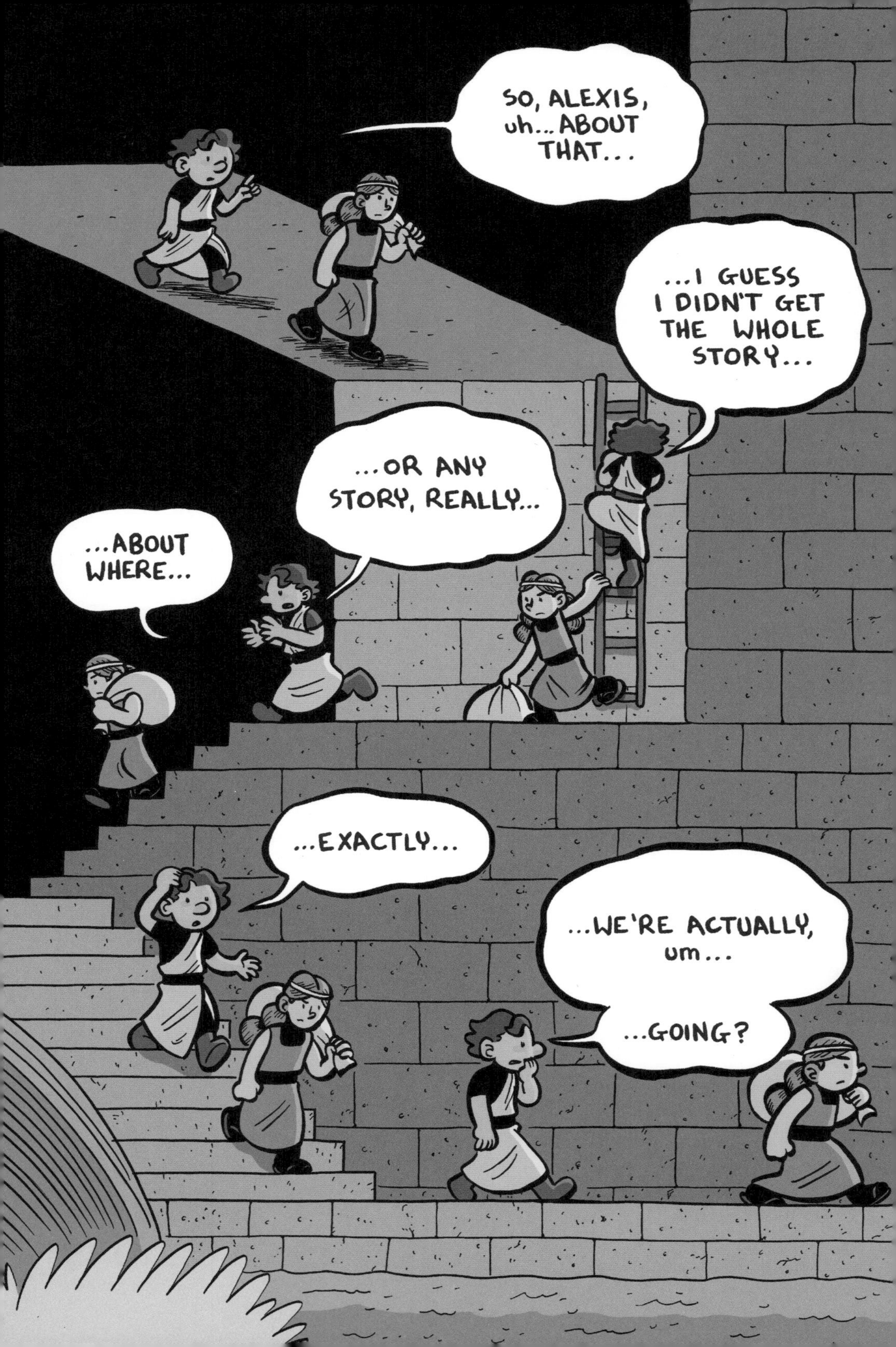
SO, ALEXIS, uh... ABOUT THAT...
...I GUESS I DIDN'T GET THE WHOLE STORY...
...OR ANY STORY, REALLY...
...ABOUT WHERE...
...EXACTLY...
...WE'RE ACTUALLY, um...
...GOING?

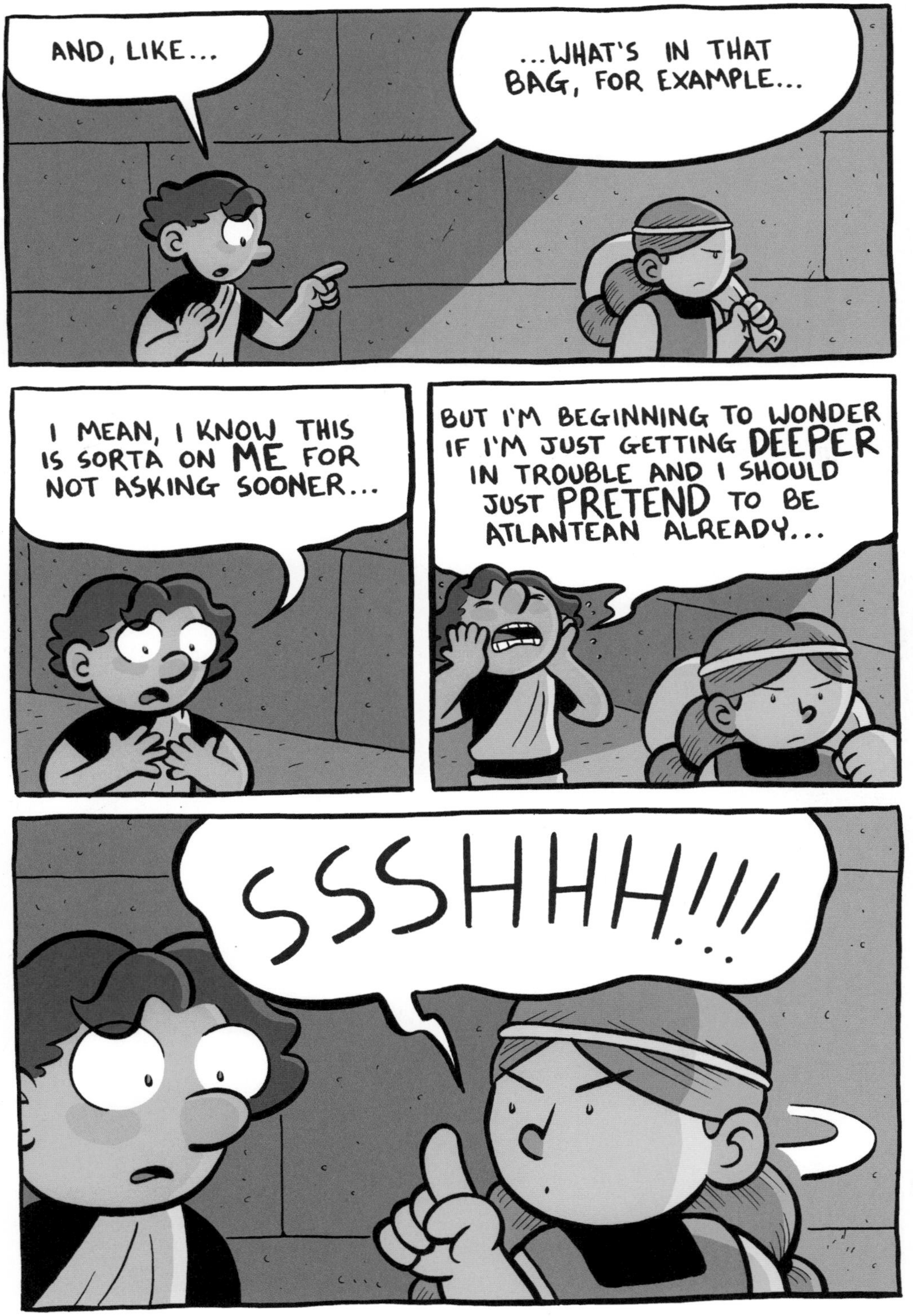
AND, LIKE...
...WHAT'S IN THAT BAG, FOR EXAMPLE...
I MEAN, I KNOW THIS IS SORTA ON ME FOR NOT ASKING SOONER...
BUT I'M BEGINNING TO WONDER IF I'M JUST GETTING DEEPER IN TROUBLE AND I SHOULD JUST PRETEND TO BE ATLANTEAN ALREADY...
SSSHHH!!!

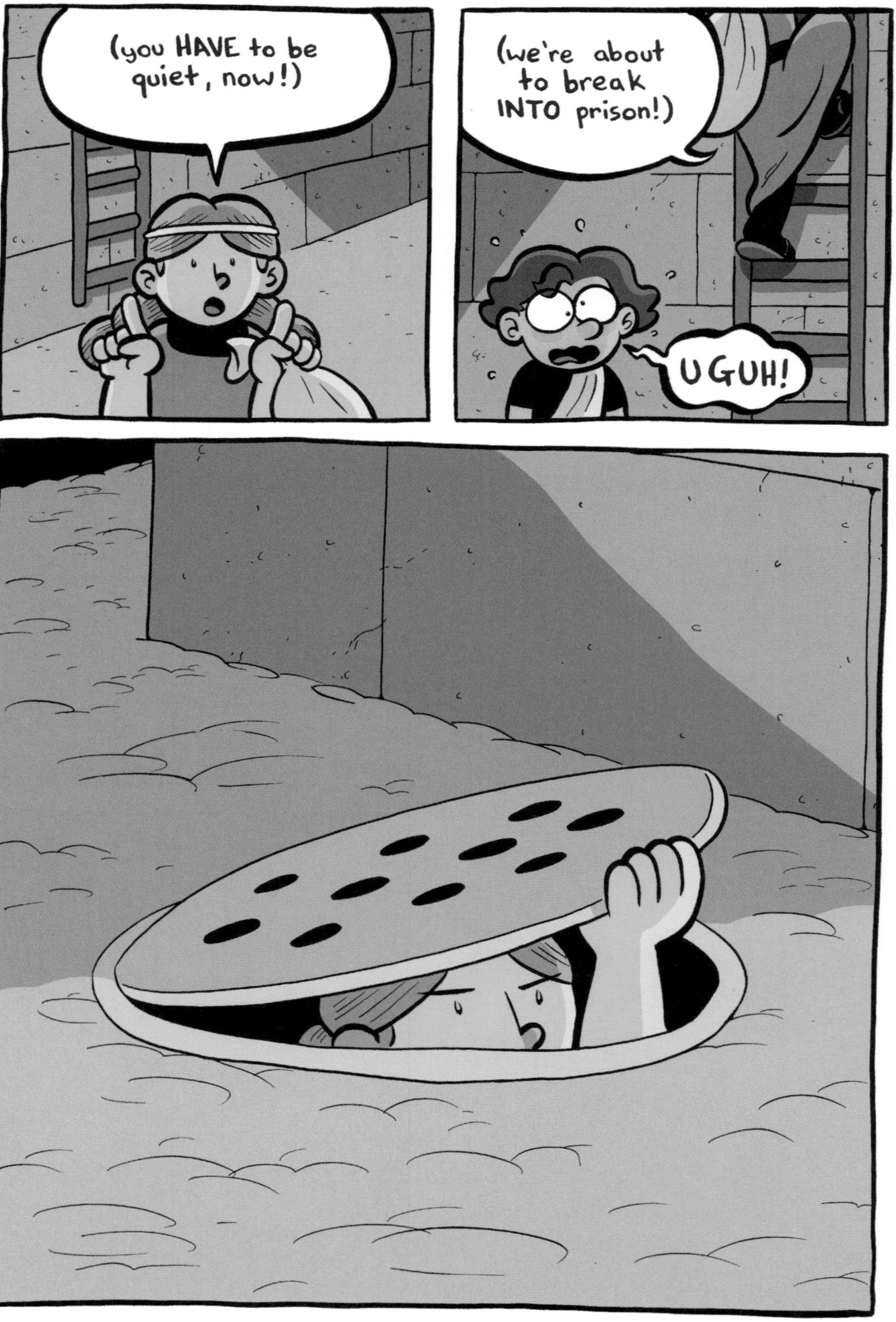
(you HAVE to be quiet, now!)
(we're about to break INTO prison!)
UGUH!

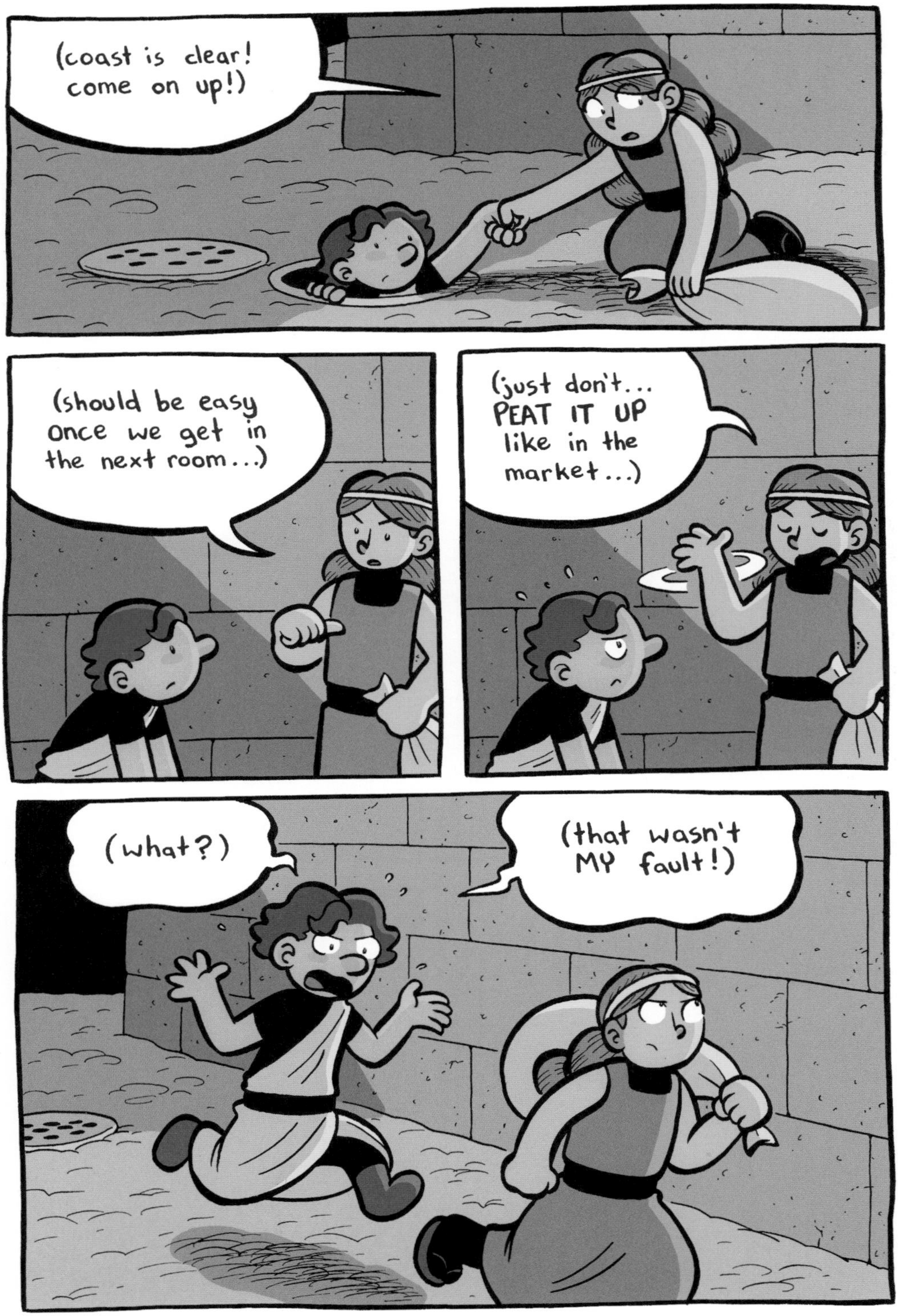
(coast is clear! come on up!)
(should be easy once we get in the next room...)
(just don't... PEAT IT UP like in the market...)
(what?)
(that wasn't MY fault!)

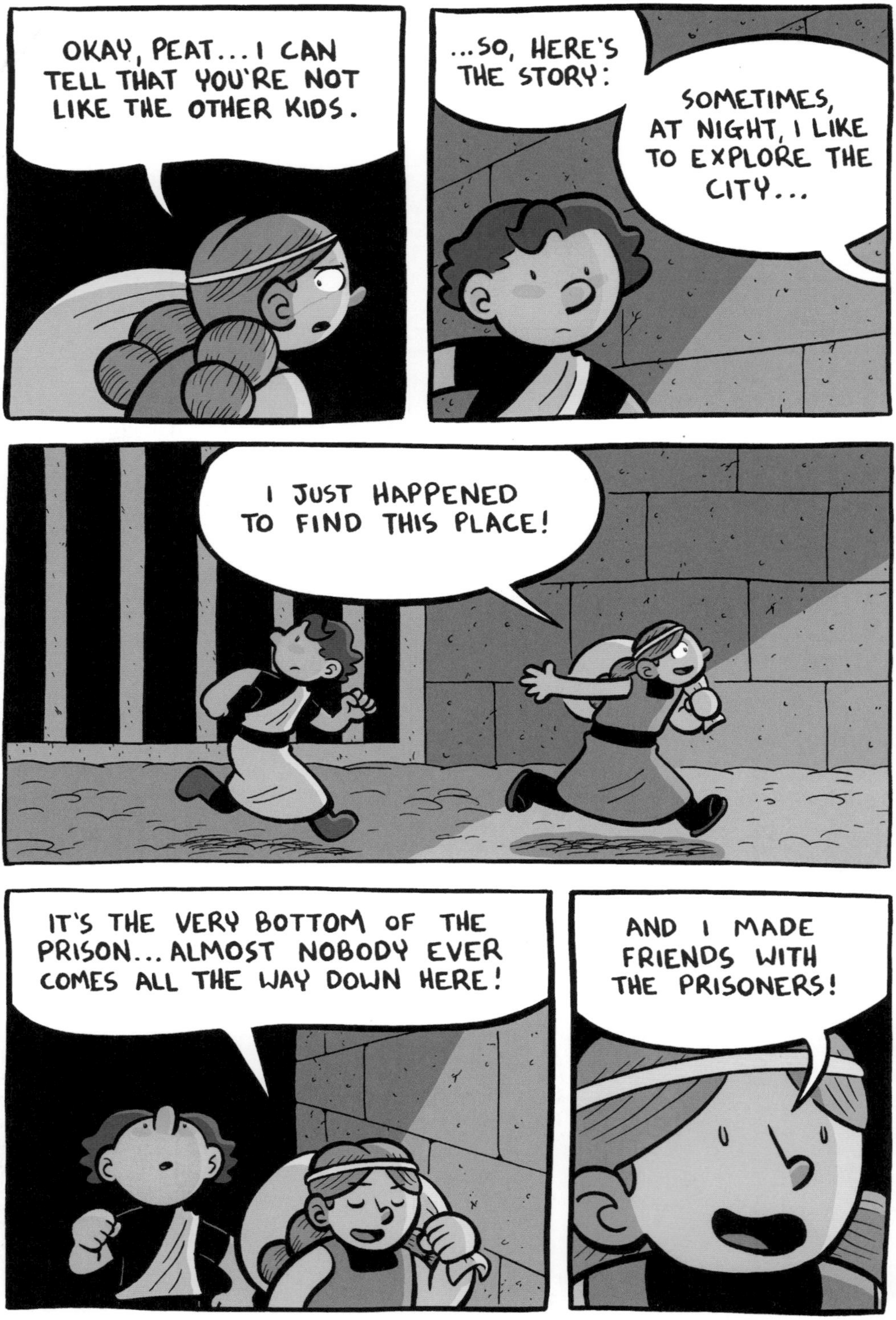
OKAY, PEAT... I CAN TELL THAT YOU'RE NOT LIKE THE OTHER KIDS.
...SO, HERE'S THE STORY:
SOMETIMES, AT NIGHT, I LIKE TO EXPLORE THE CITY...
I JUST HAPPENED TO FIND THIS PLACE!
IT'S THE VERY BOTTOM OF THE PRISON... ALMOST NOBODY EVER COMES ALL THE WAY DOWN HERE!
AND I MADE FRIENDS WITH THE PRISONERS!

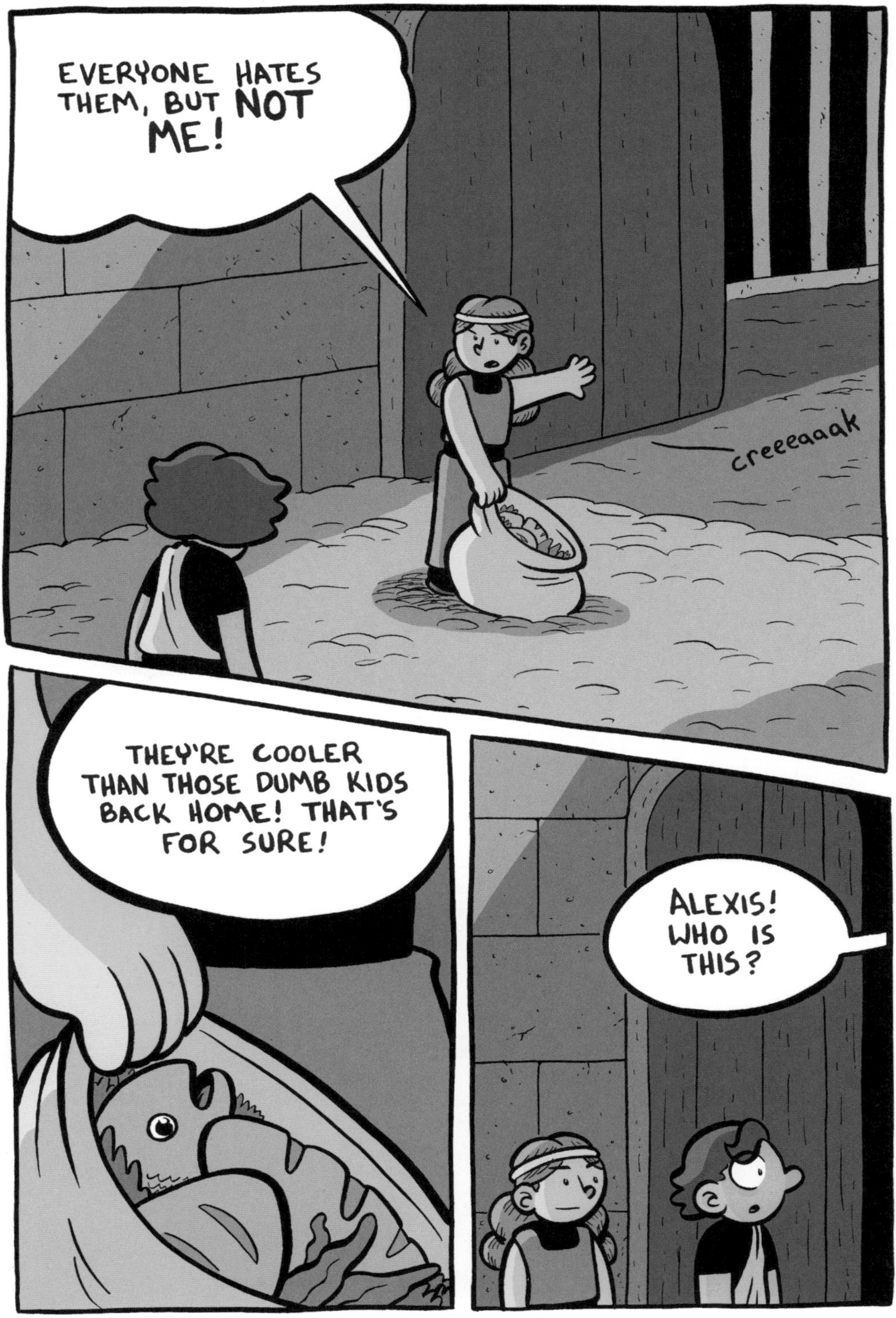
EVERYONE HATES THEM, BUT NOT ME!
creeeaaak
THEY'RE COOLER THAN THOSE DUMB KIDS BACK HOME! THAT'S FOR SURE!
ALEXIS! WHO IS THIS?

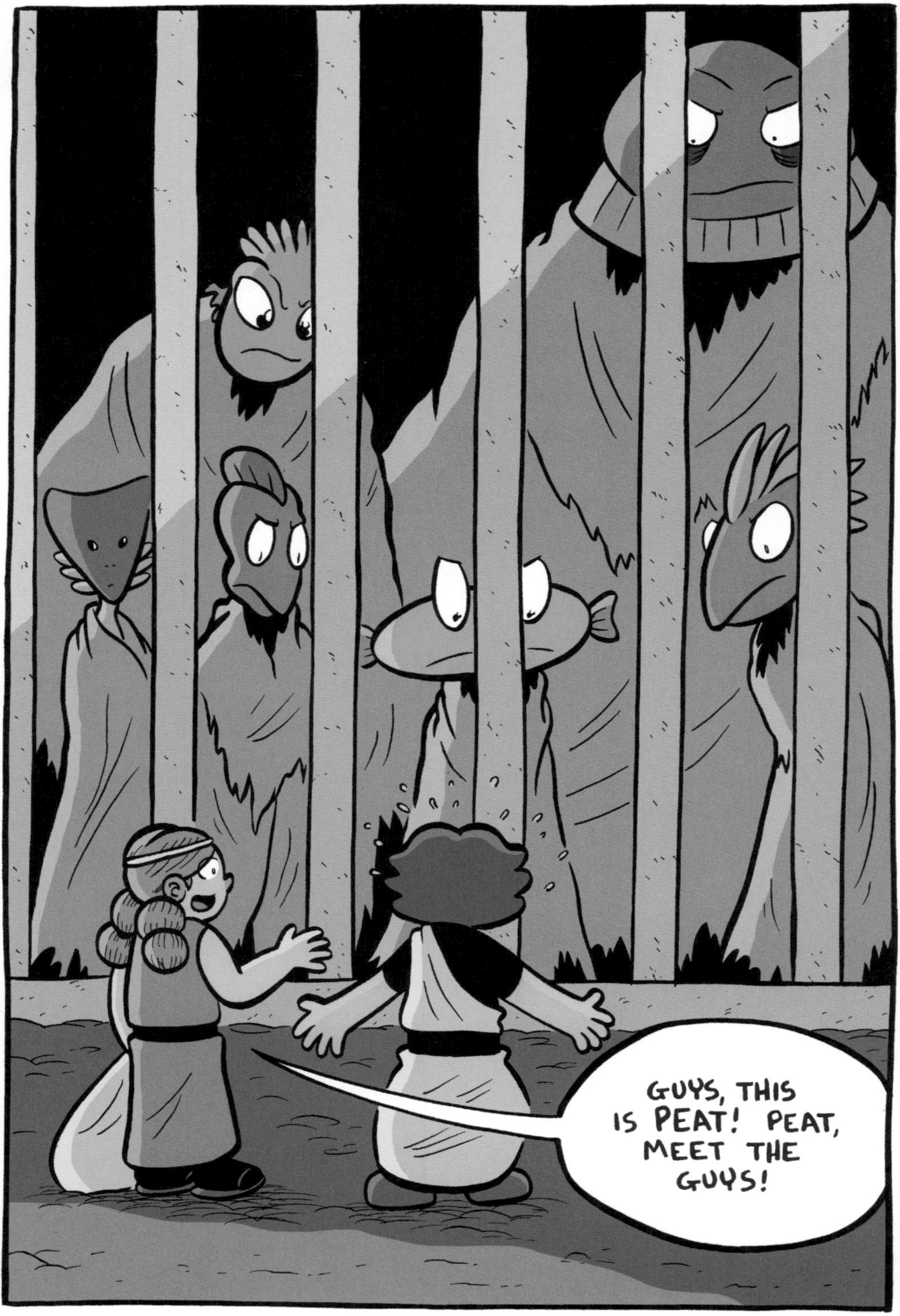
GUYS, THIS IS PEAT! PEAT, MEET THE GUYS!

CHAPTER FIVE

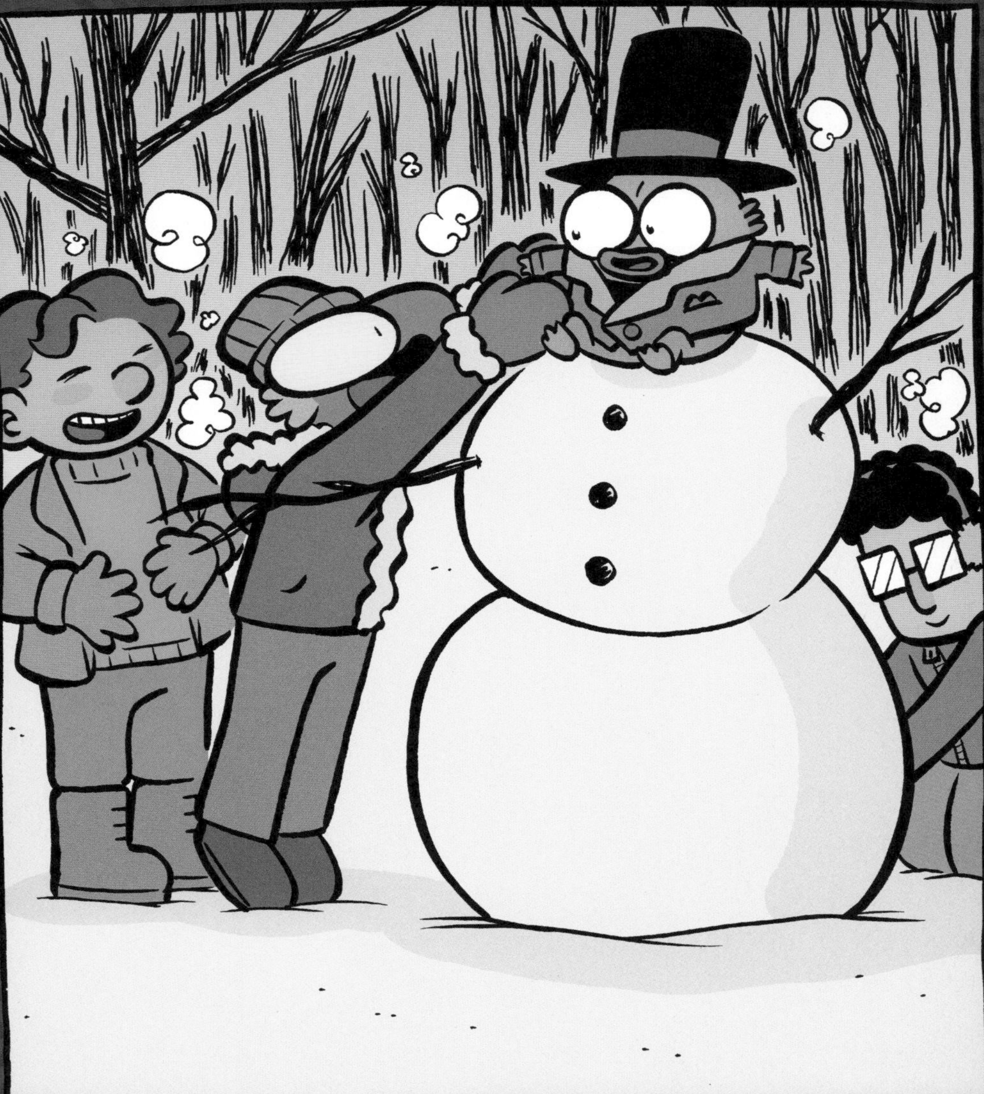

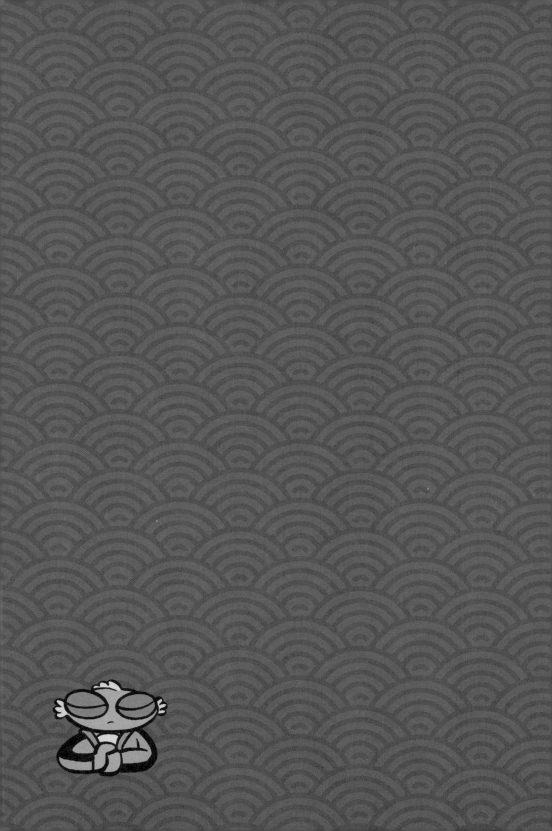

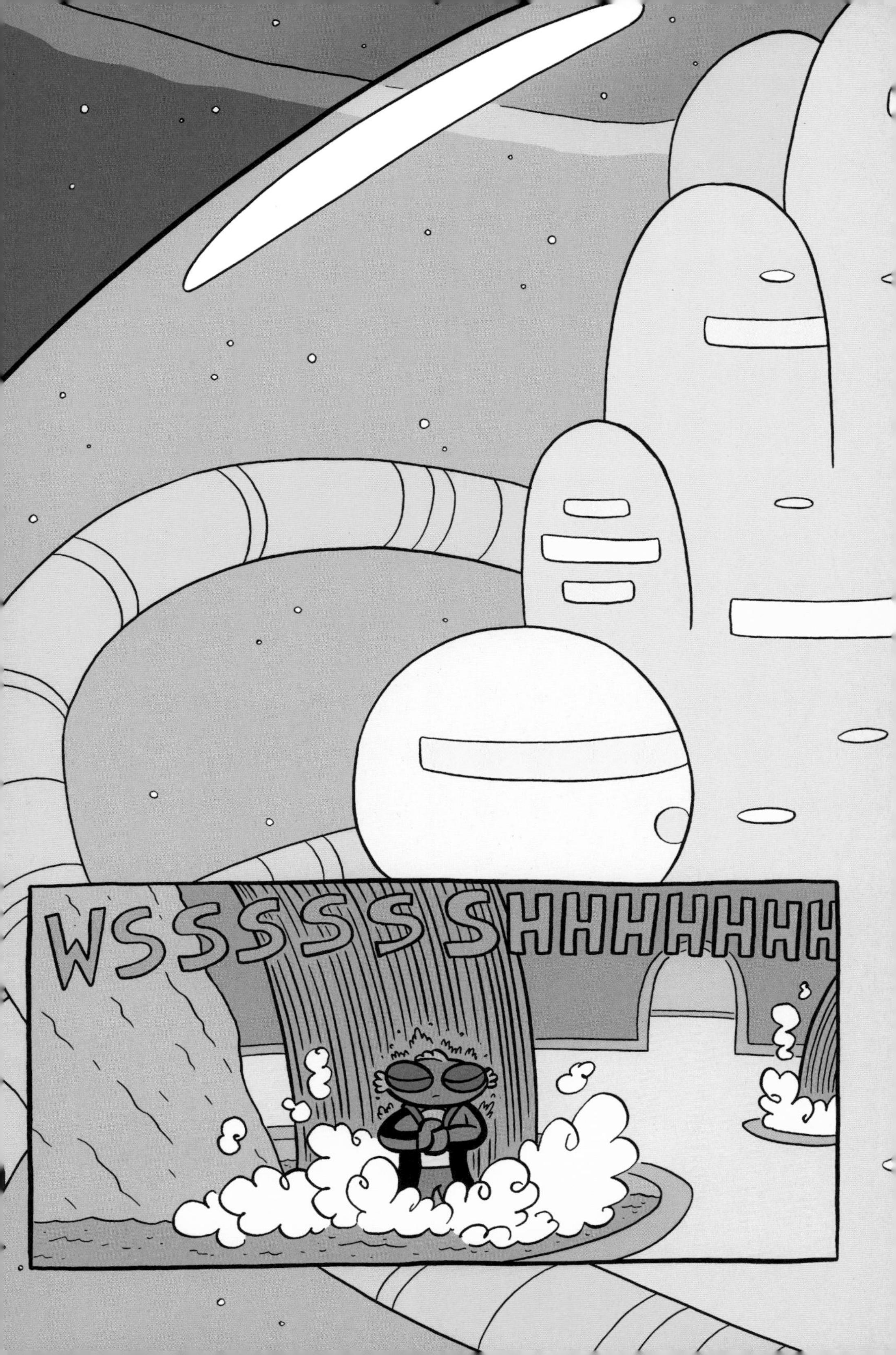
WSSSSSSHHHHHHH

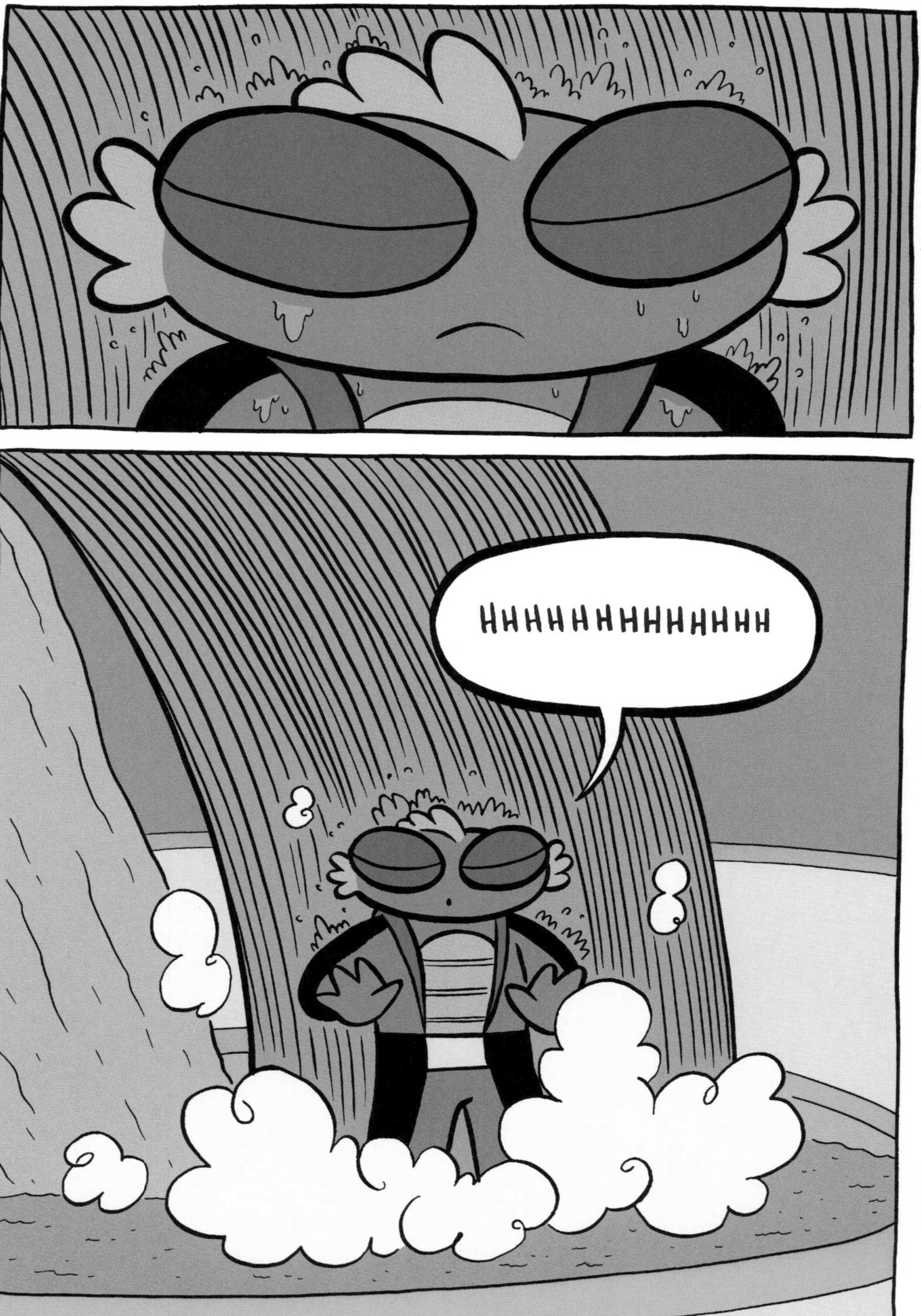
HHHHHHHHHHHHH

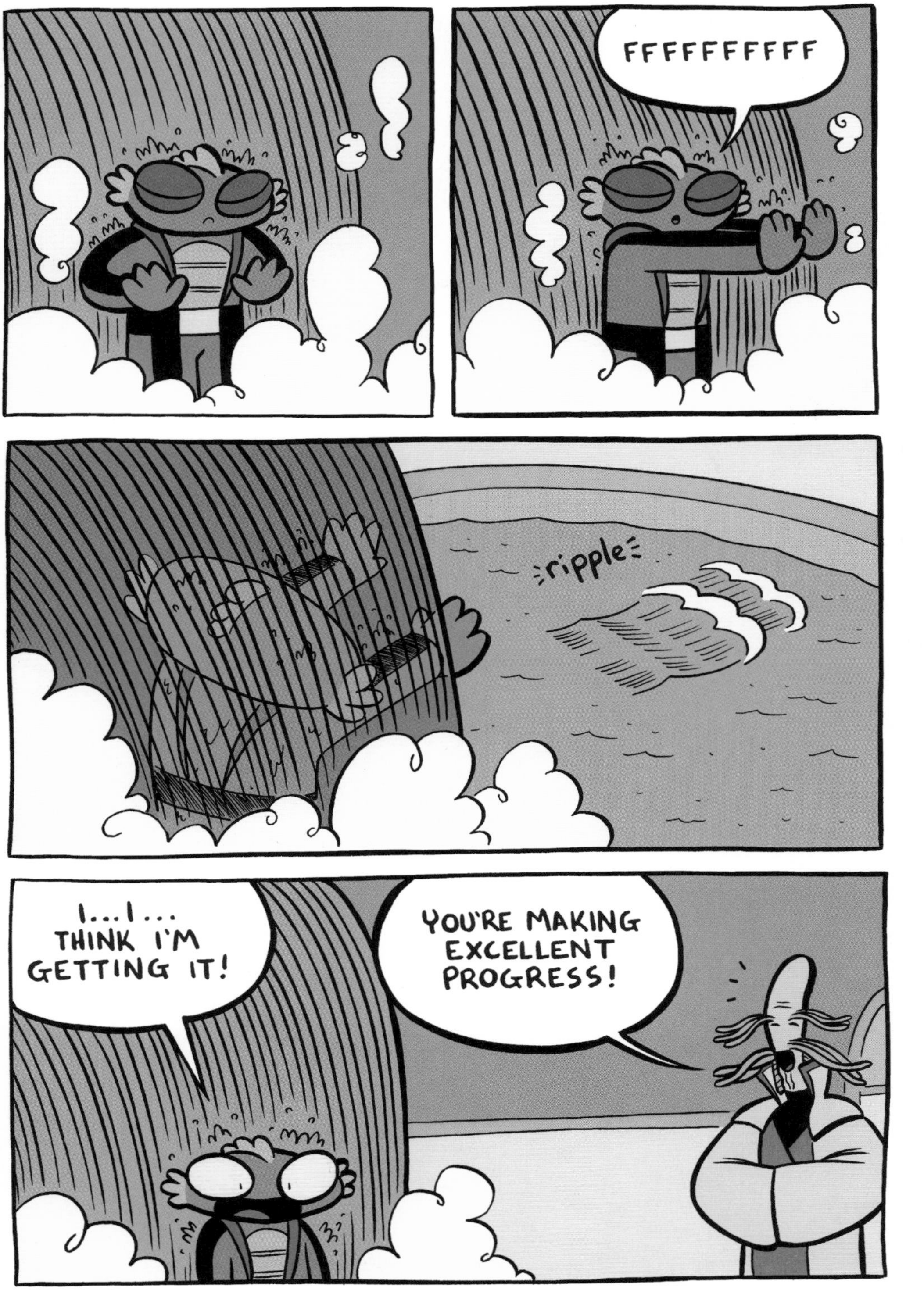
FFFFFFFFFF
ripple
I...I...
THINK I'M
GETTING IT!
YOU'RE MAKING
EXCELLENT
PROGRESS!

THAT'S GREAT TO HEAR!

D-DAD! HEY!

YES, HE IS DEFINITELY SHOWING IMPROVEMENT!

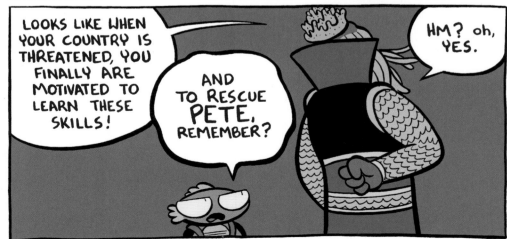

LOOKS LIKE WHEN YOUR COUNTRY IS THREATENED, YOU FINALLY ARE MOTIVATED TO LEARN THESE SKILLS!

AND TO RESCUE PETE, REMEMBER?

HM? oh, YES.

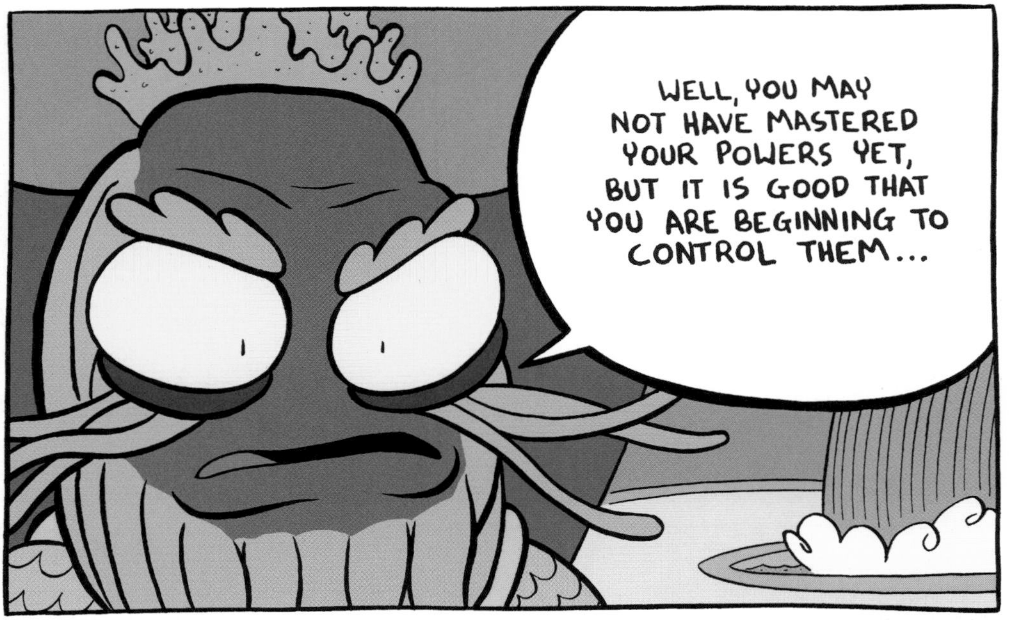
WELL, YOU MAY NOT HAVE MASTERED YOUR POWERS YET, BUT IT IS GOOD THAT YOU ARE BEGINNING TO CONTROL THEM...

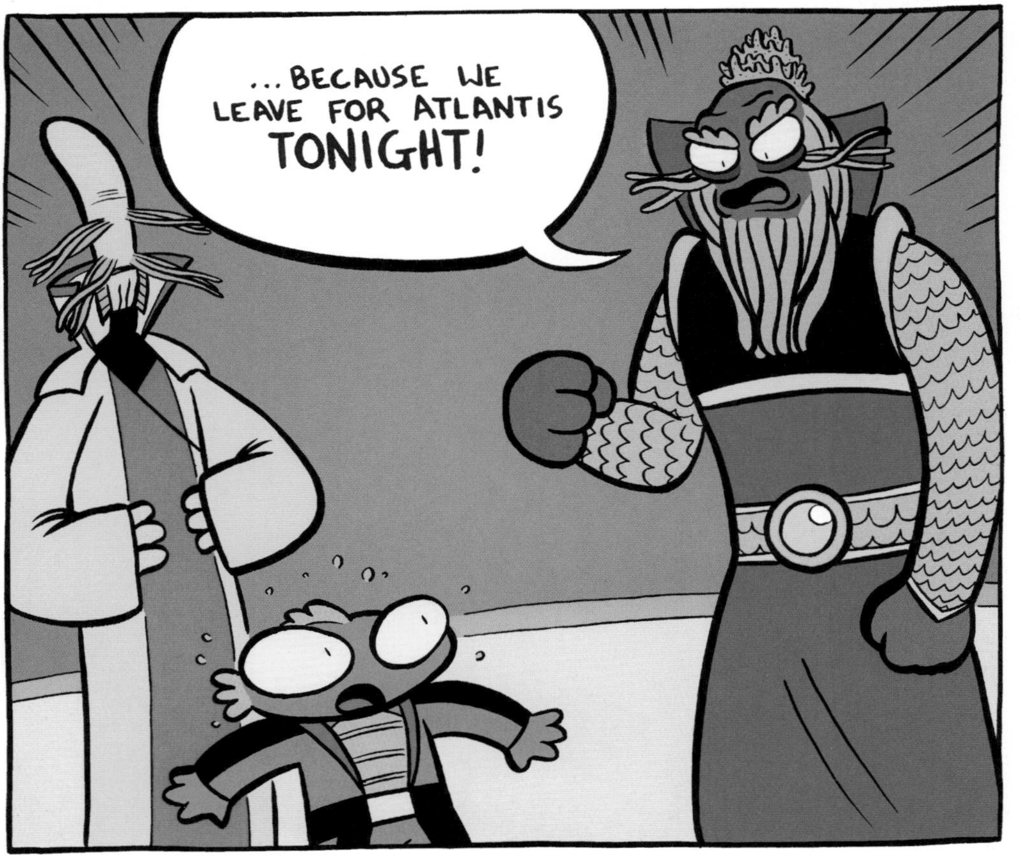
...BECAUSE WE LEAVE FOR ATLANTIS TONIGHT!

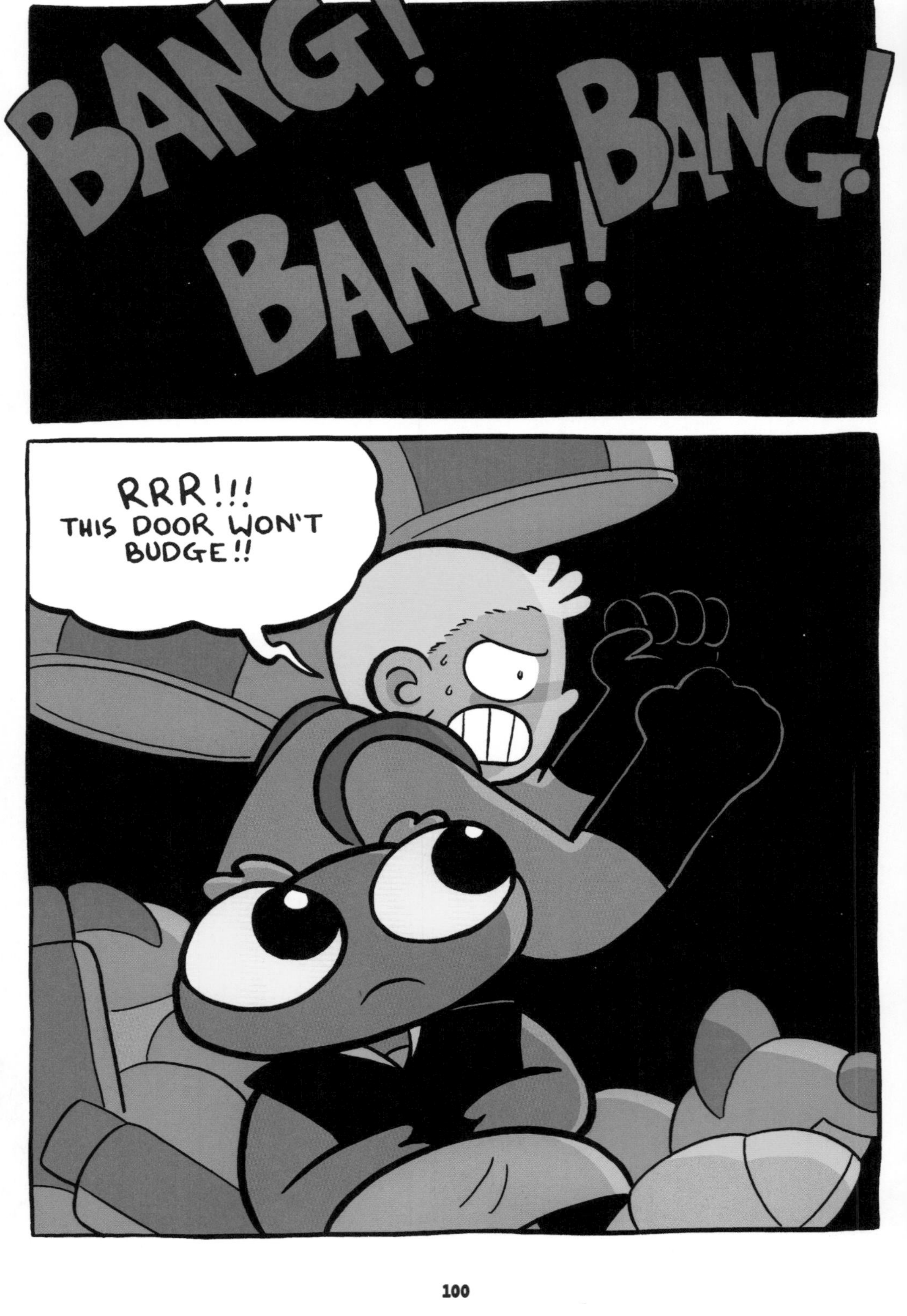
BANG! BANG! BANG!
RRR!!! THIS DOOR WON'T BUDGE!!

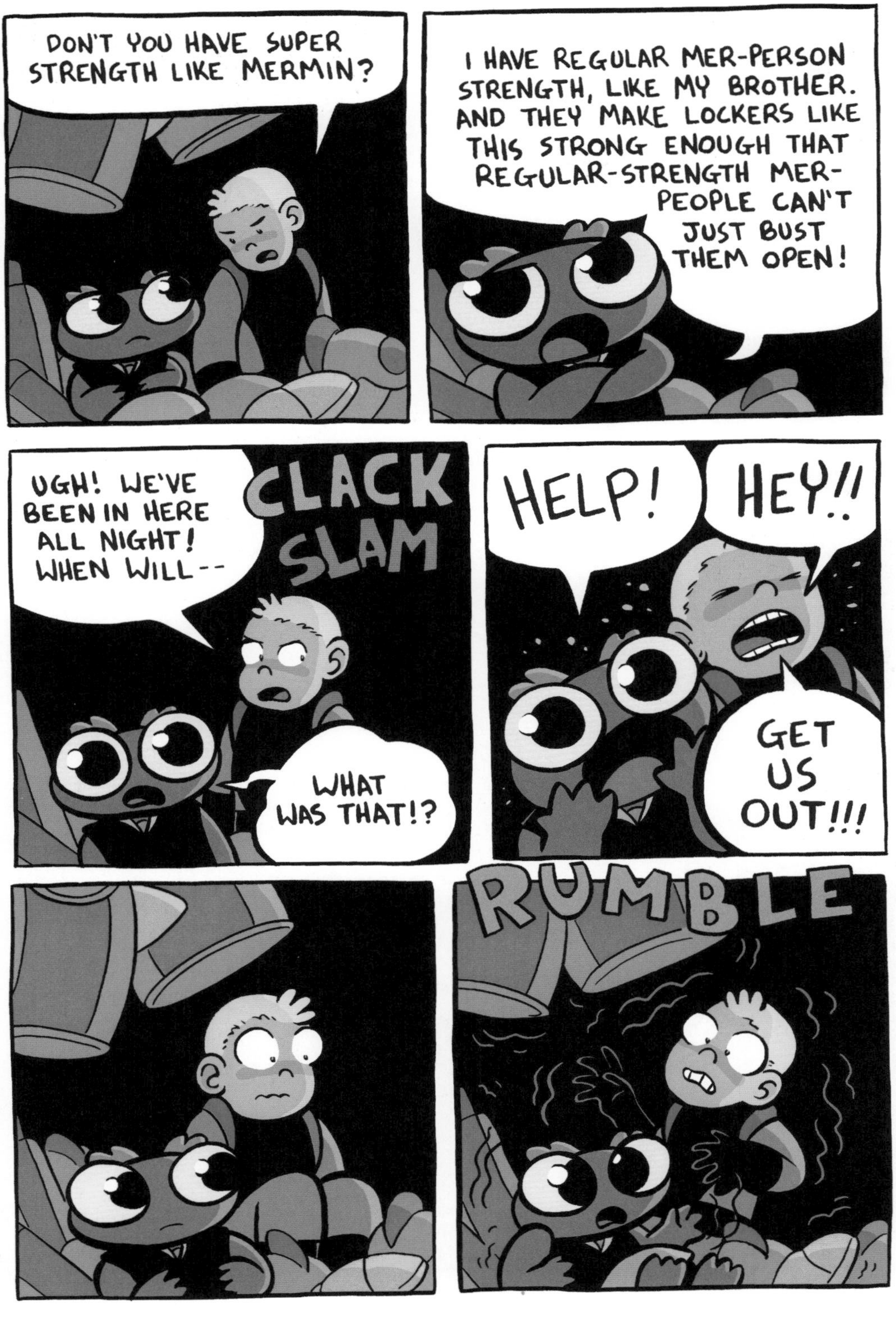
DON'T YOU HAVE SUPER STRENGTH LIKE MERMIN?
I HAVE REGULAR MER-PERSON STRENGTH, LIKE MY BROTHER. AND THEY MAKE LOCKERS LIKE THIS STRONG ENOUGH THAT REGULAR-STRENGTH MER-PEOPLE CAN'T JUST BUST THEM OPEN!
UGH! WE'VE BEEN IN HERE ALL NIGHT! WHEN WILL--
CLACK
SLAM
WHAT WAS THAT!?
HELP!
HEY!!
GET US OUT!!!
RUMBLE

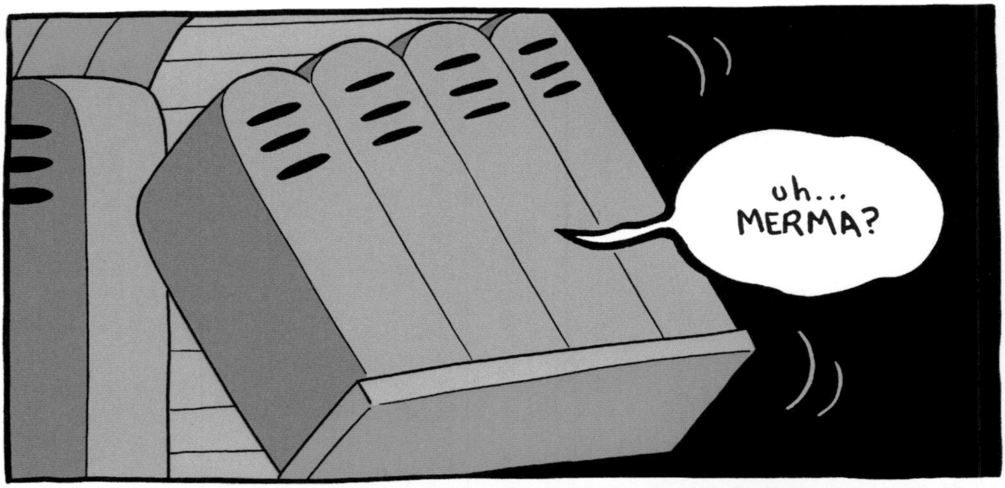
uh... MERMA?

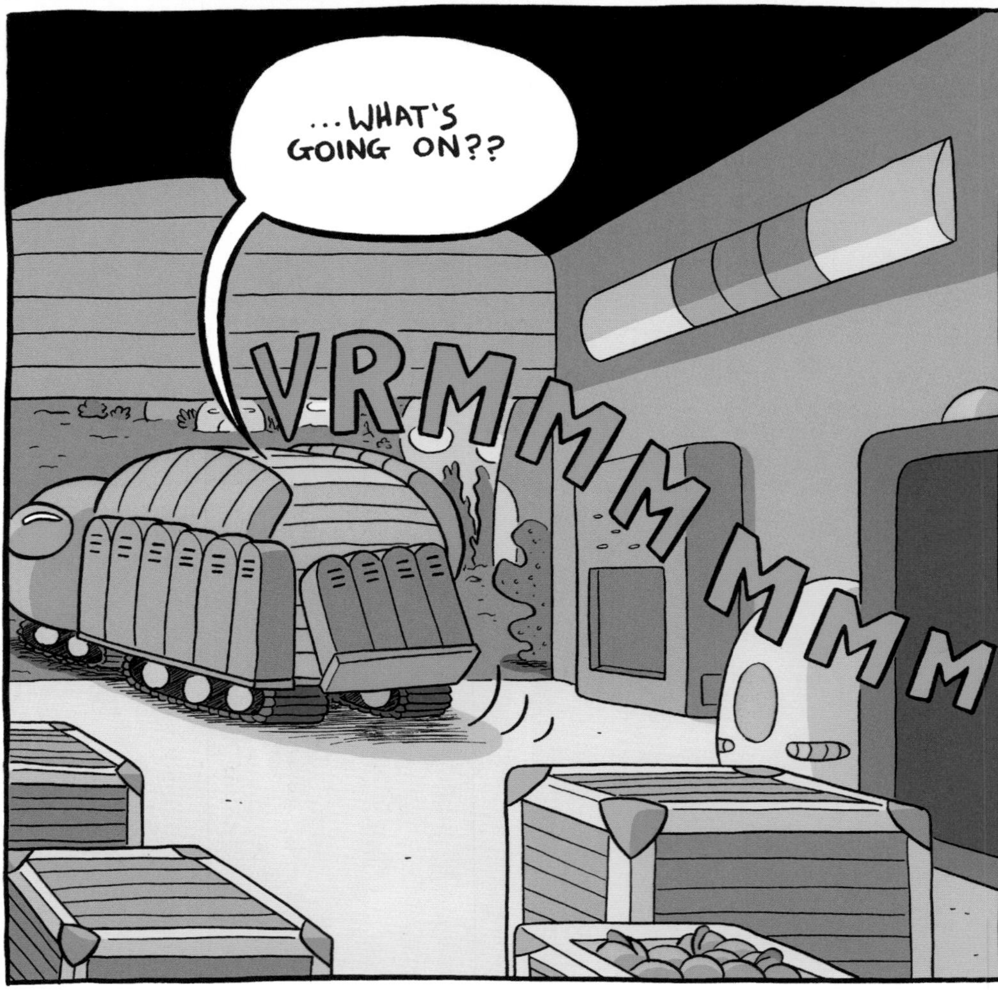
...WHAT'S GOING ON??
VRMMMMMMMM

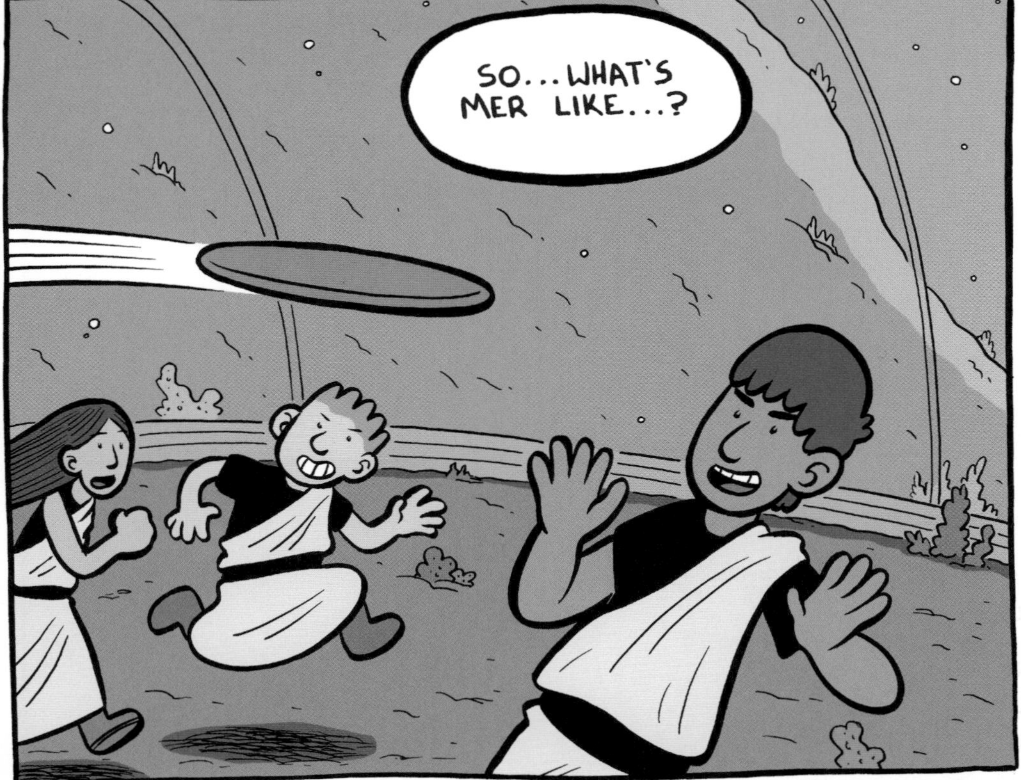
SO... WHAT'S MER LIKE...?

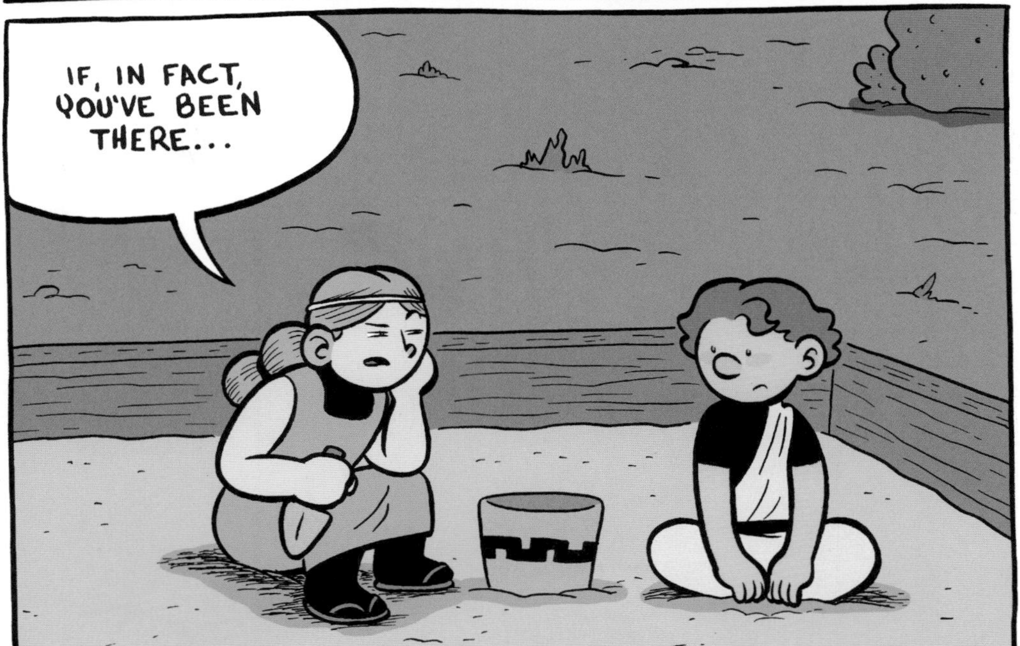
IF, IN FACT, YOU'VE BEEN THERE...

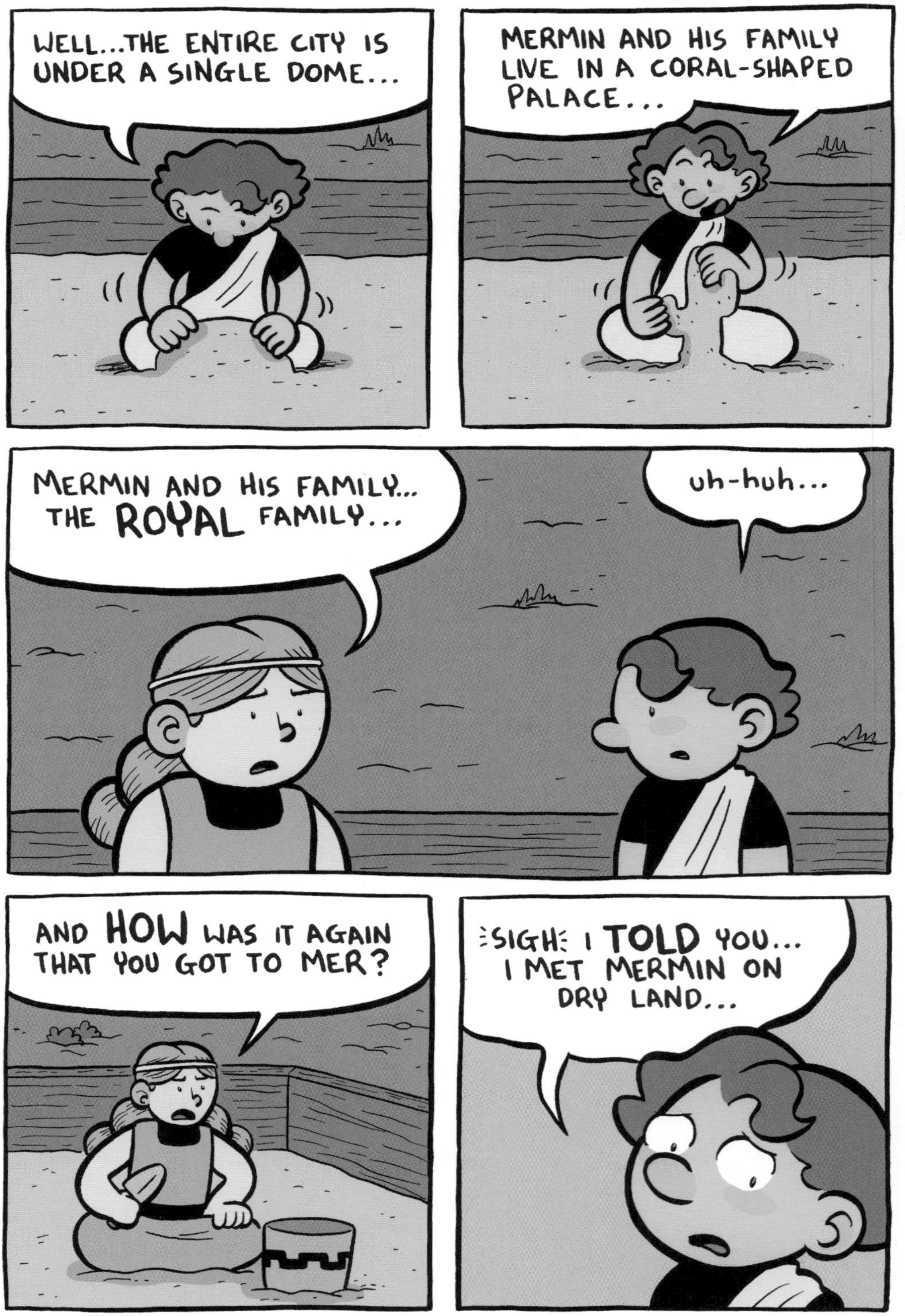
WELL...THE ENTIRE CITY IS UNDER A SINGLE DOME...
MERMIN AND HIS FAMILY LIVE IN A CORAL-SHAPED PALACE...
MERMIN AND HIS FAMILY... THE ROYAL FAMILY...
uh-huh...
AND HOW WAS IT AGAIN THAT YOU GOT TO MER?
SIGH I TOLD YOU... I MET MERMIN ON DRY LAND...

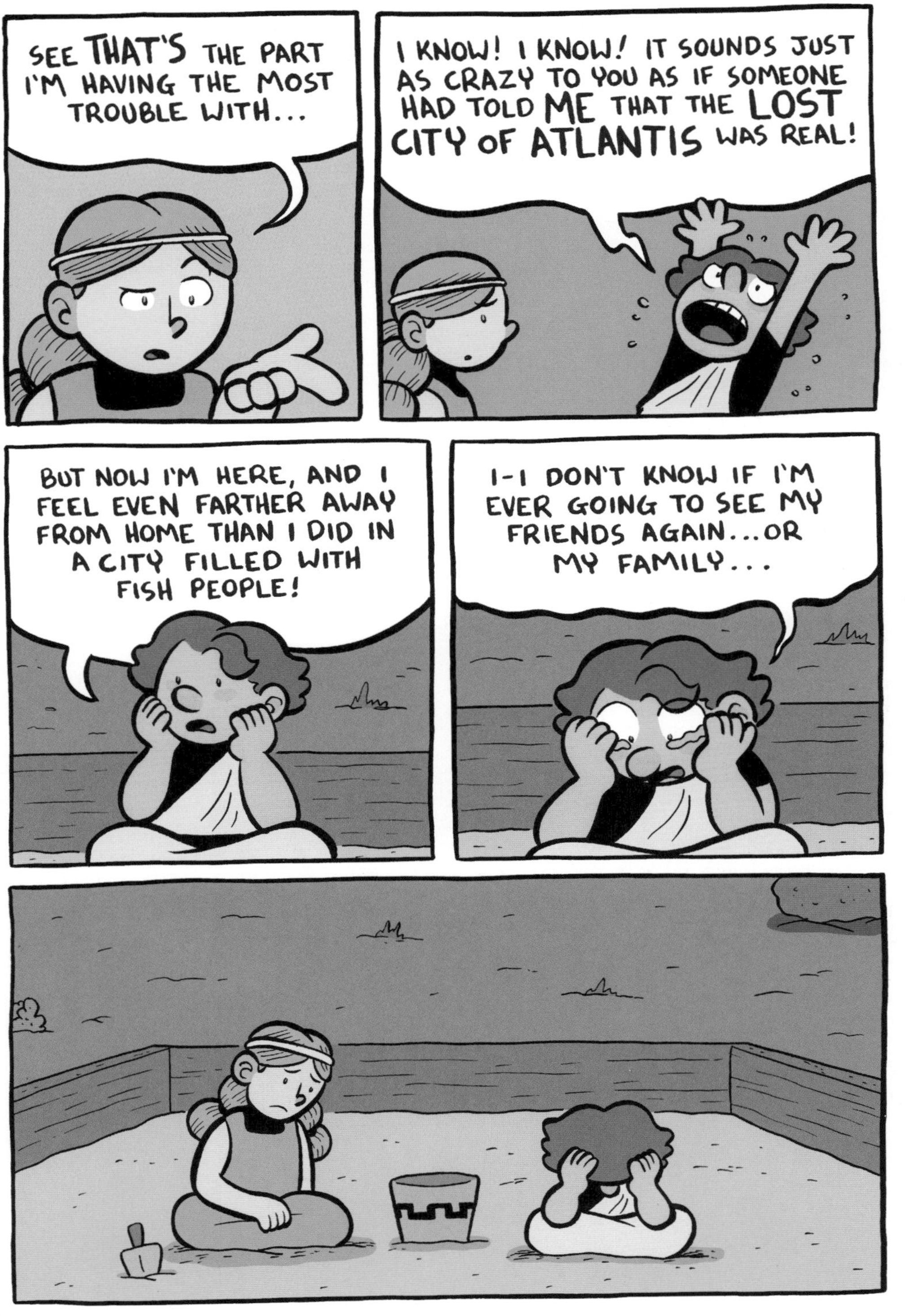
SEE THAT'S THE PART I'M HAVING THE MOST TROUBLE WITH...
I KNOW! I KNOW! IT SOUNDS JUST AS CRAZY TO YOU AS IF SOMEONE HAD TOLD ME THAT THE LOST CITY OF ATLANTIS WAS REAL!
BUT NOW I'M HERE, AND I FEEL EVEN FARTHER AWAY FROM HOME THAN I DID IN A CITY FILLED WITH FISH PEOPLE!
I-I DON'T KNOW IF I'M EVER GOING TO SEE MY FRIENDS AGAIN...OR MY FAMILY...

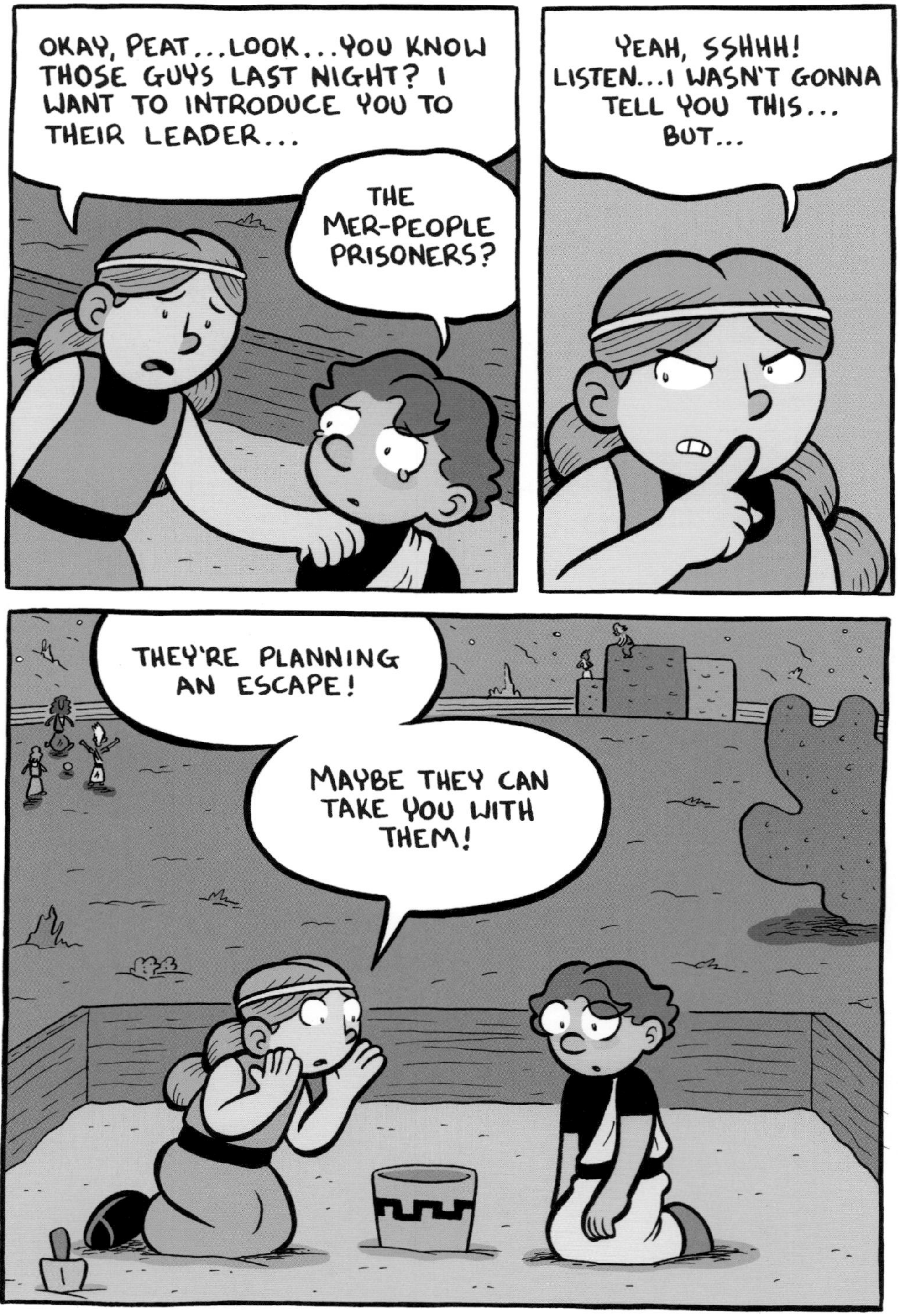
OKAY, PEAT...LOOK...YOU KNOW THOSE GUYS LAST NIGHT? I WANT TO INTRODUCE YOU TO THEIR LEADER...
THE MER-PEOPLE PRISONERS?
YEAH, SSHHH! LISTEN...I WASN'T GONNA TELL YOU THIS... BUT...
THEY'RE PLANNING AN ESCAPE!
MAYBE THEY CAN TAKE YOU WITH THEM!

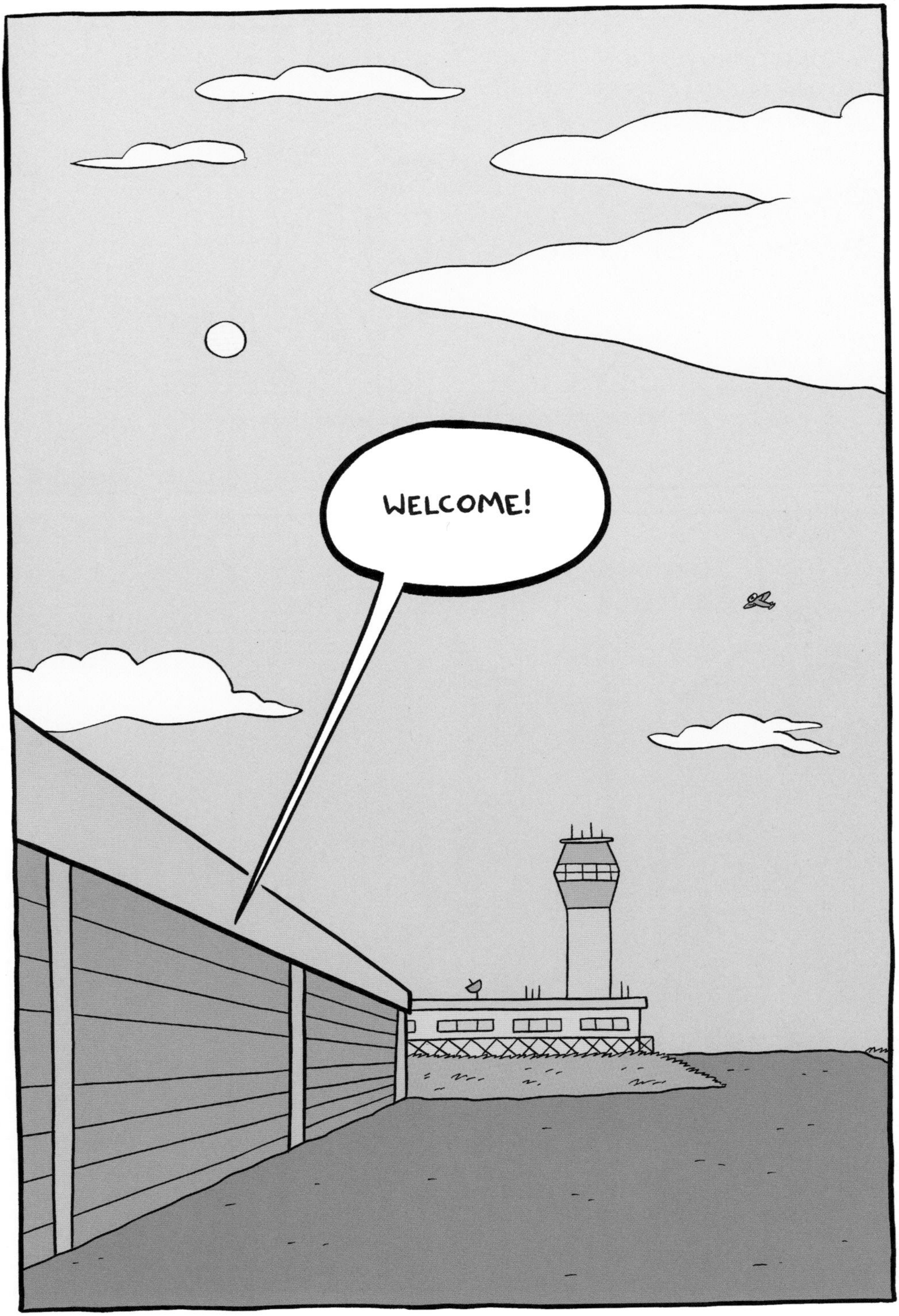
WELCOME!

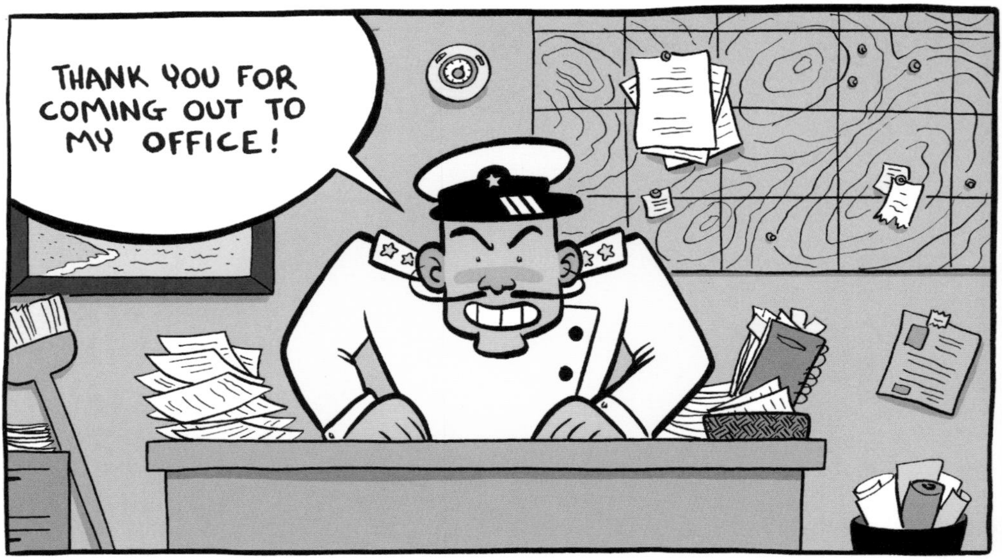
THANK YOU FOR COMING OUT TO MY OFFICE!

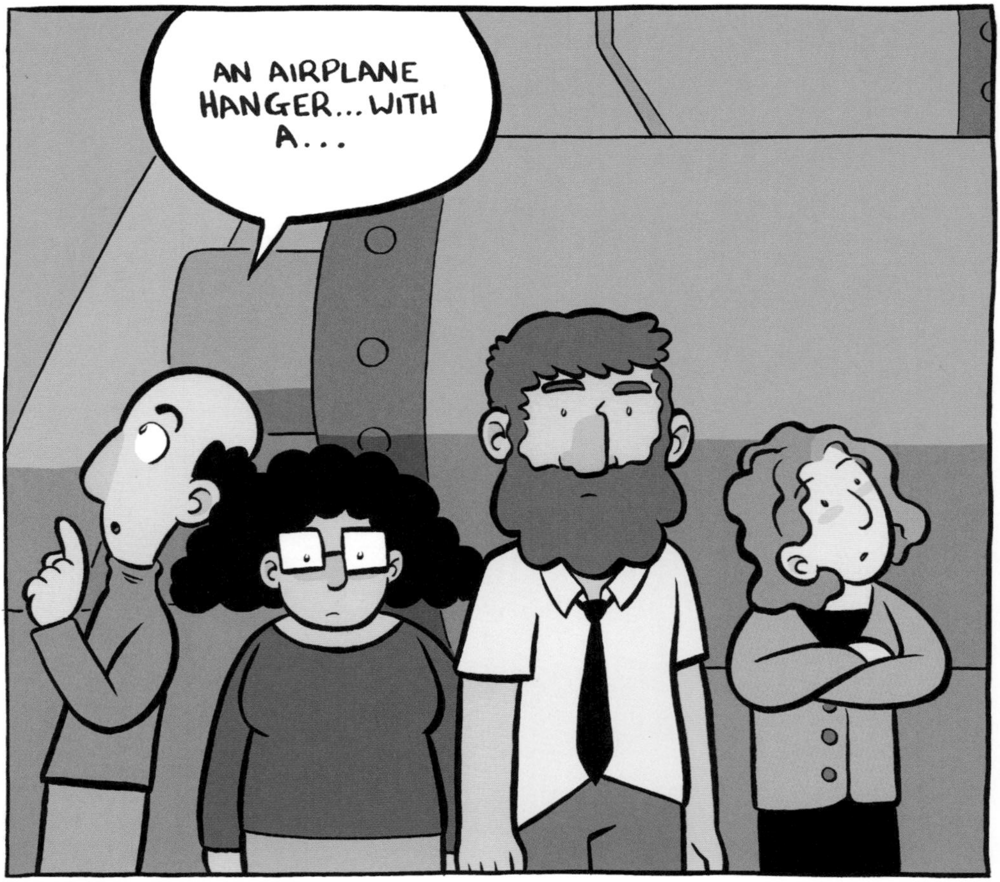
AN AIRPLANE HANGER... WITH A...

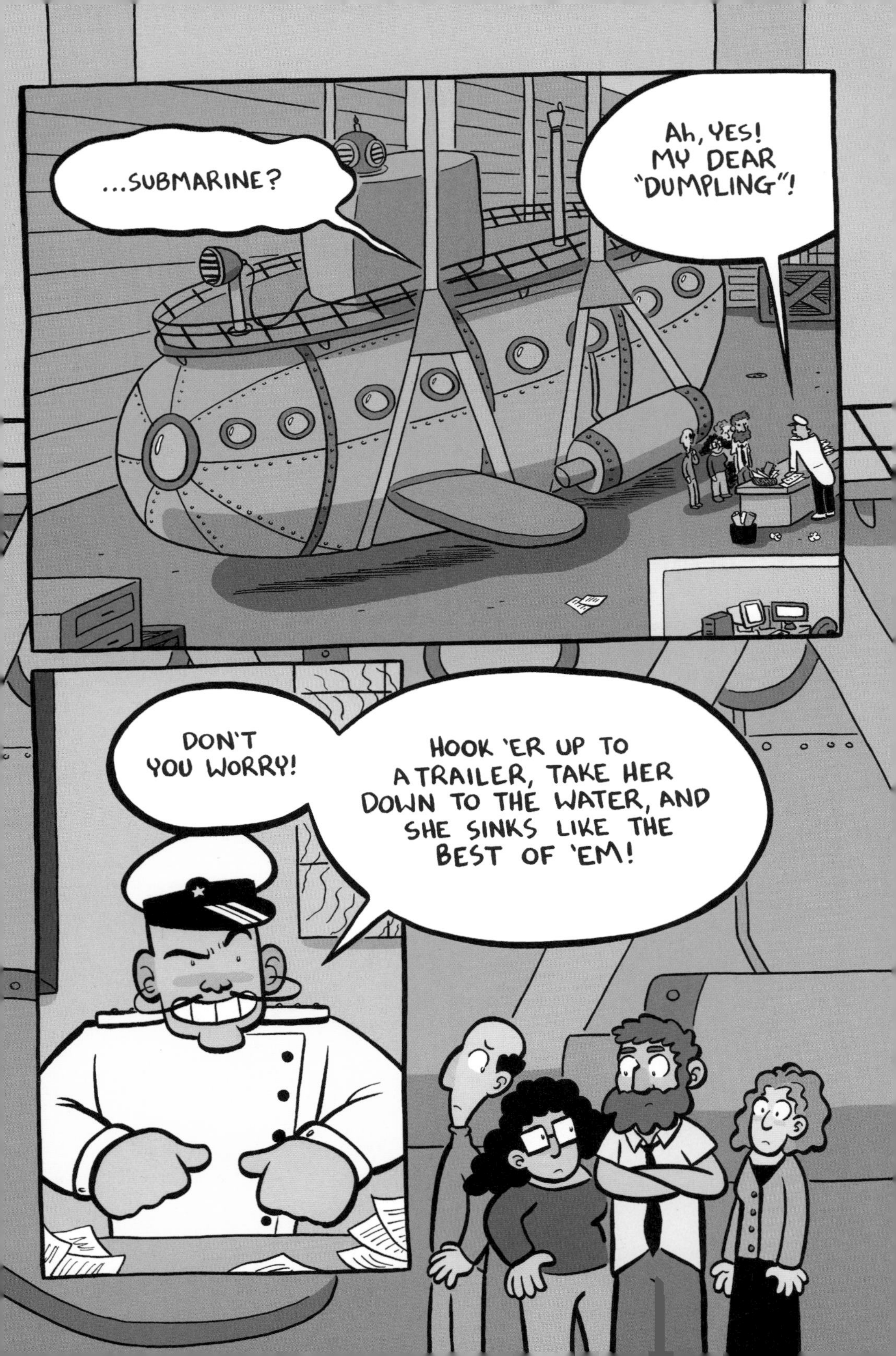
...SUBMARINE?
Ah, YES! MY DEAR "DUMPLING"!
DON'T YOU WORRY!
HOOK 'ER UP TO A TRAILER, TAKE HER DOWN TO THE WATER, AND SHE SINKS LIKE THE BEST OF 'EM!

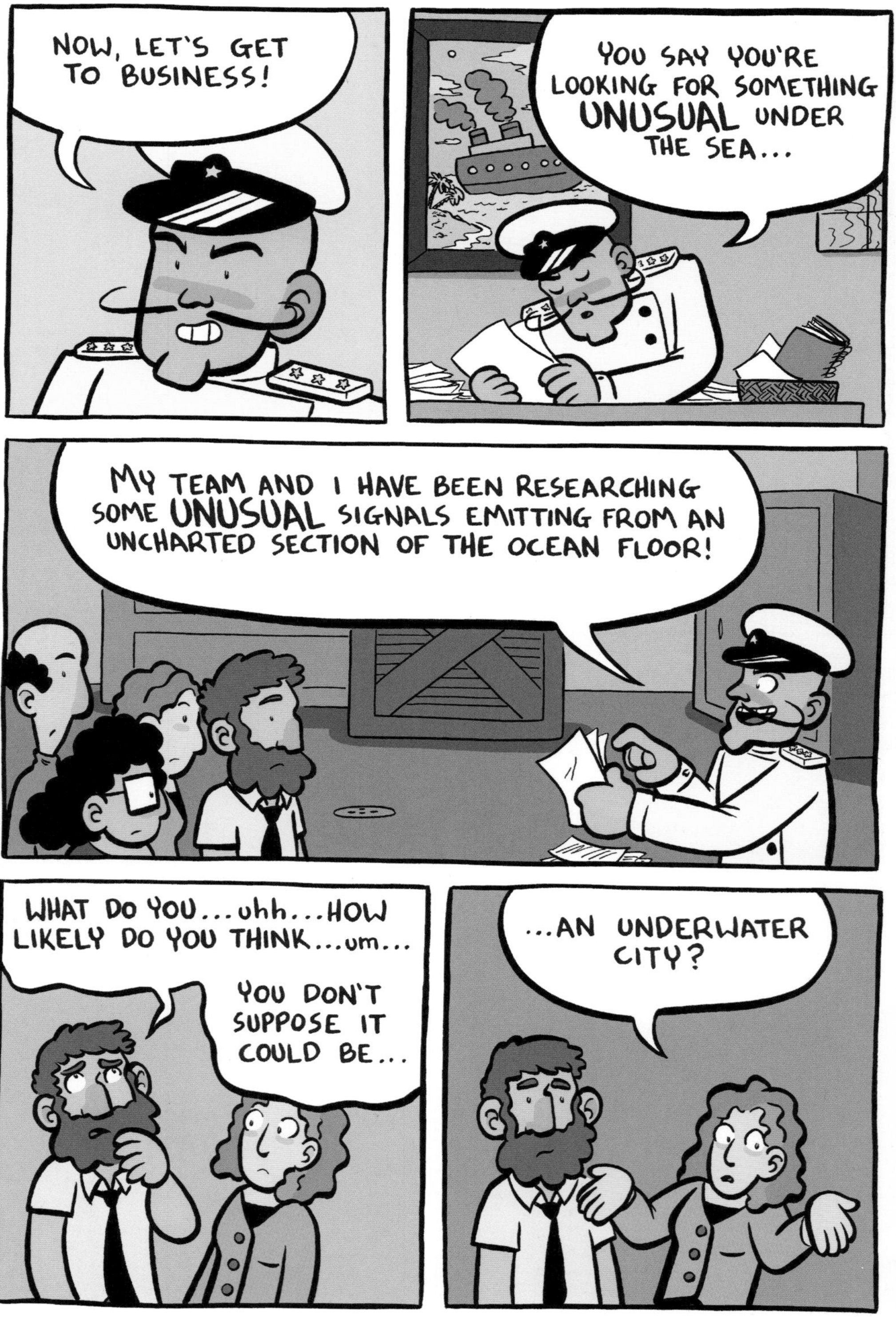
NOW, LET'S GET TO BUSINESS!
YOU SAY YOU'RE LOOKING FOR SOMETHING UNUSUAL UNDER THE SEA...
MY TEAM AND I HAVE BEEN RESEARCHING SOME UNUSUAL SIGNALS EMITTING FROM AN UNCHARTED SECTION OF THE OCEAN FLOOR!
WHAT DO YOU...uhh...HOW LIKELY DO YOU THINK...um...
YOU DON'T SUPPOSE IT COULD BE...
...AN UNDERWATER CITY?

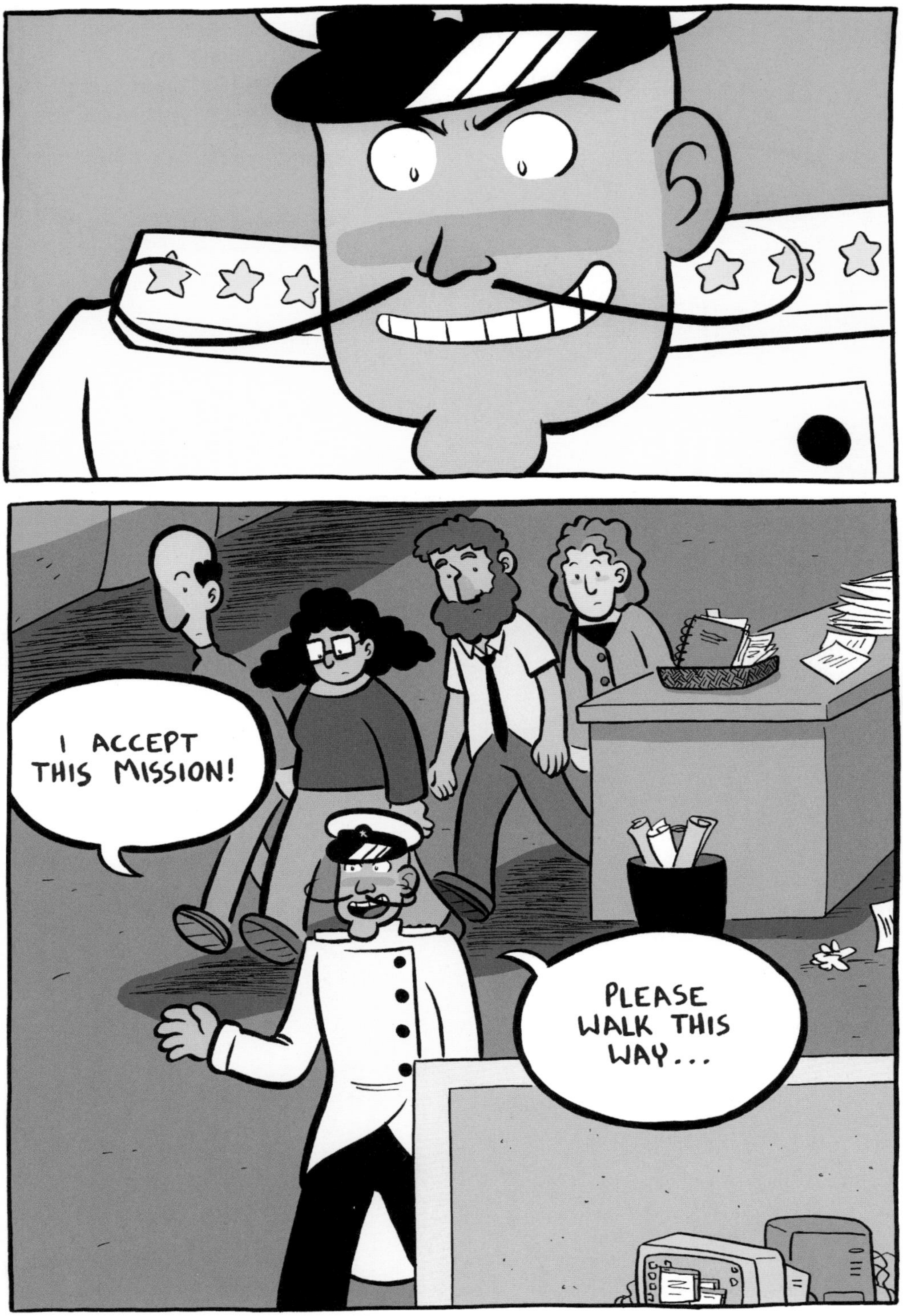
I ACCEPT THIS MISSION!
PLEASE WALK THIS WAY...

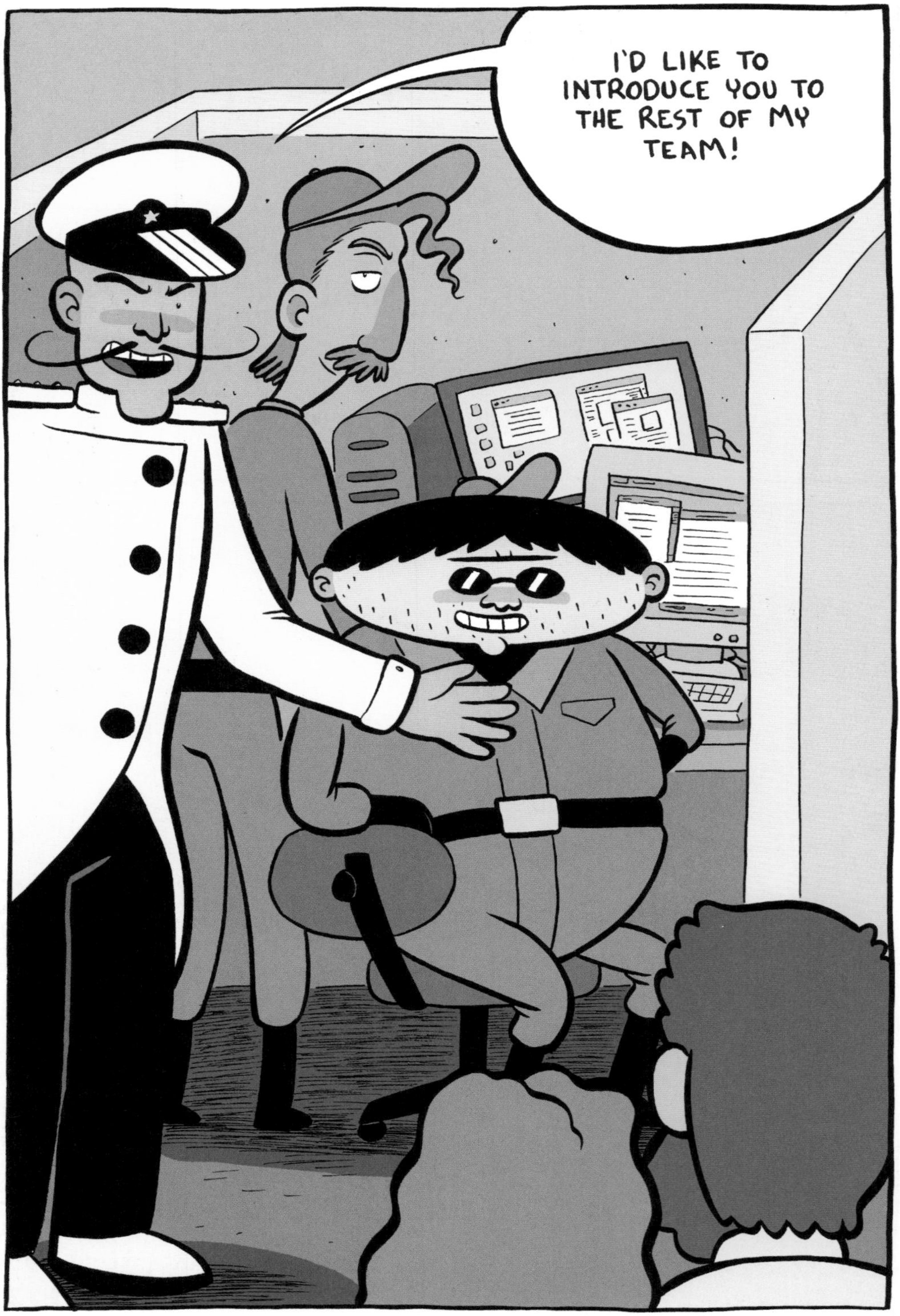
I'D LIKE TO INTRODUCE YOU TO THE REST OF MY TEAM!

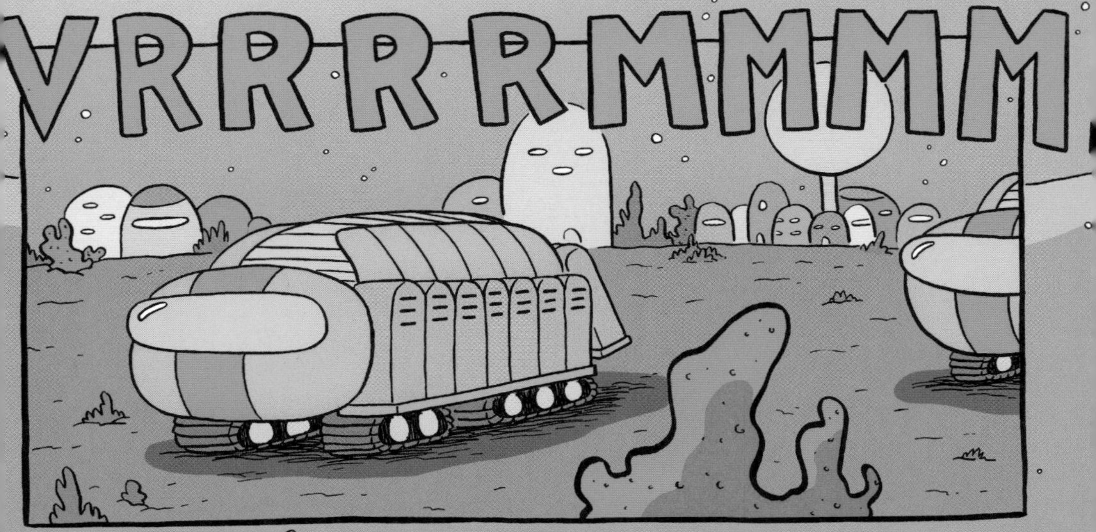
VRRRRMMMMM

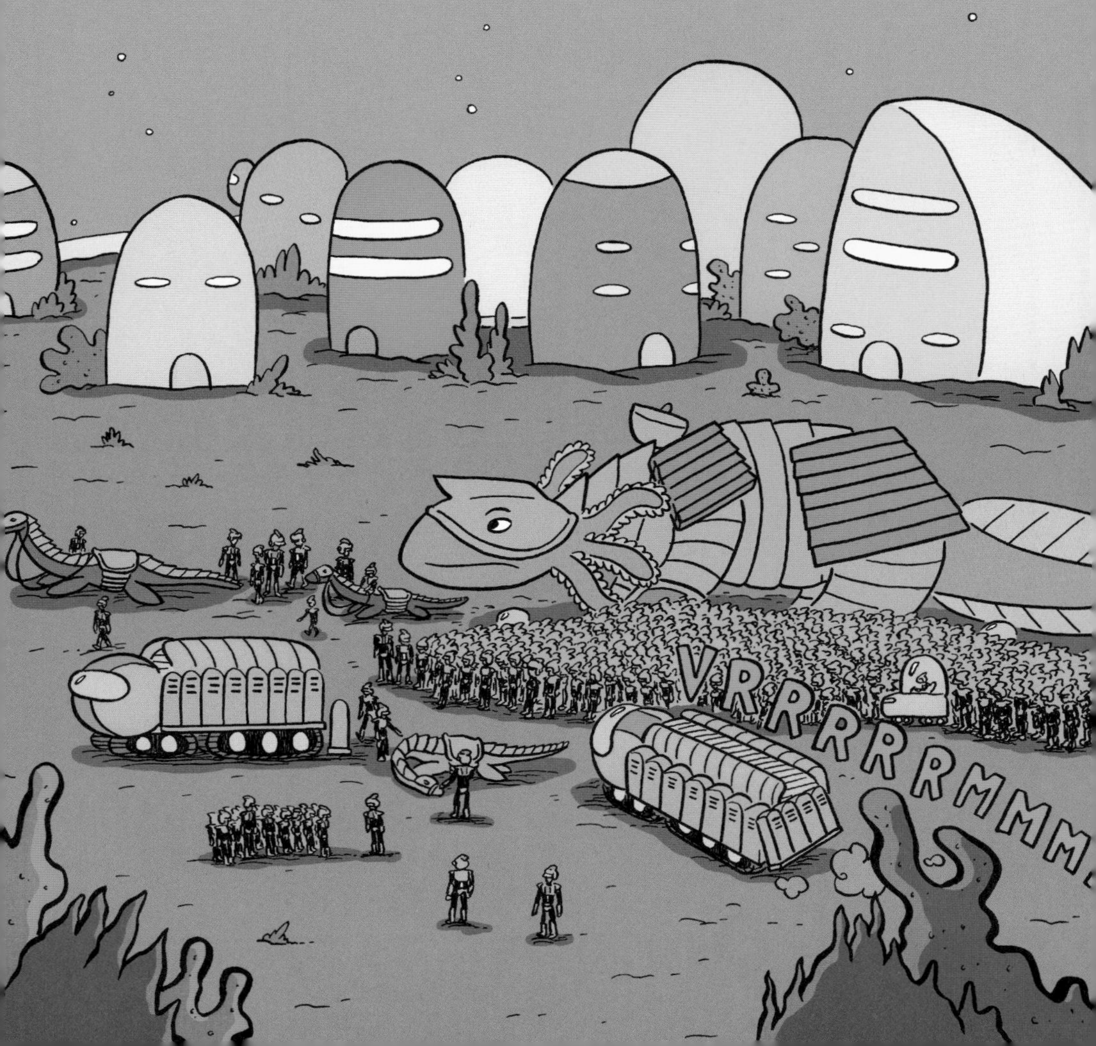
VRRRRRMMMM

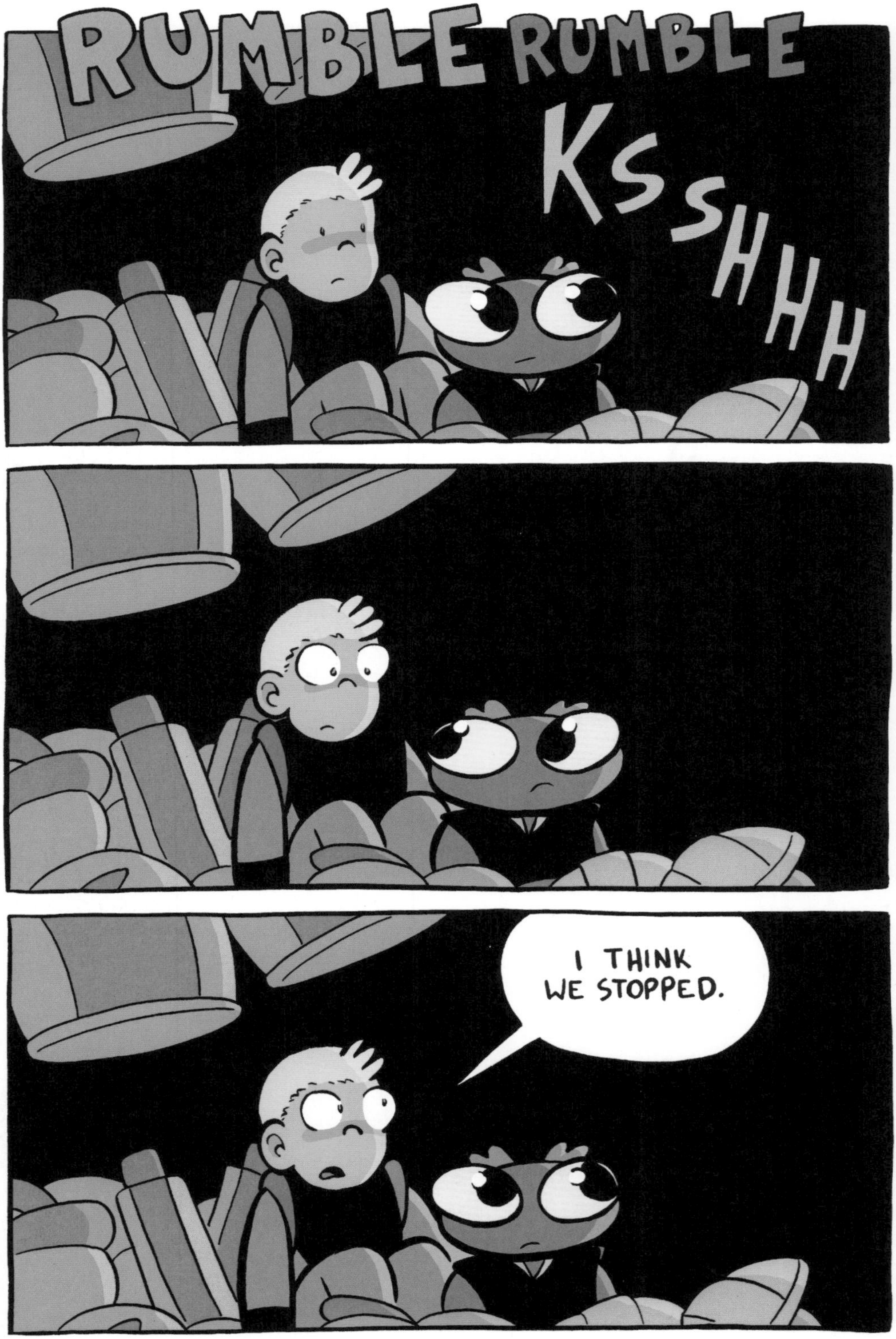
RUMBLE RUMBLE
KSSHHHH
I THINK WE STOPPED.

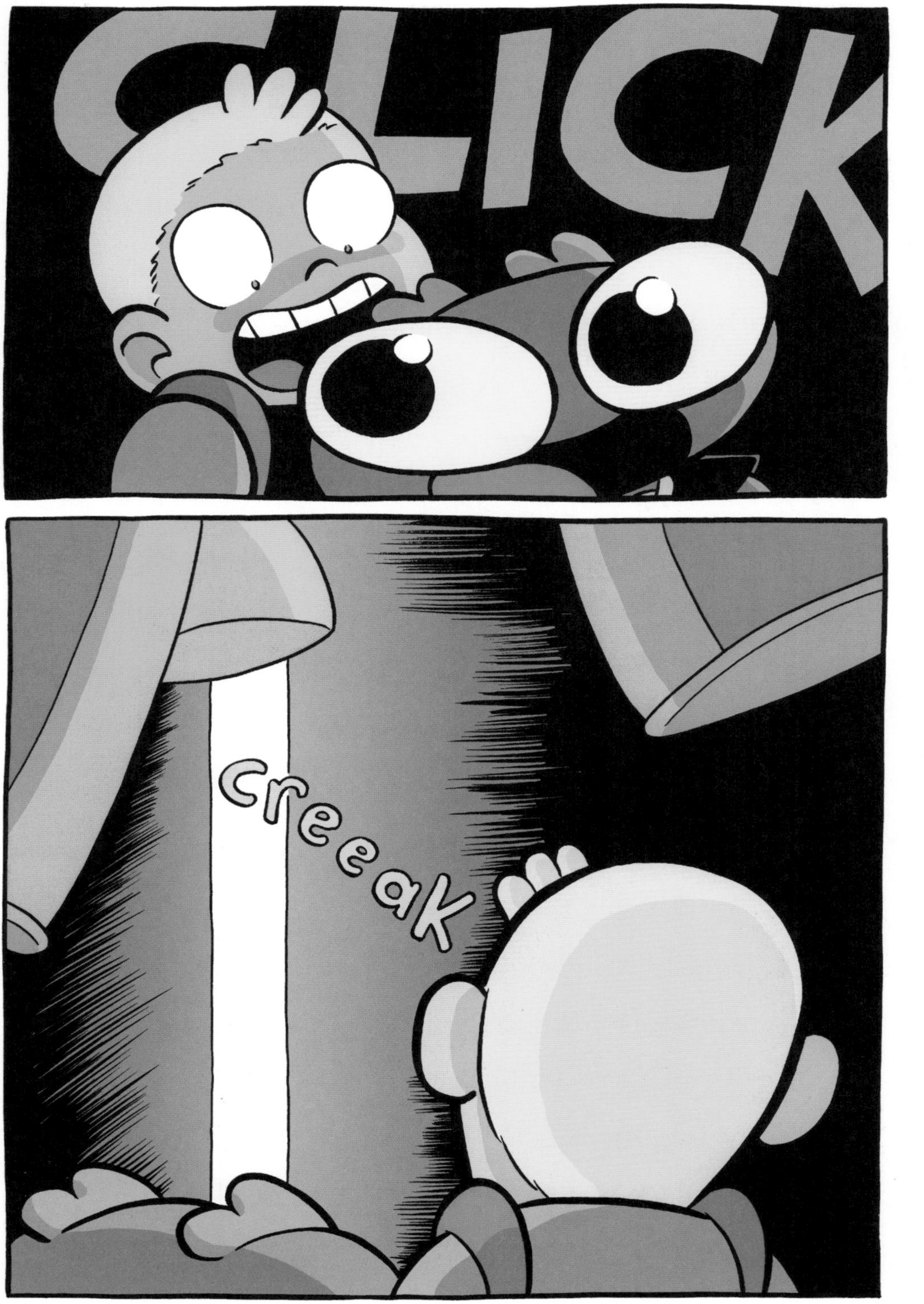
CLICK
creeak

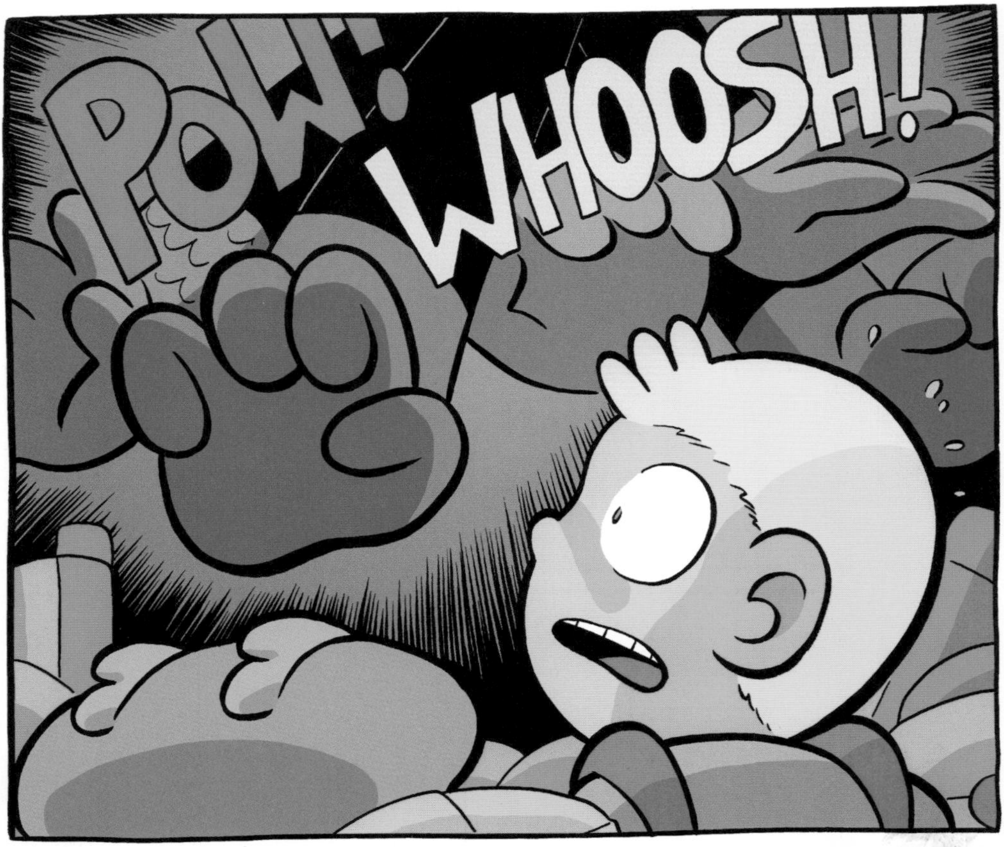
POW!
WHOOSH!

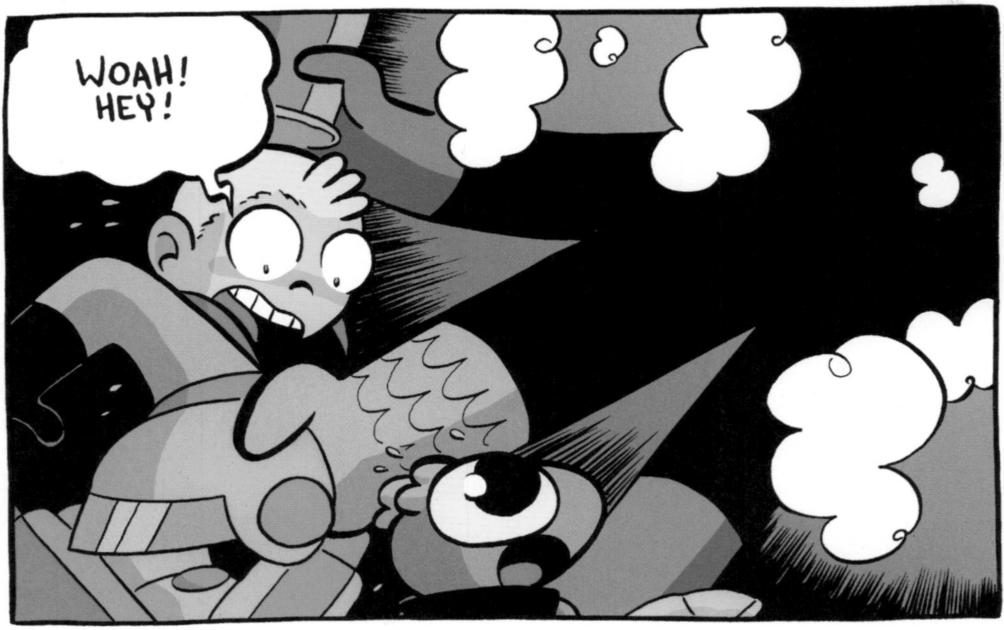
WOAH! HEY!

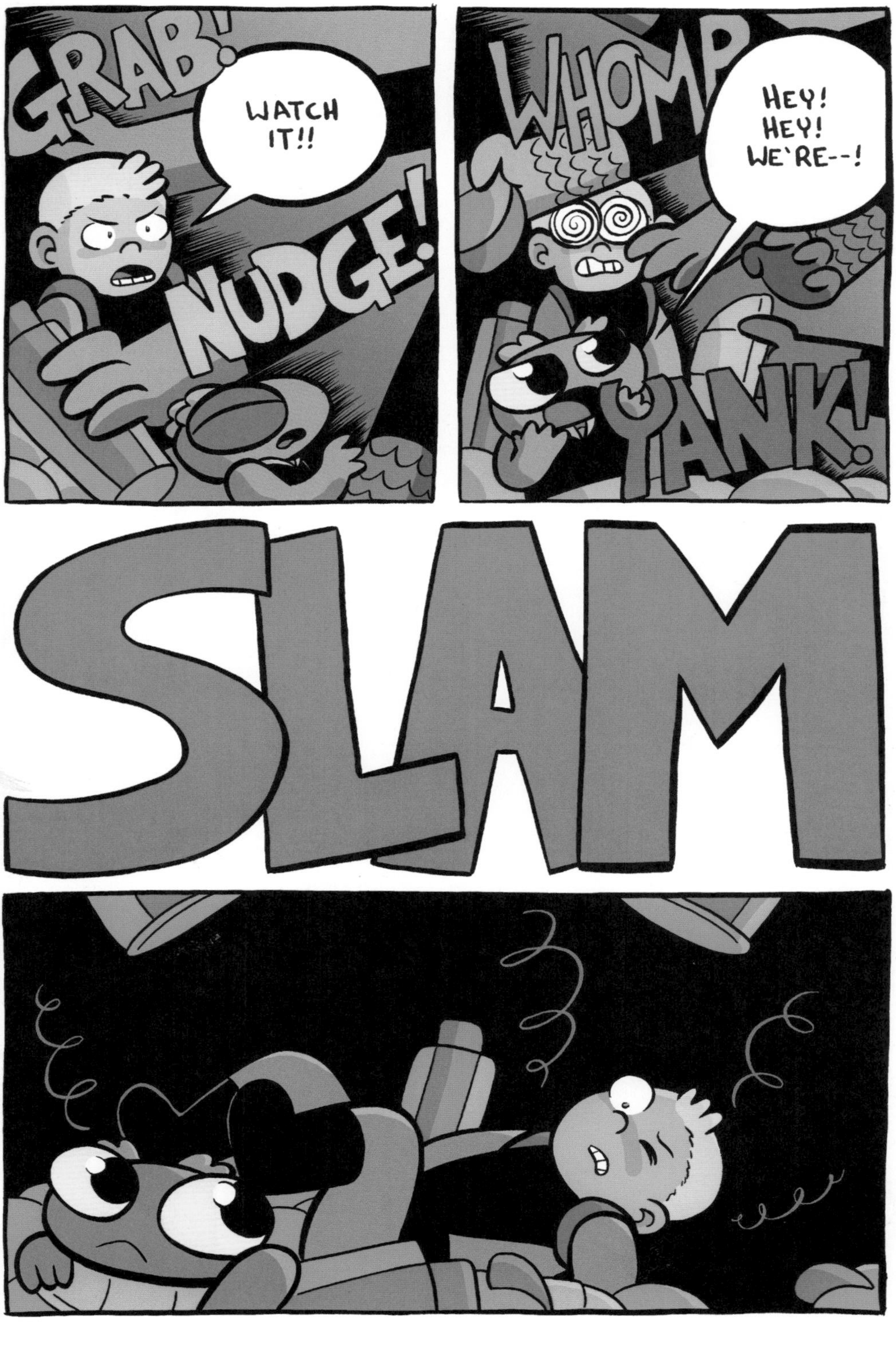
GRAB!
WATCH IT!!
NUDGE!
WHOMP
HEY! HEY! WE'RE--!
YANK!
SLAM

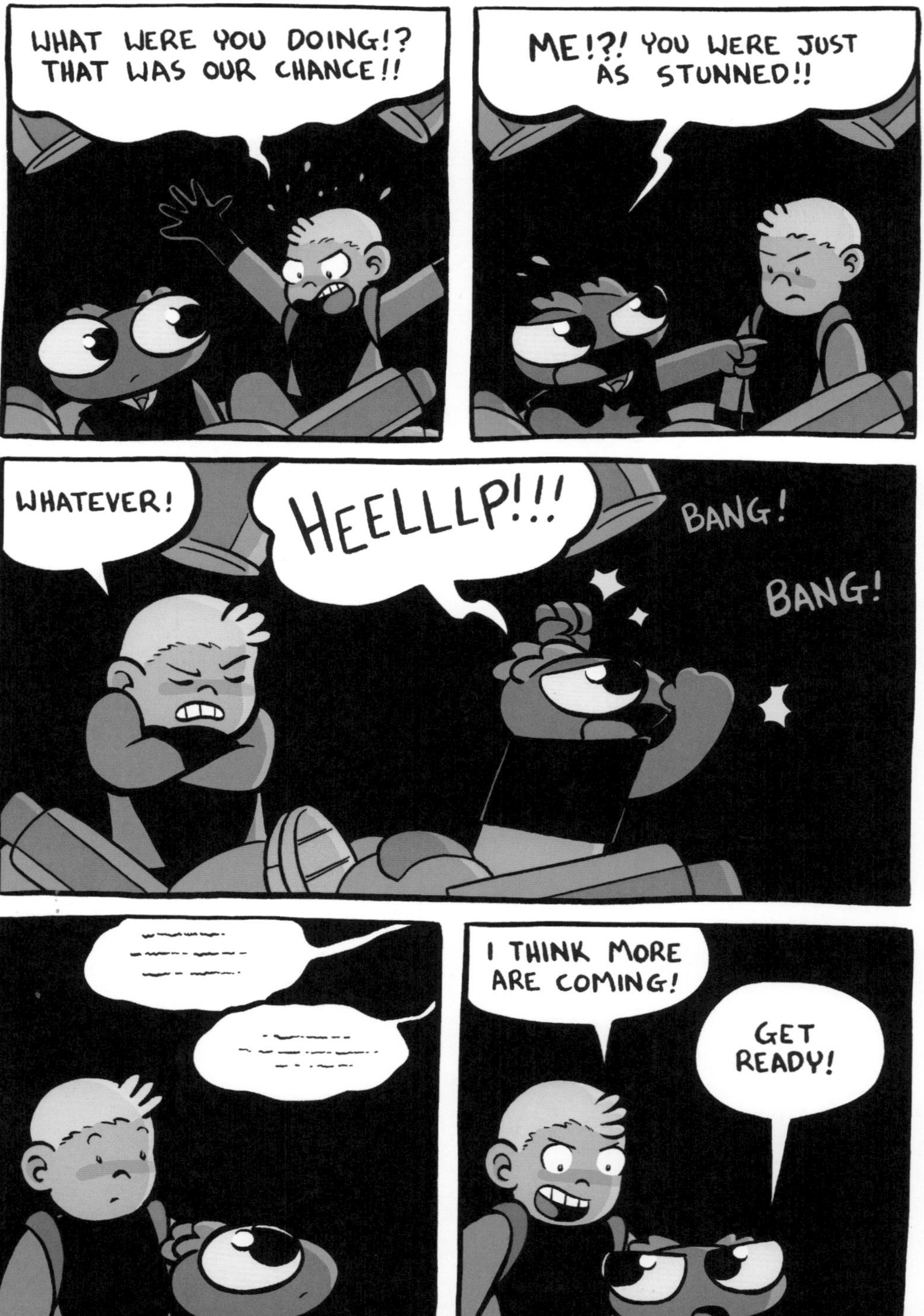
WHAT WERE YOU DOING!? THAT WAS OUR CHANCE!!
ME!?! YOU WERE JUST AS STUNNED!!
WHATEVER!
HEELLLP!!!
BANG!
BANG!
I THINK MORE ARE COMING!
GET READY!

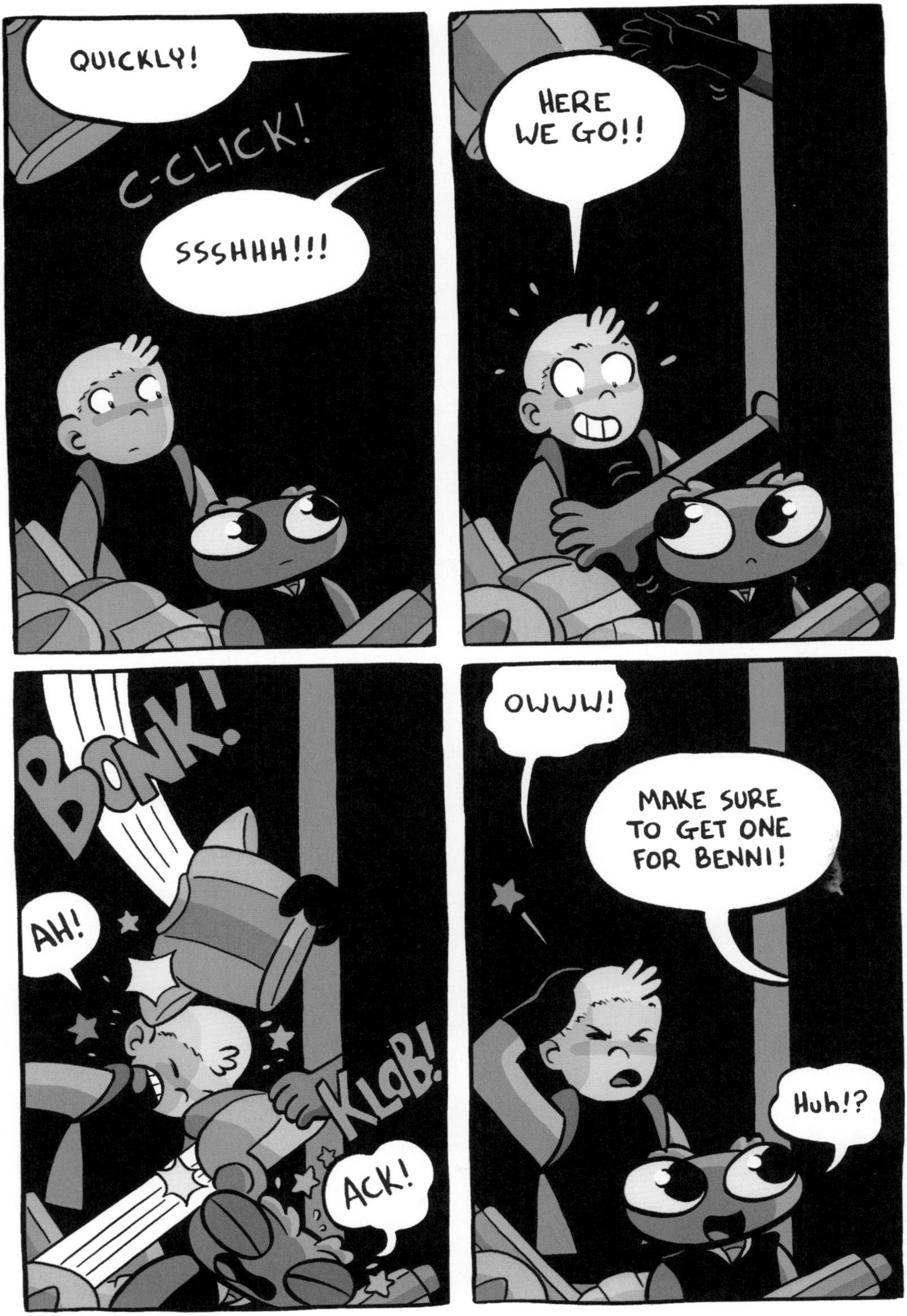
QUICKLY!
C-CLICK!
SSSHHH!!!
HERE WE GO!!
BONK!
AH!
KLOB!
ACK!
OWWW!
MAKE SURE TO GET ONE FOR BENNI!
Huh!?

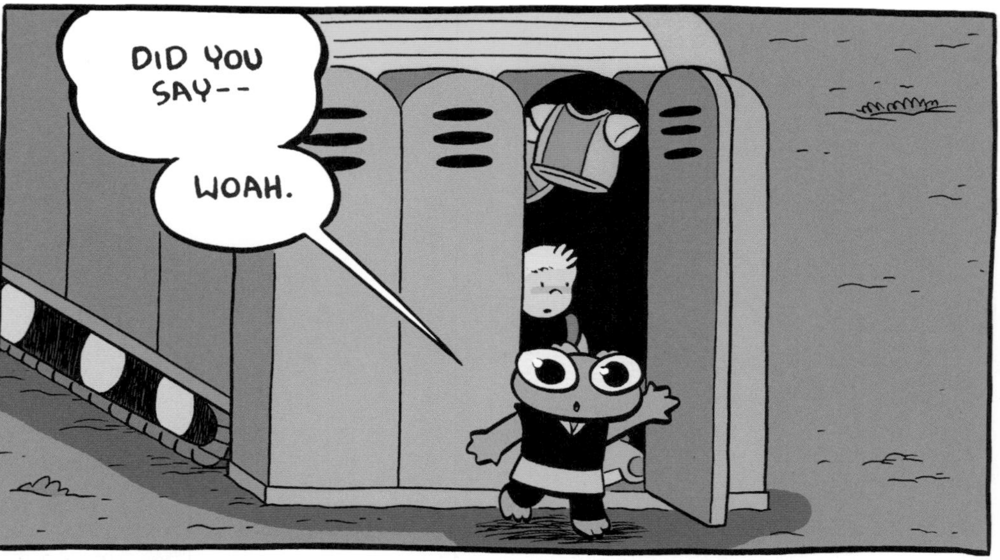
DID YOU SAY--
WOAH.

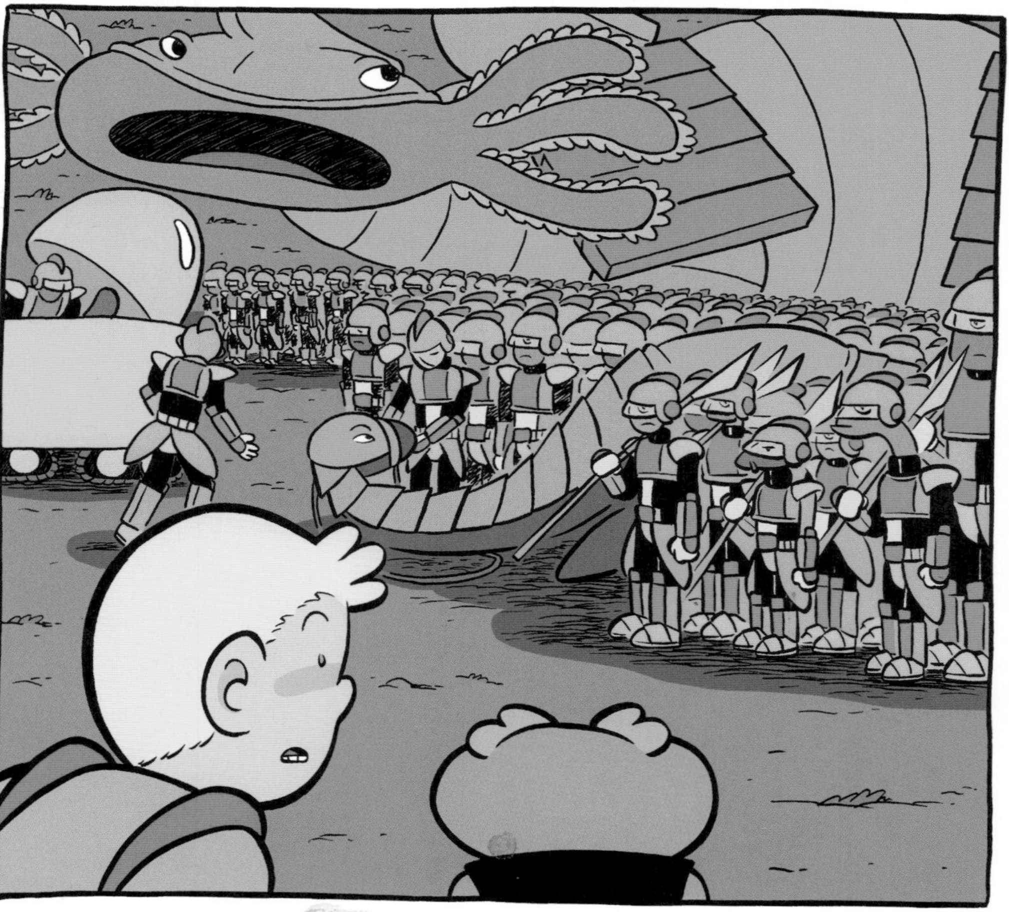

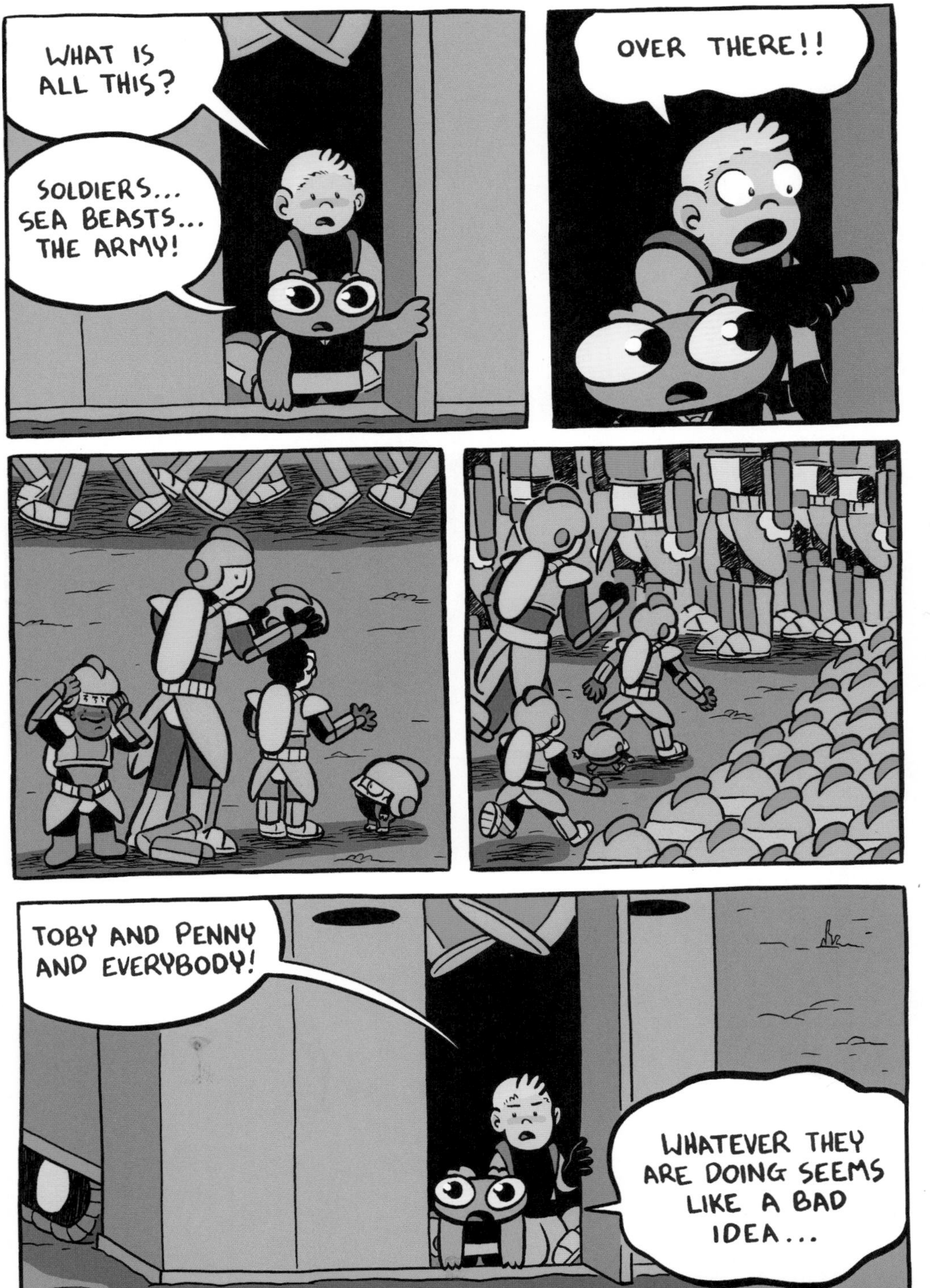
WHAT IS ALL THIS?
SOLDIERS... SEA BEASTS... THE ARMY!
OVER THERE!!
TOBY AND PENNY AND EVERYBODY!
WHATEVER THEY ARE DOING SEEMS LIKE A BAD IDEA...

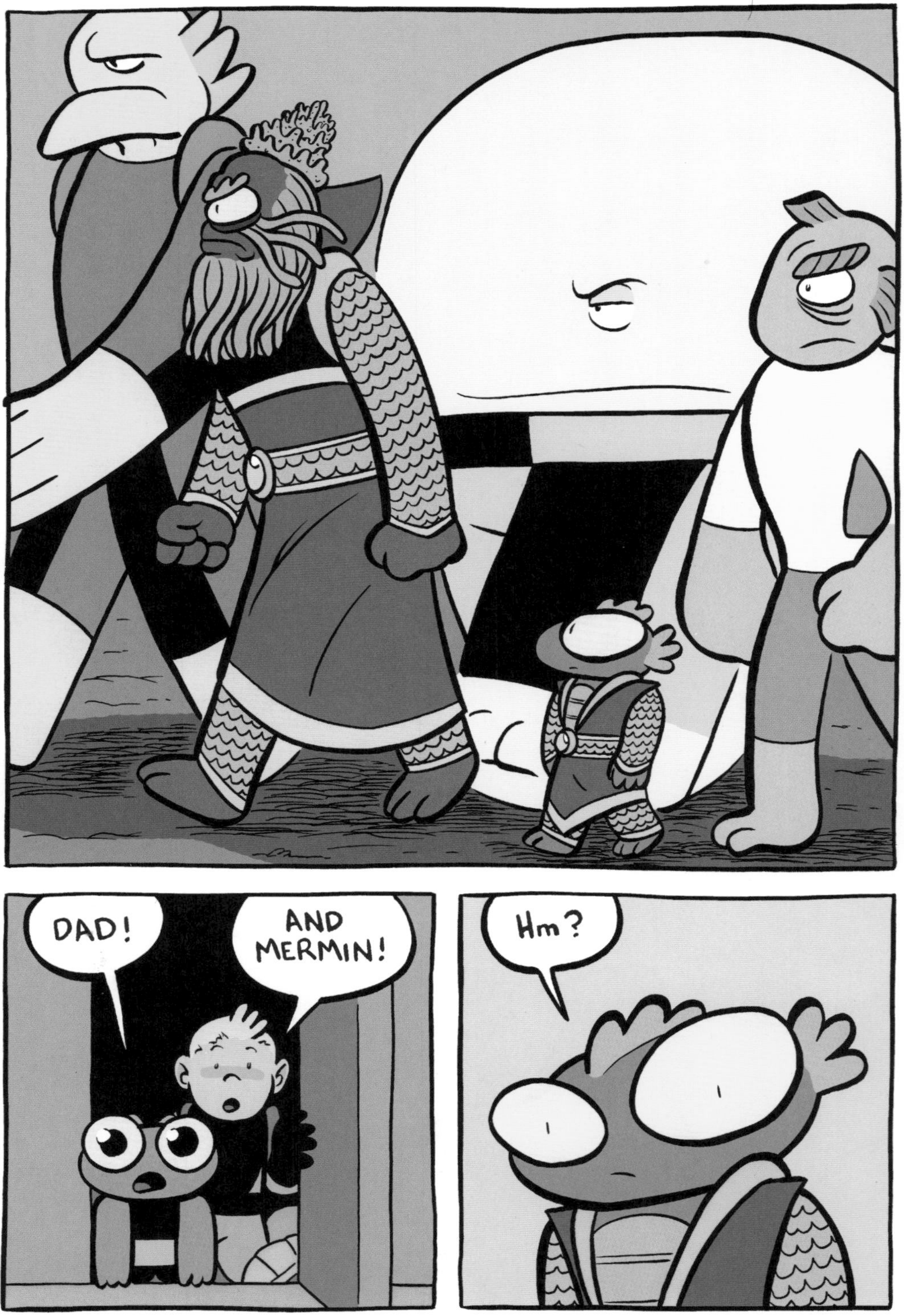
DAD!
AND MERMIN!
Hm?

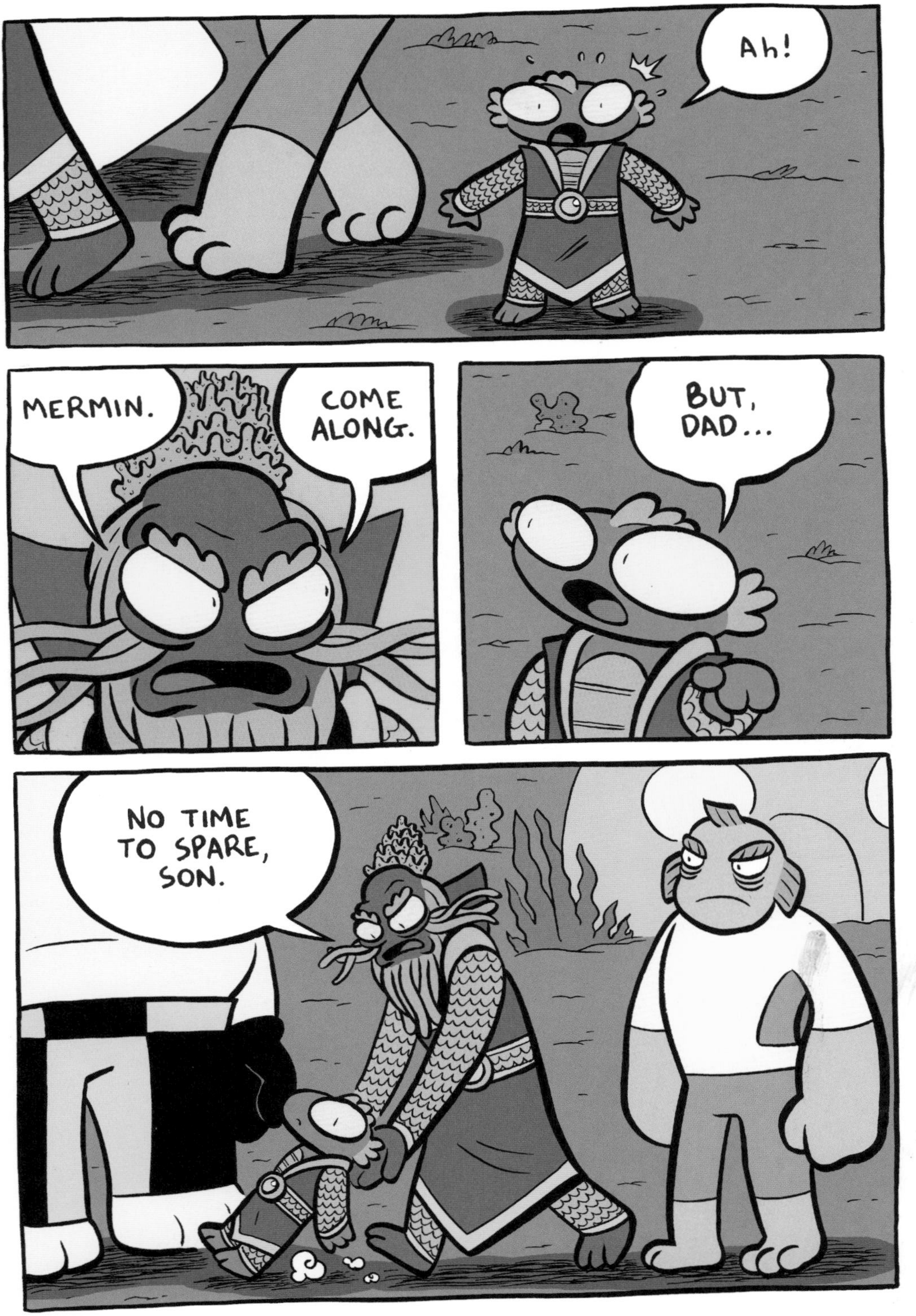
Ah!
MERMIN.
COME ALONG.
BUT, DAD...
NO TIME TO SPARE, SON.

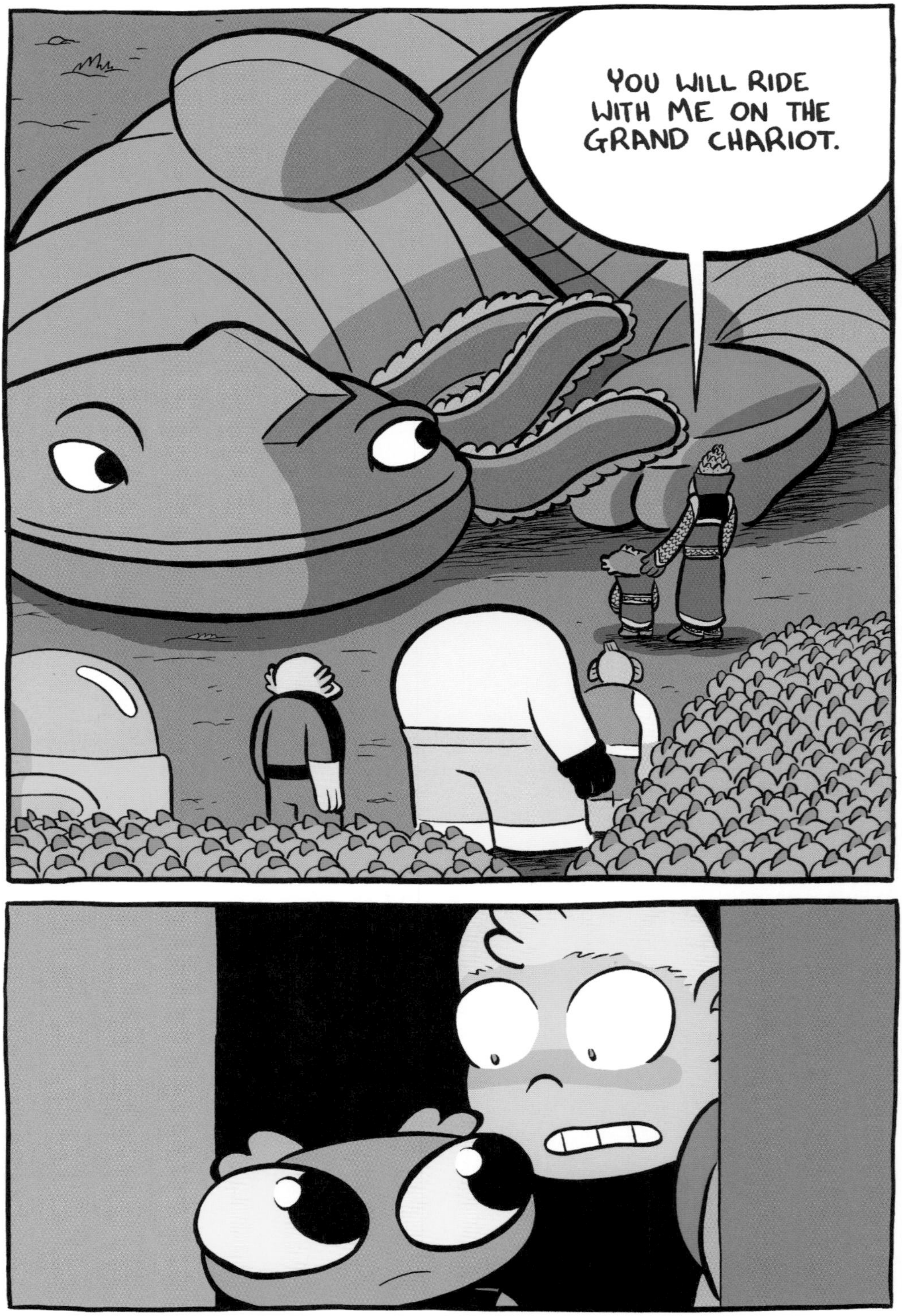
YOU WILL RIDE WITH ME ON THE GRAND CHARIOT.

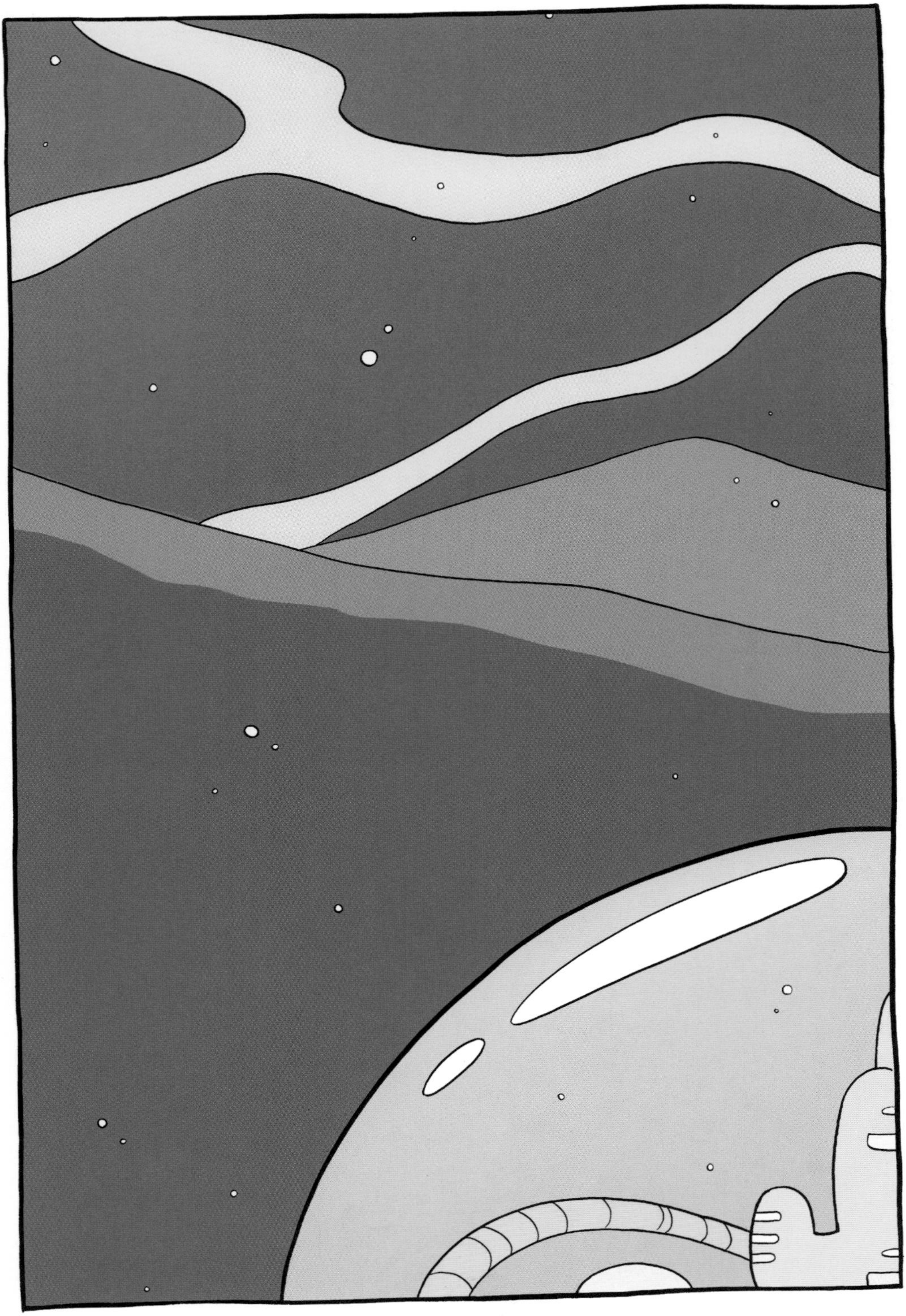

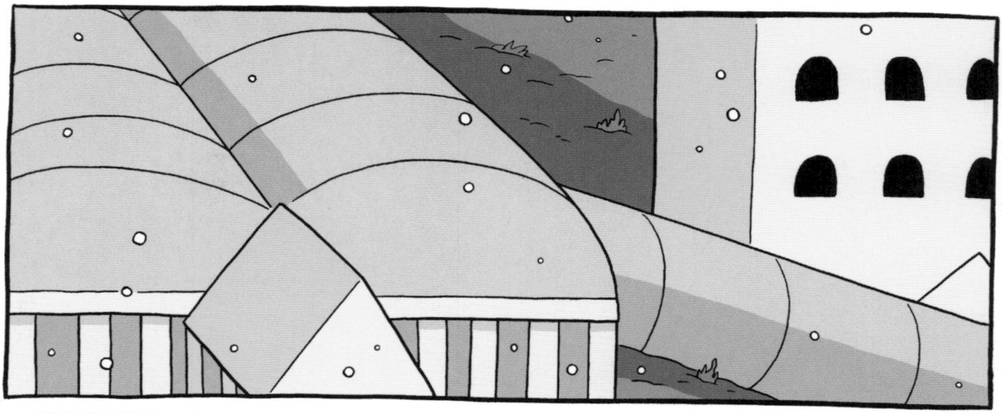
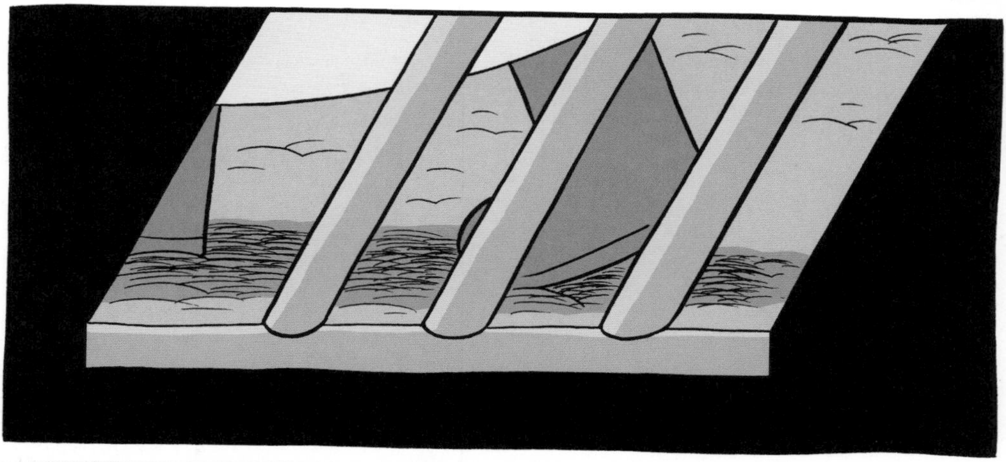
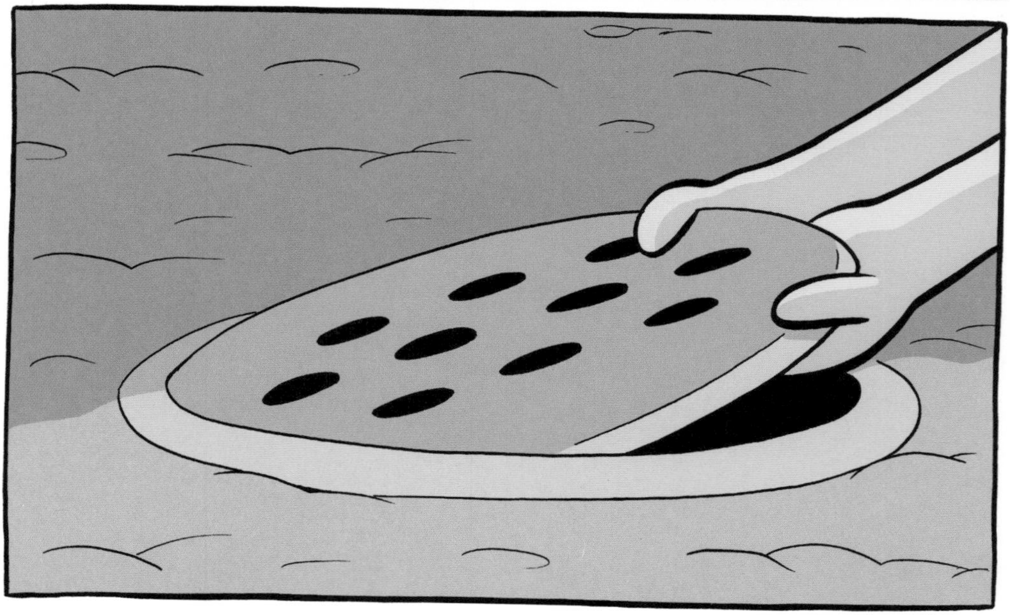

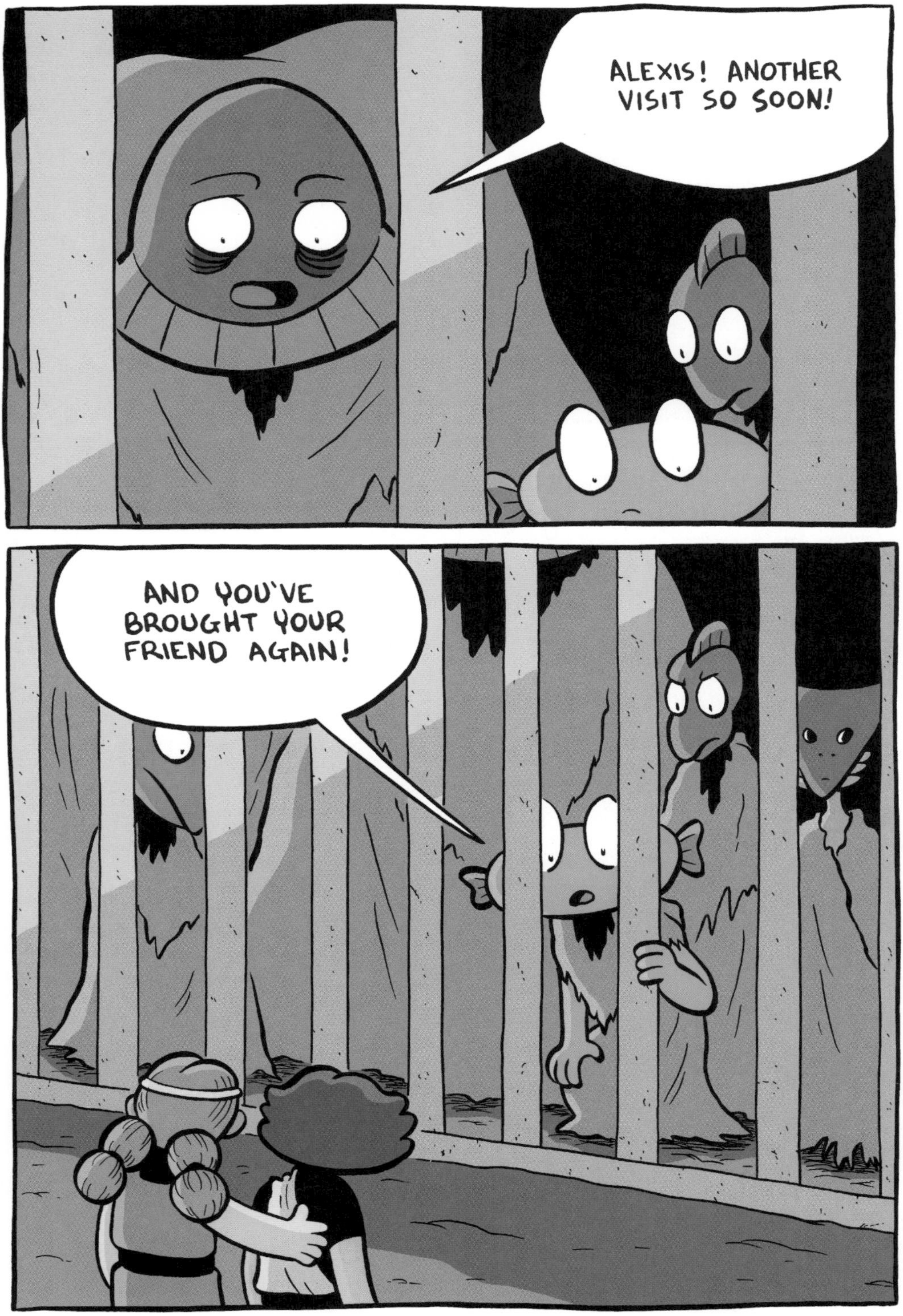
ALEXIS! ANOTHER VISIT SO SOON!
AND YOU'VE BROUGHT YOUR FRIEND AGAIN!

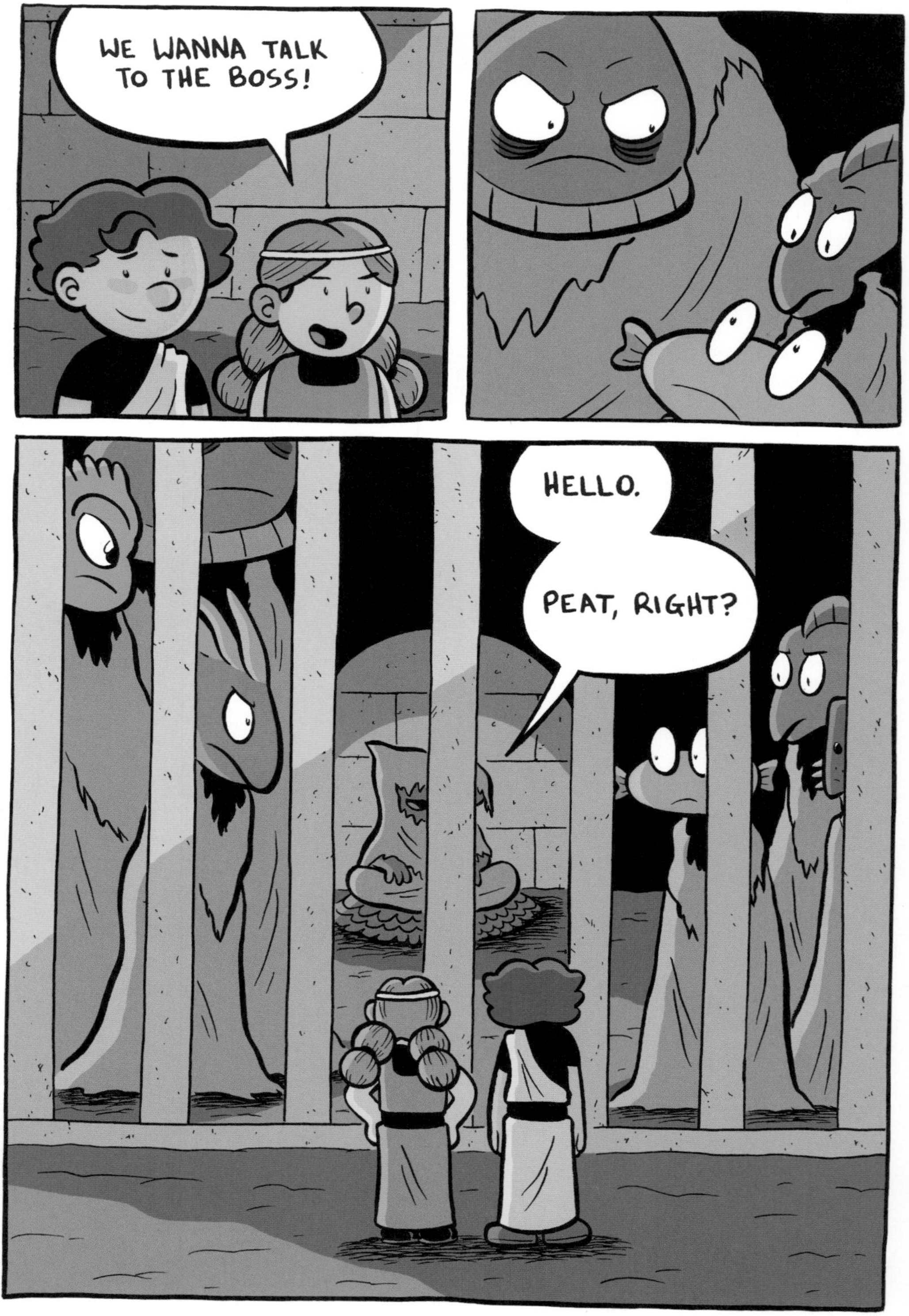
WE WANNA TALK TO THE BOSS!
HELLO.
PEAT, RIGHT?

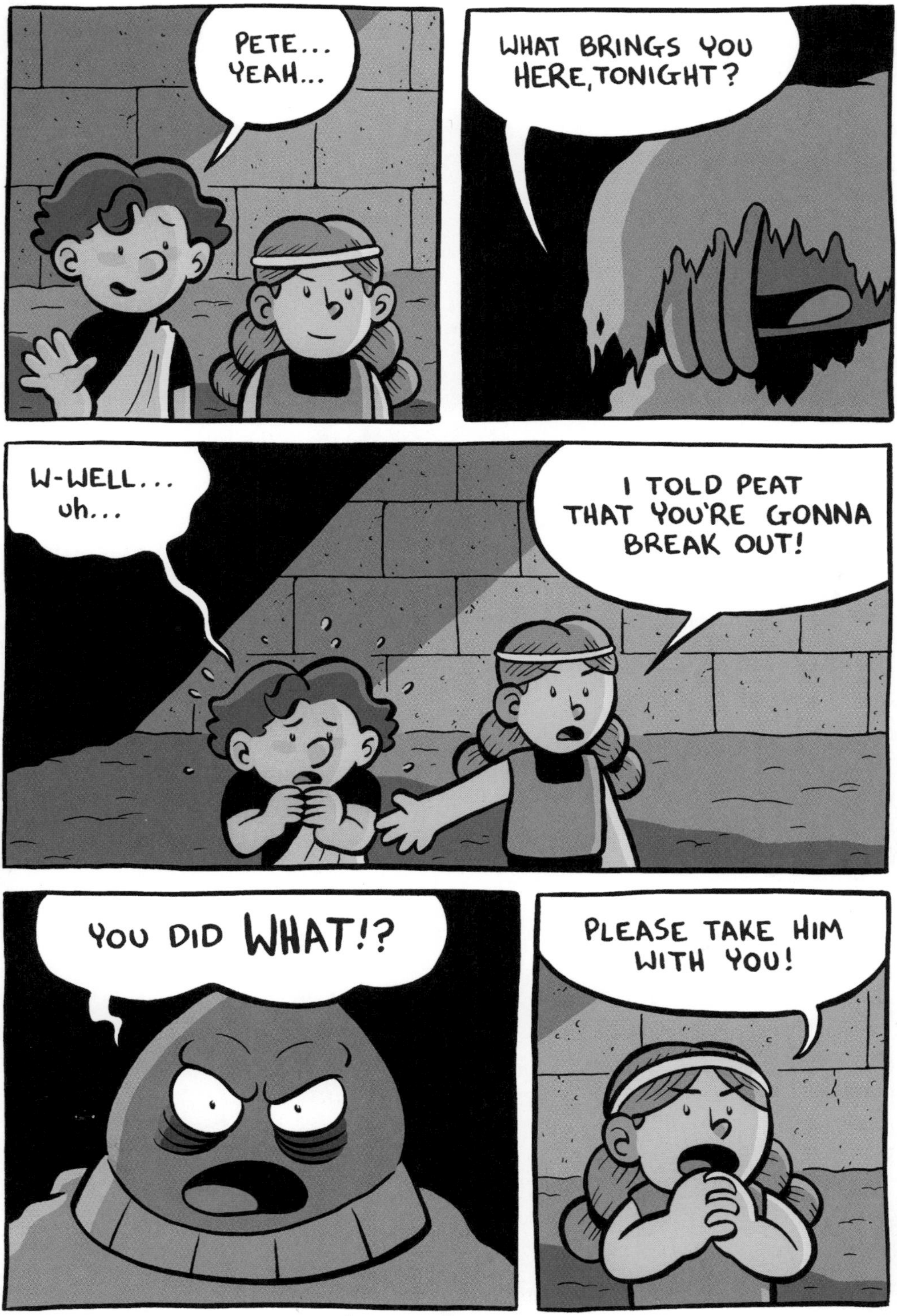
PETE...
YEAH...
WHAT BRINGS YOU HERE, TONIGHT?
W-WELL... uh...
I TOLD PEAT THAT YOU'RE GONNA BREAK OUT!
YOU DID WHAT!?
PLEASE TAKE HIM WITH YOU!

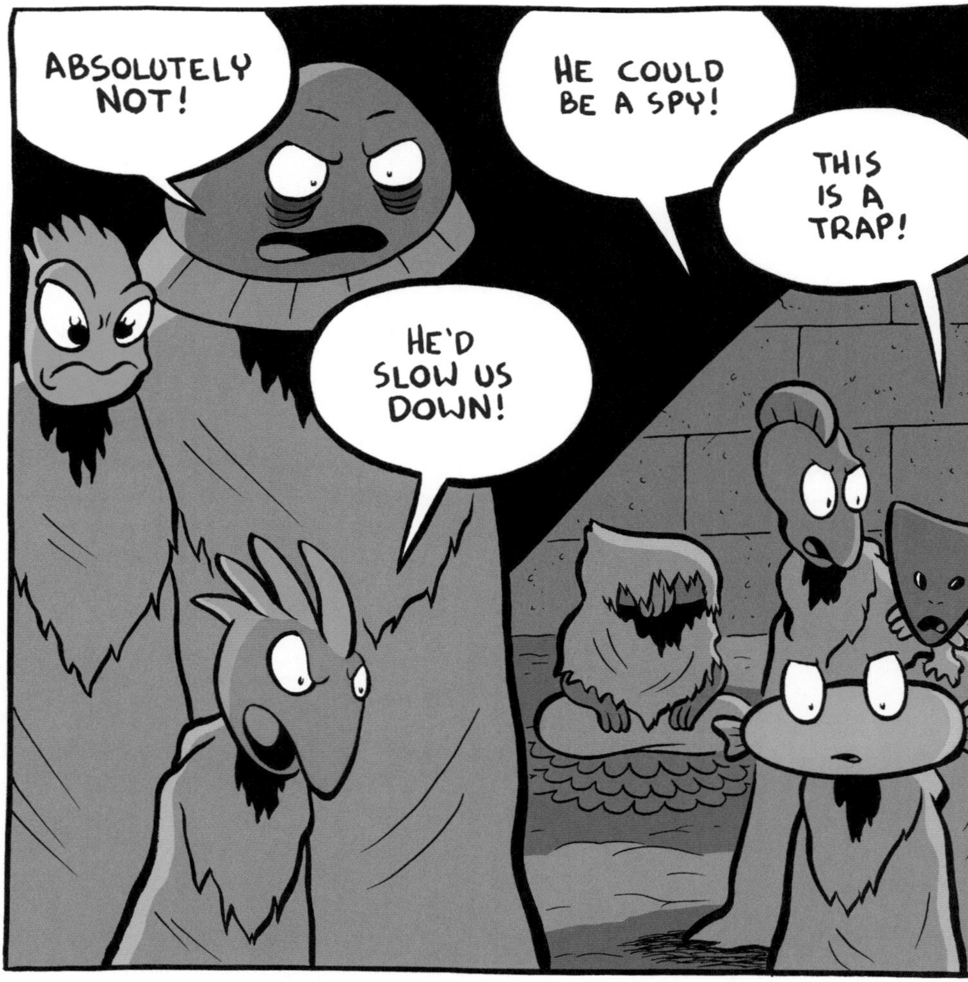
ABSOLUTELY NOT!
HE COULD BE A SPY!
THIS IS A TRAP!
HE'D SLOW US DOWN!

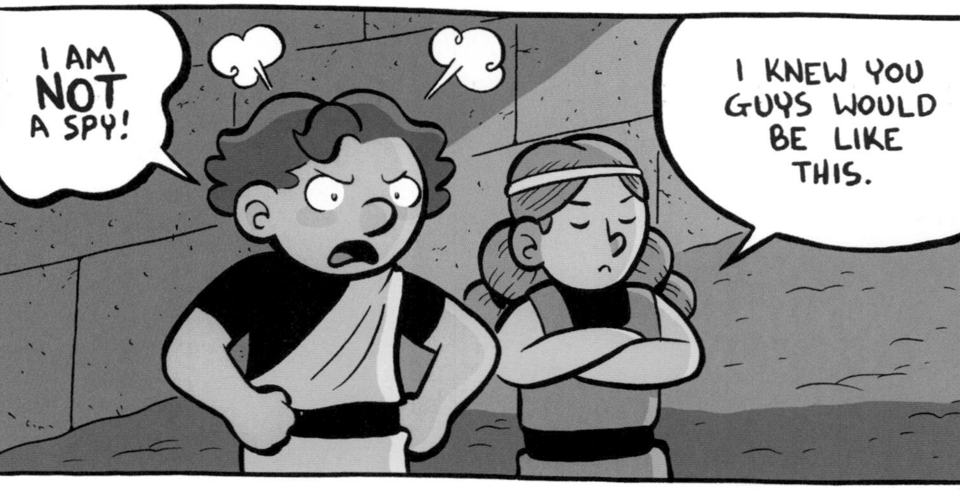
I AM NOT A SPY!
I KNEW YOU GUYS WOULD BE LIKE THIS.

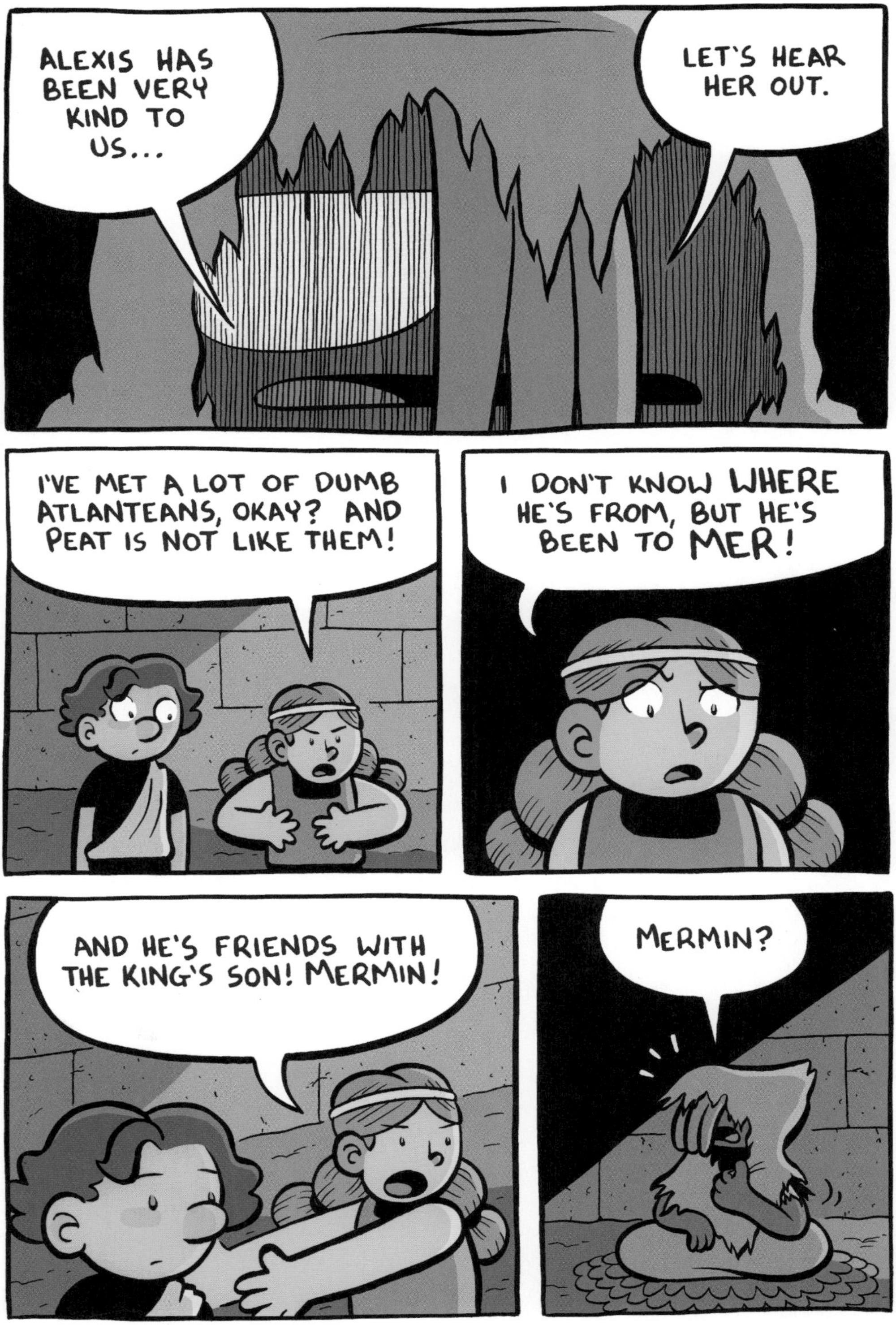
ALEXIS HAS BEEN VERY KIND TO US...
LET'S HEAR HER OUT.
I'VE MET A LOT OF DUMB ATLANTEANS, OKAY? AND PEAT IS NOT LIKE THEM!
I DON'T KNOW WHERE HE'S FROM, BUT HE'S BEEN TO MER!
AND HE'S FRIENDS WITH THE KING'S SON! MERMIN!
MERMIN?

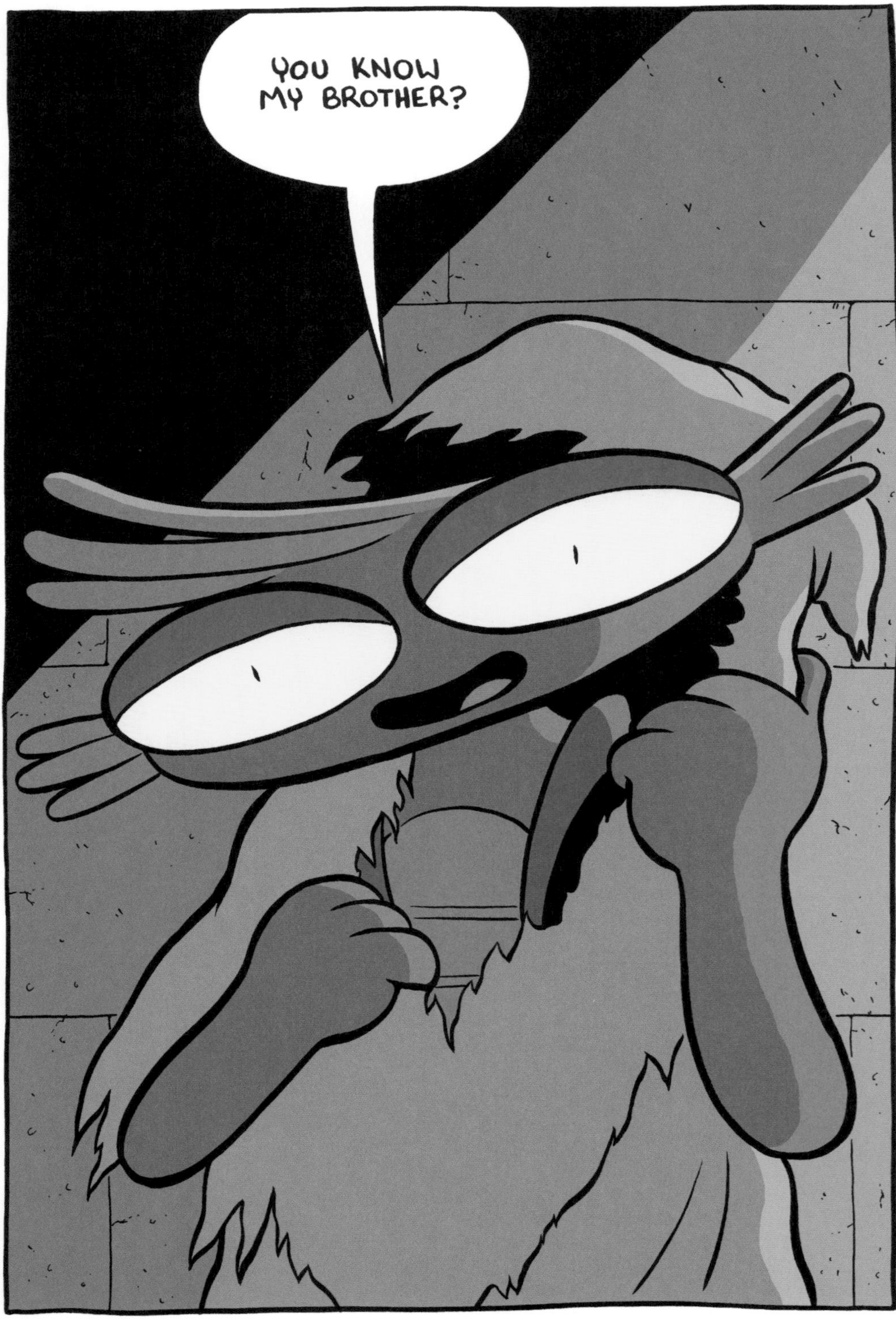
YOU KNOW MY BROTHER?

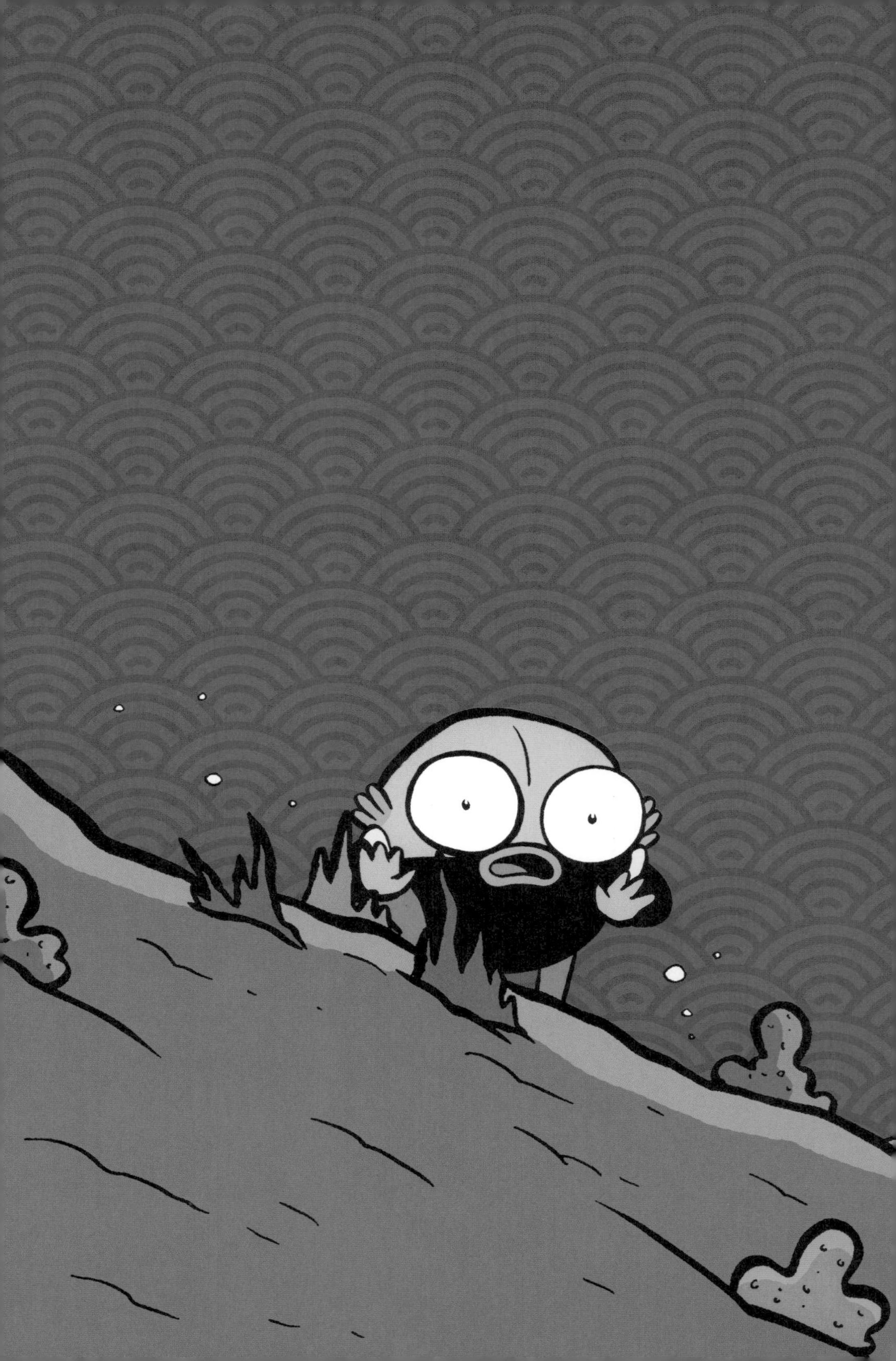

TURN THE PAGE FOR A
BONUS MERMIN COMIC
"A MERMIN HALLOWEEN!"

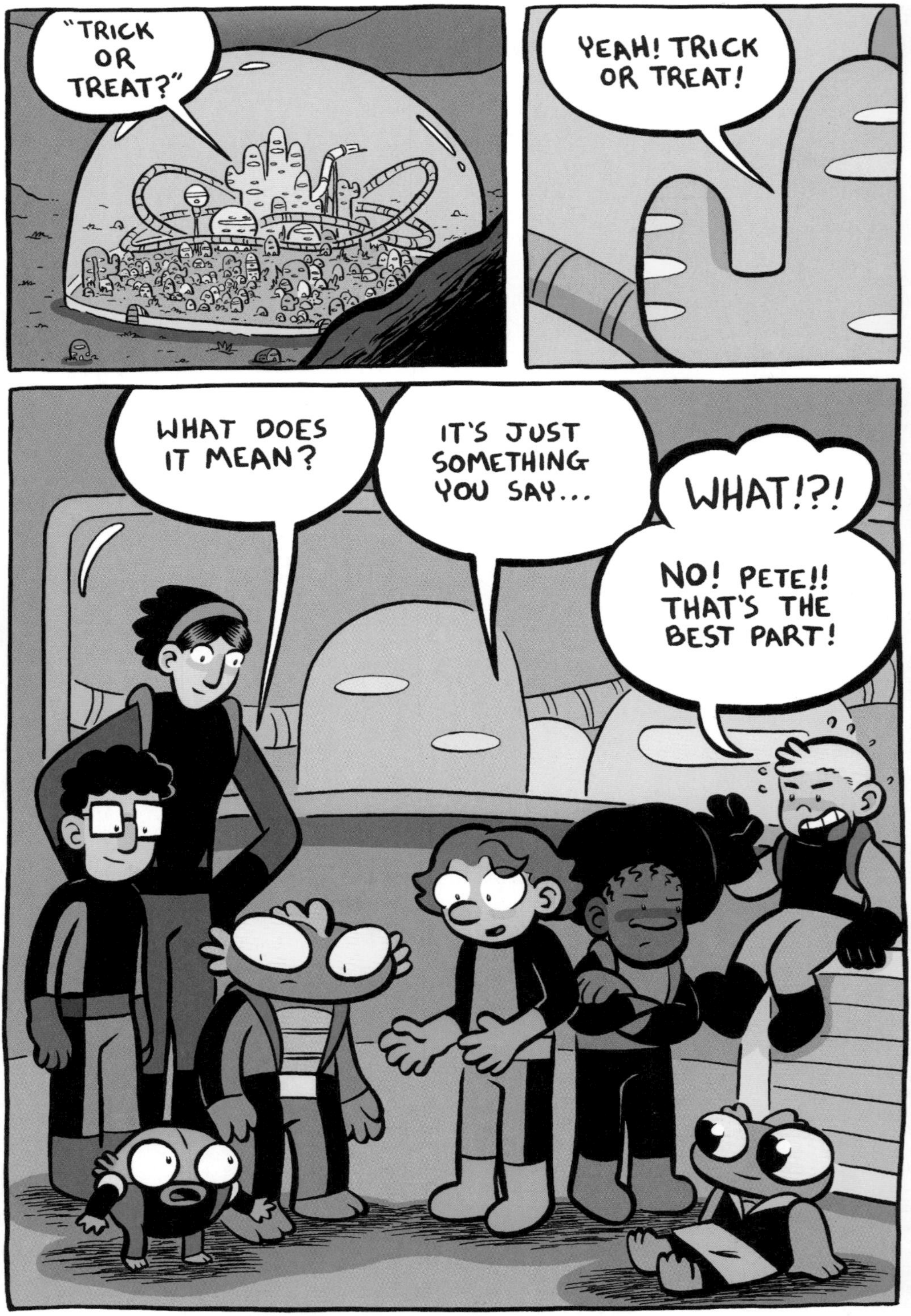
"TRICK OR TREAT?"
YEAH! TRICK OR TREAT!
WHAT DOES IT MEAN?
IT'S JUST SOMETHING YOU SAY...
WHAT!?!
NO! PETE!! THAT'S THE BEST PART!

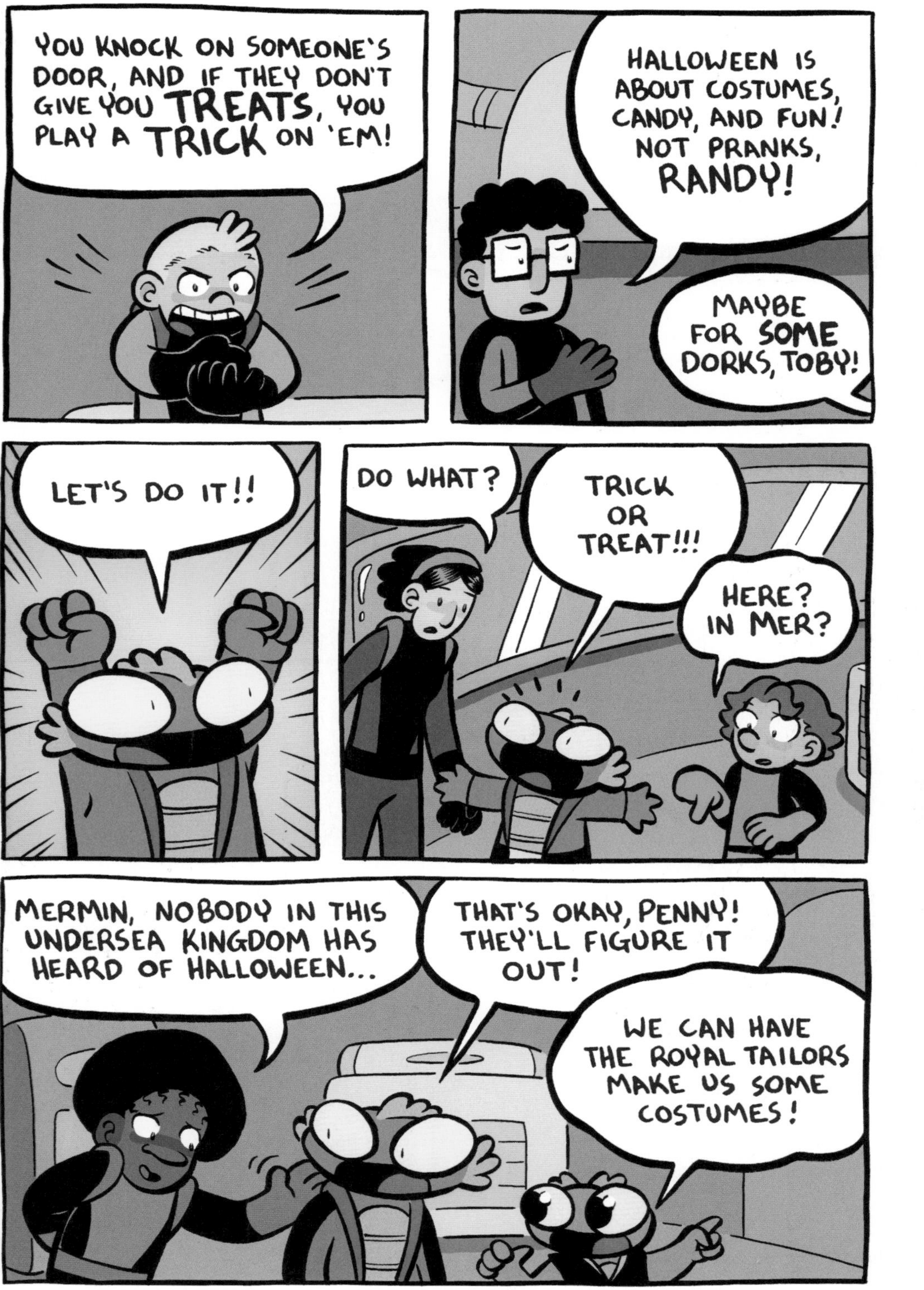
YOU KNOCK ON SOMEONE'S DOOR, AND IF THEY DON'T GIVE YOU TREATS, YOU PLAY A TRICK ON 'EM!
HALLOWEEN IS ABOUT COSTUMES, CANDY, AND FUN! NOT PRANKS, RANDY!
MAYBE FOR SOME DORKS, TOBY!
LET'S DO IT!!
DO WHAT?
TRICK OR TREAT!!!
HERE? IN MER?
MERMIN, NOBODY IN THIS UNDERSEA KINGDOM HAS HEARD OF HALLOWEEN...
THAT'S OKAY, PENNY! THEY'LL FIGURE IT OUT!
WE CAN HAVE THE ROYAL TAILORS MAKE US SOME COSTUMES!

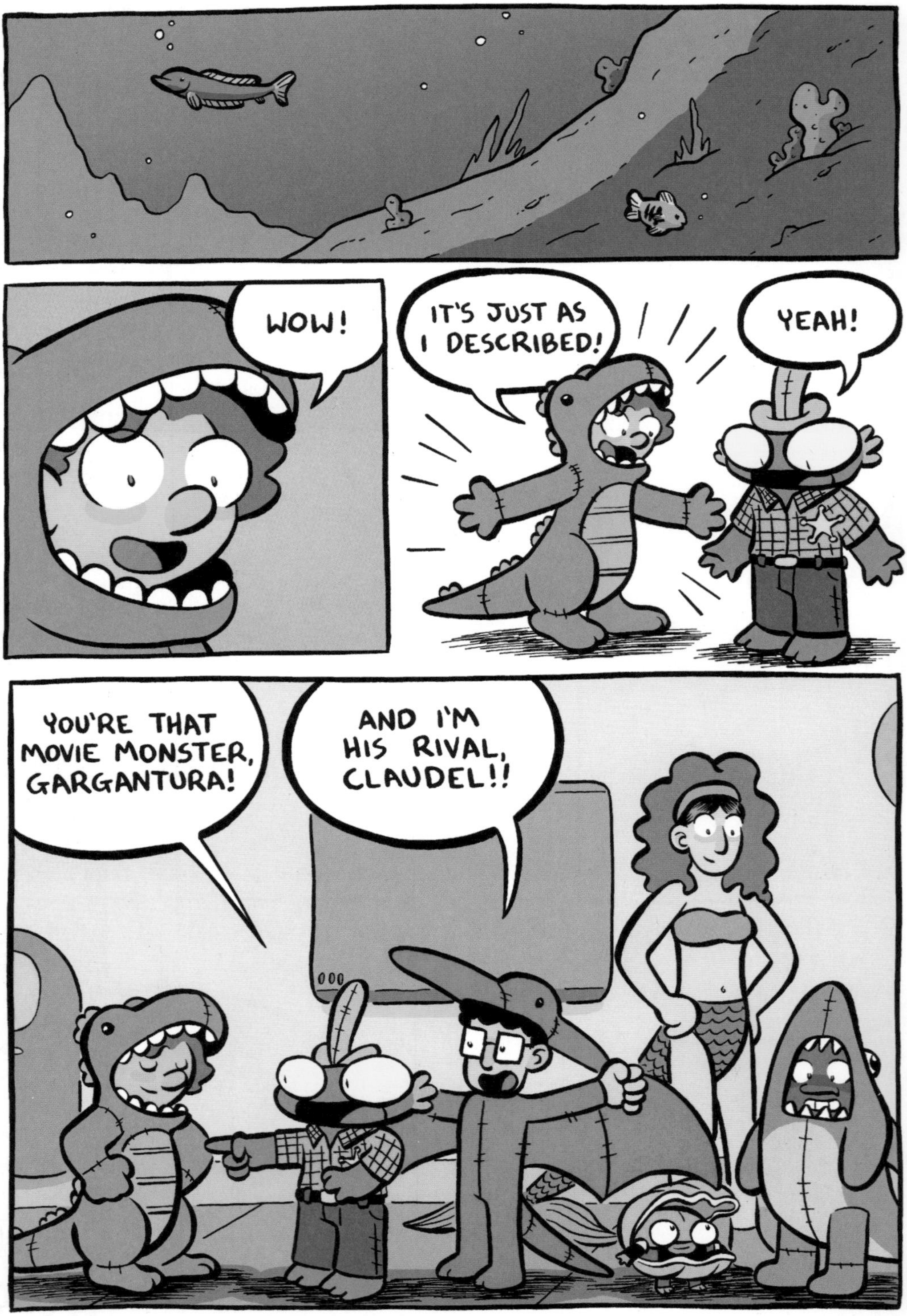
WOW!
IT'S JUST AS I DESCRIBED!
YEAH!
YOU'RE THAT MOVIE MONSTER, GARGANTURA!
AND I'M HIS RIVAL, CLAUDEL!!

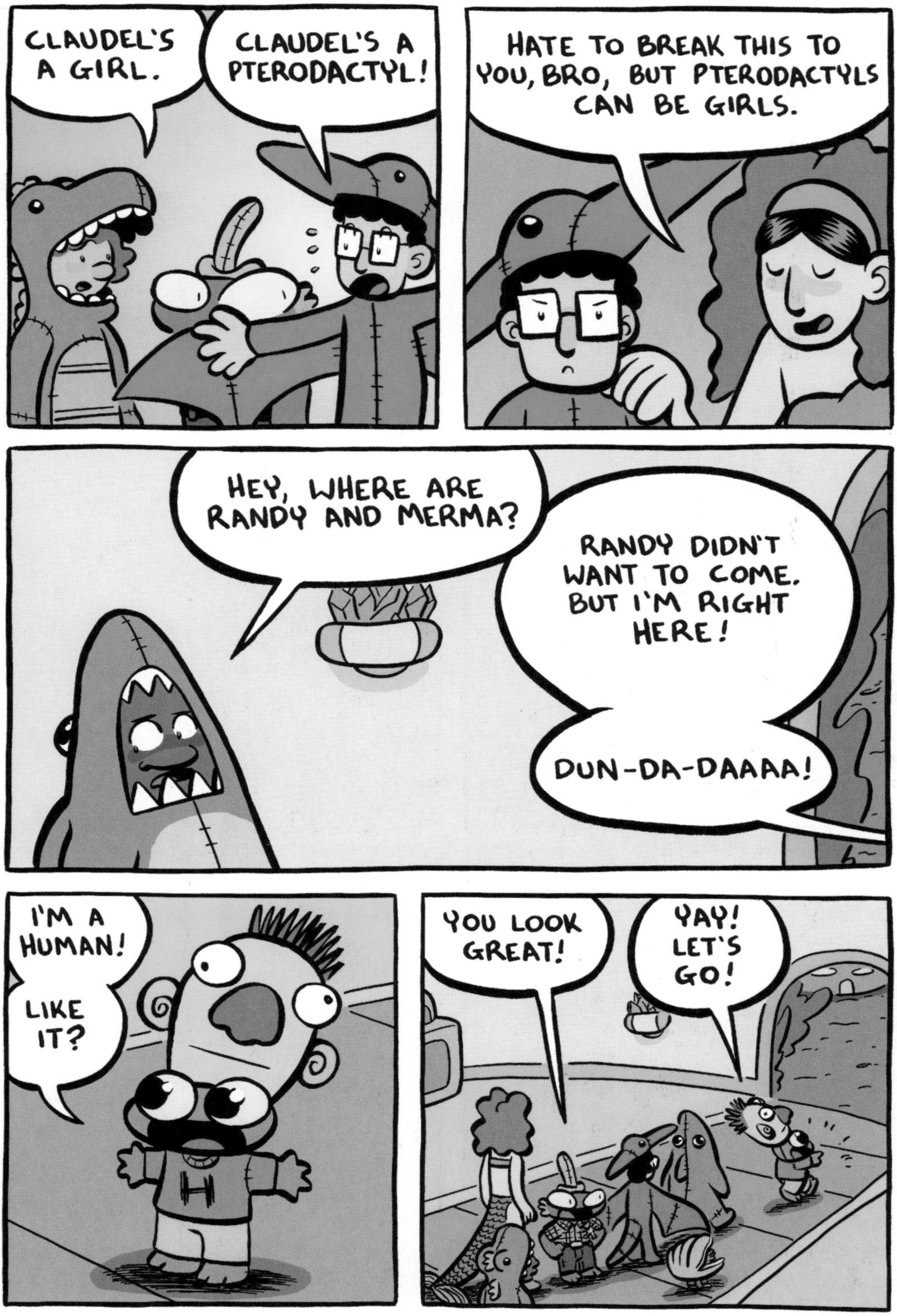
CLAUDEL'S A GIRL.
CLAUDEL'S A PTERODACTYL!
HATE TO BREAK THIS TO YOU, BRO, BUT PTERODACTYLS CAN BE GIRLS.
HEY, WHERE ARE RANDY AND MERMA?
RANDY DIDN'T WANT TO COME. BUT I'M RIGHT HERE!
DUN-DA-DAAAA!
I'M A HUMAN!
LIKE IT?
YOU LOOK GREAT!
YAY! LET'S GO!

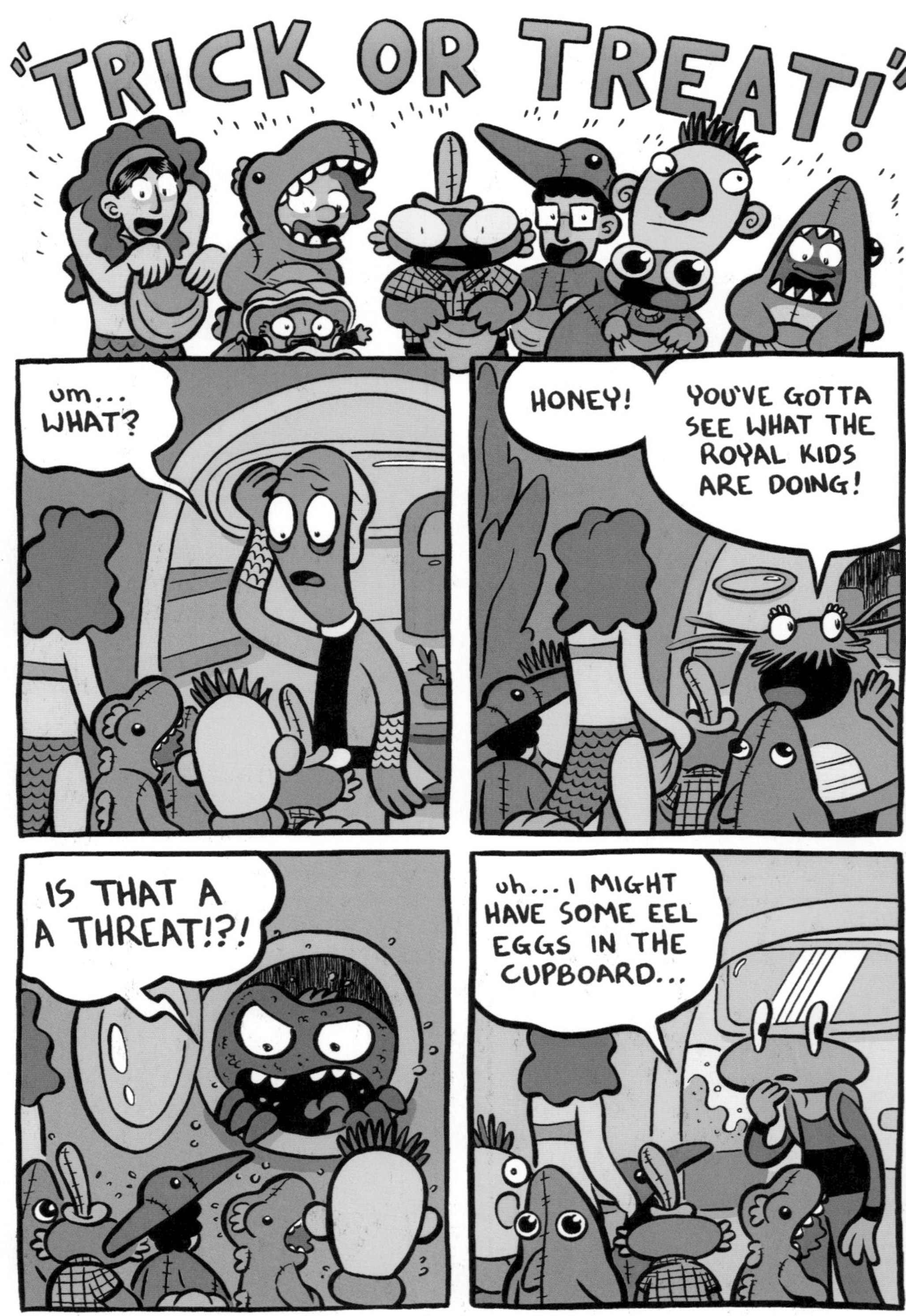
"TRICK OR TREAT!"
um... WHAT?
HONEY!
YOU'VE GOTTA SEE WHAT THE ROYAL KIDS ARE DOING!
IS THAT A A THREAT!?!
uh... I MIGHT HAVE SOME EEL EGGS IN THE CUPBOARD...

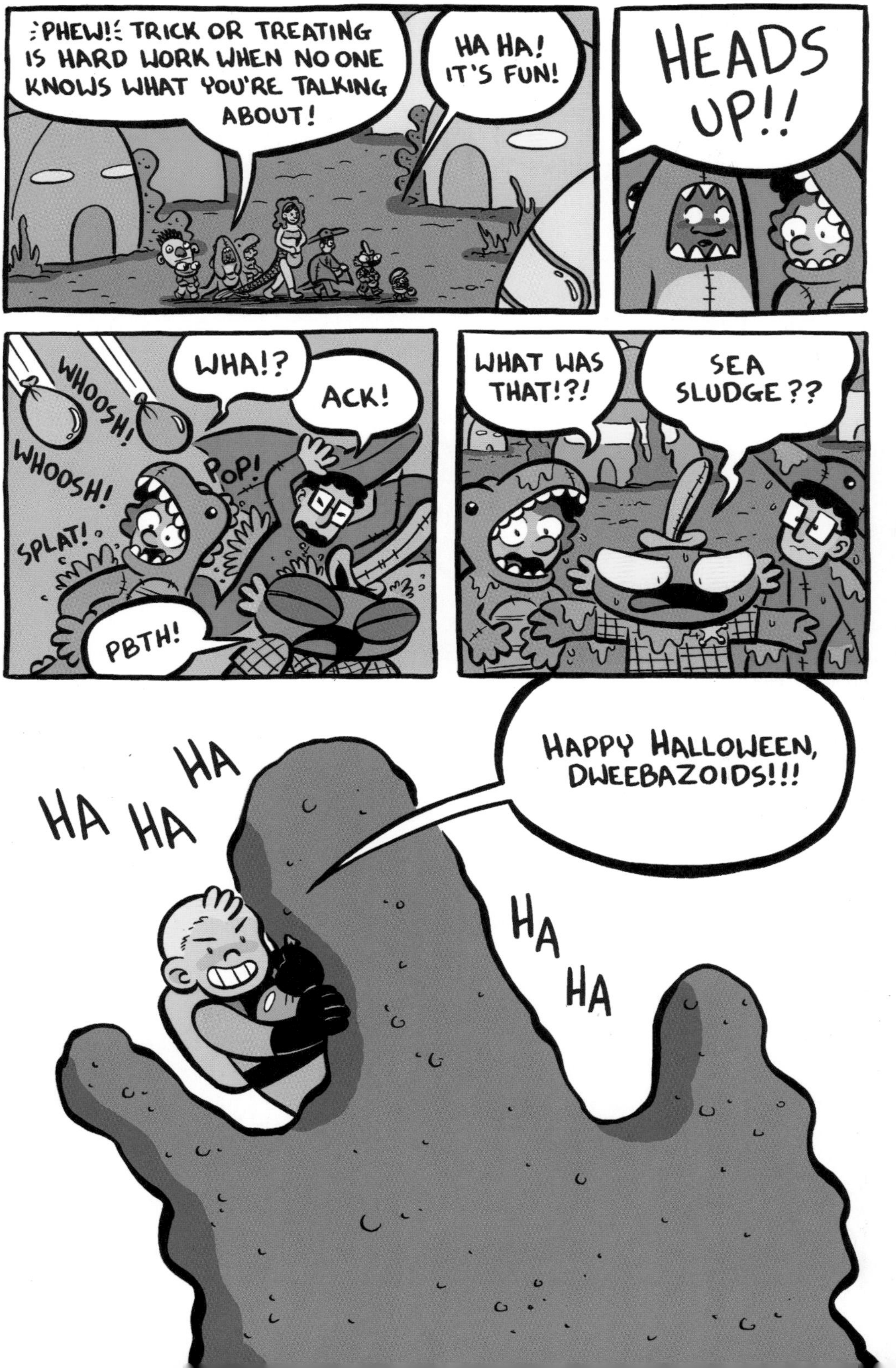
PHEW! TRICK OR TREATING IS HARD WORK WHEN NO ONE KNOWS WHAT YOU'RE TALKING ABOUT!
HA HA! IT'S FUN!
HEADS UP!!
WHOOSH!
WHOOSH!
WHA!?
ACK!
POP!
SPLAT!
PBTH!
WHAT WAS THAT!?!
SEA SLUDGE??
HA HA HA
HAPPY HALLOWEEN, DWEEBAZOIDS!!!
HA HA

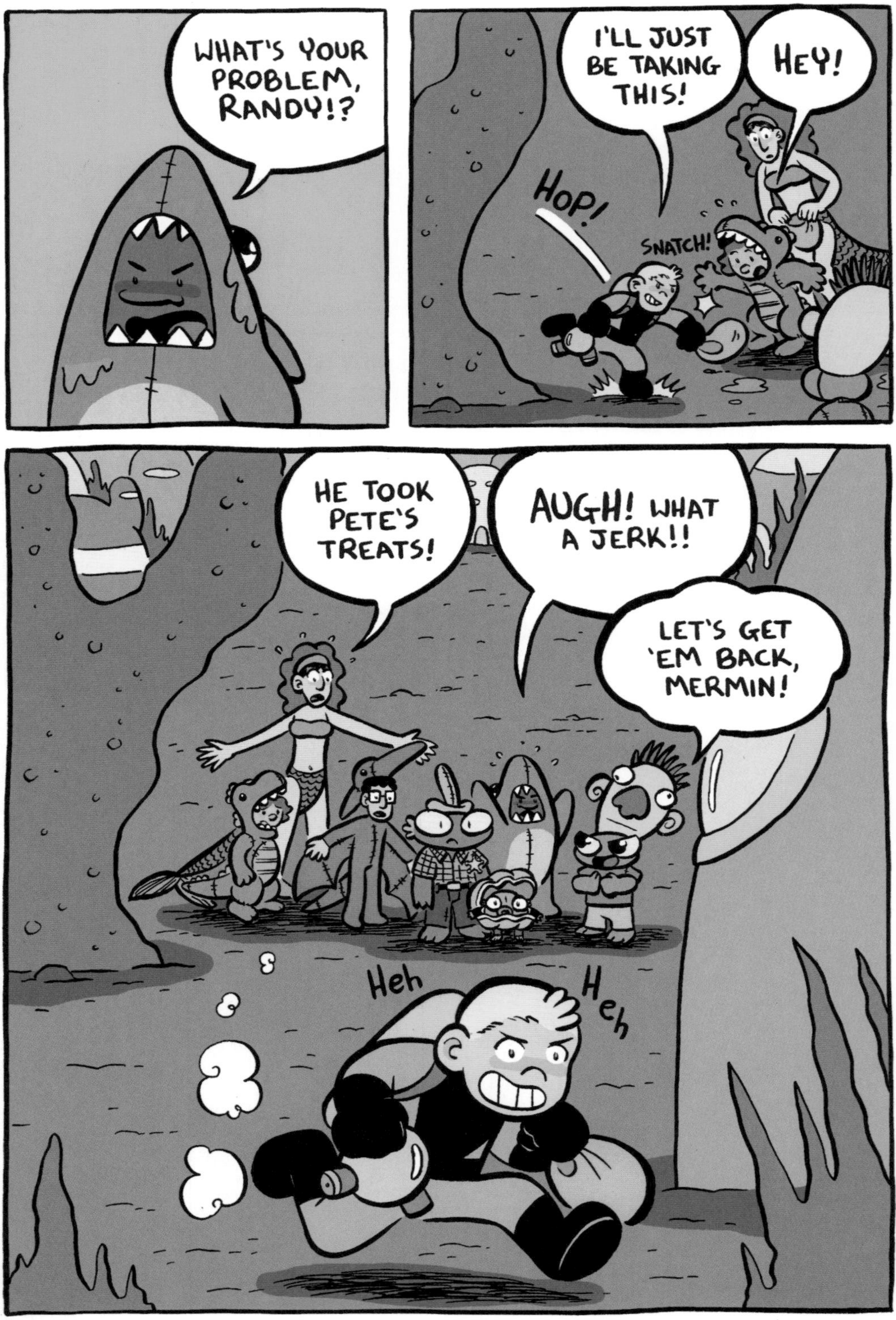
WHAT'S YOUR PROBLEM, RANDY!?
I'LL JUST BE TAKING THIS!
HEY!
HOP!
SNATCH!
HE TOOK PETE'S TREATS!
AUGH! WHAT A JERK!!
LET'S GET 'EM BACK, MERMIN!
Heh
Heh

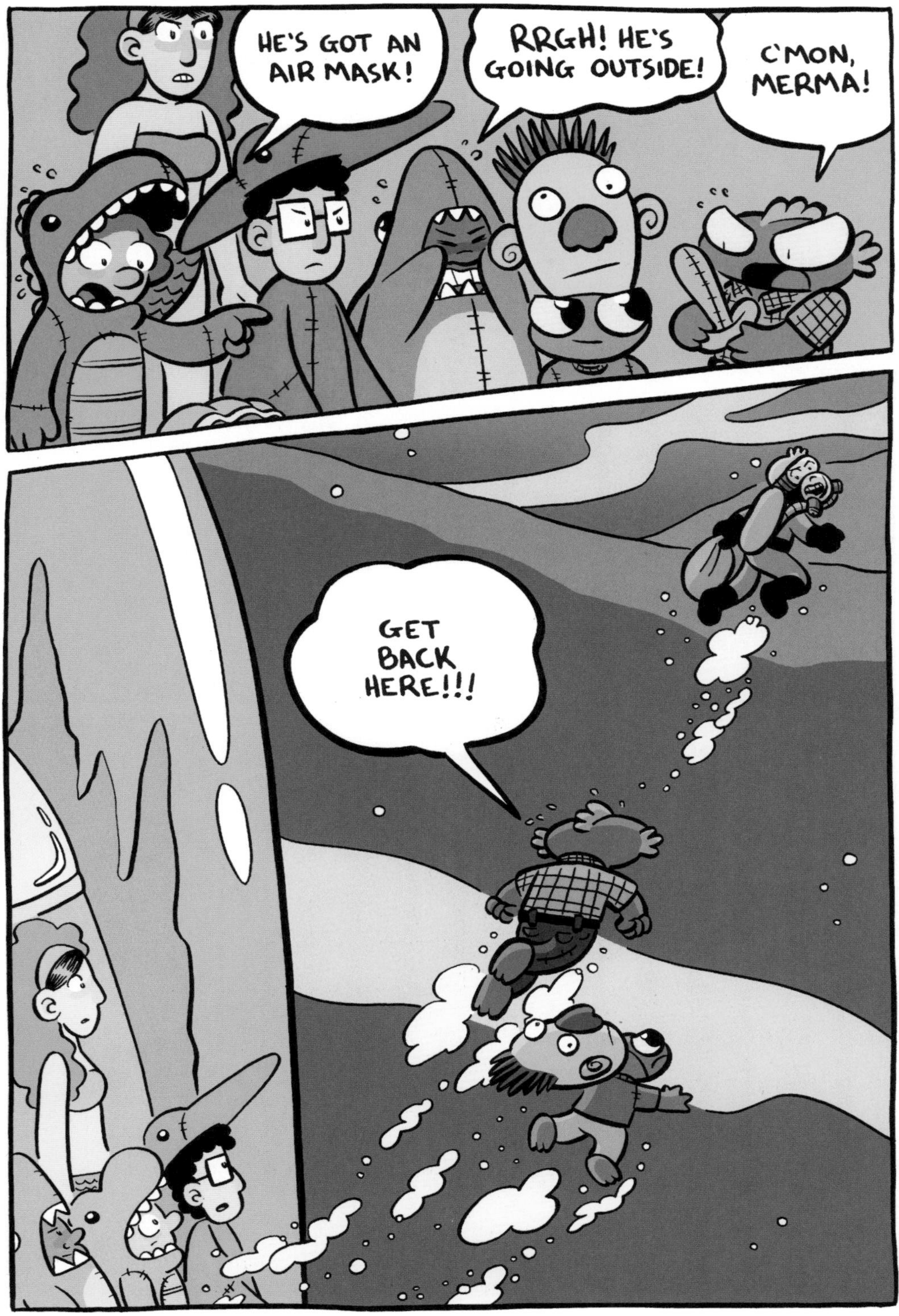
HE'S GOT AN AIR MASK!
RRGH! HE'S GOING OUTSIDE!
C'MON, MERMA!
GET BACK HERE!!!

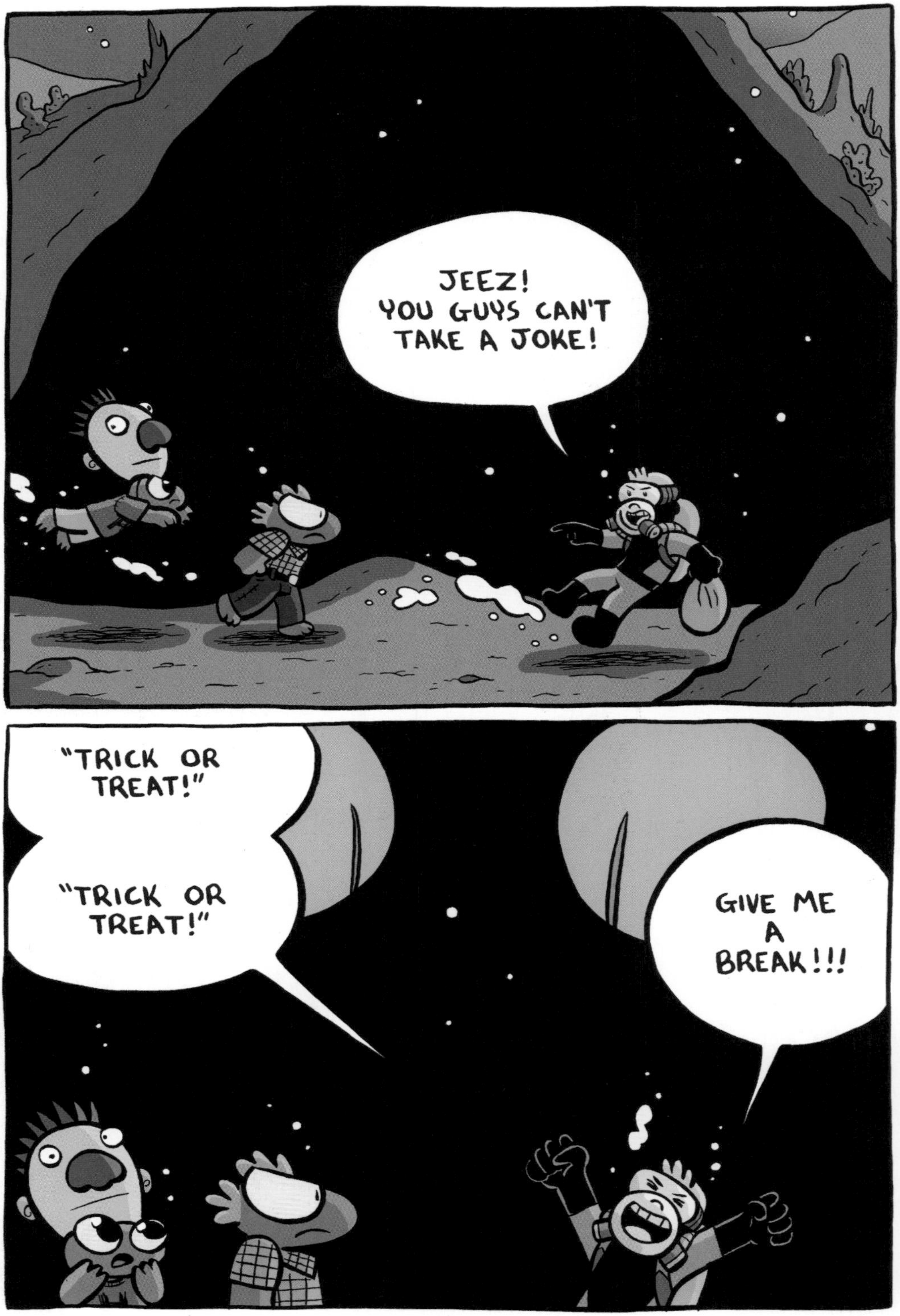
JEEZ! YOU GUYS CAN'T TAKE A JOKE!
"TRICK OR TREAT!"
"TRICK OR TREAT!"
GIVE ME A BREAK!!!

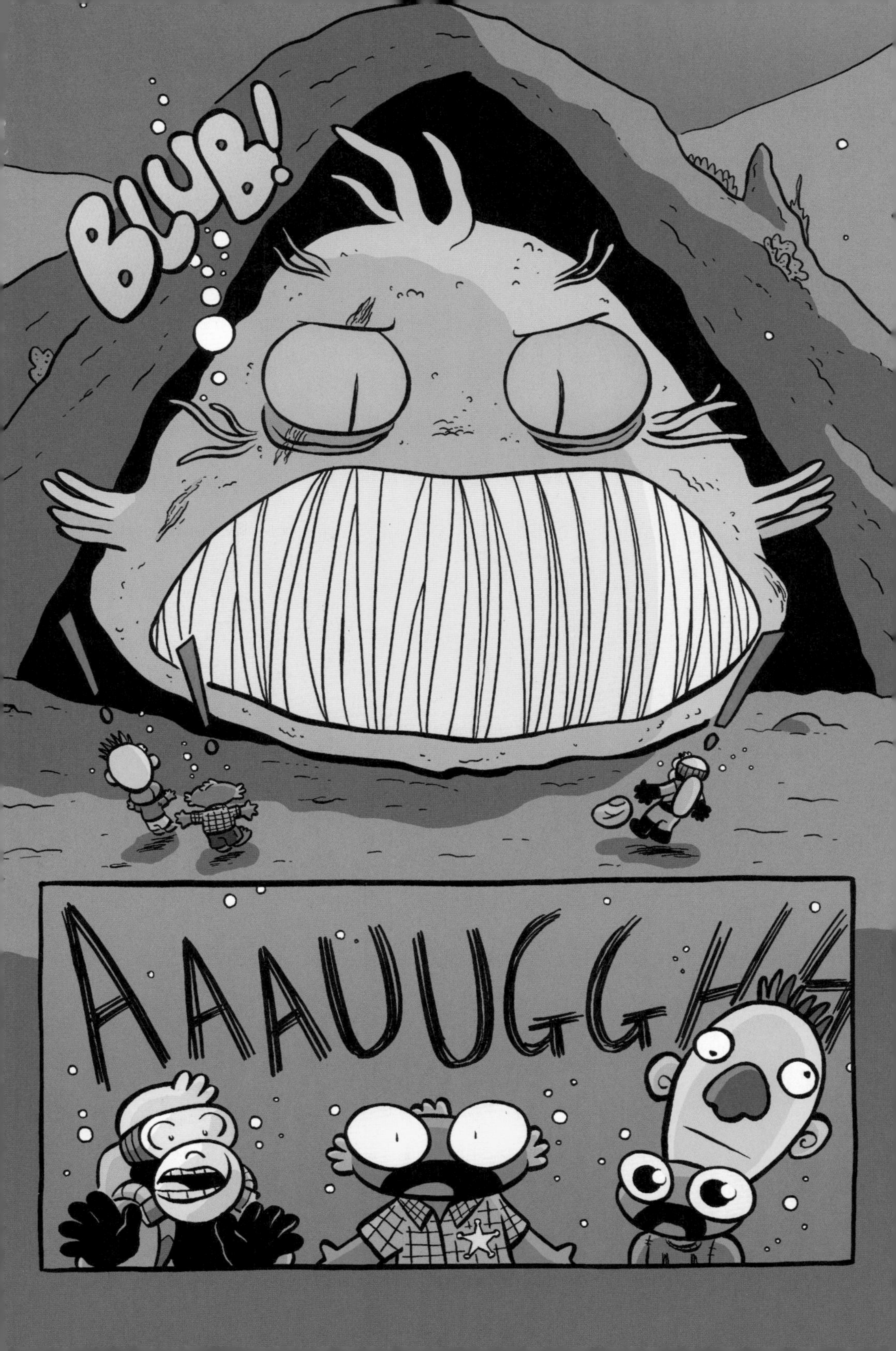
BLUB!
AAAUUGGHH

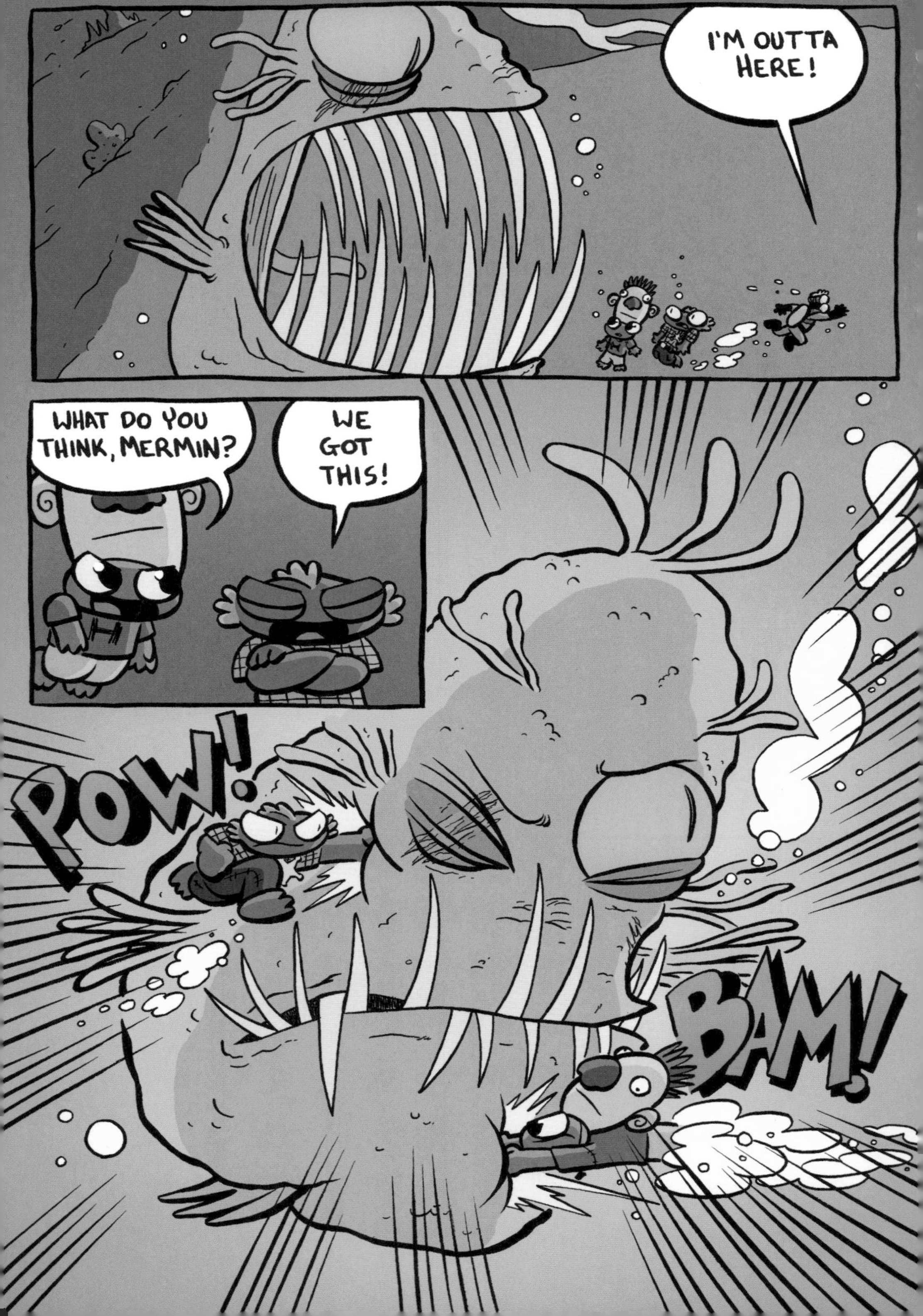
I'M OUTTA HERE!
WHAT DO YOU THINK, MERMIN?
WE GOT THIS!
POW!
BAM!

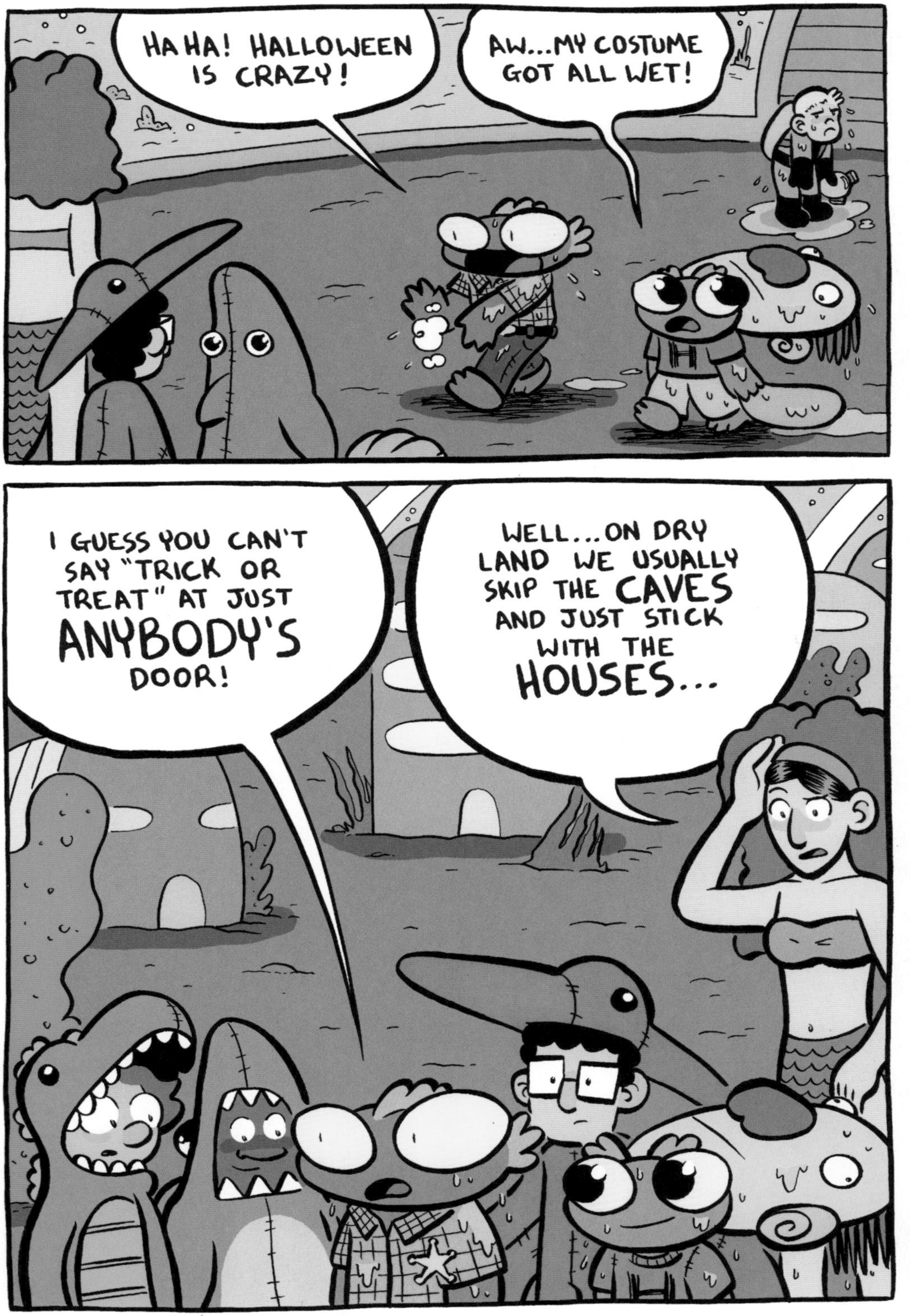
HA HA! HALLOWEEN IS CRAZY!
AW...MY COSTUME GOT ALL WET!
I GUESS YOU CAN'T SAY "TRICK OR TREAT" AT JUST ANYBODY'S DOOR!
WELL...ON DRY LAND WE USUALLY SKIP THE CAVES AND JUST STICK WITH THE HOUSES...

MERMIN™

SKETCHES

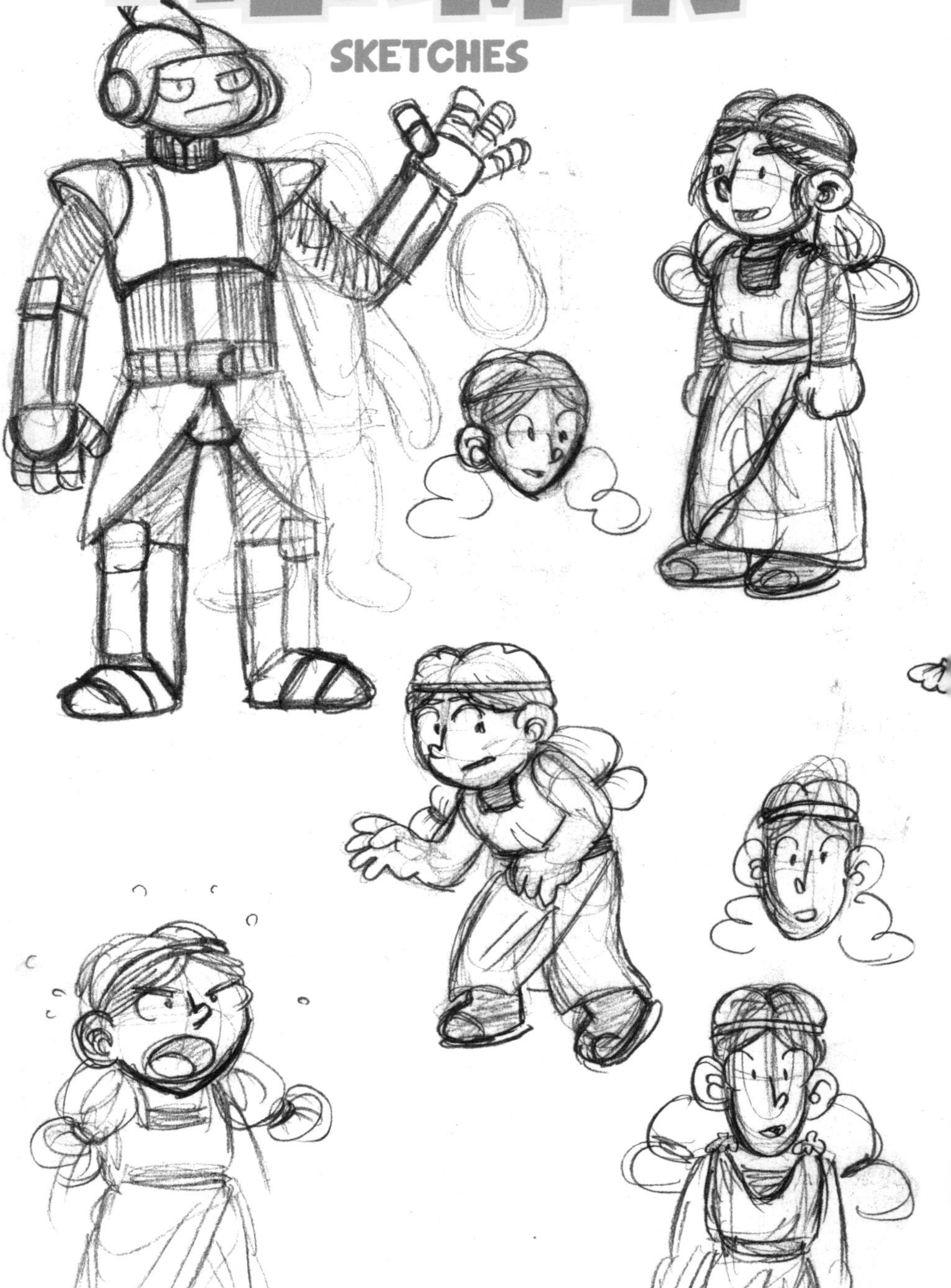

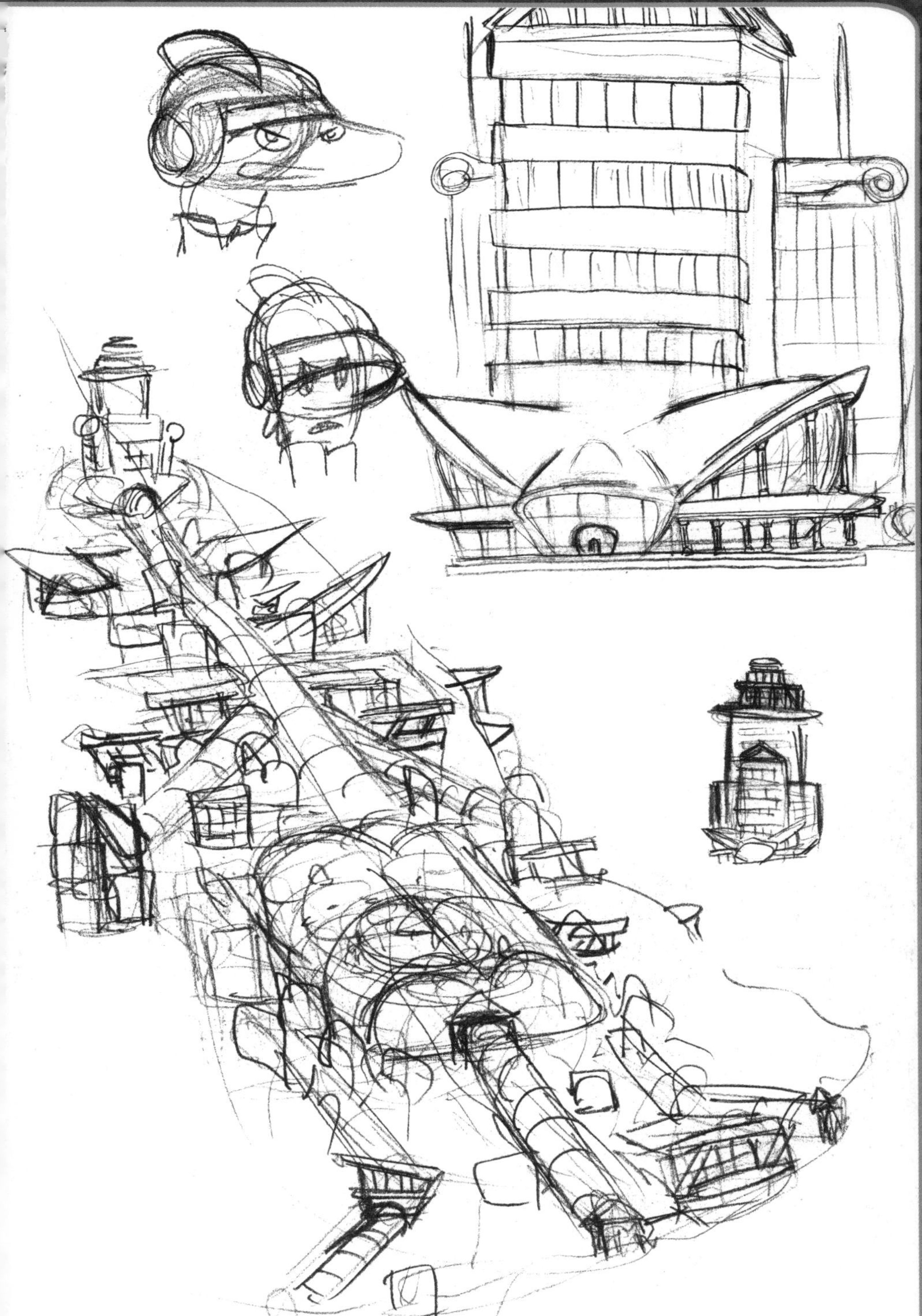

Joey Weiser's comics have appeared in several publications including *SpongeBob Comics* and the award-winning *Flight* series. His debut graphic novel, *The Ride Home*, was published in 2007 by AdHouse Books, and the first *Mermin* graphic novel was published in 2013 by Oni Press. The third *Mermin* graphic novel was nominated for a 2015 Eisner Award. He is a graduate of the Savannah College of Art & Design, and he currently lives in Athens, Georgia with his wife Michele and their cats Eddie and Charles.

GET MORE MERMIN!

MERMIN
BOOK ONE: OUT OF WATER
By Joey Weiser

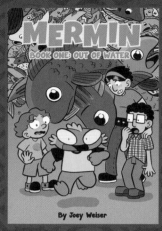

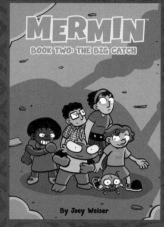

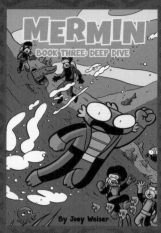

MERMIN, BOOK 1: OUT OF WATER
By Joey Weiser
152 Pages, Hardcover, Color
ISBN 978-1-934964-98-9

MERMIN
BOOK TWO: THE BIG CATCH
By Joey Weiser

MERMIN, BOOK 2: THE BIG CATCH
By Joey Weiser
144 Pages, Hardcover, Color
ISBN 978-1-62010-101-8

MERMIN
BOOK THREE: DEEP DIVE
By Joey Weiser

MERMIN, BOOK 3: DEEP DIVE
By Joey Weiser
160 pages, Hardcover, Color
ISBN 978-1-62010-174-2

"CATFOOT'S VENGEANCE IS A MARVELOUS SWASHBUCKLING TALE. CHRIS SCHWEIZER IS AN AMAZINGLY TALENTED CARTOONIST WITH AN EAR FOR DIALOGUE AND AN EYE FOR GREAT STORYTELLING."
—STAN SAKAI, USAGI YOJIMBO
THE WEST INDIES, 1701
THE CROGAN ADVENTURES
CATFOOT'S VENGEANCE
BY CHRIS SCHWEIZER

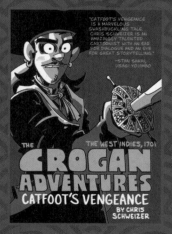

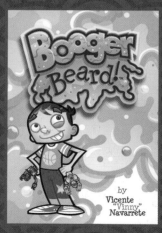

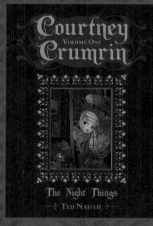

THE CROGAN ADVENTURES: CATFOOT'S VENGEANCE
By Chris Schweizer
200 pages, Softcover, Color
ISBN 978-1-62010-203-9

Booger Beard!
by Vicente "Vinny" Navarrete

BOOGER BEARD
By Vicente "Vinny" Navarrete
40 pages, Hardcover, Color
ISBN 978-1-62010-220-6

Courtney Crumrin
Volume One
The Night Things
Ted Naifeh

COURTNEY CRUMRIN VOLUME ONE: THE NIGHT THINGS
By Ted Naifeh
136 pages, Hardcover, Color
ISBN 978-1-934964-77-4

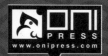

ONI PRESS
www.onipress.com

For more information on these and other fine Oni Press comic books and graphic novels visit onipress.com. To find a comic specialty store in your area visit comicshops.us.